COSMIC GATE

GALACTIC EQUILIBRIUM SERIES: BOOK ONE

ROLF F BRUNCKHORST

CHAPTER 1

Present Day 2271 A.D., Sol System
Aboard the Puddle Jumper

Chris Skylander sat in the helmsman's chair to begin the startup sequence for what felt like the millionth time. The cracked synthetic leather had long since molded to his frame, fitting like a worn baseball glove. Even though he was only twenty-one years old he'd been flying the Puddle Jumper, a Nez class cargo ship, regularly since he was thirteen.

Chris was a pretty standard kid for the most part. He stood six feet tall, weighed 160 pounds, and had dirty blond hair that was trimmed short. His sky-blue eyes were probably his most remarkable feature and he sported a clean-shaven face. For Chris, the Puddle Jumper was more than the simple smuggler ship seen moving to and from trading posts with cargo often more nefarious than its crew. It was also home. As a youth he remembered playing many simulator games, believing that one day he would pilot a fighter of his own. By the time he was ten he was asking the captain of the Puddle Jumper, Josh Hammerfist, if he could "steer." By age thirteen, if he wasn't in the pilot's seat he was disappointed and in a foul mood.

Today's mission was one they'd flown multiple times before: pick up a load of cargo from one of the stations orbiting Earth and drop it off at an outpost on Jupiter's moon Europa. They'd flown this mission profile many times because the research outposts needed regular resupply runs to stay alive. As the ship came to life, Captain Hammerfist stepped up behind Chris and put a hand on his shoulder.

"How's my ship looking, Chris? Still getting those pesky error messages from the load transducers?"

"Checking . . . no sir, looks like they're behaving today," Chris responded as he flipped through diagnostic menus.

Captain Hammerfist was in his mid-forties with a large build at six foot two and a solid 220 pounds. He had dark hair with grey streaks in it and a chiseled, scruffy jaw line, and he was the closest thing Chris had to a father figure. Chris never knew his mother or father and only had vague memories of them as a kid. Captain Hammerfist told him they were killed in a smuggling incident involving pirates. Afterward, Captain Hammerfist, who was a friend of his parents, had taken Chris in and raised him as his own.

"I should've known not to doubt Stacey. I swear that woman could fix a rocket engine with two popsicle sticks and a glue gun," joked the captain.

"Damn right I could," came a voice from the back of the bridge. "Only problem is it's getting harder and harder to keep this junker together on such a shoestring budget . . . Captain," Stacey said with a wink to the captain.

Stacey Fields was a kind lady in her mid-forties with dark hair, brown eyes, and a thin build. She was five feet tall on a good day and barely cracked a hundred pounds. She was the primary engineering officer on board and was arguably the most indispensable member of the crew. Besides an understanding of the Puddle Jumper's unique jumble of antiquated systems, she was a software coder dedicated to her craft. While that came in handy debugging ship software issues, the real magic was when the crew needed to fake manifests or bypass weak network security. She also had been "with" the captain for many years and was the closest thing to a mother Chris had ever had.

"You seem to make it work just fine. What's the problem?"

came Captain Hammerfist's response as he spread his arms almost as wide as the smile on his face.

Stacey continued, "You know damned well what I'm talking about. Typical boys, willing to spend unlimited amounts on laser turrets, but when I need a few hundred credits for new transducers it's all 'Woah, hold on now.'"

"Woah, hold on now," came Chris and Captain Hammerfist's unified response. Stacey rolled her eyes and started doing some diagnostic checks on her workstation.

Next, Captain Hammerfist made a call down to his second in command, XO Brad Singer, to check in on their payload. Brad Singer was a stringy man at five foot eight and 140 pounds on a good day, with greasy dark hair and splotchy stubble. Scars could be seen on his face from a childhood battle with acne. He essentially helped with captain duties when Josh was too busy. Usually it came down to low-level supervision of the crew.

"XO, how are we looking down there? The twins get everything secured?" asked the captain.

"Yes," came Brad's response, "I do believe they're slowly starting to figure out how to secure a load properly."

"I bet Brad has lots of experience securing loads," came a quick response in the background followed by laughter.

"Why, Captain, do you make me put up with these idiots?" was all Brad could muster.

He was referring to the twins Tim and Tom Mayberry. They were the least specialized members of the crew but could be thought of as support/muscle. The rest of the crew made sure to regularly remind them that they definitely weren't there for their brains. While each crew member had assigned duties, with such a small crew each person learned multiple jobs. It was not uncommon to find an engineer piloting the craft, or one of the twins helping fix a system or two. At the end of the day the crew did what they needed to do to get the job done.

"Because they're cheap labor and they keep each other

entertained," responded Captain Hammerfist. "Now finish up down there; we're on the move as soon as we get clearance to depart."

Chris knew the real reason Captain Hammerfist kept the twins around wasn't their low labor rates. He actually paid them fairly well considering their lack of qualifications. He kept them around because he trusted them. Not all of the Puddle Jumper's missions were strictly legal. In fact, Chris was willing to bet there was likely contraband among the cargo they had just loaded for their trip to Europa. It was simply a fact of life for many transport ships that the bottom line demanded a certain level of flexibility regarding adherence to local laws. As such, members of the crew who handled materials needed to keep their mouth shut if law enforcement ever came sniffing. Tim and Tom had gotten busted once before, and after finding out they had covered for him while detained, Captain Hammerfist had kept them on the crew ever since.

"Chris, call up the controller. Let's get out of here," commanded Captain Hammerfist.

"Yes sir," responded Chris, as he tuned in the space station's controller frequency and keyed the transmit button. "Buckeye station, this is the Puddle Jumper at dock seven requesting subspace departure as filed."

"Puddle Jumper hold for traffic," came a snappy response from the station controller. The cause of the delay was immediately clear as the controller finished his transmission. Chris watched as an Earth Force transport flanked by three Raptor class fighters came swooping behind them, flying in formation. He was mesmerized watching the sleek, shiny machines of war pass by silently.

"You're just as good as them, Chris. You just weren't born with a silver spoon in your mouth," came a familiar voice. He turned and saw the seventh member of the crew, Jordan Schmidt, standing behind him. Jordan Schmidt was an energetic engineer in his early thirties who had slowly become

Chris's best friend over time. He was not as gifted as Stacey, but made up for it with a great personality and willingness to help. When Chris needed to talk to someone other than Captain Hammerfist, Jordan was the guy.

"My dude, you ready for this trip?" asked Chris with a fist bump to Jordan.

"You know it!" responded Jordan, who then walked back to his seat to begin strapping in.

Jordan knew Chris's dream was to fly space fighters for the Earth Force, but in today's age those were only piloted by the privileged elite. This was mainly due to the fact that space fighters were extremely expensive, and the bureaucrats back at central didn't deem the occasional pirate worthy of a one hundred trillion credit space fleet. So Chris did what most young men who wanted to fly spacecraft did: he began flying a transport craft, which just happened to be the one upon which he grew up.

"Puddle Jumper, you are cleared to depart. Disengage clamps at your discretion; clearance void if not off in five minutes," came the controller's robotic voice. Chris confirmed the command and with a last check of the instruments, began disengaging the clamps to the station's airlocks. At the same time Tim, Tom, and Brad filed into the bridge and began strapping themselves into their stations. He manually started flying the ship back away from the station, and then spun it around to depart on their course.

As they cleared the station, Captain Hammerfist did some last checks to make sure the ship was buttoned up and everyone was strapped in.

"All right folks, let's get down to business. Chris, verify you have the subspace trajectory mapped into the subspace drive, destination Europa via Delta arrival."

"Confirmed Captain," responded Chris.

The Puddle Jumper sped up as the station grew smaller and smaller in the distance. After a few minutes they received jump clearance from the controller, and Chris engaged the powerful engines to the jump settings. The Puddle Jumper lurched with acceleration as the subspace drive came online. A few moments later a spinning disk of blue with a white center appeared in front of the ship, and they passed through the event horizon.

CHAPTER 2

The ship traveled smoothly through the subspace tunnel, belying the fact that it was covering over half a billion kilometers of normal space-time in less than an hour. As far as the crew on board the Puddle Jumper was concerned however, the ship was moving through the tunnel at a lazy pace. A lack of good outside references or acceleration meant their instruments were the only thing indicating their true speed. The subspace portal had bent space-time, connecting far distant points with a shorter tunnel, through which they were traversing.

Chris honestly found that despite the fantastic physics magic taking place, this was the most boring portion of the flight. He wasn't alone either. The twins almost immediately went to sleep upon entering the tunnel. This was understandable as they had been working hard loading the ship and would do the heavy lifting when they arrived. Meanwhile, Stacey and Jordan had gone off to tinker somewhere else in the ship. XO Brad Singer was polishing a set of dress shoes, and the captain was reading the news on his tablet. Chris was supposed to be monitoring the instruments, but so was everybody else. Instead, he was reading up on the latest game mods he would install on his personal console when they got done.

It was only when his master caution light illuminated on the annunciator panel that his attention was diverted. He immediately brought up the error on the screen and called for the captain's attention. Their position within the subspace tunnel was wavering, and the instruments were picking it up. They'd dealt with this before, as after reviewing the error messages Captain Hammerfist immediately belted out, "Ah damnit, not again," and started barking out orders immediately.

"Chris, pull us out of subspace. You know what happens if the tunnel deteriorates with us in it." He then followed that up with a call to engineering "Stacey, Jordan, prepare for transition out of subspace, then get up here." He was going to yell at the twins to wake up, but the XO had already put his shoes away neatly and started yelling at them.

"Have we arrived yet?" one of them muttered as he rubbed his eyes.

"Yes, we've arrived at your stop. Now if you'd kindly exit the spacecraft via the nearest airlock we'd all be a lot better off," replied the XO primly.

"Oh, are we at your mother's house, XO? Shoot, I forgot flowers," Tom shot back groggily.

The XO shot them a dark look, then turned around and tightened his restraints. They weren't really necessary, as the inertial dampers would smooth any gravity waves as they exited subspace, but they were still used as a precaution. The rotating blue disk appeared again, and a few moments later Chris was staring at the blackness of space and the sparkle of stars all around them. A few minutes later, Stacey and Jordan entered the bridge with Stacey tapping furiously at her tablet.

"Looks like one of the transducers wasn't adhered correctly. Once it heated up it started migrating and giving erroneous readings. No sweat—should be a simple fix. Worst case scenario someone takes a spacewalk," she said while eyeing Jordan. Jordan simply shrugged his shoulders and started toward the airlock where the space suits were located.

Brad noticed Stacey had put down her tablet and begun to closely monitor her station. She suddenly spoke up.

"Captain, we're getting some strange readings on the passive sensors, and a whole lot of radiation."

"What do you mean? Is there anything out here? We're in the middle of the asteroid belt, aren't we?"

"Well this is one of the most object-dense portions of the belt, but still there's something else definitely here," replied Stacey, with more than a hint of interest.

The Puddle Jumper conducted a lot of different missions, and space salvage and rescue was definitely one of them. Insurance companies paid hefty rewards for legitimate space rescues, and any salvage was property of the rescue ship. So when they caught the signals of a dying space vessel any crew perked up.

Captain Hammerfist, sitting in his command chair behind Chris said, "Go active."

Chris toggled a switch in front of him, and with an audible click the radar, along with other sensors, lit up everything within a thousand kilometers.

It didn't take long before Stacey called out the source of the signal.

"There, about three hundred and fifty kilometers away, marking the waypoint on your screens. What do you want to do, Captain?"

The captain paused for a moment to contemplate, then gave the clear order.

"Chris, proceed toward it but let's keep our head on a swivel. There shouldn't be anybody out here, after all."

"Yes sir, heading toward the signal."

Chris stared out of the cockpit and scanned around him as he steered his ship through the asteroid belt. He loved this kind of flying as it was a good opportunity to really take control and fly the ship. This was one of the most dense clusters of asteroids he'd ever seen, though. After all, the asteroid belt was mostly empty space. He weaved left and right as massive rocks flew past him. It felt like a game for Chris, as he would push the limits as far as he could, exercising his precise control over the cargo ship. Sometimes he would see how close he could get to the rocks without actually hitting them, though this was often concluded by Stacey smacking him playfully and telling him, "Cut it out."

Chris continued to maneuver the Nez class ship through the field of asteroids. The Puddle Jumper was not a huge cargo ship at only 180 meters but what it lacked in cargo space it made up for in speed and agility. Civilian transports generally required a wide range of capabilities and smuggling was one of those that necessitated speed, as opposed to a huge, slow craft that drew a lot of attention.

Chris's concentration was broken when Tom chimed in from the back of the room, "Twenty credits says Chris bangs into another asteroid."

Tim, never one to back down from his brother responded "I'll take that—it's been over a month since he French kissed a boulder."

Chris replied, "Hey that was just a nick, and besides, you try dodging asteroids coming at you a few thousand kilometers per hour in a ship sixty meters wide!"

The XO Brad chimed in with his prissy voice, "Stow it, children, we are on a mission and Chris needs to concentrate."

"Are you always this much of a downer, Brad?" Chris retorted, with a hint of sarcasm.

"Are you capable of flying and not talking, Mr. Skylander? If so I'll give you twenty credits just to shut up," replied the XO.

"Done!" Chris exclaimed with enthusiasm as he passed below another large rock's trajectory. Sometimes while conducting mining exploration missions this kind of flying could go on for hours before they would find anything or take a break. But that was the life of independent spacers. If they didn't have a cargo contract then they had to find another way to make money, as the ships didn't refuel and repair themselves.

Five minutes later in the patrol Stacey said "Picking up

better readings now. Not sure what it is but it's not an asteroid. It's definitely metal."

"Well what is it?" replied the XO.

Stacey's voice then became very concerned, "Sir, I think . . . I think it is another ship—a big one."

"Kill the active sensors and pinpoint that anomaly," ordered the captain. "I want us all quiet until we figure out what's going on here."

Chris shut off the active sensors and killed the outside running lights.

"Slow us down Chris, and take us in nice and easy. There are no transponders reporting in and no scheduled flights through this area, so I don't want anyone knowing we are here until I decide to tell them," ordered the captain.

All ships were required to have transponders installed and used in heavily trafficked areas, which respond to radar pings with the ships position and info. While transponders could be active at all times, most ship captains turned theirs off after leaving ports. Captain Hammerfist was no exception and would turn theirs off when out on their own. Of course Stacey could work the transponder to respond to pings with false info, but it was easier to just turn it off when traveling the less patrolled parts of the solar system and trying to stay quiet.

"Stacey, were you able to determine what the ship was?" asked the captain.

"Yes I believe so but cannot be 100 percent sure," she replied "I think it's an Argo class transport."

Brad then questioned, "What is an Argo class transport doing in an asteroid field? Military types usually steer clear of the belt. You must have read that wrong."

Stacey retorted while rolling her eyes, "Check the readings yourself," as she sent them to Brad's console.

"Hmmm . . . " Brad muttered, unable to disprove her findings.

The captain then ordered in his deep voice, "All right, here's the plan. I want Chris to fly us within several dozen kilometers as quietly as we can. When we get within visual range we can assess the situation and make a call on what to do. Chris take us closer. In the meantime Stacey, keep me updated on anything the passives pick up."

"Roger that," replied Stacey.

Jordan butted in saying, "Hey, if that ship is damaged and they are stranded, why is there no SOS signal? Or any attempt at requesting help?"

"Good question," the captain said. "Let's find out."

Chris cut the reactor power to 25 percent and the subtle hum caused by the power systems dimmed. Chris looked at the captain and could see the whites in his knuckles as he tensely gripped his chair. Based on the captain's reaction, Chris knew the situation was bothering him. After a few more minutes of maneuvering through the belt they reached a distance of about one hundred kilometers and the ship started coming into visual range. The whole crew sat looking out the viewing portal in suspense at what they may have found. It was definitely an Argo class transport ship that had seen better days. As a matter of a fact, when looking through the zooming optics the ship had been under heavy fire from what appeared to be lasers. Argo class ships were not well armed, but at about six hundred meters in length they were decently armored, typically escorted by fighters, and definitely not worth the effort to bring down for pirates.

The pock marks and venting gasses along with the slow but constant spin were strong signs of the ship's critical damage. As the Puddle Jumper moved in they were eventually able to identify the name of the craft: The EF (Earth Force) Big Guppy. Sensors eventually confirmed that life support had failed and their communications array was down. Structural integrity was surprisingly good, however, despite the beating the ship had obviously taken.

"Chris, close to three clicks and then give me a three-sixty orbit of the ship. I want to know exactly what we're dealing with here," explained the captain.

"Roger that," Chris said.

As they got closer the size was truly impressive. The Argo class ship was over three times the length of the Puddle Jumper and much wider. It was intimidating seeing the dark grey hull spin slowly.

"Gasses are still coming out of the hull, which means this must have just recently happened," explained Brad.

"Who do you think would have done this? I mean, that's an Earth Force vessel. You would have to be an idiot to attack an Earth Force vessel. They surely had to know that Earth Force will send reinforcements and arrest or kill whoever did this," questioned Jordan.

"Judging by the fact that it's out here all alone, it looks like the distress call never made it out," answered the captain.

"Whoever did this was smart and took out the communications arrays first. Now it will be hours or even days before Earth Force wonders where its transport is located. Basically they will notice it didn't show up at its scheduled time wherever it was supposed to go," Chris pointed out.

As Chris brought the Puddle Jumper close to the Big Guppy the captain ordered him to go active with the sensors again. The details regarding the carnage of the big ship became clearer to Chris as the sensors provided more information.

"It looks like the escape pods were jettisoned, but there are no SOS signals in the area. This is getting weirder and weirder," chimed in Stacey.

"Keep your eyes peeled Stacey. I want to know if anyone else is coming while we go aboard," proclaimed the captain.

"We're going aboard an Earth Force ship!?" both the twins blurted out.

Chris laughed. "What's the matter, you girls scared of a derelict ship?" although inside he had to admit he was pretty creeped out.

Stacey jumped in, saying, "I'm a girl and I am not afraid of that ship, so what are you trying to say, Chris?"

"Hold up Stacey, you are a woman. The twins are girls," Chris replied.

The twins both gave Chris the middle finger salute while Stacey chuckled.

Chris wasn't super familiar with military freighter architecture, but it didn't take long for him to identify a docking hatch in part of the ship that wasn't too badly damaged. He maneuvered the ship in close to the docking hatch while matching the relative movement of the larger ship.

Bang! The ship shuddered as the Puddle Jumper's docking hatch clanged against the Big Guppy's docking hatch.

The captain smiled and stated, "Here we go."

CHAPTER 3

Captain Hammerfist briefed the team while they suited up in protective gear for the exploration of the Big Guppy.

"Listen up! I want two teams for this expedition. XO, you take Chris, Jordan, Tweedle Dee, and Tweedle Dumb." Everyone except for the twins chuckled. "I want you to see if you can find anything valuable in the cargo hold worth bringing back. Meanwhile, Jordan and I will make our way to the bridge to figure out what happened to our derelict prize. Stacey, you will stay with the Puddle Jumper to guide us and monitor for trouble."

"You mean hide back on base avoiding danger while we go on the big spooky spaceship!" Tim butted in, to the amusement of his brother.

"Perks of sleeping with the captain!" added Tom.

Stacey jabbed an elbow into Tom's gut and he keeled over on the floor. The rest of the crew laughed.

At this point Captain Hammerfist stepped in.

"All right, that's enough. We have to get our game faces on. This ship could spell big money or big trouble for us depending on what's inside and who's looking for it. Stacey will guide us based on scans and data of the ship's layout, while keeping an eye on the sensors for any signs of company. If anyone shows up and we can't bug out in time our story is we stumbled on the ship while scouting for mineral-rich asteroids. As good members of society we immediately offered assistance and boarded looking to rescue survivors. Any questions?" The crew remained silent as the thought of answering questions in front of global-level court was not a pleasant one. "OK, good, let's suit up!"

Chris liked the captain's plan and didn't have a problem with it other than being in a group with the XO. Brad was a power-drunk asshole when left in charge. Chris started getting into his exosuit, which he liked to think of as a badass suit of armor but was actually no more than a beefed-up utility suit. Still, it was made of a lot of carbon fiber and titanium and was powered, which gave him superhuman strength, albeit not much in terms of speed. Most importantly, however, it had magnetic boots, which would allow him to walk around even if the artificial gravity had failed. Last but not least a comm system allowed him to track the rest of his crew, and vice versa. When he was a young kid Chris would get in the exosuits and walk around the Puddle Jumper, pretending to be a Space Force Marine. After accidently breaking a former crewman's arm, however, he was denied access until he was older.

Chris powered it on and the heads-up display came to life. Chris heard the familiar noises and gears beginning to turn as the machine turned on. Power was at 68 percent, which was more than enough but pissed him off because someone forgot to charge the suit.

"Some dickhead forgot to charge the damn suits!" said Chris.

"Fuck me, mine is at 59 percent," replied Jordan.

"Tim and Tom, what the hell guys?" asked Brad.

Both the twins looked down as they knew they were the ones who were supposed to charge the suits after loading the ship back in Earth orbit.

Chris then reached into his locker with his armored arm and pulled out a small Laz Tech laser pistol. The metal claw lifted the gun and he placed it into a custom-made holster attached to his exosuit.

"What are you bringing that for Chris?" questioned Brad.

"Well we have to keep the twins in line somehow," replied Chris as he unholstered the gun and spun it around in the exosuit's hand, mimicking an old western cowboy. Chris finished the move by holstering it again, demonstrating his control over the equipment.

The twins both chuckled.

"That really isn't necessary Chris. There are no life signs aboard and even if people do show up from another ship your one laser pistol is not going to stop them," explained Brad in a prissy voice.

Chris was getting sick of Brad's constant nagging and disapproval but knew there was nothing he could do since Brad was the XO. He thought of Brad as a consummate suck-up, who exhibited the associated trait of regarding his lessor crewmembers as brainless idiots.

"I'd rather have it and not need it, than need it and not have it," is all Chris said in response.

Tim chose that time to chime in, saying, "It's free space, XO, people are allowed to have guns out here according to the Earth constitution! We are a gun-loving race!"

"Ya!" added Tom.

"Fine, you want to bring extra stuff along then so be it," resigned Brad.

Chris shot the twins a wink when Brad had turned back around. The three of them as a rule tended to team up when it came to arguing with their XO.

The teams set off and began clanking down the hall on the way toward the airlock. Once they got there, Captain Hammerfist turned around and boomed through the helmet speakers, "All right, let's stay alert and be ready to bail at a moment's notice. I don't think this ship is going to remain here undetected or undisturbed for long. Remember, this is a smash and grab folks, not a full-length salvage op. You guys are going to the cargo bay to grab whatever looks valuable as quickly as possible while Jordan and I head to the bridge to figure out what happened. Maybe we'll get lucky and find something valuable on the ship's computers for us to download and sell on the dark web. Any questions?"

There was just silence. Chris looked around and saw nervous twitches and sweat droplets forming on people's brows. There was a tense feeling in his belly, and he hoped it was nothing, but had to admit to himself the situation was weird.

"All right, let's move out!" said the captain.

Chris slammed the open button on the airlock and the crew slowly filed in. Chris could almost taste the nervousness in the air. Sure, they had been on dozens of salvage operations, but usually they were on asteroids or an independent civilian ship—never on an Earth Force ship. This was illegal in every way they knew, but in a spacer's world, you didn't pass up on free loot. So despite the nervousness, they knew the job could pay off well. The computer chimed and said "Pressurized" and then the door to the docking tunnel opened. The corridor was fairly wide at about four meters but in their exosuits the crew couldn't walk more than two abreast.

"Magnetics on!" yelled the captain and the whole crew toggled on their mag boots. Based on the lack of power they knew the Big Guppy probably didn't have its artificial gravity online. There were some windows in the tunnel and Chris had to admit to himself the view was stunning. Two large ships next to each other spinning in unison in the middle of an asteroid field. Earth's sun Sol could be seen in the distance when it wasn't covered up by an asteroid, brightening up all of the rocks and ice chunks around them.

Once everyone was inside the tunnel Stacey closed the door back to the Puddle Jumper. Clanking down the hallways the two teams made their way to the airlock on the other side. Jordan hooked up his computer to the Big Guppy's interface and after a few clicks the interface turned red and displayed an error message. He turned around to address the crew, "The other side of the door isn't pressurized. If we're going in I need to depressurize the tunnel so we don't get blown through the door by equalization."

"Everyone check your suits," came a quick command from the captain, "OK Jordan, do it."

Jordan keyed a few commands on his tablet and suddenly the air could be heard leaving the tunnel. Space suit or not, it was disconcerting for Chris to walk around in vacuum. Like going over the edge of a cliff with a rope and harness, you knew you were OK, but still . . . A few moments later and Jordan was again keying the door interface. After another prompt, the door slid open, revealing the interior of the ship to them.

Darkness was all they saw until a few red tinted lights flashed on and off as the power went in and out. Red lights, while they helped keep vision adjusted in the dark, tended to give the ship a less-than-friendly appearance.

"Lights on!" boomed the captain and everyone toggled the lights on their exosuits. Everyone made their way into the airlock and the captain cycled the door on the other side, which granted them access to the ship. Chris stuck his head through first. Everything went from pitch black to very visible when his suit lights hit the background. He didn't see anything alarming outside of a few dangling wires with sparks coming off them so he waved the crew forward. The door had opened up into a hallway that went left and right of their position.

"Directions would be real helpful here, Stacey," mentioned the captain.

Stacey came over the comm, saying, "Sorry, Captain. Take the hallway to the left. That is where we need to go according to my schematics."

The team began clanking slowly down the hallway to the left, looking all around for any signs of trouble. Clearly the ship had been in a fight and was on the losing end. The lights that did work were the red emergency types and would flicker on and off in irregular intervals, making the hallways look like scenes from a classic horror movie.

After about two minutes of walking down hallways silently Jordan quietly said, "Halt here. This is the junction. Captain, we need to go right to reach the bridge elevator. Team two will go left, and after a couple hundred feet should reach the cargo bay."

"Stacey, how do the sensors look? Are we still clear?" asked the captain.

"All clear up here. I am picking up some weird readings coming from the cargo bay, but they are extremely faint and I'm not sure what to make of it. Probably nothing," replied Stacey.

"That's a big ten-four," returned the captain. "All right, Brad, you lead team two to the cargo bay and go find us some nice expensive Earth Force toys we can commandeer. Make sure the twins don't wander off and get lost either. Jordan and I are going to make our way up to the bridge and figure out what happened. If you see anything valuable like firearms, flag them to grab on the way out. Don't move anything until I say so—a lot easier to claim search and rescue if we don't yet have stolen military firearms on our ship."

"Yes sir!" said Brad. "Chris, you take point and try not to get lost."

Chris started clanking down the hallway and the two teams split up.

"Where are the bodies?" asked Tom.

"Good question," said Tim.

Brad answered their question. "They have been spaced—at least the ones in the hallway. If we were to follow this hallway to the end you would see a large hole in the superstructure which vented all the atmosphere . . . and bodies."

Chris shuttered at the thought, then looked down the hallways and the walls and realized what he was looking at. There were dark spots here and there on the walls, floor, and ceilings that were puddles of blood sticking to the walls in the zero G. Little goblets still formed above the surface of the puddles but stayed attached to the rest as there was not enough force in the zero G to break the tension. Chris did his best to avoid the almost-floating splotches of blood, as did the rest of the team. After another thirty seconds of clanking they came to a door with the label "Cargo Hold" above it.

Tim exclaimed, "I bet this ship has a billion credits worth of Earth Force guns and weapons on it!"

Tom replied, "I bet it has two billion worth of Earth Force gear!"

Tim responded, "I bet it has T-800 suits of armor. If it does, I'm calling dibs on one, putting it on, and I'm bringing it back on the Puddle Jumper!"

Brad had to step in to ruin the twins' dreams. "No you are not, Tim. If we find a suit you can bring it back to the Puddle Jumper in a crate, but you will not be wearing that suit on board the Jumper because you will probably find a way to put a hole in the ship and then your brother Tom will get sucked out. You being the moron you are will try to save him and both of you will end up getting sucked out and I will be left to patch the hole in the ship."

"Well aren't you just a bundle of joy," said Tim.

Chris jumped into the conversation and explained, "Guys there are probably not going to be a ton of weapons on the ship. It's in the asteroid belt for some reason, and I can't think why a military vessel would be here, let alone with a lot of guns. I mean who would it be bringing them to?"

The twins looked at him with disappointment on their faces and Brad gave him a look of approval before saying, "OK, Chris, time to get us through this door. Can you hack into it?"

"No," Chris responded with a smirk on his face, "but I can hit the open button." Brad was clearly oblivious to military vessels. While Chris had no more experience, his fascination with researching Earth Force ships had taught him that military vessels had very few locked doors. After all, it was real inconvenient during a battle to forget a door combination or key.

Brad then said, "All right team, let's keep it together as we don't know what we will find behind the doors. That being said, I want the standard search, sweep, and recover. We need to try to find as many of the most expensive containers the ship has as we may not have long to be here before someone comes looking and we need to go."

The whole team nodded their heads and threw in a grunt or two. Then Chris walked up to the touch pad and hit the open button. The cargo doors began to slide open and the team got to see for the first time what was inside.

CHAPTER 4

"**M**y God," was all the Chris could say when the doors opened and his exosuit lights lit up the cargo hold. The sight made Chris want to vomit. Several smashed up and bloody bodies floated in front of them in the cargo hold. Others looked like they had died of asphyxiation. Bulging, wide open, bloodshot eyes were an easy give away. Even those who managed to get on oxygen masks had cracks in the visors and air had leaked out. What made matters worse was the bay was relatively empty. There were only four cargo containers that were several dozen meters in the back of the massive hold.

"Ohhhh man," sighed Tim.

"Well that was a waste," replied Tom.

"Ya I'm not going to lie this was not what I expected," replied Chris, "We will have to take a look at the four containers, I guess. Should I radio the captain and let him know what we have here, XO?"

"No, I'll take care of that," replied Brad and he stood still for a minute in his exosuit. Moments like this seemed awkward if you didn't know what was going on but Brad had opened up a private channel and was talking to the captain without transmitting it to the rest of the team.

Chris began clanking further inside, shoving bodies aside with ease thanks to his exosuit. He was looking for something else just in case there was more inside the cargo hold than the four containers. The twins made their way straight to the containers to begin scanning what was inside. As Chris looked at the walls he quickly realized there was not much to see other than the occasional body. The big hold was empty for the most part. "Such a disappointment," he thought. "Why would this big military cargo ship be here in the asteroid belt with a cargo hold that had just four containers?" It just wasn't adding up for Chris.

The twins had reached the cargo containers and they began scanning the first one. Drilling supplies and equipment were inside, according to the scanner. It even spat out an estimated worth of the equipment inside at 150,000 credits.

"Well that's not going to make us rich," commented Tom. They then began looking at the next container. The four of them stood there looking at the containers as the next scan completed. It more or less was the same thing—more drilling supplies, but this one was worth 160,000 credits.

"Fucking waste of time man!" yelled Tim.

"Come on maybe the third one has something in it worth checking out," encouraged Tom.

"Ya right, and maybe I'm going to get promoted to XO," Tim replied.

"Ha!" laughed Chris, although he thought to himself that while he liked Tim a lot more than Brad, Tim was a moron. Brad was a dick for sure, but he was at least intelligent.

They began scanning the third container and after about five seconds the scanner said, "Unknown, failed scan."

"What?" said Tim.

"Stupid thing must be broken," returned Tom.

"Try the fourth container," ordered Brad.

The twins followed orders and started to scan the last container. Again, after about five seconds the scanner repeated the previous message: "Unknown, failed scan."

"What the hell man?" yelled Tim and he started tapping the side of the scanner like that would fix it. After another try and the same response Tim looked like he was going to chuck the scanner at the wall.

"Hold on," said Chris. "I bet these containers are shielded. I have never seen the equipment that can shield against a scan but I have heard it exists and the Earth Force surely has it. Try the first container again and see if it works before you go chucking our only scanner into the wall."

The twins did as asked and sure enough the scanner worked.

Brad had watched the whole sequence of events and after they finished the scan he spoke up, "OK, if they took the time to shield those two containers then the cargo is either extremely dangerous or extremely valuable—probably both. Either way I want these containers loaded up ASAP. Tim and Tom, you get the fourth container and Chris and I will grab the third container."

"But the captain said not to move anything until he gave the word," complained Tim.

"Just get them moved toward the cargo entrance. We won't put them on the ship just yet," assured Brad.

Chris and the twins went to the containers' touch screens and began unlocking the containers from their moors. For safety reasons containers were always moored down in case the artificial gravity went out. They were also equipped with repulsers so they could be moved with relative ease once unlocked. Even in an exosuit it could be tough to move more than ten thousand pounds. As the two containers had started moving through the long bay the captain's voice came in over their intercoms.

"You boys are not going to believe this—I'm not sure I do," said the captain. "These guys are out here, according to the ship logs, because some autonomous probe found an asteroid with strange readings. They came out here to check it out and when they did they found two objects made of refined alloys partially embedded in the asteroid. Here's the kicker though—the objects had been embedded in the asteroid for thousands of years."

At this last statement Tim and Tom looked at each other, and then looked directly at Chris. He knew what that look meant. Tim and Tom were the in-house conspiracy theorists, and were always telling Chris all about how aliens were real. Chris figured they were real as well, but was not on the same level as the twins. He knew when this was done they'd never stop talking, but before they could get started the captain continued.

"Anyways these guys extracted the objects, got them locked in containers, then brought them on board and that's when all hell broke loose. Pirates showed up claiming to be from the Gate Keepers, which is some looney religious group, and opened fire. The last couple of logs show there was an order to send out a distress call and then after the GK's were done they jumped out. I'm guessing since they disabled the ship they are planning to come back and get their prize."

The twins couldn't take it anymore. They blurted out in a jumbled unison: "Chris! Aliens! We told you!"

Before they could get any further Brad cut them off, "Shut up you two! Captain, how do we play this? What should we do?"

"Find those two containers, then we get the hell out of here," was his quick reply. With that the comm link cut out.

"Dude, they are alien artifacts!" yelled Tim.

"No, they are of an unknown origin," explained Chris. "They may be alien, but they may also be man-made or a result of some natural phenomenon. We don't know what they are yet."

"Whatever dude, they're alien," replied Tom.

Chris rolled his eyes but had to admit he wanted to see what was inside those containers.

Just then Stacey came in over the comms, "Guys, we have incoming subspace signatures! Somebody knows we're here!"

The captain then added, "Forget the containers and get back to the ship immediately!"

Chris stopped pushing his container and began to take off with the twins toward the exit when Brad gave them an order, "Get your asses back here and help me with these containers."

Chris replied "But sir, the captain said—"

"I don't care what the captain said, I'm giving you a direct order. We are bringing these back to the ship immediately! Do you know how much these could be worth?" interrupted Brad.

There were several grumblings but Chris and the crew complied as Brad had blocked their communications with the captain. When they got back Chris swore he would make sure the captain heard about this. Whoever was coming would not take kindly to a salvage team looting an Earth Force ship. Best case scenario it was Earth Force, who would only arrest them. Worst case scenario it was pirates back to collect their prize and would kill them—or worse. Chris had heard horror stories about pirates who took people alive.

They quickly worked their way to the entrance of the cargo hold, tossing floating bodies aside, and got the containers out one by one. Their suits could move surprisingly fast but Chris knew they didn't have a lot of time. If Stacey could pick up the subspace signatures, whoever it was couldn't be far away. They moved as fast as they could, and less than a minute later they were making their way through the hallway where they had split up. The containers were smashing into the walls left and right during their frenzied retreat but neither Brad nor anybody else seemed to care as long as they didn't get smashed themselves. Another thirty seconds later and they were at the airlock where they saw the captain and Jordan waving at them.

"Let's go!" boomed the captain. "What the hell took you guys so long and why do you have those containers? Never mind, just keep bringing them here. Chris, you take off down the hall. Get to the bridge and get us out of here!"

Chris immediately took off in his robotic sprint. He made it through the Big Guppy's airlock and about most of the way down the tunnel between the ships when out of the corner of his eye he saw subspace portals opening. "Shit," he thought. That meant he had approximately one minute at most to get out of the suit, down the hall, up the ladder, into the bridge, and finally to the helmsmen's station. Time was not adding up in his favor but with the adrenaline pumping he thought he just might be able to do it.

He clanked his way into the airlock of the Puddle Jumper, waited for it to pressurize, thankfully a fast process, and then into the hallway, where he didn't even bother to stow the exo-suit. He just got out of it and left it standing in the middle of the hallway. He looked back down the tunnel, through a viewing port, one last time to see the rest of his crew bringing the two containers along. Chris sprinted toward the ladder. They still had ladders in space for when the elevators or turbo lifts failed, and in this situation, the ladder was faster. After he was up the ladder he made it to the bridge of the Puddle Jumper, where he saw Stacey at the Pilots station.

She looked pale as she jumped out of the pilot seat and in a frantic voice yelled, "It's too late! I started powering everything up but they're already here!"

Chris ignored her and jumped in the seat. He brought up his controls and flight stick and checked to see if the captain and crew had made it out of the tunnel into the airlock. They had made it into the airlock, shut the hatch, and were beginning to retract the tunnel so he slammed the throttle forward. The thrust might damage the tunnel but they had bigger problems.

What happened next was one of Chris's favorite things. The Puddle Jumper lurched forward at a few G's and Chris's stomach went to the back of his chair. When coming from a dead stop and giving it full power the Puddle Jumper's inertial dampeners struggled to compensate for the change in momentum. What was in real life about six to seven Gs of acceleration still felt like almost two to three Gs. Chris could only imagine the chaos going on in the airlock and hoped that nobody was between the cargo containers and the aft wall when he hit the throttles. Even in an EXO suit a man could be squished by containers with that much mass.

Chris checked his radar indicator on his HUD and saw there were at least twenty ships, all of a fighter configuration with the exception of one Tumbler class transport vessel. Chris was a very confident young man and wouldn't admit anyone was a better pilot than him. That being said, even he had doubts about getting out of this one alive. He pushed down on the stick to avoid hitting one of the big asteroids and the Puddle Jumper's maneuvering thrusters did their job, sending the big ship at a downward angle.

Just then a comm request came across, blaring on all frequencies. Captain Hammerfist opened the channel and a man with a scarred face and black, short-trimmed beard with grey streaks came up on the Puddle Jumper's HUD and communications. The transponder program identified him as "Zion."

"Surrender now and I will spare your life," ordered the bearded man. "You are meddling with things you do not understand. We just scanned your ship and we know you removed two containers that do not belong to you."

The captain sent a private message to Chris before addressing Zion, "Chris, don't slow down. Charge the drives and get us the hell out of here. They won't destroy this ship if they want that cargo."

Then the captain replied, "Listen, Zion, we are just a civilian craft and we have no hostile intentions toward—"

Zion jumped in, "You are stalling—open fire."

Chris dodged left but it was no use. One big freighter, even if it was a fast one, was no match for twenty Skimmer class light fighters. Skimmers were an older generation fighter but still had incredible speed and agility compared to a freighter. While one didn't pack a lot of firepower, twenty were more than enough to destroy the Puddle Jumper. Rumbling began to be felt throughout the ship. Chris knew she was taking fire. He figured his best bet was to continue at full burn until he could get clear of the asteroid field and enter subspace.

The captain and the rest of the bridge crew began trickling into the bridge at this point but struggled to get to their seats as Chris kept changing direction in an effort to avoid the fire he was taking.

"Captain, I should have us out of here in about thirty seconds and so far the armor is holding but there won't be much left when we jump," urged Chris between clenched teeth.

"That's fine—now get us out of here!" replied Captain Hammerfist.

Another series of shudders came and Chris checked his status display. About 50 percent of the armor had been destroyed on the rear half of the ship. Soon some of the shots would start making it through to their key systems.

"They're targeting the engines!" yelled Chris.

"They're trying to take us alive and get their loot back. Let's not let them have it!" replied the captain.

Chris weaved again past another asteroid and then he saw it: the clearing he needed to hit subspace. Boom! Another shudder shook the ship and Chris saw he had lost one of his engines.

"Engaging drive!" yelled Chris.

The familiar noise of the subspace drive came on as it began discharging enough energy to create a temporary wormhole and bring the ship into subspace. Another engine was taken offline, which left them with only two, but Chris knew as long as they had enough forward momentum they wouldn't need their engines to get out of there.

Just then the familiar blue and white spinning disc of a subspace portal began to grow in front of the Puddle Jumper.

Just a few seconds more and they would be out of there! Another couple of shudders and Chris saw the remaining two engines had been taken offline and the armor was down to as low as 10 percent in some sections. Chris looked up one more time and then all the noise and chaos seemed to stop as a white glare enveloped them.

CHAPTER 5

A Brief Review of Human Space Exploration
(Excerpt from UCE standard history book)

At the time of this writing, 2271 A.D., human space exploration has been an ongoing effort for well over three cen-
turies. It is also fair to say that it has reached higher levels of
investment, exploration, and intensity over the last fifty years
than any time before. What was once the world economy has
become a solar system economy. In order to understand where
it is going however, one must first take a look at the past.

2016–2040 A.D.

In the late 2010s the United States of America saw the
space race reborn. Instead of competition between countries
however, the battle was between companies. At the time it
was considered to be the biggest push to get to space since
the Apollo missions to the moon back in the 1960s and 1970s.
Compared to modern space exploration it now seems trivial,
but at the time the world was clamoring for someone to further
the human race in terms of exploration. The economy was doing very well and there was a brilliant businessman name Elon
Musk who owned a company called Space X. Despite claiming
he would put a man on Mars by 2024, in typical Musk fashion
he was late but still delivered, fulfilling the promise in 2026.
Once mankind was able to become a multiplanetary

species its appetite only grew and grew. Because of the limited technology and resources of the time, only another fifty missions were ordered back to Mars between 2026 and 2040. During this time, however, valuable strides were made in creating a viable base of operations on the Red Planet. First, basic life-support equipment and scientific instruments had to be transported. This supported the first people who set foot on Martian soil but proved ineffective for long-term occupation. Next came the arrival of farming solutions, complex equipment, and the first true Martian settlers. By 2040, a permanent base of operations had been formed, creating a beachhead of human interplanetary exploration.

2040–2093 A.D.

Once a permanent base was in place and the technologies for getting there had matured the base on Mars grew quickly. Not only did other countries race to plant their flags, but many multibillionaires used this opportunity to cement their legacy. Mars grew from being one base, to eventually a town under a bubble, and by the 2090s it was a small city. The foundations for the terraforming seen today were even started during this time.

In 2048 the United States established the first base on the moon and began building mining colonies soon after. In addition to building bases on the moon, the human species began sending unmanned ships to the asteroid belt and the many moons of the gas giants. These asteroids were often densely packed clusters of exotic elements, worth untold sums in days past. Like all flights before the development of fusion engines these missions could take anywhere from a few months to a few years.

One other interesting piece of information that remains unconfirmed but is a very popular conspiracy theory is that in 2046 while digging the foundations for a high-rise in the outskirts of Chicago, something with ancient writing was uncovered from a metallic pod. It was initially believed to be from an ancient Native American civilization, and this is the current government position. Many groups, however, claimed it had to be alien as it was quickly removed by the United States government and its current whereabouts are unknown. These groups go further to claim that many of humanity's recent scientific advances can be linked to info gathered from this ancient artifact. This is called the Ancients Theory.

2093–2142 A.D.

In 2093 mankind was finally able to crack the code to fusion technology and create its own unlimited supply of clean energy. This revolutionized space travel and caused what used to take years to now take months or even weeks. Missions to Mars were no longer a thing that took extensive planning based on when the Earth and Mars were close together. Now even when the planets were at their furthest apart the journey only took a couple of weeks. With fusion engines the human race was able to move at a small percentage of the speed of light. Even today the concepts developed during this time are used to power the largest, most powerful ships.

By 2110 spaceships equipped with these fusion reactors were becoming numerous and hundreds of new expeditions and mining colonies had been launched. The asteroid belt was becoming a huge metal mining belt full of companies. At this point Earth was even populating some of the gas giants' various moons.

In 2130 mankind sent out its first interstellar mission to Alpha Centauri. The journey would take around twelve years each way. This marked the first time humans would become a multi-solar-system species.

2143–2209 A.D.

In 2143 the first worldwide government was formed. It was simply named the United Countries of Earth (UCE) and about 80 percent of countries on Earth willingly signed up. The other 20 percent remained under the jurisdiction of the UCE but were not always willing participants. The UCE was formed due to the growing populations around the solar system, and in particular Mars. It is still the governing body behind the Earth Force space military. By 2143 Mars was home to three hundred million people and regularly supported as much as half a billion people (including labor and tourists). They wanted their own independence from Earth, which led to the first interplanetary wars and the creation of their own government. The Asteroid belt and even the moons of Jupiter and Saturn eventually would do the same.

Two additional solar systems were colonized, Sirius and Epsilon Eridani, but due to the many years it took to get there they remain on the fringe as lowly populated colonies. Even after the discovery of subspace these colonies remained years away.

The Sol system continued to grow in population and evolve technologically but humanity was about to take its next big leap forward.

2210–present day 2271 A.D. as of the writing of this article

In 2210 the discovery of subspace was made real. This changed space travel forever. Instead of ships spending days building up speed and then days slowing down to go from one planet to another, ships were able to open a wormhole into subspace and travel from one destination to the next in minutes. This changed everything, from ship design to ship warfare. Gone were the days of having to anticipate where a ship would be by the time you fired your weapon. Conflicts where ships would fly past each other in the blink of an eye and be hundreds of kilometers apart in seconds were over. While ships are still capable of building up that kind of speed there is often no need to as they are able to create artificial wormholes that can take them from Earth to Mars in mere minutes.

Subspace also brought the different governments in the Sol system much closer together. UCE was quickly able to extend its influence and vast resources where it felt it was needed. Either you became an ally of UCE or you were banished to the fringes of the solar system. UCE became the most powerful form of government in Sol with United States of Mars (USM) in a distant second place.

All this became possible through the understanding of how to manipulate gravity. This also led to the ability to create artificial gravity in spaceships. There was no longer a need to spin a portion of the ship in order to generate gravity, leading to another evolution in ship design.

Unfortunately, subspace was not the be-all and end-all mankind hoped it would be. There were limitations on distance, meaning you could not open up a subspace portal from Earth and go to Alpha Centauri. The biggest distances traveled were the equivalent of going from our sun Sol to Neptune. After that, the artificial worm holes became unstable and could not be traveled safely. Many ships have been lost trying to create wormholes that went even further, never to be heard from again. In addition, wormholes cannot be created too close to large gravity wells, such as planets or moons, as they are too unstable. This is why the three colonies in other solar systems remained small, lacked the ability to significantly impact the human race, and remained self governed. Even when taking many small jumps through a subspace portal, it would still take multiple years to reach the nearest colony in Alpha Centauri. Until the next giant leap in science, mankind has been largely limited to the Sol system. It is estimated by the years 2400–2500 A.D.

the three colonies will be large enough to support their own fleets and contribute to human exploration.

With subspace the human race again reached new levels of productivity within the solar system and continued to massively push space travel in the solar system to new levels. With subspace it became possible for people to take a weekend trip to Mars or even Saturn.

Interestingly enough, no one man or company is credited with discovering subspace. Many have claimed to be responsible for it but have been unable to show proof of how they did it. This has led to many people giving fuel to the Ancients Theory that something in the pod discovered in 2046 led to the breakthrough. This has been dismissed as a simple conspiracy theory by UCE officials.

CHAPTER 6

The white began to fade away and Chris was able to see the familiar sight of a subspace tunnel. It looked like a cylindrical tube that the ship was going through, with blue and black walls that flowed past the ship in a spiral pattern. In the center at the end of the tunnel was a bright white circle that would be the other end of the wormhole. He knew that they had several minutes in subspace before reaching the other end. Even though wormholes folded space spanning incredible distances, it still took some time to traverse the length of the tunnel. Chris wasn't sure how or why this happened but after a brief adventure into astrophysics he decided to stop asking that question. Chris exhaled and in his mind he said a prayer and thanked God he was still alive.

"WOOOOHOOOOO!" yelled Tim.

"Damage assessment!" yelled the captain.

"Armor is pretty much gone in the aft of the ship and down to 30 percent in many of the other sections toward the rear. Engines one through four are out but we have enough momentum to carry us through the portal. All other systems are nominal," replied Stacey

"That was amazing Chris!" yelled Tom.

"Stow it guys, we have jobs to do," barked the captain. "All right, Jordan, grab the twins and get to the engines and see how bad it is. We need to get those online and get back to a

♦ 38 ♦

base for repair ASAP."

The three of them moved out and the crew went to work figuring out what the next move would be. Chris watched as the Puddle Jumper continued to drift down the subspace corridor.

"Chris, where did you plot the jump for us to come out?" asked the captain.

"I just picked a random spot in space that was about a million kilometers below the orbital planes of the planets below the asteroid belt. I figured that would keep us out of harm's way and nobody would be able to find us in a random place in the Sol system," Chris replied.

"Ya but on the other hand unless we send a SOS signal nobody is going to come to our aid either," criticized Brad.

"Well Brad, I didn't exactly have time to plan out the pleasure cruise you so desperately wanted. In case you didn't notice I was flying while getting my butt shot off!" Chris shot back.

"It's fine. I want everyone at their stations so we'll be able to figure out what's going on when we get out of subspace," remarked the captain.

Another thirty seconds went by and the ship was once again enveloped in the white glare of the portal threshold. When they emerged the team began assessing how they were going to get the engines online. Jordan reported back saying the damage to the engines was bad—really bad.

"Basically we have enough spare parts to bring two of the engines back online and by get them back online I mean we have to swap them out." The Puddle Jumper was large enough to include a small but decently equipped machine shop on board. This enabled Jordan and Stacey to do surprisingly extensive repairs without having to pay for the work elsewhere. "I'm going to need at least two days though around the clock to get them functional," explained Jordan.

This was not a problem, as the ship had enough food to last

them a couple of months, and with the recycling systems on-board air and water were a renewable resource. Chris got up from his console to help out as he knew there was no piloting needed at this time. All they had were maneuvering thrusters and that wouldn't help them get anywhere significant so he figured he could help with repairs.

Chris was just about to walk off the bridge when Stacey announced, "Captain, I am picking up some weird readings."

"What is it?" asked the captain.

"Not sure yet but it's some type of signal coming from our ship," replied Stacey.

The captain wrinkled his forehead in thought for a brief moment, but suddenly jumped out of his seat, shouting, "Stacey locate that signal now! Brad look through any external cameras we have still working at the back of the ship. Look for something that does not belong!"

"It's coming from just above where the number three en-gine exhaust is located," Stacey said in a worried tone.

Brad continued to work his console, sliding through differ-ent camera feeds. Chris knew this couldn't be good, so he got back in his helmsman chair.

"Shiiiit," said Brad in a worried voice. "There is something that looks like it latched on to the back of our ship."

"Everyone get back to your stations! I want Jordan and the twins to the turrets! Chris you can run the fourth one from your helmsman console. I believe they hit us with a tracker, which means any minute now we are going to have company again," commanded the captain.

If there was one place the captain had not skimped it was the ship's defensive firepower. Life as a freelancer ship doing occasional smuggling runs wasn't the safest line of work. Sure, 95 percent of the time their trips were uneventful. The XO even complained periodically that they were wasting money preparing for a gunfight that would never come. Every so of-ten, however, another ship would show up to the same site claiming they'd been there first. At that point the captain could usually talk them off with strong words. Sometimes though they'd run into an especially insistent (usually Martian) salvage ship that wasn't turned away so easily. Usually Chris learned later these were pirates, trying to get close enough to size up their prey. At that point the captain would fire a trio of rapid-fire warning shots, demonstrating their firepower, and that would usually end the matter.

The Puddle Jumper was equipped with four medium-class laser turrets. Normally these were already powerful weapons. Stacey and Jordan had worked together, however, to increase their power and cooling abilities, turning them into weapons of devastating effectiveness. Individually they were strong enough to punch through almost any light fighter in a few shots. With coordinated fire they could even damage other freighters, and with enough time theoretically a capital ship— not that the Puddle Jumper could survive long in a fight with a capital ship, but it did usually help deter pirates, knowing the Puddle Jumper would punch back.

In addition to those turrets the Puddle Jumper had four more point-defense cannons, which could take out incoming missiles. These batteries were automated though, as missiles moved too fast for a human to track. They could, however, accept human inputs regarding target prioritization. In summary, the captain, as a point of pride, had made sure the Puddle Jumper was well protected from any normal threat they would encounter. No other ship yet had pushed the issue further once the captain ordered a warning shot. Chris thoroughly enjoyed watching antagonists back step, close the link, and fly away. He even caught Brad smiling after watching them scatter before their superior firepower.

Today Chris had never been happier that when it came to arming their ship, the captain had stuck to his guns, quite literally. He could tell, however, that what they had might not be enough for what was coming their way. This suspicion was confirmed when the captain turned off the comms device and calmly looked at Brad.

"XO, I need you to start preparing for a boarding party. Start by setting up a barricade around the main docking hatch. If they do find us—and God help us if they do—they'll have to make it past our turrets. If they get past those the docking hatch will be where we make our last stand. Godspeed, Brad."

It was at this point that Chris, for the first time in a long time, felt true fear. Chris had flown this ship through asteroids, made questionable subspace jumps, and even dealt with a few pirates. But never in his life had he been outmanned, outgunned, and had to deal with the possibility of someone boarding his ship. They should have been safe after they hit the jump. Nobody carried trackers capable of reporting the result of a subspace jump, as they were expensive and the military kept pretty tight control over them. Chris sat back down in his console and just stared at his hands as they shook slightly. It felt like there was a fifty-pound weight in the middle of his chest. Just then he felt a warm hand on his shoulder.

"Son, you are going to be OK," comforted Captain Hammerfist. "I'll get us out of this, but I need you to be on your game with that turret. Remember, they need the cargo inside our ship, so they won't destroy us. We just need to make this ship too much trouble to be worth it for them."

"Dad," said Chris quietly. Chris didn't call the captain "dad" when the rest of the crew was around but in private he always referred to the man who had raised him as dad. "How are we going to make it out of this? Should I send an SOS out?"

"No, not yet. If they come we will send out an emergency signal, but there is still a small chance we got something wrong and they're not going to follow us. Just remember, they have to get through me before they can get to you and I don't plan on going down easily," replied Josh.

This comforted Chris, and Josh's strength reminded him

that while Chris knew he was a great helmsman, he was not yet ready to be a captain.

Just then Stacey chimed in, "Sir," she gulped, "I am detecting several subspace signatures."

The captain returned to his station and keyed up the comms one more time. "Boys, we have company inbound. I'm not going to bullshit you. This is going to be tough for us. But we do have a couple of cards to play." The captain signaled Chris to send out the SOS. "We all need to be on our game here so clear your minds and stay focused. Fear is the mind killer, the enemy of the mind, and you must be ready to face it. When those ships start coming through the subspace portals I want them to be lit up with laser fire. They want what we have, which means they will have to disable us to get it. We sent out an SOS, which means they won't have forever to disable us and get on board. Our goal is to either A, make this cargo not worth their time by causing as much damage as possible, or B, hold them off long enough to avoid being boarded while we wait for the authorities arrive. Those of you manning the cannons light up the nearest ship when you get the chance. If we do for whatever reason lose our weapons, we will all retreat toward the docking hatch area where the XO is preparing a secondary defense. This is it, boys; it's time to make our stand."

Chris noticed his hands had stopped shaking and he continued to calm himself. He began to look through his turrets camera and started furiously looking for the first subspace signature to emerge from subspace. He was going to light up anything that came through the portal. It took another thirty seconds but once it started he knew the race was on and only the winner got to live.

Just then he saw a flash followed by a little blue portal open up about three thousand meters off the port side.

"First one's coming through, nine o'clock low!" he heard the captain call out.

Chris was controlling the lower turret and he wheeled it to face where he expected the first skimmer to come out of the subspace portal. About a second later the small silhouette of a Skimmer began to emerge while at the same time Chris's targeting reticule turned red over the object. This meant he had a lock and since the cannons effective range was about ten thousand meters he was well within range. Chris squeezed the trigger and saw the lights dim ever so slightly with the large demand of power the lasers demanded. Out of his peripheral vision he saw the amber streaks of the other turrets firing as well on the main display.

As the Skimmer finished emerging from the portal it was showered by no less than three direct beams. Even with the fighter's armor the pilot never stood a chance. The three beams immediately lit the small craft up. Chris could see the metal of the ship turn bright orange, then white as it slagged off. Internal systems must have been damaged as evidenced by the sparks flying off the ship and the gasses leaking. Chris watched the beams punch through the other side of the ship and extend into space before cutting off to recycle.

"WOOOOHOOOOO!" yelled Chris.

"Hell ya, nailed that pirate bastard!" added Tim.

Their excitement quickly died as ten more subspace portals began opening up.

"We have incoming, guys! We need to synchronize our attacks," shouted the captain. "I'm highlighting the first target—light 'em up!"

The crew knew some basic tactics when dealing with subspace attacks. Ships were their most vulnerable right after they emerged from a subspace portal because they were going slow and in a straight line. That's when you hit them. Otherwise, after they emerged the pilots would typically hit full burn and accelerate at extreme rates, making them tough to shoot. Even autotargeting computers had limitations and they couldn't predict a pilot's maneuvers.

Chris saw one of the emerging ships highlighted blue as the captain had targeted that ship for them to attack. He didn't know what prior sin that pilot had committed to receive this fate, but the turrets had gone through their cooling cycle and were ready for round two. As soon as the enemy ship emerged Chris depressed the trigger again. Once more, the pirate's vessel went white-hot from the simultaneous fire, but before the beams were able to punch through Chris was blinded by a white light.

He immediately covered his eyes but it was too late. Even as the light died away he was seeing stars.

"What the hell—I can't see anything!" shouted Tim. Tom echoed the same sentiment.

"Stow it boys—the reactor went supercritical. Get over it! I've highlighted your next target. Open fire now!" ordered the captain.

They were able to open fire on another ship, but before it was destroyed it managed to get away, albeit with significant damage. The enemy ships had seen what had happened to their comrades and were clearly being more cautious. The Puddle Jumper's crew fought valiantly, but Chris knew it was nine fighters versus one transport ship. They had sucker punched the hell out of the first two fighters, but that card had been played. The enemies were taking evasive action and surely planning on how they were going to rip off the Puddle Jumper's claws.

The team did manage to pick off another ship but that's where the good news ended. To make things worse two more subspace portals opened out of range of their laser canons. One was another Skimmer and the other was the Tumbler class cargo ship. Tumbler class ships were great multipurpose ships that were small at only forty meters but thick with armor and could carry lots for their small size. Chris knew this ship probably had a boarding party on it.

A familiar deep scratchy voice with a southern accent came

over the comm systems. "Surrender now Puddle Jumper, and I'll spare y'alls lives." This familiar voice belonged to Zion, the head of the pirate band they were dealing with.

"Go to hell!" replied Captain Hammerfist. "Keep on them boys!"

"Have it your way, Captain," sighed Zion.

Chris began tracking his next target. It was a Skimmer flying in a formation of two. He was having trouble getting a target lock and fired twice, both shots missing their mark. Just then the fighters turned in unison right toward the ship. Chris fired again and hit one of the ships with a glancing blow. It was enough to deter the fighter from coming at him this pass, but Chris knew he was not out.

There were several more shudders and Chris knew the Puddle Jumper was taking fire. It also made lining up precise shots difficult. He knew the ships armor wouldn't last long in the aft section as it was already thin there. Lucky for the crew the turrets were in the mid-section of the ship and that armor was relatively undamaged. Chris felt the ship shake more from incoming fire and watched the status indicator for Tom's turret turn yellow to indicate it was taking damage. An exasperated cry from Tom emphasized the impact. Chris lined up his reticule on the other ship coming toward him and fired again. Direct hit! Chris watched as much of its frontal armor was vaporized and the ship veered off course. It was damaged but not out of the fight.

Chris again checked the status indicator and Tom's turret had gone red, meaning he was out of the fight. In addition, Jordan's turret status was now yellow from taking fire. One of the ships attacking Jordan's turret was highlighted, and the crew immediately synchronized fire. Chris didn't know if the pilot was reckless or just slow, but he veered away late as all three remaining beams opened up on him. By the time the ship had turned its engines sputtered out, spelling doom for the pilot.

COSMIC GATE

Chris almost felt bad as the turrets cycled, knowing their next blow to the fighter would spell death for the pilot. Just then he saw a small puff, and the pilot's capsule detached from the enemy skimmer. The pilot had ejected. The captain must have seen it too, because another target was immediately highlighted. The Puddle Jumper wasn't full of saints, but they weren't murderers either.

Chris scanned for the next target and saw a skimmer that had just finished its attack run on Tom's turret. Four enemies were down, but there were still eight fighters remaining. At this point all parties knew the captain's targets were mere suggestions, as there was no way he could keep up with all of the actions. Chris lined up his sights on the next available target, fired, and missed. He lined up again as the fighter pulled up, knowing it was being targeted. Just as he fired another shudder hit the ship knocking his hands around, causing him to miss.

"Dammit," Chris whispered under his breath.

The point defense cannons, or PDCs, were chattering away doing their best to help but the small fire did not do a lot of damage and mostly just caused the pirates to bail on their approach and line up again.

Chris saw his target turn away from him but the target made the mistake of flying in a straight line. Chris lined up and fired as the ship was approaching the limit of the lasers range. At the very moment one of the other turrets must have seen the same thing. Multiple beams slammed the rear of the fighter and two of the three engines sputtered out. Chris realized he had bought himself a couple of minutes with that ship as it would need to figure out the extent of the damage the Puddle Jumper had done before coming back around for another pass.

A few shudders later and Chris saw that Jordan's turret was offline and Tim was in the yellow. Tim made sure through shouts of rage that everybody on board the Puddle Jumper knew he was in trouble. That left two turrets versus eight Skimmers, some of which were damaged, plus the enemy Tumbler lurking just out of range.

A few seconds later a formation of four Skimmers came into view on his display. Much to his dismay Chris saw they were aiming directly for his turret. He began targeting the lead Skimmer as all four ships opened up fire on his turret. The lasers had an amber tint to them to help the shooter see the path they were taking. Despite amber-tinted lasers landing all around his viewing camera, Chris lined up his shot and squeezed the trigger. Boom! The lead ship took the brunt of the attack and broke off before Chris could do more damage. There was no time to celebrate though. Chris lined up the next ship behind the lead and tried to get it to peel off as well. More rumbling from laser fire prevented Chris from getting a second good shot and before he could even get the sights on the next ship the turret's camera went out and his console went red. His turret was finished.

Tim's turret was the only one left and it was in bad shape. The crew knew it was only a matter of time before Tim's turret joined the rest. Nevertheless the crew cheered their companion onward. After a few more rumbles and shudders the Puddle Jumper went quiet as the defenses were disabled. Even the point defense cannons were down.

"Everyone, it's time to meet Brad down at the airlock. Grab weapons and get moving!" ordered the captain.

Chris got up from his console and was first to the ladder. He slid down it, followed by Stacey and the captain. Chris knew the crew had to make their last stand at the airlock and was happy they had prepared. As they made it down the hallway the captain unlocked the armory and the three of them grabbed six T-22 assault rifles and several battery packs. These weapons were frowned upon by most governing bodies, but Chris knew the captain cared about that about as much as he cared about what he flushed down the toilet each morning.

The further away from civilization, the less the rules mattered. In deep space they were almost nonexistent. Chris noticed one assault rifle was missing and assumed Brad had already gotten his in preparation for the oncoming assault.

T-22 assault rifles may not have been the latest or best assault rifles on the black market, but they sure packed a hell of a punch, and they were very accurate. As they carried them to the docking hatch they saw Brad had thrown down various shelves and cargo boxes in the hallway, forming a barricade. They would have a great line of sight from which to fire at whatever came through the docking hatch. Chris wasn't a fan of the man, but he had to admit he had done an admirable job.

Tom, Tim, and Jordan made their way to the barricade and took up their weapons next to Brad, who was still throwing items down to take cover behind. Chris looked around and realized he was not the only one who was totally worried about what was going on. Pale sweaty faces with large eyes were all around. Thoughts raced through Chris's mind on what the pirates would do to them. Surely they wouldn't kill them, right? Or would they? He looked and saw the rest of the crew was very shaken, and just then a voice cut through the chaos going through everyone's mind.

"Listen crew," commanded Captain Hammerfist in his deep booming voice, "this is where we make our last stand. We have some nice weapons, a tactical advantage in terms of position, and we just have to hold out long enough to either make this trip not worth it for them or until the Earth Force arrives, which could be any minute."

"Or never," Chris thought in his head, but didn't vocalize. At least the captain seemed calm and ready to go. The crew around him had wide eyes and Stacey began crying.

"Captain, let's just give them the cargo and then they will leave!" Stacey sobbed.

"Ya, we don't need to do this, Captain," said the twins in unison with desperate looks on their face.

The captain's chiseled jaw line began to move as he explained, "Team, I know you don't want to hear this, but these are the pirates who took out an armed Earth Force vessel. The only thing keeping us alive at this point is that cargo. Otherwise they would destroy us immediately. Do you think they want any witnesses remaining who can point out what has happened both here and on the Big Guppy?"

No one on the crew said anything but Chris could tell based on a few nods and looks on their faces they believed him.

Stacey continued to sob a bit and the captain went over to her to console her.

"I have your back as long as you have mine," a voice whispered into Chris's ear. He looked suddenly to his left and saw Jordan with a very serious look on his clean-shaven face.

Chris nodded and powered up his gun. Then he remembered something and immediately asked, "XO, what did you do with our power suits?"

Brad didn't answer at first because he was obviously distracted by the current situation. After Chris shouted it at him a second time he looked back and said in a quick sharp voice, "I moved them around the corner of the hallway so I could set up this barricade."

Chris nodded and told the crew he was grabbing something from his exosuit. As he ran around the corner he saw his exosuit and grabbed his Laz Tech laser pistol out of it. Strapping it to a band on his inner leg he covered it back up with his pants. He came back and the captain began circling his team up to brief them. Before the captain could begin, a familiar southern-accented voice came over the comms in the hallway.

"Now listen carefully, my difficult and slightly stupid friends. Despite you destroying valuable property and killing my pilots this can still end peacefully if you just cooperate. Like it or not, my crew is going to board your ship. If you peacefully show them to the cargo you stole, you have my word they will not harm you. Once they verify you have not tampered with our property we'll be on our way. Y'all can go free and back to whatever existence you pathetic smugglers like. If you are difficult, however, I will kill each and every one of you and then take the cargo. And if you really piss me off, you'll wish I'd just killed you. Now let's not go down that road and instead take the easy peaceful path. Now whadya say, can you behave?" asked the pirate Zion over the ship's comms.

The captain motioned for the crew to remain quiet and spoke to the comms, "All right, if we let you in here and stay out of your way, you will guarantee our safety and let us go afterward?"

Zion's reply came over the comms a second later, after he got done laughing, "I see you dummies do have a few brain cells and can listen to the voice of reason. Yes, you have my heartfelt guarantee. What I want is much more important than your lives. Now unlock the hatch and let my men pass freely and we can all go our separate ways."

"Done," replied the captain. "We will unlock the hatch and stay out of your way. The cargo hold is all yours. We just want to go home at this point," replied the captain.

He shut the comms down via his handheld terminal and the crew looked at him with puzzled looks.

"I thought you said they would destroy us if we gave them the cargo?" asked Tim.

The captain looked at them all and said, "Nothing has changed. I just want them to think we are not going to put up a fight. It will delay them and we can hopefully take a few out before they know what is going on."

"Ohhh," muttered Tom in a dumb voice.

The captain got them in position behind the barricades. Tom, Tim, and the XO Brad were together on one side. Jordan and Chris were in the middle, and Josh and Stacey were on the other side. All seven of them had their guns primed and ready.

The next few minutes seemed to take a lifetime. The team

sat there ready with sweat trickling down their faces, anticipating the need to pull the trigger. Chris figured it was as good of a time as any to start playing some music over the ship's speakers and keyed his personal terminal to start playing Eye of the Tiger. The rest of the crew at first looked at him like he was nuts, but he just owned it and started bobbing his head. Within about twenty seconds all seven people were bobbing their heads, and even Stacey had snapped out of her scare. The captain wore an approving expression on his face.

"Risen up, back on our feet," is what came over the speakers when a shudder was felt throughout the ship. Chris killed the music as he knew that meant the Tumbler had docked with the Puddle Jumper.

CHAPTER 7

Everyone held their breath with anticipation of what was coming next. Sure enough, after a few tense seconds they heard the outer door unlock. Several more clangs later they knew there was a group of pirates in the airlock. All that stood between the crew and the pirates was about ten meters of hallway and a door to the outer side of the hull. The pirates hit the access button and the door shot up into the ship.

The captain whispered, "Hold your fire till they come out all the way."

Just then three scruffy-looking pirates wearing grease-stained jumpsuits clumsily walked out into the hallway like they owned the place. All of them looked like they had not taken a bath in a long time and were armed with laser rifles of their own.

"Fire!" ordered the captain.

The sound of seven laser rifles shooting at once was not something Chris had ever heard before. Right before he squeezed the trigger he saw the whites of one of the pirates eyes as he realized they had not stepped on a whimpering enemy's ship but had instead walked into a kill zone. The pirate began bringing his gun up but it was too late. In the same instant that Chris had completely depressed the trigger a couple dime-sized holes had already been burned into the pirate's head. Vapor trails pouring out of the newly created holes. The pirate's body flopped to the floor, as did the two behind him.

Smoke emanated from the wounds in the pirates as they cauterized from the burn. Laser weapons were a popular choice for battles on the inside of ships as their firing distances could be varied to prevent significant damage being done to the hulls of the ships—that and the amount of energy required to melt through skin and bone was far less than the armor plating of the hull.

"You dumb backwater piece of shit smugglers!" yelled Zion over the comms in his southern accent. "That cargo was all I wanted! All you had to do was step aside, but now look what you did! You signed your own death warrants!"

The crew reset themselves as they waited for the next wave of pirates to come in. The wait was not long as the next group was ready about a minute later.

Chris sat with his sights on the edge of the doorway waiting for the next pirate to stick his head out. What came next was not as easy of a target. An arm with body armor on it and a laser rifle at the end of it stuck out and started blindly firing at the Puddle Jumper's crew. The shots were not accurate but nonetheless the crew was startled and hid behind cover. Chris blindly fired a couple of shots back but nothing hit.

The captain stuck his head up behind the sights of his gun and pulled the trigger.

"OOWWWWW!" screamed the pirate who had his armored arm shot. It didn't kill the man or even put a hole in his arm thanks to the armored glove he had on but it was enough to make the pirate drop his weapon and bring his arm back around the corner.

A few seconds later though his arm quickly reached out again and snatched the rifle up before anyone could hit him with another salvo.

The firing stopped for a second and the team continued to look downrange for any targets. They only had to wait for another ten seconds before one man dove from out of cover with a light armor suit on, shooting as he fell to the ground. Immediately following him were two other men in light armor suits with rifles raised and firing.

Chris squeezed the trigger over and over at the man who hit the floor while the rest of the crew intermittently fired or hid behind cover. The man who dove out first stopped firing and died from the laser fire. Wounds were smoldering all over his armored body. One of the two who had come out charging behind the fallen pirate went down to his knees but still had some fight in him. It was the last guy, though, who despite taking some fire managed to get a shot in of his own. Tim came out from cover with his rifle raised when a laser bolt hit him directly in the forehead. He went down with the wound smoking. Tom jumped up in a fit of rage but before the man could move his rifle in Tom's direction a trio of laser bolts from Brad, the captain, and Chris penetrated his armor and finished him off. Stacey and Jordan finished off the man on his knees.

Chris exhaled and Tom grabbed his brother and began doing anything he could to try to save him. It was too late. The laser shot had gone directly into his head and his lifeless eyes said all the crew needed to know. Tom began crying as he held his brother's head in his lap. He kept saying, "No no no! This can't be! Why, God! NOOOO!" as tears came down his face.

Stacey immediately came over and began to console Tom. She was doing her best but it was just too much too quickly for Tom. Chris watched in horror as one of his closest friends fell to pieces in from of him. That's when Captain Hammerfist stepped in and did what the team needed him to do.

"Tom! You need to snap out of it! I know it hurts but there will be time for mourning later!" Tom looked up at the captain but didn't say anything. The captain continued. "That anger you feel inside of you, use it! We are not finished here and your brother would want you to live! Do it for the crew! Do it for Tim! Do not let your brother's sacrifice go in vain!"

With that Tom wiped his eyes, snatched up his rifle, and growled "I'm going to kill them all. Every last one of those motherfuckers! They are dead!"

The captain motioned for him to take his position again. Brad and Jordan moved the body out of the way and took up their positions again as well. A wave of two additional pirates came out and the crew lit them up and disposed of them with relative ease. Only Jordan and Brad took glancing blows, but other than some minor burns they were fine.

"Is that it?" asked Stacey with a note of optimism in her voice.

"I don't think so," replied the captain. "Everyone remain ready as that ship is capable of holding a lot more than eight men."

Chris heard another shudder go through the ship but was pretty sure it had originated from the Tumbler docked to them. He wondered what the heck was going on out there.

"I got a bad feeling about this," said Jordan, but he remained calm and ready.

"Everyone stay where you are and be ready for more people to jump out. This is not over yet!" barked the captain.

The crew managed to keep their focus despite all the adrenaline flowing through their systems. All was quiet for about five more minutes before they began to hear some clanging coming from the airlock that was connected to the Tumbler. During this time the crew checked over their weapons, adjusted their cover, and Tom looked over his brother.

Then the crew heard a voice, but it wasn't coming through the comms. It sounded like it was coming from speakers within the airlock.

"Sorry it took so long for me to join the party, but I had to dock to our ship in order to get in my favorite new suit. You will have to tell me if I've dressed up for the occasion properly," came Zion's familiar voice, immediately followed by diabolical laughter.

Chris began to wonder what Zion was talking about when the clanging started up again. It sounded like footsteps getting closer and closer. Sweat began trickling down Chris's head and he wiped it away. He thought, "What is that?" Then a long metallic object that looked like a big mechanical leg from a robot stuck out of the airlock. Then he saw the rest of it as it emerged from the airlock into the hallway. Zion was wearing a T-800 military exosuit. It was painted all black and was basically a heavily armored and weaponized version of the crew's exosuits. The suit made a man stand about seven and a half feet tall and Zion was fully encased in the suit with no obvious weak spots. The suit had hands at the end of its arms but they were too long for actual fingers to be inside. Instead they were mechanical hands controlled from inside. Mounted to the left arm was a laser rifle of some sort and on the right arm it had a multitool pack and what looked like a grenade launcher, as far as Chris could tell. It was an Earth Force issued standard suit that ground pounders used, but he had never seen one on anyone outside of the Earth Force.

Chris and the rest of the crew began firing at Zion with everything they had. Several lasers reached out at the target but even with six laser rifles it would take several seconds to wear down the deflective armor Zion had on, and Zion wasn't waiting around. He raised his left arm, locked onto his target, and pulled the trigger. A large amber laser bolt lit up the room. Despite being behind cover meters away, Chris could feel the heat from the beam before it went quiet.

Tom slumped to the floor with a portion of his upper head gone, vaporized into smoke.

Chris stared, slack jawed at how quickly two of his friends had perished. He was shocked and didn't hear the captain yelling at him and the remaining crew to fall back. It wasn't until the captain yanked him from his spot behind cover that he realized the crew was retreating around the hallway. They ran for all they had but it wasn't enough. Right before they reached the bend in the hallway he saw Jordan go down with a hole in his back.

As Chris rounded the hallway he looked back at Jordan. He could still see his friend's eyes open and blood coming from his mouth as he lay sprawled on the floor dying. He was mouthing, "Help me," but no sound came out.

Chris tried to go back for Jordan, but Captain Hammerfist still had his arm in his grip. Chris yelled, "NO! I have to get him—I told him I have his back!"

"We have to go!" screamed the captain.

Chris tried to get back to his friend but the captain was overwhelmingly strong. Instead he screamed toward the advancing suit, "You'll die for this, Zion. You hear me! You'll die!"

With that last shout of defiance Chris stopped resisting the captain and ran down the hallway. As they made it down the hallway Chris could hear the sounds of laughter booming from the speakers in Zion's suit. It was at that moment Chris swore to himself he would kill Zion, no matter what it took.

The remaining crew of the Puddle Jumper made it to the ladder leading up to the bridge. The captain yelled at them to climb it while the clanging around the bend in the hallway got closer. Brad, Stacey, Chris, and finally the captain all made it up though.

"He shouldn't be able to get up here via the ladder, as the opening isn't big enough for that suit to fit through. He'll have to take the elevator. Stacey, get to the controls and lock out the elevator and lock down the bridge," ordered the captain while breathing heavily.

Stacey did as she was told, even though it took her a couple of tries as her hands were shaking so badly. Even Brad the XO was shook and had a look of terror on his face. Everyone with the exception of the captain was terrified. Chris wondered what the captain had seen or done in his past that allowed him to remain so calm.

"It's done!" cried Stacey and she immediately picked up her rifle again. They could hear the familiar clanging sound of Zion in his T-800 armored exosuit as he made his way toward the elevator.

"What do we do now?" asked Brad.

"I need a minute to think," replied the captain.

Chris looked over at one of the screens on the bridge and toggled it into shipboard sensors. He looked at several camera feeds as about a dozen more of Zion's troops came on board with the light armor the second wave had been wearing. He warned the captain what was going on and watched as they all gathered around Zion, who was standing in front of the elevator. Zion then proceeded to order one of the troops to get the elevator open. The poor man was given an impossible task, as the controls were locked out. Chris could see him over the display pounding furiously at the controls. After about thirty seconds of trying and not getting anywhere Zion knocked him over with one of his big powerful suit arms. The man scrambled back into formation with the rest of the troops.

"You have five seconds to unlock this door before things get real nasty!" boomed Zion from his suit speakers. "Remember the part about if you really piss me off? Well, you're getting there real quick. What I have to do requires the cargo you have stolen from me. I will not stop until I have what my people need. I didn't want to do this, but you leave me no choice. I will execute you person by person until I get the cargo. Captain Hammerfist, I saw that girl you had with you. I'm thinking I'll start with her."

The captain looked at Stacey and shook his head. Then he said, "Listen, he's just trying to scare us into making things easier for him. He'll kill us immediately if we give him the chance."

Zion announced over his speakers: "Five . . . four . . . three . . . two . . . one. You backwater dumb shits just don't know what's good for you." Zion then proceeded to order his men around as half of them ran off in different directions and the other half followed Zion.

Chris could hear the clanging from Zion's suit as he watched Zion walk over to the ladder he and the remainder of the Puddle Jumper crew had climbed up.

"What's he doing? He can't fit up the ladder. Right?" cried Stacey.

"I don't know. I don't think so," Chris responded.

Chris watched the screens and Zion stuck out his right arm and then raised it over his head. For a few seconds nothing happened. Chris and he rest of the crew stood there watching, wondering what Zion was doing. Then they started to notice a glowing dot on the floor near the ladder. The dot got brighter and brighter until smoke started coming up from the glowing dot.

Chris yelled "He is using a plasma cutter to get through the floor! What do we do now, Captain?"

"I want all three of you guys to make your way to the escape pods on this floor. Just head out through the doors. Remember you will need to unlock them, as we locked down the bridge."

"You don't have to tell me twice!" replied Chris.

He ran over to the door which led to the hallway where the escape pods were located. He began initiating the unlock sequence when Brad commanded, "Wait, check the camera on the other side of the door!"

Chris did and his mouth dropped. There were three armored troopers with rifles raised on the other side waiting for him to step out.

"Shit!" Chris remarked "What are we going to do? We are trapped on the bridge. They have guys surrounding all exits with guns and Zion's cutting a hole in the floor near the ladder!"

"Stay calm," commanded the captain, "I want the three of you to spread out and train your laser rifles on the floor where

Chris hadn't even noticed them enter the room from up the ladder they had been guarding moments before.

As the troops surrounded them Zion tossed Chris to the ground near where the captain was.

Chris coughed and spat blood onto the hard ground of the bridge floor. After he was able to catch his breath enough he crawled over to where the captain lay. He was still alive but looked like he desperately needed medical attention. The pool of blood under him was growing faster than Chris believed was possible. There was a large hole in his side and back where the laser had gone through him. The burned flesh was nauseating but Chris knew he had to get to his dad. As he crawled up to the captain he could see his father was still conscious.

"What can I do to help?" cried Chris as tears began to well up in his eyes.

"Live son, live. Do whatever you have to, to survive this. I am sorry I failed you and cannot do more for you," replied Josh Hammerfist.

"You didn't fail me and you're going to be all right," sobbed Chris.

Captain Hammerfist used all of his remaining strength to pull at a chain he had on his neck. It snapped and Josh handed him what was in his hands. It was three dog tags: one from his mother, one from his father, and Captain Josh Hammerfist's own tag.

"No, my time in this solar system draws to an end," the captain said as he coughed up blood. "Take this and remember I am proud of the man you have become and will be. Do not look back, Chris. Be bold, your destiny lies . . . ahead . . . of you."

With that the captain was no more. His eyes stared up at Chris but they no longer saw.

"Foolish man, he brought this onto all of you," sighed Zion. "Secure this bridge, take the rest as prisoners, and get the cargo. I'm going back to my ship and preparing for the next stage."

With that Zion turned and walked away, leaving Chris in tears. Zion's pirates rounded them up and put them in cuffs, including Brad.

"Wait!" said Brad suddenly. "Captain Zion, I can be of use to you."

Zion hesitated, and after a moment turned to Brad.

"How?" he asked impatiently.

"I'm a skilled leader of men. I know this business. I know ship systems. I'm interested in what you're doing. And if you ask me, you seem a helluva lot smarter than the guy dying over there," replied Brad.

"Why shouldn't I just kill you where you stand?" asked Zion. "You've caused me a lot of trouble today. Besides, who's to say you won't betray me like you did your captain?"

At that Brad walked up to Zion's suit. Zion immediately pointed a suit cannon at him with a puzzled look on his face. Brad kept walking, however, and when the barrel was inches from his nose he spoke.

"I hereby pledge my services to you, Zion. If you wish to kill me you can, but as long as you are not a fool like the previous captain I served I'll be your biggest asset. Besides, I have a feeling you are part of something bigger than a random pirate or small group of smugglers. On top of that, the cargo we have is clearly worth many lives and a lot of equipment. I want in. Will you have me?"

Zion starred Brad down, contemplating his next move. Then he barked to Brad, "Open these doors and allow my men in to secure the area. After that we might discuss your employment terms, if there are any."

Chris couldn't take it anymore. He turned from his father and through clenched teeth raged, "I swore I would find a way to kill Zion and you just got added to that same list, Brad! Know this though: you will die a painful death, and unlike what you did to the captain, mine will not be a surprise attack at your back. I will look you in the eyes and watch as the life drains from them, just as I had to with my father's!"

"What do you think this is?" Brad shot back, "Some kind of fairy tale? I just saved us all from death over a box we don't know anything about. Your 'father' was a fool and would have killed us all. At least now we have a chance—or at least I do. You'll probably be a slave—or more likely they'll kill you the first time you open your mouth. You want to talk about revenge? You should start with appreciation if you hope to live much longer."

With that two guards grabbed Brad and escorted him off the bridge. The next couple of guards went over to Stacey and grabbed her and dragged her off the bridge. The two guards responsible for Chris had the decency to give him a minute before they said, "Hey kid, time's up. Let's go."

Chris looked up with hatred in his eyes but knew enough to not say anything. The two guards put handcuffs on Chris and began walking him off the bridge. He knew that despite what had just happened, he needed to keep his wits about him. After all, how he played this out would likely mean life or death. As they made their way to the Tumbler, Chris did all he could to learn as much as he possible. To his disappointment, before the Tumbler doors opened a bag went over his head and everything went dark.

CHAPTER 8

Chris could not see anything through the heavy hood over his head, but he could still feel the motion of the ship. After all, inertial dampers were good, but not that good. He knew they had gotten on the Tumbler docked to the Puddle Jumper and he knew he was traveling with Stacey as he could hear her quiet sobs. He sat on a bench with his head leaned back against the hull. Chris himself was destroyed emotionally but he also knew this was not the time to grieve. He would not get his revenge by mourning. There would be time for that later, if he lived through all of this. He was just so mad that Zion had walked into his life and taken everything he had ever known away from him. On top of that, Brad had betrayed him, his father, and their whole crew. It was just so much to take in all at once.

"What now?" Chris thought, "What do I do even if I get out of this?" He had his own credit account but it wasn't anywhere near enough to buy a ship. He knew he could survive for two or three months paying for food and water but that was about it.

Chris shook away those thoughts and tried to focus on his father's dying words: "Do not look back, Chris. Be bold. Your destiny lies ahead of you."

At that point Chris heard a clanging noise underneath him, which meant the Tumbler was landing. Despite being blindfolded and cuffed he knew those sounds from years of smuggler life. He felt himself being shoved around like cattle until he came to what he assumed must be a holding area.

When the hood came off he found himself in a room that was about three by three meters. There were steel pillars along the entrance side of the cell and the same generic metal walls found on most ships on the other three sides. In his cell were a bunk bed, a toilet, a sink, and two chairs. Stacey was already on the bed curled up in a ball with her head buried in a pillow. When Chris turned around he saw two guards exiting the cell and shutting the door. The guards then walked down the hallway to the right and disappeared from view, never looking back. Naturally Chris tried to open the door but it was locked shut. He yelled out the cell for someone to tell him what was going on. Where was he? Where were they going? All the usual questions prisoners ask. As expected, nobody responded and he was left to sit there with his grief.

It was at this time Chris finally let the door in his mind burst open—all the grief, all the heartache, all the loss. It washed over him in waves. Stacey even came out of her stupor when she saw his racking sobs. She came over and put an arm around him, and they just sat there for a while. After a time, they lay down and Chris fell into a fitful sleep. He dreamed of giant machines, gunfights, and worst of all, his father's dead eyes.

Chris awoke what must have been a couple hours later. Stacey had moved to the other side of the cell and was quietly sleeping. He felt oddly refreshed having had the chance to grieve; the sleep couldn't have hurt either. He could feel his mind beginning to work again. He knew he was on a large ship, but he had no idea what kind. It looked to be a military vessel, based on the lack of comforts and the fact that he appeared to be in a holding block. Civilian vessels tended to have no use for a brig. He couldn't be sure though.

Chris next began trying to figure out how to get out of the

cell. He again tried opening the door but it was locked shut. "Duh," he thought to himself. His eyes next traced the whole cell. He looked for weaknesses in the walls, looked at the plumbing of the toilets. He jiggled them to see if they would come loose but he knew even then he wasn't going to get out that way. He couldn't fit through a four-inch diameter hole. By some miracle he still had his pistol, which was tucked into his pant leg. Thank God for the small compact design. Through all the confusion and chaos they had neglected to search him for any other weapons before bagging him. The people who did this surely were not professional soldiers. However, he didn't think this was the time to pull out his ace in the hole. At this point Stacey began to stir.

"I would offer coffee, but I've got no beans, no coffee maker, no coffee mug, and we're in a jail cell," joked Chris.

Stacey and Chris laughed about it, but while Chris was feeling better he could tell Stacey was still bothered. They spent some time talking and Chris was happy to have a bit of normal injected back into his life. Stacey slowly started coming around.

After an hour or so the conversation came to an abrupt halt with the sound of a door opening. He then heard footsteps as several people walked toward his cell. Chris stood up but kept his distance from the entrance of the cell. He didn't know what was coming and figured having some steel bars in between him and whatever it was couldn't hurt. Stacey went quiet again, as she usually did in stressful situations.

Rounding the corner was none other than Zion himself, followed by Brad and four guards. Chris was surprised by Zion's size. Till now Chris had only seen him through his heads-up display or in a T-800 suit, which made any man look big. Outside of the suit Zion still stood a solid six foot five inches and must have weighed in around 220 pounds. He wore an all-black spacer suit but had the posture of a career military man. He had a neatly kept trimmed crew cut of black hair. The grey in his beard told his age. The scarred face was very clear now and Chris could tell Zion must have been in a knife fight. The most prominent scar went from his top left eye across his nose and down into his right cheek. His eyes were a dark brown and the left one had a slight discoloration from where it had been sliced, most likely from the knife that had caused his main scar. There were other scars too, but they were less significant.

Zion walked up to the cell with a twisted smile on his face. Brad, meanwhile, looked like he had been roughed up. He had a black eye and several bumps and bruises on his face but he too had a smile. Chris guessed this was from some sort of initiation.

"Well well well, what do we have here?" questioned Zion in his southern accent. "Good to see my old friends from the— what was it? The Puddle Jumper? You caused me a lot of trouble you know, but luckily it all worked out in the end."

Chris replied, "All worked out? Are you fucking serious? You killed our whole crew; everyone I cared about was on that ship!"

"Well boy, I didn't kill all of them," replied Zion with a smirk. "Your former crewmate Brad took care of your precious captain." Zion then chuckled.

To everyone's surprise Stacey screamed through tears at Brad, "Why? Why did you do it?"

At the same time Chris grabbed the bars and yelled "You piece of shit! The captain took care of you and you shot him in the back for it! If there weren't bars in the way you'd have a lot more to worry about than some bumps and bruises. I would rip you to fucking pieces, you backstabbing coward! Why don't you step in here and we can settle this man to man?"

As Brad began to step forward Zion raised a hand to stop him.

"Easy boy," chuckled Zion. "I haven't decided exactly what to do with you yet, but I'm sure a few of my associates have ideas of what to do with your crewmate here . . . Stacey is it?"

Stacey immediately backed away, behind Chris.

"Remember when I told you not to piss me off? Remember that I said this could be easy and I just wanted the cargo? Well, you killed a lot of my associates, and they want payback," stated Zion.

"You will have to go through me to get to her," Chris replied.

Zion, Brad, and the guards laughed. Then Zion announced, "Oh you are a noble lad, aren't ya? Well, I don't think you will stop my merry band of pirates from having their fun with her. Besides, a pretty girl like that won't last long with this crew."

Chris, through clenched teeth, rumbled, "You fuckers better keep your hands off of her."

Zion laughed, "Oh don't worry boy, there are surely some here that will take care of you too. You're not my flavor but someone on my crew is bound to want you."

Chris had a look of confusion on his face. Then he began to smile.

This clearly caught Zion by surprise, as he immediately asked, "What's so funny boy?"

Chris chuckled and declared, "So wait, are you telling me you are the leader of a bunch of butt pirates?" He then broke into hysterical laughter.

Zion slammed his hand on the cell pillars and shouted "Quiet! Laugh it up because you won't be able to once these men break your jaw. Open this cell and have your way with the prisoners. I have more important things to do than listen to this ignorant boy!"

One of the guards stepped forward, and right before he unlocked the cell a warning sound came over the speakers in the cell block, "Warning—all crew to battle stations."

Zion remarked, "Saved by the bell, but my men will be back for you two."

Chris replied, "I don't fear your gang of merry butt pirates!"

With that Zion turned, growled, and began to walk off,

signaling his men to follow him. The guards and Brad joined him, but before they were out of sight Brad turned around and flicked Chris off while walking away.

"You shouldn't have done that," moaned Stacey, "They will be back and now pissed off more than ever. We are going to be raped and killed. Probably not quickly, either, and making them angrier won't help."

"That's not going to happen, Stacey," explained Chris, "I will find a way to get out of here. As a matter of a fact, I think I already have. I've just been waiting for the right time."

"What? How?" questioned Stacey.

Chris walked up to Stacey, who was red faced from the tears, and whispered to her, "Those idiots never did a thorough search of us before throwing us in here. Instead they just grabbed the guns in our hands and locked us up. I'm beginning to think they are a bunch of dumb pirates with the exception of Zion. Before we got into the shootout on the Puddle Jumper, I stashed my laser pistol in the lower leg of my pants." As he showed Stacey, her eyes went wide when she saw the glint of metal. He continued on: "We can use this pistol to melt the door lock and hopefully sneak out of here. The only problem is if we are spotted we won't be able to engage in a gun fight for long. The pistol has a limited battery pack and is no match for their weapons."

Stacey asked, "Well what if they catch us? They will surely do even worse things to us!"

Chris remembered how his father had been under dire circumstances only hours before, and realized it was time for him to grow up and be brave too. He put his arms on her shoulders and in a consoling voice he explained, "Stacey, we are as good as dead here. We have to try to find a way out. I promise we will be OK. Just trust me." Chris was not nearly as confident as he portrayed, but he knew he needed Stacey to believe they had a chance, even if he didn't believe they had a chance. It was what Josh would have done.

"OK," replied Stacey in a resigned, but strengthened tone.

With that Chris turned back around and started thinking. He told Stacey, "We just need to figure out when is the right time to make our move."

As if on cue, there was a rumble felt throughout the ship. The battle station sirens were still going on and Chris figured this would be his best chance, while everyone was focused on whatever was going on outside.

Chris lifted up his pant leg, pulled out his laser pistol from his leg strap, and began to aim at the locking mechanism. He dialed the setting to a continuous beam. Then he pulled the trigger. A faint, light red streak showed up in front of his gun and stretched all the way to the door lock. Chris held the trigger down for a second and let up.

The locking mechanism, which was made of steel, had melted away significantly and was now only held together by the molten slag the laser had left behind. Chris stood back and kicked out at the door. Chris felt some resistance but the door gave way, turned on its hinges, and banged into the pillars when it reached the end of its rotation.

Chris listened for a second in case anybody came into the cell block wondering what that noise was. As he guessed, they had bigger problems, and nobody came. He waved at Stacey, signaling her to follow him.

Chris approached the open door and slowly stuck his head out into the hallway. He first looked to the left and saw about twenty meters of generic white ship hallway and several cell blocks. To Chris's surprise they were all empty. Then he turned his head to the right, and about six or so meters in front of him were several steps leading up to a grey metal door.

Chris exited the cell with Stacey right behind him. He pressed his back up against the pillars and kept his laser pointed in front of him. After passing two more cells he began to make his way up the stairs with Stacey in tow. Chris reached the door and reached for the open button on the side of the wall. He pressed it, and to his dismay he heard an annoying chirp sound from the access panel followed with an: "Access denied."

"Shit," muttered Chris. "Guess it all couldn't be that easy. I could try to use my pistol again, but I would probably run down the battery pack on this door and still not get it open."

"Oh come on," Stacey said. "These doors aren't as tough as they look. They usually have an exposed locking mechanism if you look hard enough. Peek through the cracks and see."

Just then another rumble could be felt as the ship shook from something. Stacey looked at Chris with wide-open eyes.

Chris did as she said and started looking through the gaps on the edges of the door. After a few seconds he saw that it was locked by two metal bolts, one at about head height and one slightly below the waist. Like with the cell door he raised his pistol, pointing toward the top bolt, and pulled the trigger for about a second.

The metal glowed red and sagged down. It still connected the door to the wall, but as long as Chris hurried the metal would not cool fast enough to harden significantly. He lowered the pistol and fired again at the lower bolt. Again, the metal glowed red and sagged down.

"I can help you kick the door down," offered Stacey and she lined up next to him.

"Wait," replied Chris, "if there is someone in the hallway and they hear the door slam open we will surely be toast."

Stacey nodded, realizing what he was saying.

Chris then explained, "We need to open the door slowly and not let it bang against the wall."

Chris put his hand in the cutout for the door handle and grasped it with his hand. Then he braced his shoulder up against the door and began to push. Nothing happened, so Chris began pushing harder and harder. The red glowing metal connecting the door began to stretch but still didn't break. Stacey began using her body weight to open the door as well and the metal elongated even further. As it stretched though it was cooling at a faster rate and Chris wasn't sure they would be able to open it. Right before he was about to give up another large shake in the ship could be felt, which caused them to smash into the door harder and break the metal cleanly. Unfortunately though, the quake caused Chris to lose his control of the door and it slammed open, making a loud banging noise against the wall. Chris and Stacey fell down and out of the door due to the lack of balance.

In that moment Chris freaked out thinking, "Oh shit, I just ghosted us. Everyone in this hallway will be looking at us." As Chris and Stacey looked around they only saw a white hallway with red lights and a battle station siren going off. Chris picked himself and Stacey up off the ground and checked the charge on his pistol. He was down to 20 percent, which would be enough for several blasts at a person but that was it.

The hallway they had fallen into went both left and right. Chris asked Stacey, "Well, which way do you think is the nearest way to the closest emergency escape pod?"

Stacey looked around and said, "Well I don't know what kind of ship this is, but it seems to be pretty big. My best guess is to pick a direction and keep going with it until we can get to the outer hull of the ship. That's where the escape pods will be, but I have no idea if that is left or right."

Just then another big rumble shook the ship. Chris, in a worried tone exclaimed "We better move quickly. Sounds like Zion is getting his ass handed to him and I don't want to be here when this ship comes apart."

Chris grabbed Stacey's hand and began running down the hallway to the right. Just before they rounded the corner Chris slowed up and pressed his back up against the wall before looking around the corner. Stacey followed suit and did the same. As Chris was peering his head around the corner he heard footsteps running toward him. He quickly pulled his head back and waited. Three people came running by but luckily they did not turn or look down the hallway they were in.

Chris could overhear one of them yelling, "Get to the turrets! I'll make my way down to engineering."

Before Chris could speak Stacey shot him a quizzical look and said, "Wait, were those guys wearing Earth Force uniforms?"

Chris quietly responded, "I dunno? I didn't have time to study their outfits, if I'm being honest. Anyways, this must be a big battle. We need to move now before the distraction ends." Stacey just nodded and squeezed his hand.

Chris looked around the corner one more time and stated, "All clear."

With that he rounded the corner, going right again. As they sprinted down the hallway Chris saw a viewing port coming up on the left side. Most military ships obviously didn't have windows in the traditional sense. Large wall screens were connected to sensors on the outer hull and a virtual image was displayed on them. Often these screens were interactive and gave viewers the ability to cycle multiple cameras, or in some cases even control systems.

Chris and Stacey almost tripped and fell as the ship was rocked again by something. As they approached the viewing port Chris slowed down to glance at what was going on. He looked outside and saw laser bolts and plasma cannons firing all over the place. There must have been a dozen fighters flying in and around the ship, shooting at each other. Most were the old Skimmer types but he thought he saw a few advanced Earth Force Raptor class fighters that had a Panther logo on them. Chris didn't know who they were but he was glad they were giving Zion trouble.

In the distance Chris saw a Poseidon class Earth Force destroyer. Chris had only seen a few of those military ships in his life but never in action. The Poseidon class destroyer was the flagship of the Earth Force fleet and nothing in the history of

Earth could match its firepower or defensive capabilities. He knew the ship had three sections to it. The front housed the bridge and command area. The middle section was even bigger, as it was home to a small hangar bay and crew quarters, while the last section housed the engineering section, which consisted of a big fusion reactor and four engines. The massive ship was roughly 420 meters long, bristling with various-sized laser turrets, various-sized plasma cannons, rail guns, and many antifighter flak and PDC turrets. In addition, the hangar could hold a five ships, known as a wing, of fighters or bombers or a mix of the two, along with a single Tumbler. Chris didn't know what Zion had done to piss off Earth Force's military, but they were serious and Zion was in big trouble.

The Earth Force destroyer was firing at many of the small craft and whatever ship Chris and Stacey were on. As Chris continued looking around he saw another Poseidon destroyer also firing away. Chris was stunned by what he was seeing, but at the same time the view was beautiful to him in a strange way. He always wanted to serve on an Earth Force vessel, fighting against pirates. Seeing it play out in front of him caused him to fall into an almost trance like state.

It took Chris a moment, but he came back to reality when Stacey shoved him and yelled, "Chris stop looking out the damn window you space nerd and let's go!"

Chris nodded and made his way to the end of the hall and again peered his head around the corner to the right. This time they were not so lucky and instead found a bunch of people running back and forth between their jobs. Weirdly enough, a few of these guys were definitely wearing Earth Force uniforms. Chris didn't know what in the world was going on, but he wasn't trying to stick around and find out. As he scanned he saw another branch of hallway about four meters away from him on the left side that had an "Emergency Escape Pods" sign on it and an arrow pointing to the left down the hall.

Chris looked at Stacey and whispered, "We can't go yet.

There must be twenty people using that hallway. We need to find a way to get past them without them noticing us."

Stacey with a look of terror on her face squeaked, "We don't have time to figure this out. They will find us soon!"

Chris looked again down the hallway, but still wasn't sure he would be able to make it to the other hallway with the escape pods without being noticed.

He turned back to look at Stacey and was about to say something when he looked past Stacey's left ear and saw two pirates about twenty meters away jogging in their direction.

The pirates came to a stop and one yelled, "Hey! You two! Stop right there!"

What happened next was something Chris didn't understand. His adrenaline hit him like an energy blast and his mind went into automatic mode.

Chris grabbed Stacey by the hand, turned, and started sprinting down the hallway where all the people were. As he rounded the corner several of them looked up at him. Some of them gave him strange looks but others were so engulfed in their tasks they didn't even register what was happening. The person nearest Chris was an average-sized man who was looking down at something he had in his hand and didn't even notice Chris until it was too late. Chris barreled into him, knocking him on his back, with Stacey right behind him. Chris was able to maintain his balance and begin to shift left to where the emergency escape pod hallway began. With two more strides Chris was rounding the hallway. He was moving so fast that he could hear the people in the hallway they'd just left still trying to figure out what was going on.

As they sprinted down the hallway toward the escape pods Chris began searching visually for the actual escape pod hatches. The white steel walls were pretty standard and the same throughout the hallway, only separated by panel gaps and the occasional viewing port. Chris located the first escape hatch quickly but was challenged when he realized there was a pirate between him and the escape hatch.

This pirate sported a long black beard and decent-sized build and was definitely not wearing an Earth Force uniform. Even worse, he was already aware there was something going on and when he saw Chris and Stacey running toward him he quickly reached for his gun. He began unholstering it, and that's when Chris made another snap decision. Chris pointed his own gun at the pirate and depressed the trigger. Chris was impressed with himself because he nailed the pirate in the gun-carrying shoulder. Even though the pirate was only three or so meters away, aiming a gun while running and holding the hand of another was not an easy task.

The man reeled back and dropped the gun as a dime-sized hole opened in his right shoulder. Chris reoriented the gun at the man's face and pulled the trigger. The pistol made an empty pinging sound, and that was it—the battery was depleted. It didn't matter though as Chris and Stacey sprinted by while the man hit the wall, yelling in pain. Several strides later Chris reached the escape hatch, slammed his hand on the emergency button, and the doors quickly slid open. He then used all of his strength to throw Stacey inside. She yelled as she lost balance and fell in. As Chris shifted to jump in himself he felt an intense burn along his right shoulder blade. He knew he had been hit by a laser beam but it didn't slow him down. The tough bastard must have picked up his gun and shot him. "That's what I get for not finishing him off!" Chris thought.

He yelled in pain as he jumped face-first into the escape pod. He hit, arms first, onto the escape pod's floor, which was about a one-meter drop. His hands and elbows screamed in pain but he could still move them so he knew nothing was broken. Hopefully the shot he had taken had not seriously damaged anything.

Chris yelled, "Stacey, press the launch button and get us the hell out of here!"

She had already picked herself up from the floor and slammed her hand on the big red launch button. Then she turned to Chris and yelled back, "Strap in!"

A three-second countdown began from a computerized voice as Chris picked himself up and sat in the seat on the right side. Stacey had already sat down in the left seat and was pulling down her safety harness when Chris saw a laser bolt shoot down into the pod from where he had just jumped in through. It didn't hit him or Stacey but it came close and smoke came up from the floor near his right foot. Chris knew he had nothing left in his pistol, so he used his good arm to hurl it up the shaft the man had just fired from. He must have gotten lucky because he heard a man grunt in pain as the pistol ricocheted off his face. While not killing the man, it did buy Chris and Stacey a couple precious seconds because the doors to the escape pod slammed shut. Chris reached up with up with both hands to grab his harness. He again screamed in pain as his right arm began to fail him but luckily his left was able to reach the harness and pull it down.

Boom!

The escape pod launched at full burn away from the ship. Chris and Stacey both gritted their teeth as they held on through all the Gs the escape pod was pulling. Even with inertial dampeners the acceleration force could still be felt. Chris glanced at the view port and saw the giant ship he had been on come into perspective. He at first couldn't make out what type of ship it was, but as the escape pod went further and further away from the ship its whole shape came into perspective. Chris couldn't believe what he was seeing. He and Stacey were launching an escape pod from another Poseidon class destroyer! Chris immediately began thinking, "How the hell had the pirates gotten a Poseidon class destroyer from the Earth Force fleet?" Nobody in the history of Earth had ever stolen one of those, and here he was launching away from it. He immediately thought back to the men in uniform they had seen.

Chris yelled between gritted teeth at Stacey, "That is a Poseidon class destroyer!"

"What?" replied Stacey struggling to hear over the loud engines.

"That's a Poseidon class destroyer!" Chris yelled again.

"Ya, OK?" questioned Stacey.

"How the heck did he get one of those?" asked Chris.

"I don't know, why don't you go back there and ask him?" shot back Stacey.

Another five seconds went by and the thrust from the escape pod cut off.

Chris looked around at the escape pod and saw the four empty seats next to him and Stacey. There were small viewports on each side of the spherically shaped pod and in some of them Chris could see ships flying around in combat.

Just then a screen to Chris's right opened up and a familiar face appeared on it. It was none other than the scarred face of Zion. Stacey looked up and screamed for a second.

After a brief chuckle Zion began, "You backwater hillbillies are as slippery as a swamp snake. You managed to escape my grasp for now, but I'll see you in the future, boy. I wasn't sure what to do with you before but after adding theft to your list of crimes I think I've made up my mind. In fact, I think I'll echo the promise you made me: Your time in this system will come to an end and it will be by my hands," exclaimed Zion.

Chris raised his left hand to the screen and raised his middle finger.

Zion's face changed into an evil grin and with clenched teeth he growled, "You seem to like that finger. I'll make sure to break that one first."

With that the screen cut out.

Chris looked left out of the viewport and saw the Poseidon destroyer begin to open a subspace wormhole. At first it was a small blue spiraling hole. Then it grew and grew until it was bigger than the Poseidon destroyer. The white center of the spinning blue disc was almost blinding. A burst of thrust came from the four main engines and the massive destroyer lurched forward at fantastic speed. Chris could see the other Earth Force vessels shooting at it with everything they had, but it appeared to not be enough. Zion's destroyer hit the wormhole and it began to swallow the destroyer. As the ship went through the wormhole the Earth Force fighters broke off as to not follow the enemy capital ship through. Then without a sound or a flash the tail end of the destroyer went through and the wormhole closed a few seconds later. If nobody had seen the ship enter it would have appeared as if it was never there.

"It's over. Zion's gone," Chris explained to Stacey.

Stacey immediately exhaled as the adrenaline finally stopped pumping and she started coming down from all the energy. Chris tried to remain vigilant but found he too was exhausted and his shoulder had begun to throb.

"Thank God, we made it," replied Stacey. "That was some pretty slick shooting and running, Chris. Your father would have been proud. Now let me have a look at that shoulder."

Chris smiled at the thought of his father being proud of him. Unknowingly, a tear came down his eye at the same time. Stacey lifted her harness and came over to Chris to take a look at his shoulder.

"It's a glancing blow to the shoulder. It's burned through the skin but not into the bone. A doctor will be able to patch you up, but in the meantime I'll use the med pack on it," explained Stacy as she tore a med pack from the wall and began working on the shoulder. As the adrenaline wore off Chris found himself again traveling quietly through space with Stacey. The two sat in silence while the little escape pod drifted through the cold depths of space.

CHAPTER 9

Stacey and Chris were just beginning to doze off when a proximity alarm went off. It was a dull, pulsing sound and Chris reached over to shut it off. The shoulder pain reminded him of the injury he had received, despite the painkillers and skin spray from the med pack. He began looking around through the various portals in the escape pod. Nothing was visible yet, but that didn't mean much in the darkness of space.

"What is it?" asked Stacey.

"Looks like the Earth Force is finally getting around to dealing with us. Hope you've got your 'I'm not a pirate' face ready to go," replied Chris.

Stacey nodded in acknowledgement.

Chris checked out the sensor readings and saw a vessel was approaching them. It appeared to be another Tumbler class ship.

"We'll have company in a minute," whispered Chris.

Chris went over to the entry point of the pod and looked through the viewing port in the hatch. He could not see anything at first in the dark, star-filled void. Then a thruster from an incoming ship fired and betrayed its position.

Chris quietly muttered, "I think it's a Tumbler class ship from one of the Earth Force vessels."

Stacey did not seem to care as she lay on one side of the escape pod. Chris watched as the ship maneuvered itself in front of them. Just the fact that they were this close was a good sign. Earth Force could have blasted them into smithereens from a distance if they were having a bad day. Technically, there were universal laws about handling of prisoners of war. As far as the Earth Force was probably concerned, however, this was an escape pod full of pirates. The rules didn't quite apply, and nobody was likely paying attention anyways.

The Tumbler began closing in on the escape pod. It grew and grew in the view until it no longer fit into the viewing angles of the port he was looking through. Chris backed away from the escape pod entrance and even Stacey started paying attention. There was a soft thud as the Tumbler made contact with the escape pod. Then there was a hiss as the ship's atmosphere was transferred to the attach point.

"What now?" asked Stacey.

"We wait and find out," replied Chris.

Nothing happened for about ten seconds. Then Stacey and Chris began hearing clanging noises that sounded like mechanical footsteps. Light began to pour in through the viewports of the entrance doors of the escape pod. It was so bright it blinded Chris as he tried to see what was causing the noise. Then he heard the escape pod doors unlock.

"Here goes," thought Chris.

The escape pod doors slid open and the light became even brighter. So bright that both Stacy and Chris shielded their eyes and had to look away.

The next thing they heard was a deep mechanical voice that sounded like a robot talking to them.

"Good morning, fine people, have you heard the good word of our Lord and Savior?"

"Huh?" was all Chris could muster.

What followed was a sharp clang and a new voice, similar to the first.

"Jesus Christ Beis, I told you not to pull that crap. When we get back to the ship you're going on report."

Chris looked at the blinding light and saw the closest shape turn back to them. It started speaking again.

"Greetings, prisoners, you are under arrest by the orders of Captain Spear of the Earth Force vessel Leviathan. We know there are two of you in there, and if you wish to remain alive you will exit the escape pod slowly with your hands in the air. Any attempts at resistance, including reaching for that pistol on the ground, will be met with lethal force."

"OK! OK! We will not resist, but can you please turn down the lights so that I can see where I am going?" replied Chris.

"Move it kid!" came the mechanical voice back to him.

"I'll go first Stacey. Just stay close behind me with your hands up. We are almost out of this mess," Chris explained.

Stacey nodded with a look of fear. Chris began walking toward the hatch with his hands in the air in front of him, shielding his squinting eyes. His shoulder again reminded him he was hurt. As soon as he took one step forward, to his surprise, the light dimmed. After another step it dimmed more to the point where he could actually see what was on the other side.

Chris was not surprised to see guns pointed at him, but he was surprised to see it was from three soldiers standing inside the Tumbler in Earth Force T-800 suits. They looked as mean as could be and had three huge laser rifles pointed right at him. Behind the three men in suits were three more marines in light armor. They also had rifles trained on him.

"That's it kid, one step at a time," came the voice from the nearest person in a T-800 suit.

Chris ducked his head, walked through the escape pod hatch, and set his first foot on the Tumbler. He looked around and for the most part was unimpressed. It was just a standard Tumbler ship with several marines on it.

"Keep moving kid, this isn't a scenic tour. Stand over there next to Jim," came the same mechanical voice he was getting used to now.

Chris saw the man pointing at one of the lightly armored

marines. Chris picked up the pace and walked over to the man he was supposed to see. As Chris got closer the man lowered his gun and pulled out some energized handcuffs. Chris knew once they went on he would be at the mercy of his captors. The cuffs were basically metal cuffs, but they had a computer in them and could be controlled by any of the marines. If he stepped out of line, not only would the cuffs restrain him but they could electrocute him on demand and disable him. At this point Chris knew his destiny was not in his own hands, so he complied.

Chris couldn't help himself and admitted, "You know I am used to being wined and dined before I let myself get tied up at night. You boys just skip the foreplay and go straight for the prize."

Chris thought he saw one of the T-800 suits shimmy with laughter at his joke, but nobody else thought it was funny. Well, at least he maybe had one friend. He stuck his hands out to be cuffed.

"I'm sorry, please don't listen to him. He is like this all the time. I can't believe he is doing this right now though. Chris, shut up!" Stacey chimed in as she too exited from the escape pod.

The man with the sterner mechanical voice added, "Ma'am, stand over there," then turned to Chris, "So, we have a funny guy. Well you won't think it's funny when we get done with you. You guys are in deep shit."

As the cuffs went on Chris he smirked and said, "You boys are such a tease."

The marine standing in front of Chris warned, "Keep your eyes straight ahead and your mouth shut."

Chris looked forward and joked, "Easy fella I'm cooperating."

Now it was the marines turn to smirk and Chris swore he saw a look of satisfaction in the man's eye.

"What's that look for?" asked Chris.

"This," was all the marine in front of him said.

Chris felt a prick in the side of his neck. He immediately snapped his head left and shifted his weight to the right. Sure enough there was a dripping needle in the hands of one of the other marines.

Stacey screamed, as she had the same thing done to her. Chris's vision began getting blurry and he realized he was quickly losing his sense of balance.

In a slow, drugged voice Chris slurred, "What the hell are you bastards doing to me?"

Chris saw the blurry outline of Stacey struggling with the marines near her but he couldn't make out the details. He continued to hear screaming and yelling but it was getting more and more muffled.

In a slow, dopey voice, Chris joked, "You boys didn't need to drug me for this party," and with that he fell to the ground.

The last vision Chris remembered from this was looking up at the lights on the ceiling of the Tumbler with one lightly armored marine giving him a smirk. On the other side was the metal helmet of the marine in a T-800 suit. Chris's vision then went black and all the noises were silent as he went to sleep.

CHAPTER 10

Chris opened his eyes and began wondering where the heck he was. For a moment he wasn't sure if he was dreaming or if what he was seeing was real. As the effects of the chemicals continued to wear off he started remembering what had happened. He started tracing the events in his mind and when he got to the part where he came aboard the Earth Force Tumbler from the escape pod he shot up and realized he was on a bed. He looked around and saw a familiar sight. At first he thought he was somehow back aboard Zion's ship in the prison cell. Then as he continued to look around he saw a few minor differences. There were two beds in this cell and Stacey was in the other one. Other than that, it was the exact same layout as the previous cell he'd been in.

"Shit. Two cells in one day. This is not my day," muttered Chris.

He looked back over at Stacey and she was still knocked out. Chris assumed that they had given her the same drugs as him. As his wits came about him Chris threw his legs off the bed and walked over to the sink. He turned the cold water on and splashed some in his face. It felt amazing. With all the activity that had happened it felt like it had been weeks since he took a shower. Chris noticed that the wound on his shoulder was also bandaged up and was healing. They must have done some serious work on him while he was out, as it was feeling much better. That was a good omen, as they wouldn't have spent the time if they planned to push them out an airlock.

Chris thought about waking Stacey up but decided against it. She didn't need to wake up only to realize she was in a cell in the same crappy situation as before. So instead he began stretching out. He was just getting his legs loosened up when Stacey began to stir. He imagined she was probably going through the events of the last day much like he had.

Chris helped her as she came to and filled her in on what little he knew. It was during this time that an anger started to boil up from deep inside of him. He hadn't done anything really wrong, and Stacey definitely hadn't done anything to deserve all of this. It was at this time he noticed there was a camera facing the two of them.

Chris then stood up and shouted "Hey! Let us out of here! We're not criminals! We're civilians from a transport ship!"

Silence was all that greeted him. He got up and started banging on the cell pillars with his good arm but it wasn't as loud as he'd hoped. So instead he resigned to get back to his stretching routine while Stacey laid back down on her bed.

A few minutes later Chris heard a door open. Stacey sat up. Chris walked up to the cell pillars and saw six people walk up to his cell. It appeared to be three people of importance with three guards flanking them.

"Greetings," said the middle person in the front. "My name is Captain Erik Spear and you are on my ship the E.F. Leviathan. You must be the young man with the mouth my crew has been telling me about. Tell me, how is that shoulder doing?"

For some reason this Captain Spear guy seemed to put Chris at ease. He came off as a serious fellow, but someone at the same time who could lead troops out of respect, not fear. Chris found himself getting almost embarrassed for his shouting and banging on the door.

Chris gulped, "Yes sir, sorry about that. It has been a rough day and sometimes I let my mouth get me in trouble. The shoulder is much better; thank you for patching me up."

Captain Spear was only five foot ten and around 180 pounds but with his military grade posture and authoritative demeanor he easily commanded respect. Even Chris was impressed and slightly in awe. Erik wore a serious expression on his clean-shaven face and an Earth Force captain's uniform. His brown eyes were accentuated by his brown hair and slightly dimpled cheeks.

Captain Spear asked, "You claim to be a civilian, yet you were on a pirate's vessel. What is your name and what were you doing on an enemy ship?"

Chris replied, "My name is Chris Skylander and this is Stacey Fields. We were captured by this asshole—err, I mean pirate, named Zion. It's a long story, but we are not with that guy. We are part of a crew on a ship called the Puddle Jumper and our Captain is, or I guess was, Josh Hammerfist."

Chris looked down as a wave of emotions hit him with the memory of his father figure dying.

Stacey chimed in, "He is telling the truth, I swear. We aren't lying!"

Captain Spear motioned for her to calm down and in a soothing voice explained, "I know who you both are I just wanted to see if you would lie to me."

"You do?" questioned Chris.

"Yes, our facial recognition scans identified you right away. The only real questions I have are how you ended up on Zion's ship. But we will get to that shortly. While you are staying on board the ship let me introduce you to some of my command staff. To my left is my XO, Commander Ben Shafer."

Chris and Stacey looked at the man who nodded at them. He was of similar build as Erik but was an inch taller and slightly stockier. He also had brown hair and eyes but a slightly bigger head sporting a clean-shaven face and a comb over.

Captain Spear continued, "To my left is my wing

commander, John Sarner."

The wing commander was five foot nine and around 190 pounds. He sported a full beard that was trimmed neatly, with blue eyes and a crew cut.

Chris could barely contain his excitement. Even though he knew he was not a crew member these guys would have been his command staff if he was able to live his dream of flying a fighter for the Earth Force. Chris was especially excited to meet John, since that was the man who was the lead of the fighter wing.

Chris straightened up and beamed, "Uhhh pleased to meet you sirs!"

Stacey sarcastically commented, "Oh now you turn into a polite person?"

The corner of Captain Spear's mouth raised up in a barely perceptible smile, then he continued, "The gentlemen behind me are our guards and you will get to know them in due time, depending on how long your stay is with us."

"Awesome," was all Chris could conjure in response.

Stacey butted in saying, "How long our stay is? You mean you're not going to take us back to our ship?"

Captain Spear replied, "We believe your ship was destroyed based on the debris we found when we were tracking down Zion's ship. That is why we were surprised to find you two in an escape pod launched from Zion's ship. After our mission is complete we will take you back to an Earth Force station and you will be free to go about your business from there."

Stacey looked like someone had just shot her dog. Chris was not thrilled about the loss of his home, but was too enamored with his current surroundings to really care.

"Well now that introductions are complete let's discuss the series of events that led you to the prison cell you are in now."

The guards opened the cell doors and escorted Chris and Stacey to a small conference room on the same deck. Chris and Stacey began telling them their background stories and all the events that had transpired up until this point. The command staff had many questions and were generally surprised and disappointed in the different things that had happened to them. When they had finally finished answering all of the questions asked of them, Chris spoke up, "Sirs, umm, would it be possible for us to get a shower and a hot meal?"

The command staff chuckled as a whole and Captain Spear replied, "Yes I can imagine it has been a while since you had a good meal and a wash. You will be granted access to the non-restricted areas of the ship and have free reign over your person as long as you comply. You two will share living quarters that my XO will show you. Basically, living quarters and the rec rooms are all yours but the bridge, hangar, engineering, and other restricted areas are off limits. If you choose to ruin your freedom you will spend the rest of your stay with us behind these bars. Trust me, my hospitality is not offered twice."

Chris's hand immediately shot up.

"Yes Mr. Skylander?" questioned the captain.

"Uhhh sir, umm, is there any way I can check out the hangar? I would love to see what ships you have in person! I have always wanted to be a fighter pilot but it just wasn't in the cards for me," asked Chris.

"No," replied Captain Spear.

"Oh," came a deflated reply from Chris.

The captain visibly smiled then explained, "When things calm down I will set up a tour for you and you may take that tour with an escort."

Chris perked up again, realizing the captain had a dry sense of humor, and with a big grin on his face he replied, "Thank you, sir!"

"Just don't make me regret it. I leave you in the capable hands of my XO," stated the captain.

With that the captain and everyone except for two guards and Commander Shafer did an about face and walked away.

"It appears I am stuck on babysitting duty," Commander

Shafer opened up with.

Stacey placed her hands on her hips and Chris rolled his eyes.

"Come with me; I'll give you the tour," ordered Commander Shafer. "I need to stretch my legs anyways."

With that the five of them set out. They walked out of the room and began walking through a series of hallways into a turbo lift. Large capital ships typically had a few turbo lifts that were capable of going forward, backward, up, and down depending on where you wanted to go. Stacey and Chris were both impressed by what they were seeing but it was Chris who was looking like a kid in a candy factory. The men and women in their uniforms moving back and forth from their various jobs made Chris wish he could serve on a Poseidon class destroyer. "Maybe," he thought, when this is all done I can enlist, and with a recommendation from the captain they just might let me in." The only problem was how he would get that recommendation.

Commander Shafer spoke up, "Your biometric data is already being scanned so when you enter the lift it will only allow you to go to the nonrestricted areas. First up is the mess hall, otherwise known as Spacer Café. This is where you can get that hot meal you requested."

"Sounds delicious," replied Stacey.

The XO pressed a button with a fork and knife outline on it and the doors shut. Chris could tell the XO was a very serious man based on the hands clasped behind his back and his lack of pleasantries. Chris wondered if all XOs were so serious to the point where they were kind of assholes. Maybe that was why Brad was the way he was. Then Chris shook his head and remembered what Brad had done. Despite Commander Shafer's terse attitude, the two were probably not alike. There was a whirring sound as the lift took them up a couple of floors to the mess hall. Then there was a chiming noise and the turbo lift doors opened wide.

The sights and smells Stacy and Chris observed when those doors opened caused both of their mouths to begin salivating. Spacers Café was no small café. There was a large room with many different places to sit down and eat. There was lots of noise, as various off-duty crewmen walked around and socialized over a meal. In addition, the food smelled delicious. Chris had heard of military kitchens being of high quality. After all, in a ship out on a deep space patrol for months on end, having a variety of warm delicious meals did wonders for the crew's morale. Sure, it was no five-star restaurant, but it was better than almost anything Chris had eaten on the Puddle Jumper.

The XO walked off the turbo lifts with Stacey, Chris, and the guards and with a gesture of his hand he explained, "There is the line. It appears today's special is spaghetti and meatballs. Please hurry up and get your food so that we can finish this tour and I may resume my duties."

"Already on it boss," came a reply from Chris as his back was already turned and he was walking to the line.

"Sorry about him, he forgets his manners sometimes when there are distractions," explained Stacey.

Commander Shafer nodded and Stacey too took off for the line behind Chris.

They each got their meals and returned to a table, where the XO was already waiting. Chris had a huge plate of spaghetti and began wolfing it down while Stacey began a much more delicate version of eating. The commander looked at Chris with a questionable set of eyes as he scarfed down his food, getting sauce and some noodles on the tray and his face. Chris didn't care though as the food was so good and he was starving. After he finished his first plate he got up for another round. Commander Shafer sighed with a lack of patience but allowed Chris to continue. Stacey asked a few question over the meal and the XO answered them with short, direct answers. He clearly was not a fan of giving tours. Finally, with the meals done and full bellies, Commander Shafer stated, "I think now would be a good time to show you your quarters."

"I think you are right," replied Chris with a yawn.

They got up and walked back to the turbo lift. Both Stacey and Chris felt a wave of tiredness come over them. With droopy eyes they watched the XO hit the button for their living quarters.

"You will find our accommodations to be a bit Spartan but sufficient. This is a military vessel, after all," said Commander Shafer.

"All good to me sir," replied Chris.

He could see the commander cringe with the lack of military discipline in Chris's vocabulary.

"Yes, thank you again," added Stacey.

She got a polite nod from the XO as he clasped his hands behind his back again and waited.

The turbo lift doors opened up to a maze of white hallways.

"This is where your living quarters will be for the remainder of your stay. Please remember you are on a military vessel on a mission so make it a priority to stay out of people's way," explained Commander Shafer.

"Yes sir," replied Stacey.

"No problem," Chris added.

As they walked to their room the XO entered a series of commands into their doorway. Then it opened up and Chris saw a small room with two beds and a small living area.

"This is it," Commander Shafer volunteered. "It's not much but it is more than your average enlisted man gets. I have programed the room to open up when either of you approach. It will recognize your biometrics and allow you and only you two in unless there is some reason we need to get inside. There is a bathroom and wash area just down the hall on the left. It is a community shower, so don't be surprised. Also, there is a bar on another deck called the Afterburner if you are interested in taking in some spirits. Last but not least is the rec room. There is weightlifting equipment in there that you may want to investigate, Chris."

Chris thought, "Is he calling me skinny?" He started to say something but was immediately interrupted by Stacey.

"Thank you for all your help today and for saving us."

Commander Shafer nodded his head, turned around, and walked away with the guards in tow.

When the doors shut Chris joked, "Man that guy has a stick up his butt!"

"It's a military thing, Chris. These guys serve on an Earth Force vessel, not a smuggler ship like us," mocked Stacey.

"Ya true. Despite all the stuff that has happened, I have to admit this is the coolest ship I've ever been aboard," Chris admitted.

Stacey and Chris took turns going into the shower, as Stacey was kind of a mother figure to him in a way. After Chris spent fifteen minutes in a refreshing hot shower he went back to the room and opened a closet on his side. There were five pairs of standard crew uniforms that he could wear, along with shoes. He only put on some underwear, wrapped himself up in bed, and hit the lights.

CHAPTER 11

An unknown amount of time later Chris woke up. He'd had nightmares all night of Zion in a metal suit, killing his family and crew, Brad pulling the trigger and murdering his father, and his father's dead eyes. It took him a while to remember where he was, but a glance over at a sleeping Stacey in the bed next to his brought back the necessary memories. He must have slept for a while as he wasn't tired anymore despite the nightmares, and his stomach was beginning to rumble.

Chris got himself out of bed and stumbled into the bathroom. He freshened up, brushed his teeth, and combed his hair. He was amazed to see the burn in his shoulder blade had healed for the most part and only some scar tissue remained. The spray-on skin and other advanced medicine available thanks to Earth Force was simply a miracle.

Walking back into his cabin he turned on dim lights to put on the crew wear in his closet. It was a basic grey jumpsuit with the Leviathan patch on the left arm of the jumpsuit and an Earth Force patch on the right. Despite everything that had happened he felt a surge of excitement putting on the jumpsuit. He felt like he was part of the crew of the Leviathan and figured, damn it, he had a horrible time up until now so he might as well enjoy what was in front of him. Besides, after they dropped him off he was pretty sure he would never get on a Poseidon class vessel again unless it was in the jail cell.

So for the rest of his time here he was going to enjoy living the life and looking the part of a fighter pilot.

Thinking about it he walked back into the bathroom, and with a glance at the mirror he couldn't help but think, "Wow! I look pretty bad ass!"

With that he walked out of the community bathroom, put his hand on his hips and asked himself, "Where to now?"

His stomach rumbled as if answering his question, so he decided to get some chow. He began walking down the hallway with a long, prideful stride. Crewmen were passing him by and for the most part ignoring his big smile and almost bouncy stride. He rounded the corner to get to the turbo lift and boom! A shoulder plowed into him and the next thing he knew he was staring up at the ceiling.

"Watch it, kid! You're going to see stars if you don't pay attention when a big dog walks by," said a tall, strong man with blond hair.

Chris spoke up, "Oh, sorry sir—didn't see you there."

The man made a PFFFing sound with his lips, turned around, and kept walking. Chris heard him laugh and say, "Dang noobs. I guess they're taking them straight from the cradle these days."

Chris picked himself up and went to introduce himself but the man was already fifteen paces away chuckling to himself and wasn't slowing down. He brushed himself off instead of getting mad, put on another smile, and turned around to continue his day. He made his way onto the turbo lift, where he ran into several more crewman. He greeted them but they did not respond and kept their heads forward. Chris began to realize the crew must have all been warned about him and Stacey. He also figured out that nobody seemed too eager to meet the new young civilian smuggler on board. So Chris just hit the button to the Spacers Café and waited for his ride to arrive.

Ding! The lift came to a stop and the doors opened up. Before Chris could take one step several crewman shoved their way past him off of the lift.

"Hmmm," Chris thought. "Are they trying to piss me off or do they just want nothing to do with me? Well either way, someone has to be slightly friendlier around here."

Once at the café Chris made his way to the line and waited. He gathered as much bacon as he could and some eggs and stood with a tray trying to figure out where he was going to sit. He surveyed the scene. Most people were eating in groups. Chris assumed they were part of a team or people who knew each other, but he did find one person at a table by himself.

"Well here goes nothing," Chris thought. With that he walked himself over to the table and asked, "Can I join ya?"

The man looked up at him and said, "I don't know, can you?"

Now at this point Chris had about had enough of the negative attitudes he was getting from the crew so with a determined mind he replied, "Yep, I can!"

He sat down across from the man, stuck out his hand, and beamed, "Nice to meet you! I'm Chris."

The man across from him stared back with the gaze of a person who'd seen years in the service. He had a salt-and-pepper colored trimmed beard and was slightly overweight. He looked to be in his late forties with greying, long-cut hair. His brownish green eyes and round face made him look friendlier than he was acting. Chris noted the red jumpsuit he was wearing and a mechanics badge on his jumpsuit.

After a second of awkward staring the man reciprocated the handshake and introduced himself. "I'm Veteran Justin Patterson, but most people just call me Whistler. I'm the lead mechanic for the fighter squadron."

The man's handshake was a firm one and full of stringy muscle and callused skin. Chris could tell these hands had held many wrenches in their day and he had no doubt the man knew what he was doing.

"You work with the fighter squadron?" Chris asked. "That

must be awesome!"

Whistler, with his southern accent, responded with a grin, "Ya, I know the flyboys. But I wouldn't call it working with them. They mostly ignore what I say, fly my birds, and hand them back to me broken."

Chris chuckled at the response and in between bites began to tell him how he wished he could have been a fighter pilot.

"Well if you want to meet the fighter jockeys they tend to hang out in the Afterburner lounge between flights," explained Whistler.

"Well Whistler, I appreciate that. Hey, do you think I could get a tour of the hangar?" asked Chris.

"Heh heh heh!" Whistler bellowed. "You sure are persistent, kid. The captain warned us about you. No tours till he gives the green light. Nice try, though."

Chris questioned, "Warned you about me? Personally? Did he warn the rest of the crew as well? Cause I have been ignored and. . . ."

"Whoa, whoa, whoa there killer—one question at a time. The whole crew was warned about you through our nanite software package. Basically it was a ship-wide update. It mentioned you had a curiosity about the hangar. People are aware of who you are, and frankly you will find if you're not one of the crew, then you are in the way. Don't take it personally," Whistler explained.

"I've heard of nanites being used before but they were always too expensive for me. It must be awesome having that in your head, updating you on the latest information. Heck, I'd be twice the pilot if all the information was directly downloaded into my brain," commented Chris.

"I guess so," replied Whistler, "Sometimes I wish I was off the grid. Would be a lot easier to get some peace and quiet. With these nanites I am expected to digest information quickly and act even faster. But complaining won't do any good I suppose."

Chris smiled and ate another bite. While chewing he asked, "Have you ever gotten to fly one of the fighters?"

Whistler frowned and in his southern drawl stated, "Now that would be against regulations. Only pilots have a normal need to fly those ships."

Chris understood, but it was the frown on Chris's face that made Whistler laugh.

"But . . . that being said sometimes I need to fly the ships to understand exactly what went wrong, you know?" Whistler added with a chuckle.

"That must be awesome! What is it like?" questioned Chris.

"It's a lot of fun. I wish it happened more often sometimes," laughed Whistler. "That being said, my true passion is fixing the ships and that's where I get my jollies. Besides, those flyboys are built differently than me. I like having this massive ship around me keeping me safe, not being out there shooting at pirates in a small tin can. Don't see too many flyboys with grey hair like me."

Chris laughed at that and stated, "I understand. You guys are lucky to be on this ship. It is a dream job!"

With that Whistler stood up and cautioned, "We need more guys with your attitude. That being said, just remember the grass is not always actually greener on the other side. It was good to meet you, Chris. I have to get back to the shop but look forward to seeing you on that tour."

They shook hands, and with that Veteran Patterson left Chris to finish his meal.

Chris finished up his plate, walked it to the dishwasher, and set off to his next stop. Chris remembered the XO making fun of him for needing to hit the plates, so the gym was his next destination.

Back on the Puddle Jumper the ship had some old equipment left in one of the storage rooms. Chris had worked out there before, but it was nothing like a serious gym. Most civilians didn't have weight rooms on ships, so the fact that they had a few dumbbells and universal machines was better than nothing. He and the twins used to make bets about who could lift more, but nobody was particularly strong. The exception, of course, was Captain Hammerfist, who lifted with that small amount of equipment regularly. If you needed cardio, he would just say jog in the halls or in the cargo bay. If you needed more weight, they could just turn up the artificial gravity. Because of the lack of equipment and the lack of need Chris never worked out too seriously. "Why workout when you could play space simulator games?" Chris would tell himself.

Chris took the turbo lift to the rec room, and when the doors opened he took in the scene. The room was impressive. There was a ton of cardio equipment, but what Chris really liked was the weights. It made him smile that as far as mankind had come they still used good old-fashioned steel dumbbells. The place had multiple sets ranging from five to two hundred pounds. Next to that were the squat racks, bench presses, and other barbell setups. Following that were the cable machines, and last but not least a large open area for stretching, yoga, and bodyweight exercises. Even with all this equipment, the place was busy. Chris could tell the weight room was a popular attraction on Poseidon class destroyers, and the Leviathan was no exception.

Chris was not sure where to go first so he did what most young guys do. He walked up to an empty bench. The equipment was newer than anything he had seen before. It appeared to be a leather bench press with two plates on each side. Upon further review though, there was a screen at the base of the bench that controlled the equipment. He started playing with it and realized that the bench utilized artificial gravity to control the weight. He dialed up 155 pounds and proceeded to lie down.

Chris wrapped his hands on the bar, lifted it up, and started repping it out. He thought the first few were pretty easy but quickly realized he did not have the endurance and after the tenth rep he racked the weight again. Once it was in place he sat back up to recover. His timing couldn't have been more perfect. When he looked up he saw a dream of a woman walk into the room. She was roughly five foot four, with blond hair pulled back in a ponytail and chocolate brown eyes. When she walked her hips swayed in a way that hypnotized Chris.

Now Chris was no virgin, but to say he had been with lots of women would be a lie. It was tough being a spacer on board a small ship with only one woman on the most recent crew. That woman of course was Stacey, who could have been Chris's mother and was already in a relationship with Captain Hammerfist. Chris was used to docking with a space station though, or landing at a local city on Earth and taking a couple days of leave. These stations were great at comforting spacers and smugglers for a short time with bars, nightclubs, and even brothels. The further from Earth, the less laws applied. For someone with Chris's way of life, however, settling down was a rare commodity.

Since he'd boarded the Leviathan he'd seen dozens of women walk by, many of whom were quite easy on the eyes. This girl was different. She was drop-dead gorgeous in his opinion. So he did what came naturally to him. He quickly sat back to crank out another set on the bench. Hopefully she would notice him and be impressed. After he pushed himself hard, putting up another eight reps, he sat up to take in the praise for his physical accomplishment.

To his disappointment the mystery lady was gone. He looked around and spotted her warming up at a different area. "Damn," he thought, "she didn't even look my way. What a waste." Chris was not to be deterred that easily, however. He finished another set on the bench and walked up to the dumbbell rack, which was conveniently three or so meters away from where the lady of his interest was stretching.

Chris quickly grabbed the thirty-five-pound dumbbells and started repping them out to the best of his ability. "Surely she will be impressed by the bicep curls," he thought. Again, she didn't even look his direction. Instead, she continued stretching her legs with her head down. Her flexibility was very impressive and it only made Chris more attracted to her. He racked the weights and looked over at her shapely posterior. It was amazing in those tight, form-fitting pants. This process of her moving to different areas repeated again, and again Chris moved into a different area with a nice view of her.

When he completed a set on another machine and sat up to admire the view a voice a foot away from his head chimed in, "So you like Melissa?"

Chris looked to his left in surprise and saw an average-sized man in his mid-twenties with a shit-eating grin on his face looking at him.

He started to ask, "Are you talking about the—"

Before he could finish the man responded, "Ya I'm talking about the hot blond you keep undressing with your eyes."

Chris blushed a bit and muttered, "Well sure but I didn't realize I was that noticeable."

The man blurted out, "Dude you are the only one in this room that is not part of the crew. Everybody notices you. Plus that girl is a fighter pilot. You think she hasn't noticed you out of the corner of her eye?"

"Oh shit," Chris managed.

"Hahaha relax dude, she is a super friendly girl. The name's Mike, by the way," Mike explained.

"Chris," Chris replied, and they shook hands.

Mike seemed like an honest guy. He had short brown hair, a couple of tattoos, and sported a neatly trimmed goatee.

"Listen," Mike said, "She is a dove of a girl. Very friendly. You should introduce yourself to her and invite her for a drink at the Afterburner. She is probably just as curious about you since you're not part of the crew."

"Oh," Chris muttered, "You're probably right. I guess that does make me a bit unique."

"Ya man, you got this. Do it now—she's looking this way!" Mike cheered.

Chris looked over at her and sure enough she was watching the two of them out of the corner of her eye.

"You gotta go now," Mike added, "If you don't it will seem like you're weird and just staring at her. Just believe in yourself."

"All right, I got this. Just give me a second," Chris responded.

With that Chris got up from his machine. He could feel a lump in his throat and butterflies in his stomach. He had never done anything like this in the past—just walk up to a girl and straight up ask her out. "Was that what he should do?" Chris wondered. Chris figured that maybe he should start by introducing himself and ask her if she would be up for a drink. He took a few steps forward. The pressure was just building in him and he started to second guess himself. This girl was not only hot, she was also a pilot. If he screwed this up it would be such an embarrassment if he ever got to talk to the pilots later. In his nervousness he looked back at Mike.

Mike had a smile on his face and flashed him a thumbs-up sign. Chris reactively gave him a thumbs-up back.

"Well I guess I'm committed," Chris thought.

He started walking again and saw Melissa flash him a glance and then keep looking forward. As he made his way up to her he cleared his throat and attempted the calmest semi deep voice he could conjure.

"Uhhhhh. Hi," Chris sputtered. He immediately regretted saying that and kicked himself internally for not having a good opener. He then added, "I'm Chris," and stuck out his hand.

Melissa rolled her eyes turned around and gave Chris a venomous stare.

"Um, this is the part where you introduce yourself," Chris encouraged.

"Yes I know!" Melissa spat. "Let's just fast forward to the

part where you ask me out and I shut you down. Now can I continue my workout in peace?"

Chris was stunned and looked like he'd had his lunch money stolen from him by a schoolyard bully.

"Uh, ya it's cool," Chris said in defeat, feeling like it was most definitely not cool.

He turned around and was about to walk away when Melissa added, "Wait. Listen, I don't date people on this ship and certainly not a temporary visitor. I'm sure you are a good guy but Mike likes to mess with people. This isn't the first time he has sent a person over here to ask me out. It gets annoying."

Chris replied, "Hold on, this is not the first time?"

"Hell no," Melissa responded.

"Fair enough. I think it's awesome you're a pilot though, and I'd love to hear about it sometime," Chris explained.

Melissa smiled and looked at him for a quick second, then turned around and continued her workout.

Chris looked back at Mike, who was dying of laughter. He wanted to go over and punch him, but besides the fact that Mike would probably whoop his ass, he knew he would get sent right back to the cell if he attacked a crew member.

With his pride destroyed Chris walked over to another machine and sat down to keep working out on his own. These people did not respect him and he just had to come to terms with that fact. At least Whistler was willing to talk to him. The rest of the crew was just not happy to have him aboard and wanted him out of the way.

Chris continued his workout and kept thinking about his next moves. He knew he had to earn the crew's respect somehow if he wanted to fit in. He had to find a way to get on this ship on a more permanent basis. He had to become a fighter pilot. "What did he have left to lose?" Chris thought.

After this ship finished its mission he was going to be dropped off at a local space station with a few credits in his name and nothing other than the clothes he was wearing. That was a horrible deck of cards to be dealt. People without any-thing often ended up with terrible lives in today's society. He had no formal higher education, no skills other than piloting a ship, and no credits to invest in anything. The prospects were depressing and he was just beating himself up thinking about it. Chris continued working out for another several minutes before he decided he should just shower up.

Just then he observed something. Mike just happened to be working out at the bench he was at before. This gave Chris an idea. Chris waited till Mike laid back and lifted the bar off the bench. Chris quickly and quietly started walking over to the bench. Mike then noticed him out of the corner of his eye.

"Wanna spot?" Chris offered.

"Sure, I could use some negatives," grunted Mike after the fourth rep.

Chris walked up like he was about to help but instead he reached down toward the screen that controlled the weight of the bench. He quickly dialed up to four hundred pounds.

"There you go bud, thanks for the tip earlier," grinned Chris.

"Huh?" questioned Mike.

Chris hit engage and watched as the weight went falling down toward Mike. He saw the safety stops engage before the weight crushed Mike and then he walked away chuckling.

"Hey!" yelled Mike. "Get this thing off of me!"

"You got it! Just believe in yourself!" laughed Chris as he walked toward the turbo lift.

"Oh you asshole!" yelled Mike as he struggled with the weight.

Chris looked over and saw Melissa watching him. He even detected a faint smile on her face.

Chris thought, "Maybe I will fit in here somehow." Then he got on the turbo lift and went up for a shower.

CHAPTER 12

The next several hours were pretty boring for Chris. The exhilaration of being on an Earth Force ship was wearing off. He couldn't go where he wanted, and nobody would really talk to him. He mostly just sat around his room and talked with Stacey. While she was happy to be alive, she was becoming a little stir-crazy from being cooped up on the ship.

Chris laughed when she summed up the situation as: "The prison warden rescued us from the executioner."

Chris didn't hold it against her. Not only did she not share the same fascination with military life, she knew she had to start over and wanted to see family after the whole ordeal. Meanwhile Chris was in a sour mood because nobody would tell him what was going on. He had picked up bits and pieces of conversations from people as he passed them by in the halls or at the Spacers Café, but couldn't put all the pieces together. He tried at one point to log onto a data terminal, but nobody had given him login credentials for access. After thinking about the circumstances bringing him to the ship, he wouldn't have given himself the ability to log onto the ship's intranet either.

One comfort available on the ship was the availability of civilian and military news channels. Most of the time the talking heads were discussing mindless fads, celebrity nonsense, and taking potshots at their political rivals. Occasionally, almost by accident, it seemed they behaved like the journalists they claimed to be and discussed current events. Chris learned that the Gate Keepers were a rogue element of the military. This explained why there were people wearing military uniforms on Zion's ship. Apparently they believed humans had made contact with aliens in the past, and worshipped them as gods. While this made Chris laugh a little he couldn't help but think back on the strange things they had found on the Argo class freighter a few days ago.

Chris also learned, with no great surprise, that Zion was the leader and face of the Gate Keepers organization. Before the current rebellion, he was a former admiral in the Earth Force Navy. When reporters tried to investigate his previous assignments, however, the Earth Force had claimed everything was classified—typical Earth Force secrecy.

There had been hundreds of arrests since the beginning of the rebellion, and for the most part the news had portrayed the conflicts as just minor skirmishes. Chris couldn't believe how soft the media was being on Zion and his terrorist group. He almost shouted at the display when they claimed the "minor rebellion" had "intensified" after the Gate Keepers destroyed a space station orbiting Saturn, killing thousands. Another key piece of information was that an Earth Force task force had been sent to squash this rebellion and reclaim the stolen property.

It didn't take long for Chris to realize that he was a guest on board a ship that was part of that task force. From listening to crew member conversations, the Gate Keepers had deep ties within Earth Force and crew members were always a little suspicious that there might be Gate Keepers insiders within their midst. That was apparently how they got a hold of a Poseidon class vessel in the first place. The Gate Keepers vessel he'd been aboard was called the "Iceni" and had gone rogue several months prior. This paranoia also explained why crew members weren't excited to talk to the new guy they picked up from the very ship they were chasing.

Chris was in his bunk, just about to doze off while watching the talking heads, when suddenly an alarm went off. This was followed with a sudden jolt and strange tingly feeling he was all too familiar with that he got when making a subspace transition. The Leviathan must have just exited subspace. Most people were able to feel the effects of subspace transitions but to this day the phenomenon could not be explained scientifically. The lights dimmed and switched to a red tint. A loud voice came over the ships intercoms: "Battle stations, battle stations, this is not a drill!" it repeated.

Chris ran out into the hallway and began trying to figure out what was going on. People were sprinting back and forth between rooms and turbo lifts. He did his best to keep out of the way but sometimes they ran into him anyways. Chris decided the best thing he could do was head to the observation deck. At least there he might be able to piece together what exactly was going on with his ship and if they were about to attack Zion.

He waited until he found an empty turbo lift and took it up to the observation deck. As he got off the lift he stepped out and surveyed the scene. For the first time since he had been on the ship the observation deck was empty. This meant he could manipulate the walls/screens to see whatever he wanted to see. Chris quickly located the observation deck control panel and began his programming.

The cool thing about the observation deck was that the walls could be turned into screens that portrayed what was going on in the outward direction each wall was facing. Meaning the room could mimic what it would look like around you as if the ship were completely transparent. You could zoom in on objects if you wanted to see details or keep the view from a distance as if you were looking out of a window from the deck. Most of the time people would come up here if they wanted to see what was going on in the solar system around them. For example, if the Leviathan was in orbit around Saturn, people would come up here and program the walls to display the beautiful planet, its rings, and its many moons. For the most part it was used as a tool to keep the crew happy and sane during long voyages. The optics were impressive too. You could zoom in and see neighborhoods on Earth from orbit if you wanted. Or in the previous example you could zoom in on the rings of Saturn and see the individual rocks float by in orbit.

Chris had a different idea today. He set it up so that all the walls would portray what was around the ship. This created a 360-degree view of the battle that was about to play out in front of him. If the crew of the Leviathan wasn't going to tell him what they were doing, he would just figure it out for himself. Besides, the captain didn't say the observation deck was off limits.

After he plugged in the commands he looked up and the soft grey walls of the ship began to change into transparent screens. Even the floor and ceiling were capable of this transformation. It took them a couple of seconds to load what was visible outside of the ship and even then a few more seconds to display details as the resolution sharpened up. Pretty soon Chris found himself standing in what looked like outer space. He could still see gridlines that represented the floor he was standing on and below that a transparent image of the ship around him. The Leviathan was an impressive ship in its own right. At 420 meters long there was a lot of ship to take in and its long structure bristling with turrets looked fearsome. In the aft direction he could make out the transparent image of engineering and the reactor houses. The image even showed the blue glow of the engine exhaust from the Leviathan's four fusion engines.

Then something out of the corner of his eye caught his attention. He looked over his shoulder and saw the exhaust plume of the engines coming from a Raptor class medium fighter. It was leaving the hangar headed out on its mission.

The four engines (two on top and two on the edges of its wings) of the Raptor class vessel burned hot with white centers and blue outlines for each plume. The Raptor class fighter was a blend of firepower, speed, and maneuverability. It came equipped with four banks for cannons, which could either be set up for lasers or rapid-fire rail guns. At twenty-one meters long it was a big fighter that could house several missiles of various types. The Raptor was the image of the modern Earth Force fighter. There were a couple of other types, but more often than not Poseidon class destroyers preferred to go with the Raptors. This was due to its multimission capabilities and its deadly weapons load out.

The pilot of the vessel must have hit afterburners as the exhaust plumes stretched from three meters long to about fifteen. The exhaust also changed color from blue, to orange, to red, as the fighter sped away from the hangar and began banking to the left. "Wicked!" Chris thought. Just as the first Raptor left the hangar another one emerged in the same fashion. The process repeated itself until all five of the Leviathan's complement of fighters were launched. Chris knew the Leviathan also was capable of carrying a Tumbler class transport vessel in addition to the fighters and sure enough, shortly after the fighters launched, it did too. Chris looked around and saw Neptune in the distant background. It was about the size of a quarter on one of the wall screens. After that he couldn't see any other signs of where they were, with the exception of their home system's sun Sol burning on one of the other walls.

After that Chris directed his attention forward in the direction the Leviathan was traveling. He didn't know what the mission was but if he could figure out where they were going he could venture a guess. Sure enough, many kilometers in front of the Leviathan was another Poseidon class vessel. Chris immediately zoomed in on the ship to try and identify it. As the zoom increased so did the size of the vessel. Within about a second the resolution sharpened up and Chris was able to identify it. Just as he had hoped, they were chasing down the Iceni. The Iceni, however, didn't appear to want to fight as it was hauling at full burn away from the Leviathan.

"Yes!" Chris yelled as he thrust his fist in the air. "Get that bastard! Woohoo! Go Earth Force!" he yelled as he jumped with excitement.

Chris watched as the Iceni appeared to be fleeing from the combat zone. Then he realized if it was a Poseidon versus Poseidon matchup, who would win? Chris had to gamble on the Earth Force trained crew running their ship better than a bunch of Gate Keepers rebels. Still it would be a tough match-up, and if Zion was an ex-Earth Force admiral he would know what tactics and armaments Captain Spear would bring to bear.

That's when Chris noticed two more flashes to the Leviathan's port and starboard sides. Two massive subspace portals began to open up. The familiar blue swirls with white centers were almost hypnotizing to Chris. Now the only question was what was going to emerge from those portals?

Seconds later the forward sections of two more Poseidon class destroyers made their way through the portals. "OHH YAA!" yelled Chris "Time for Earth Force to open up a can of whoop ass on you, Zion! I just wish I was one of the pilots who got to pull the trigger on your ship!"

Chris zoomed in on each of the new Poseidon destroyers and saw one was called the E.F. Olympia and the other was the E.F. Oxford. "So it will be three on one," Chris thought, "I like those odds."

Sure enough, in similar fashion the two additional destroyers began deploying their fighters. They had slightly different compliments of fighters. Instead of five Raptor class vessels like the Leviathan had, they deployed three Raptors and two Lightning class fighters.

Lightning class fighters were the replacement to the Skimmers that had been used by Zion when he attacked the

Puddle Jumper. The Earth Force always had the latest and greatest equipment and every decade or two it tried to update its equipment. The Lightning class fighters were designed to be fast-attack intercept ships. They often doubled as scouts since they had high top speeds, brutal acceleration, and were the lowest-cost ships out of all the Earth Force fighters. Lowest cost was relative though, as they were bristling with the latest technology. The model also had four engines but they were centrally located in the back. Lightning class fighters were also twenty-one meters long like the Raptor, but unlike the Raptor they sported a narrow shaped fuselage with small wings coming off each side. As a result they contained far less mass than their heavier Raptor counterparts. A tradeoff of this lower weight, however, was that they also sported less armor and only two banks of cannons. They carried missiles, but a smaller amount than the Raptor was capable of carrying.

Chris watched as the fighters sped off in the direction of the Iceni. He looked again at a zoomed-in picture of the Iceni and saw it had ten Skimmer class fighters guarding it. Those ships broke off from their escort duty to intercept the incoming Earth Force fighters.

Chris wished he had some popcorn and soda because this fight was going to be a good one—that is, for the Earth Force anyways. There was no way the Iceni would be able to take on the combined might of three Poseidon destroyers and their more modern fighter compliments. The only thing Chris didn't understand was why the Leviathan also launched its Tumbler transport. That thing was not intended for combat. Just like that, it hit him.

"Duh," Chris mumbled.

He bet the Earth Force was not trying to destroy the Iceni, only disable it. From there the tumbler would dock and probably take the cargo back. Or even better, bring Zion back alive for interrogation purposes and to face justice for the crew of the Puddle Jumper!

Chris pondered as he watched the ships closing in on each other. "What was so important about that cargo?" he thought, "Could it really be an alien object? No that's just so far-fetched. It has to be something very valuable. Maybe a special research project. Heck, maybe a special research project that Zion was working on. But then how did it get in an asteroid belt?" Chris shook his head as he realized he was not going to figure it out. Instead, he turned his attention back to the battle that was about to unfold.

Flashes of amber light began to be seen from the Leviathan. That meant she was in range of the incoming fighters. In addition, missiles began firing, along with several rail guns. Within seconds the Earth Force fighters and Gate Keepers fighters began firing at each other as well. It looked like a beautiful mess of light and ships moving around in a big sphere. Chris would have given anything at that point to be in the cockpit of an Earth Force fighter.

Between all the lasers, rail guns, and missile explosions there was no way to keep track of the individual battles. Chris basically watched it all play out and looked for the larger explosions as they would probably be the first fighters blowing up.

Sure enough in less than thirty seconds after the initial battle started the first Gate Keepers fighter went supercritical and exploded. It was a beautiful sight to see, as whatever ordinance it was carrying along with its fusion reactor exploded in a flash of light. Chris had heard stories of fighter pilots shooting down another fighter only to get caught up in the destroyed fighter's explosion and lose their own fighter to the damage.

To Chris's delight none of the Earth Force fighters were close enough and they got out of the way. "These guys are pros," Chris thought.

The battle continued on and two more of the Gate Keepers

fighters were destroyed. It was at that point that Chris realized five of the Raptor fighters had broken off from the battle and were headed straight for the Iceni.

The Iceni was on a full burn away from the incoming Earth Force fleet. At this range only missiles from the Leviathan would be able to do any damage and those would probably be taken out by the ships point defenses, which were small laser batteries designed to take out missiles as they approached. That was probably why the Leviathan had not attacked directly.

The five Raptors, however, were much closer to the Iceni and began opening fire on the Iceni with their lasers and rapid fire rail guns. They couldn't do much damage to the massively armored ship in the short run, but continuous barrages would add up over time. The Raptor pilots were probably targeting subsystems like defense batteries or the engines themselves. The Iceni was not a punching bag, though, and it returned fire with everything it had. Missiles were launched at the Raptors. Defense lasers and their amber glow could be seen hitting the incoming fighters, causing them to break off of their attacks. Chaos was all around the Iceni.

Chris guessed the Iceni was making a run for it and the incoming Raptor fighters were trying to stop them. Two more of the enemy Skimmers were taken out, which left the enemy with five Skimmers and a fleeing Poseidon class destroyer. There was no way for the Gate Keepers fleet to win; it was only a matter of time. That's when Chris saw what he had been hoping wouldn't happen.

A small blue portal opened up in front of the Iceni. The subspace portal grew to its proper size and the Iceni generated a burst of thrust from its main drives, pushing it toward the interdimensional portal.

"Dammit!" Chris cursed as the destroyer began to disappear inside the swirling blue and white portal. The ship's long, sleek structure was being swallowed by the subspace portal quickly. The weapons fire of the Raptor fighters could do nothing to slow it down.

Seeing their command ship flee, the Gate Keepers pirates in their Skimmer vessels began their retreat into subspace. All five of them opened up portals but they didn't have the armor or the distance between them and the other Earth Force fighters that the Iceni had.

As the Iceni finished its transition into subspace the Skimmers portals reached full size. They were overwhelmed though by the Earth Force fighters, which were unloading everything they had into them. The thing about retreating into subspace was during the transition the ship had to fly straight into the portal, which meant the path was very predictable. Round after round of rail guns slammed into them and three of the five fighters never made it into their portals. The other two escaped with likely heavy damage.

All of the adrenaline and excitement that had been worked up in Chris immediately stopped. He exhaled in disappointment and his head slumped down. The Iceni had gotten away again and was still at large. Chris was sure that Captain Spear would continue to pursue the fleeing ship, but it would take time before they were able to get close enough to engage them again. He exhaled and watched as the fighters turned around and began flying back to their respective home ships. For the most part the fighters were very lightly damaged with just some nicks and dings from stray rail gun or laser fire impacting the armor. However one of the Raptors had taken a hit directly to the cockpit and apparently the pilot was in bad shape as the ship was not moving under its own power. He could see the tumbler craft using its tractor beam to tow the respective fighter back to the Leviathan. The cockpit of the fighter appeared to be breached, from what Chris could see.

Chris remained on the observation deck while the fighters flew back to their respective ships. It was a beautiful sight to watch and normally would have lifted Chris's spirits, but he couldn't get the images of Zion killing his crew out of his head. He told himself then and there he was done being a useless passenger. Zion, Brad, and all the other rebels aboard that ship would answer for killing the only family he had. With that he shut down the observation deck programming he had made. The walls and floor in all of their fine details faded back to plain old white ship walls. Chris got on the turbo lift and made his way back to his cabin, thinking about his next move. Maybe, just maybe, he would find a way to get involved.

CHAPTER 13

Several hours later Chris found himself staring at the ceiling of his room while lying on his bed. He had been bouncing a tennis ball off the ceiling as a way to pass the time and alleviate his boredom. He also used it as a way to concentrate and think. While Chris considered himself to be a reasonably intelligent man, he was struggling to put a plan together. He knew what he wanted but he needed more time to figure out how to get it.

Stacey had already gotten up and left. On her way out she expressed her displeasure at Chris's habit of bouncing the ball off the ceiling and catching it over and over. Chris had ignored her and kept concentrating at the problem in hand. After several more bounces a chime came through the room's speakers.

"Uh, hello?" Chris managed to say.

A pleasant voice over the speakers replied with, "Chris Skylander, will you please meet Major Sarner at the turbo lift in front of the hangar. He is ready to give you a tour."

"Awesome! I'll be right there!" Chris shouted.

With that he hopped out of bed, got himself together, and proceeded out of his small room toward the turbo lift. Chris had to stop himself from breaking into a full-on sprint. All he needed to do was run into one of the crew, injure them, and have them complain about the civilians on board. He thought about searching for Stacey first but he didn't want to make the

Stacey hesitated, then returned with a smile of her own and proceeded forward.

They went aboard through the cargo hold and the major pointed out various bits of equipment used during assault missions. Chris was very impressed with the different assault rifles and armor suits that were stored on board. They even had some of the T-1000 model exosuits, the latest upgrade to the T-800 exosuits, which Chris knew were the previous generation.

"All this equipment must make taking over another ship pretty easy?" Chris asked.

"Theoretically, as long as you've disabled a capital ship's external defenses, the assaults are pretty straightforward. After all, nobody really flies around prepared to repel a full company of marines wearing exosuits. You yourself have seen how devastatingly effective they are against light infantry." Chris winced at the reference, but Sarner continued, "In Zion's case, however, we are taking on what we assume is a fully staffed Poseidon class destroyer with much of the same equipment. Nobody really knows how it will go, as we've never run into this scenario outside of an exercise before now."

"I've been inside that ship and I can tell you it's not fully staffed by trained professionals of the Earth Force. There were a lot of people who looked like they were not supposed to be on a military vessel." Chris added, "If I were a betting man I would put my money on the Earth Force in this battle."

"I'll second that," Stacey chimed in.

The major had a thoughtful stare going on and Chris could tell something was bothering him.

"It's no secret that Zion is ex Earth Force and that he took the ship you saw with him when he defected. But your report of your time on board the Iceni is unnerving, especially the part where you said the majority of the personnel on board were nonmilitary. Zion would have needed a majority of the crew on his side to take the ship, so where were they?"

questioned the major.

"Well Stacey and I didn't get to see the whole ship, as we were kind of in a hurry, but they may have kept some key staff members around to navigate the ship and replaced all nonessential crew with others," Chris suggested.

"Yes, but why would you replace a fully functional and trained crew with a bunch of thugs that amount essentially to pirates?" questioned the major.

"Good question," Stacey added.

"Hmmm . . ." was all Chris muttered.

"Well, I'm not going to bore you guys with that question. Let's move to the cockpit and see how you guys like the Tumbler's flight interface," beamed the major.

They moved on to the cockpit, but Chris couldn't help thinking about the major's question. The more he got to know the wing commander, the more Chris wished he could serve in his wing. The guy was obviously dedicated and knew how to fly, but he also looked at the big picture.

They went into the flight deck of the transport and Chris got his first chance to check it out in real life. He enjoyed himself, and even Stacey seemed to be having a good time. Then the major said, "All right, now let's move on to the main part of the tour."

"The main part?" Stacey asked.

"He means the Raptor fighters! At least I hope he does," Chris exclaimed.

"You guessed it," replied Major Sarner with a smile.

With that they exited the Tumbler through the cargo doors again.

"Watch yourself," the major warned as they made their way into the heavy traffic of the hangar.

Chris dodged left as he rounded the corner of the Tumbler and two maintenance technicians rushed by them carrying some type of equipment. He watched as the major seemed to navigate the hangar bay with ease. Stacey was in tow right behind the major and made sure to stay close. Chris never was one to follow and for that he almost got crushed by another person in an exosuit clanking by with a missile in his mechanical grip.

The major had made his way back to the front of the Tumbler's exterior and gestured in the direction of the Raptors.

"I'll show you my Raptor, as my pilots have already left the hangar for some R and R," stated Major Sarner.

"OK," replied Stacey with a smile.

They began walking down what would be the main path of the hangar. Four of the five Raptors looked good, minus a few small nicks and dings. The wing commander's fighter was the closest to the exterior main hangar doors, which was also the farthest from them. They continued to make their way down the path toward the fighter, dodging when necessary any oncoming mechanics.

The Raptor to Chris's immediate right was the one that had to be towed in by the Tumbler. Chris could see a large melted hole in the thick cockpit's transparametal canopy. Transparametal was the latest transparent material ships used instead of glass. Glass, despite all the improvements that had been made, was still no match for an oncoming rail gun or laser shot. Even random space debris could prove detrimental to reinforced glass when traveling at high speed. So transparametal was the Earth Force's solution. It was not invincible by any means, but it did provide far better protection then the old glass canopies. On top of being transparent, it had active coatings on the inside that could dim incoming sunlight and display information on it just like heads-up displays of the past.

Chris could only guess the ship in front of them had taken a direct hit from a laser bolt and the bolt was strong enough that it had penetrated through into the cockpit where the unfortunate pilot was located. Chris could only imagine how bad the laser and radiation burns were for the guy. No wonder he was unable to pilot the ship back. The guy was lucky to be alive at all, considering how big the hole was in the canopy. Chris stopped walking as he saw several mechanics unfastening the main bolts that held the canopy's transparametal frame on the Raptor.

"Is this the ship the pilot in med bay was piloting?" Chris asked.

Major Sarner stopped and turned around to look at what Chris was referring to.

"Yes. That was Corporal Higgins' ship," the major responded.

"He is lucky to be alive," Chris added.

"Multiple shots at almost point-blank range got him. Could have happened to anyone in a dogfight like the one we were in," Major Sarner explained.

"I'm sorry to hear that," Stacey said solemnly.

"It's OK; comes with the job. I just need to make sure his sacrifice is not in vain," Major Sarner replied. The major portrayed confidence but Chris could see in his eyes that he was not happy about what had happened to his pilot.

"It's just one more reason for me to take Zion out," Chris announced. He looked Major Sarner in the eye when he said that and the major returned the stare.

"You planning on taking him out in a way I don't know about, Chris?" the major responded.

"No, I guess I mean when you take him out," Chris replied in a dejected voice.

"It's all right, Chris. I'll get that asshole; don't worry," the major asserted.

"Please do. He's a horrible man," Stacey added.

Chris turned and watched as the mechanics in their red jumpsuits used a crane and began lifting the cockpit off the Raptor. That's when he looked a little closer and spotted a familiar-looking bearded face.

"Whistler! How are you?" Chris shouted.

The mechanics turned their heads to see who had yelled at their lead. Whistler said something to them and they went back to what they were doing. Then he waved down to Chris and yelled, "Be down in a second, Chris."

Stacey and Major Sarner gave Chris a puzzled look.

In defense Chris threw up his hands and explained "What? He is one of the few people on the crew who will talk to me and not treat me like I am some traitor or civilian who doesn't matter—besides you and the captain, of course."

Major Sarner smiled and shook his head.

"Look at you Chris, making friends already," Stacey laughed.

They watched as Whistler finished up with his crew and came down a ladder. He walked right up to them and in a southern accent said, "Major, I see you were given the tour duties."

"Yes Whistler, I get all the good jobs around here," Major Sarner chuckled.

"Chris, I see it didn't take you long to get that tour you wanted," Whistler stated.

"No sir!" Chris beamed.

"And this lovely lady must be Stacey?" Whistler asked.

"Yes, I'm sorry, but I don't think we've met," Stacey responded. She stuck out her hand to shake Whistler's.

He took her hand and kissed it instead of shaking it, replying, "Pleasure to meet you, ma'am. I'm Veteran Justin Patterson but everyone calls me Whistler."

Stacey blushed and pulled her hand away but did manage to say in a slightly embarrassed voice, "Nice to meet you, Whistler."

Chris rolled his eyes and the major chuckled at Stacey's obvious discomfort. Chris had been shipmates with Stacey for so long he knew she wasn't used to chivalry—though he did see a slight smile on her face.

"Well out of all the Raptors to take a look at, this is the

wrong one," Whistler warned.

"Yes, we were on our way to my Raptor when Chris spotted you," Major Sarner explained.

"How long till you can get that thing functional?" questioned Chris.

"Well we will have the canopy replaced in a couple hours, but the real work will be on the inside, where we have to replace a lot of circuitry. Without going into details there is also a lot of mess in there. I'd say my crew and I can have it functional within twelve to sixteen hours," Whistler put forth with pride.

"Dang, that's fast," Chris replied.

"Well, when you have a full crew, spare parts on hand, all the hours on the clock, and me running the show you'd be amazed at what we can do to fix these things," Whistler taunted with a wink at Stacey.

"So then next time I bring in a ship with a couple of holes in it I expect you to be happy about the opportunity to demonstrate your team's ability," Major Sarner remarked with a slight smile on one side of his face.

"Whoa now, let's not get out of control!" Whistler cautioned with his hands raised. "We are good, but are not begging to prove how much we can fix. Besides, you guys need to treat these babies with more respect!"

Major Sarner laughed and said, "Roger that, Whistler."

Chris knew there was an interesting relationship between a pilot and his mechanic. They had to trust each other, but the nature of their jobs meant they butted heads sometimes.

"Well I don't want to hold you guys up from the rest of your tour, and I have a lot of work to do on this bird. So with that, I will bid y'all *adieu*," Whistler announced.

"Nice to meet you!" Stacey replied with a smile on her face.

With that Whistler got back to the damaged Raptor and began barking out orders to his team of mechanics. Was that an extra pep in his step Chris saw?

"Shall we?" Major Sarner asked.

Stacey and Chris nodded and then began following the major to his Raptor.

As they were walking toward the Raptor Stacey asked a question: "What do all the different-colored jumpsuits mean? Some people have blue, some green, and some red. I have even seen people in grey jumpsuits."

"Good eye," replied the major. "Red is what our mechanics wear, and green is a color designated for the pilots—although when we have marines on board they wear green as well, but the suit is very different from a pilot's. Blue is for the higher ups or the command staff, if you prefer. Last but not least are the grey suits, and they are for all the other support staff we have on board."

"Oh, I see," Stacy stated.

"That's why we have grey jumpsuits then! We are support staff!" added Chris.

Major Sarner looked at Chris and shook his head then offered, "Nice try, Chris. Guests get to wear grey jumpsuits if they don't have their own clothing."

"Hey at least we're guests and not prisoners!" Chris joked.

Stacey smacked him on the shoulder and cautioned, "Let's not push our luck, Chris!"

Major Sarner laughed and continued walking toward his Raptor.

They continued walking and dodging mechanics in their exosuits until they made it to the far end of the hangar where the major's Raptor was located. Chris knew the last Raptor belonged to the major because it had the major's name stenciled under the canopy. He didn't want it to show too much, but he was green with envy.

"I park my Raptor next to the exterior hangar door because as wing commander I expect to be the first out into the danger zone," Major Sarner explained.

"That's very admirable of you to do," Stacey noted.

"Also I don't have to fly over the other ships on the way out of the hangar," Major Sarner quipped.

Chris and Stacey laughed.

"Well Chris, do you want to do the honors of explaining what my ship is called, since you seem to have its stats memorized?" Major Sarner teased.

Chris took in the sight of the silver and black ship. At twenty-one meters long the Raptor was a large piece of equipment. It was considered a medium-class fighter, however, since there were bigger ones in existence. The main fuselage was a sleek shape that stretched all the way to the back. It had wings with large engines mounted on the ends. In front of these engines were forward-mounted cannons. It even had two additional large engines on the top of the fuselage that gave it the thrust it needed to be a space superiority fighter.

Chris, after waiting a second to take in the ship, started spouting information like he was reading from an encyclopedia.

"This beauty is a Falcon industries SF-15a Raptor. It's Earth Force's primary space superiority fighter. It has a total of four mounts for either lasers or rail guns. It also has sizable bays for whatever type of missiles you want to add to it. Duranium armor surrounds the hull so it can take some serious damage, but it still maintains relatively great agility and speed."

Stacey had already tuned Chris out and proceeded to walk up to the Raptor to put her hands on the hull.

"Well you are right, Chris, but you bored the lady to death, so that doesn't count as a win," Major Sarner stated.

"That's not fair! Stacey ignores me most of the time anyways," Chris responded.

"That's because it's usually just a bunch of hot air coming out of your mouth!" Stacey chimed in while looking away from them and at the ship.

The major just laughed and Chris knew it was time to cut his losses and look at the ship in detail.

They spent the next fifteen minutes looking at the Raptor in detail. The major explained the many facets of the ship's exterior and even managed to keep Stacey's attention while doing it. Chris was stoked, regardless of the conversation, because this was the first time he had ever put his own hands on an SF-15 Raptor. In the many video games Chris had enjoyed on the Puddle Jumper he had often selected the Raptor as his fighter of choice. Its blend of speed, agility, toughness, and firepower was too good to pass up.

Right when Chris thought the tour may come to an end, he figured he would go for broke and ask the major if he could get a chance to sit in the cockpit and check out the controls. The major gave him a hard stare and Chris started wondering if that was a mistake. Stacey even shook her head at Chris, but he figured, what the hell? Worst thing he can say is no, right?

"Ya, let's make that happen, Chris," the major stated bluntly.

"Awesome!" replied Chris.

Major Sarner pulled up a ladder to the Raptor and climbed up it with Chris and Stacey in tow. He began pressing a button and watched as the canopy opened up and Chris put his eyes on a real Raptor cockpit for the first time.

Chris had seen some pictures of a Raptor cockpit before, but they were usually altered slightly as the military didn't want everyone knowing what was going on inside.

"She is ready, Chris. Go ahead and have a seat," Major Sarner insisted.

Chris threw a leg over one side, then the other, and sat down in the synthetic leather seat, careful not to touch any of the controls. As he slid into place the seat began to conform to his body automatically. Chris was shocked at how natural it felt.

Major Sarner started going over all of the controls and they spent a solid twenty minutes doing it—so much so that Stacey finally chimed in with, "OK, boys, you two have fun. I'm going to the Afterburner for a drink." Then she walked off.

After Chris and Major Sarner finished the tour of the cockpit and Chris was sure he knew how to fly a Raptor, in theory of course, he thanked the major for the in-depth tutorial.

"I'm going to practice flying this thing in the simulator. It must be awesome flying the most advanced fighter in the fleet!" Chris beamed.

"Haha it is, I won't lie. But it's not all fun and games. There is a lot of responsibility leading a wing into battle. I hold myself accountable for what happened to Corporal Higgins," Major Sarner stressed.

"I can only imagine how you feel. I was just the pilot on the Puddle Jumper, but my father Captain Hammerfist always seemed to be carrying a weight on his shoulders whenever he would bring the crew into a dangerous scenario," Chris remarked.

"It's the burden of command. Sure, we get the best parking spots, but we're also responsible for everyone's life under our command. I can only imagine how Captain Spear feels. I have five other pilots; he has hundreds, including me, under his command," Major Sarner concluded.

"Well I am sorry for what happened to Corporal Higgins. I'm sure he was a good man. I hope he recovers from his wounds and flies for you again," Chris sympathized.

"I hope so too. But even if he does recover it will be months before he is back in the cockpit. I'll just be happy if he can fly a desk in the future. Anyways, Chris, it was a pleasure getting to know you and Stacey. Tell her I said that," Major Sarner insisted.

"I will Major," Chris replied and stuck out his hand.

"Also, Chris, we could use some good pilots in the future. You should consider joining the academy," Major Sarner noted and shook Chris's hand.

"I already tried but I can't afford it and I have no one left to give me a recommendation besides Stacey," Chris explained.

"Behave yourself and that may change in the near future. I have some old friends there that I can talk to. They give free rides to those who are elite-level recruits," Major Sarner specified as he gave him a wink and let go of his hand.

Chris was dumbstruck. Was the wing commander hinting he might help him get into the Earth Force's Space Academy?

"Uh, um . . ." Chris muttered.

" 'Thank you, sir,' are the words you're looking for, Chris," Major Sarner announced.

Chris threw up his best salute and rigid posture and beamed, "Thank you, sir!"

The wing commander smiled and said, "All right, the tour is over and I have duties to perform. Let's get out of here and let Whistler and his crews work."

With that they made their way out of the hangar deck. Chris was genuinely pumped, but also a bit conflicted. An idea had been brewing in his head and he wasn't sure if he could pull it off. Just then Chris heard the last words of his father, "Do not look back, Chris. Be bold. Your destiny lies ahead of you." He knew what he had to do. It was only a matter of when, not if.

CHAPTER 14

That evening Chris decided it was time to make his way to the Afterburner lounge to have some beers. Chris knew this is where the crew went to let off some steam and was hoping he might catch Major Sarner and his pilots there for some conversation. If not that, then at least the crew might be more open to talking to him there. He was getting bored of having only Stacey to talk to and the observation deck to entertain him. Worst case scenario he could still get drunk and relax.

Chris walked through the bulkhead door into the Afterburner lounge. It wasn't a huge bar but it did have a relaxed atmosphere with some smooth jazz playing in the background. The deck also had several wall screens imitating windows out of the ship. Currently there were no planets or objects nearby so the view was just a bunch of stars in the background. Several groups of people were sitting down at tables and a few glanced in his direction when he walked in, but for the most part he was ignored.

Chris scanned the area and found a group of people in green jumpsuits sitting at a table near the bar and mentally said, "Bingo." Chris immediately recognized two of the pilots. Mike and Melissa were there along with the tall man who had knocked him on his butt earlier and almost knocked him over coming out of the turbo lift on his way to the hangar tour.

"Shit, he's a pilot," Chris thought.

There was a fourth guy in a green jumpsuit at the table as well, who Chris didn't know. Major Sarner was nowhere to be found, unfortunately. The table was engulfed in a lively conversation—pilots exchanging war stories or fighter tactics by his estimation, based on the hand gestures. He thought back to his old crew, and how people's eyes glazed over when Chris would start talking pilot stuff.

Chris made his way toward the bar and grabbed a seat. It was a very nice bar with a large, lengthy oak wood surface where many could grab a drink. Behind the bar were row upon row of bottles, several beer taps, and an array of garnishes. Above the bar were racks that had many different shapes and sizes of glasses for people to pour their drink into. It really was a nice place to enjoy a peaceful beverage, let off some steam, or enjoy some company in relative privacy.

Chris wasn't here to let off steam tonight, however. He was on a mission, and that mission was to get in with the pilots. He figured the combination of alcohol and the fact that he was a pilot, too, just of a different variety, was just what he needed to break the ice with the pilots aboard this ship.

Chris overheard the pilots laughing at some joke the taller man was making, and with that he turned his attention to the barkeep, who had just made his way over to Chris.

"What can I get for ya?" questioned the barkeep.

The barkeep was a heck of a tall man. He must have been six foot six or six foot seven, but maintained a thin body type. He was a light-skinned African American man who had a clean-shaven face and brown eyes. He was the only crewman who wore a nice suit with a black tie.

"Hi, do you have any amber ale?" Chris requested.

"Say no more, I have just the beer for ya," the barkeep responded.

The barkeep was gone for several seconds before returning with an amber-colored beer.

"This is a classic. It's called Fat Tire Amber Ale and it's

been around for hundreds of years. Great stuff," explained the barkeep.

"Awesome, I've never had it before but it looks great," returned Chris.

"That'll be five credits," the barkeep responded.

"Uh . . . are you sure? I thought things on the ship were free?" Chris guessed.

The barkeep just stared at him. Even the people in the immediate vicinity seemed to stop and look at Chris, including the pilots. He began to feel that familiar weight on his chest again.

"All right, my bad, I don't have any credits so I'll just get going," Chris groaned. He felt like he had already missed his opportunity and embarrassed himself in the process.

Then the barkeep laughed and the rest of the crowd did as well.

"I'm just messing with you, friend. The name is Bill Bronx and I am the ship's bartender," Bill comforted as his hand reached out.

Chris shook his hand and introduced himself to the man.

"I was wondering when you would show up here," Bill mentioned.

"Really? Nobody else seems to take an interest," Chris replied.

"Well that's cause they're busy military folks. I'm the bartender, so keeping an eye on the comings and goings of the ship is part of my job," Bill explained.

"Is that why you don't have a jumpsuit on and wear a suit and tie instead?" Chris asked.

"Yep, it helps with the vibe around here. People are looking to escape from the day-to-day grind of living on a military vessel, and I try to help with that," replied Bill.

Chris took a pull from his beer and exhaled. "Well, you're doing a good job with that. Also, this beer is delicious!"

"Thank you, I figured you'd like it," Bill said.

"I have another question. What happens in an emergency if people are here drinking and they need to get to battle stations or something? Won't they be intoxicated?" asked Chris.

"Well, the nanite packages everyone has can help sober you up, and if it's real bad we have some injections I keep under the bar here. One shot from this bad boy," Bill held up a syringe, "and you will be sober in about a minute," Bill explained.

"Oh, that's pretty awesome!" exclaimed Chris and he chugged the rest of his beer, "On that note, I'll have another please."

"All right, coming right up," replied Bill.

They continued having a conversation for a while. Chris explained how he came to be on the Leviathan and what had happened to him on his previous ship, the Puddle Jumper. Bill was a good listener, which kind of made sense when he thought about it. Bartenders were like therapists that could prescribe alcohol. He liked Bill right away, and could see why this was a good fit for him.

Before too long a guy sat down next to Chris and ordered four beers and four shots of whiskey. Chris looked over and it was none other than Mike, the man who had pranked him at the gym.

"Hey dude," Mike opened with.

"Hey Mike," Chris responded with a bit of caution in his tone. He wasn't sure how Mike felt about Chris leaving him trapped under four hundred pounds and a wisecrack.

"Hey, we're good, right? No hard feelings or anything?" Mike asked and raised a fist up to Chris to bump.

Surprised, Chris responded with, "Ya man it's all good," and then returned the fist bump.

"Cool. I have always said if you're gonna dish it out, you gotta be able to take it," Mike explained, "and on that note, Bill, get this man a shot as well please."

The barkeep nodded and went about his business.

"Hey man, sorry to hear about your friend. That sucks he got hurt. I hope he's all right," Chris mentioned.

"Ya it does suck, but he will pull through. We went to see him before we came here. As a matter of a fact, we were about to toast to him. You up for joining us?" Mike asked.

"It would be my pleasure," Chris responded, trying to hide his enthusiasm.

Bill came back with four beers and five shots of whiskey and added "Enjoy, gentleman."

"Oh we will," laughed Mike. "Chris, help me carry all these drinks to the table and I'll introduce you to the rest of the pilots on board."

"Hey Chris," chirped Bill as they began gathering the drinks, "don't let these hooligans trick you into a drinking contest. They've got the nanites—you don't."

Chris and Mike grabbed all the drinks and Chris cautiously walked over to the table with the beverages. All the while he kept saying in his head, "Don't screw this up. Don't screw this up. This is your chance to meet the pilots."

"Boys, let me introduce you to my friend Chris," Mike loudly asserted as he started distributing drinks around the table. Chris quickly followed suit and put his on the table as well.

Mike started going around the table, "Chris, this is our Tumbler pilot Sergeant Casey Hogan." Chris shook the hand of a man roughly six feet tall with black combed hair and brown eyes. Casey sported a neatly trimmed full beard and a broad cheerful face.

"Nice to meet you, Casey," Chris greeted.

"Likewise," Casey responded.

"Next up we have the best-looking pilot on the ship that you've already met AND been turned down by, the stunning Melissa Lawson," Mike provoked.

The rest of the pilots laughed with the exception of Melissa, who rolled her eyes but did shake Chris's hand. Chris couldn't help but blush a bit. Nonetheless he grabbed her hand and gave her a firm but not harsh shake.

Chris couldn't help but think, "Wow, she is beautiful." Those skintight clothes around her shapely hips and well-rounded chest were impossible to ignore. She had a mesmerizing effect on Chris that he did his best to disregard.

"All right, Chris, let's get to the rest of the team before you start pitching a tent under the table," joked Mike. Again the pilots laughed and even Chris got a chuckle out of the joke. Mike was just a jokester at heart, but he was a good guy, Chris began to realize.

"Last but not least, we have our second in command, Lieutenant Sean Quick," announced Mike.

Chris walked over as Sean stood up. He was a full six foot four and had a muscular build. His blond flattop haircut added at least another inch or two. He had green eyes and sported a blond goatee on his chin, which helped add to the effect of his angry-looking face.

"Nice to meet you, Sean," Chris mumbled.

"Well, kid, turns out you have a name after all," replied Sean. Chris reached his hand out and Sean's hand grabbed it in a strong grip. Chris could tell Sean was testing him as Sean began squeezing harder and harder. Chris knew this was a critical moment so he squeezed back and stared Sean down. After an awkward couple of seconds Sean realized Chris would not break so he released his hand and sat back down.

"Thank God," Chris thought and they all grabbed a seat. Chris shook his hand out under the table so nobody would know that he had almost broken the grip.

They all grabbed their shots of whiskey, and Sean proposed a toast, "To Andy Higgins! He may be the most unlucky pilot, but he is a damn tough son of a bitch that I am proud to serve with!"

Everyone except Chris acknowledged the toast with a, "Here here." Chris figured it was not his place to agree or disagree. Then they clanked their glasses together and took their shots.

Chris downed his and felt the whiskey burn going down his throat. Chris had tried whiskey before, but rarely shot it. The Puddle Jumper crew was more of a sip-your-whiskey crew than a shoot it. It burned going down and Chris grimaced, but he held it down.

"Kid, this will put hair on your chest. When Casey first got here he was just a hairless boy," Sean mocked. Casey flicked him off with a smile on his face. "But now after all this whiskey he has a full beard and a hairy chest!" Sean continued.

"Ewww," Melissa murmured.

"Don't act like you don't like my hairy beard and chest," Casey quipped.

They all laughed and began sipping on their beers.

They started another conversation and Chris for the most part just observed. It was a bunch of banter that he struggled to relate to, not being part of the fighter squadron and all. Most of it was storytelling, however, and in true pilot fashion it was embellished—a lot. Sean even mentioned how he once got two smugglers to chase him and collide into each other, blowing them both up. Sean said that's how he, "Got two kills without firing a shot!" Melissa and the other pilots called bullshit but Sean swore it was true.

Then Chris chimed in and asked, "Do you guys all have call signs? In all the video games every pilot has a call sign."

The pilots began laughing before Melissa finally answered, "Yes Chris, we all do. Mine, much to my dismay, is Ice Queen, or simply Ice when we are in combat."

"Can I ask why it is Ice?" Chris asked.

"Cause she keeps shutting everyone down on the whole ship," Mike blurted out and they all laughed with the exception of Melissa.

"Well can't you change it?" asked Chris.

"Not until you become an officer. Until then you're stuck

with what your wing decides is your call sign," Melissa replied.

"Ohh, I see," Chris acknowledged. "Well what is your call sign, Casey?"

"I'm Husky, since I fly a," Casey put his hands up to quote, " 'big fat tumbler.' "

"No it's because of that beer gut you've been working on," Mike laughed.

"Hey!" Casey responded, "I have a four pack still." Casey lifted his shirt up to show off his abs.

"Put that hairy thing away!" Melissa mocked, "Or we will change your call sign to Shaggy or Wooly."

Chris and the pilots got a laugh out of that one.

After another pull on his beer Chris asked, "Sean, what is your call sign?"

Sean had been sitting back in his chair with his arms crossed but when he was asked he leaned forward, grinned, and provoked him with, "I'm Maniac, otherwise known as 'The Maniac Man.' "

"Ohh God here we go," agonized Mike, "You shouldn't have asked, Chris. Once he became an officer he changed it to that. Before his promotion his call sign was Asshole."

The whole table laughed at that while Sean flicked Mike off.

Sean continued, "It's because I'm the baddest dude on the ship! When I enter battle I become an efficient killing machine. Nobody on the other side is safe. Remember that, Chris, next time you break the law smuggling and the Leviathan's crew is on your tail."

"Oh my God," Melissa groaned, "You should have changed your call sign to Ego."

"What?" replied Sean as he threw his hands up in a gesture, "Check out that kill board over there. Only the wing commander has more kills than me, and he has been here longer."

"I'm gunning for you, so don't get too big for your britches there, big guy," added Mike.

"Besides being an awesome pilot and bodybuilder," Sean explained as he flexed his arms, "The Maniac Man has a way with the women that only adds to my mystery."

"Well easy there, Maniac. You've been barking up Melissa's tree ever since she got here and you haven't scored yet," added Casey.

"Don't worry, I haven't given up. The Ice Queen can only resist for so long," joked Sean.

This time it was Melissa who flicked Sean off, then contended, "Oh ya, it's getting harder and harder to resist." Melissa rolled her eyes as she made her statement.

"Oh my God," laughed Chris. "I had no idea figuring out call signs could be so funny and humiliating at the same time. All right, last but not least, what is your call sign, Mike?"

"Really, Chris, you couldn't figure his out?" probed Melissa.

"Umm, ADD?" Chris answered.

The table laughed at that one, even Mike did.

"Good guess," Mike explained, "but it's Joker!"

"Oh, makes sense," replied Chris.

"I coined it," added Sean

"Well when I make it to officer ranks, I'll be like Sean and change it to 'The Joker,' or 'The Joker Man,' " Mike said sarcastically.

The table laughed again and Sean didn't seem bothered.

They all ordered another round of beers and shots and the conversation continued on. Chris had to admit he was feeling the booze at this point. The other pilots seemed to be doing pretty well. Maybe it was the nanites or maybe, Chris started realizing, the pilots had built up a tolerance from drinking on the ship regularly.

When Mike's story came to an end Chris blurted out, "What's it like flying for Major Sarner?"

Sean spoke up first, "The wing commander is a badass. He sometimes sticks to the book too much, but there is nobody I'd want to fly with more into combat."

"Agreed," added Melissa. "He can be very serious but he really does look out for us as pilots. I wouldn't be surprised if he was checking up on Higgins right now. He cares a lot."

"He also leads the kill board, so there's that." Mike commented.

"Ya but I'm catching up to him!" Sean replied.

"Sean, he leads the kill board while coordinating attacks, relaying commands, and making sure we come home safely. You just go try to get kills regardless of what the rest of the wing is doing," Casey quipped.

"Boys, how many times do I have to explain this to you? If I kill all the bad guys, you will be safe!" Sean joked.

"What if you are on an escort mission? Isn't it more important to protect the ship you are escorting?" Chris asked.

Sean gave Chris a look that said, "You're overstepping your bounds."

"Chris, you're smarter than you look!" added Melissa.

"The Maniac Man is a glory hound!" laughed Mike.

"There is a reason I'm second in command!" Sean replied. "It's because I am a lethal killing machine when I am in a Raptor."

"Ya, that's true, you are pretty good. But you're still no Major Sarner," commented Melissa.

"I have a couple of kills myself—not bad for a guy piloting a transport ship," stated Chris.

"How in the hell did you get a couple kills in a transport?" asked Mike. "Are you talking about turret kills?" He laughed.

"Well ya, but I did manage to weave through some asteroids being chased by a pirate and he couldn't hang with me. He ended up smacking his ship on the side of an asteroid after incorrectly guessing which way I was turning," explained Chris.

"Not bad," commented Mike.

"Ya and just so we're clear there is nothing wrong with turret kills," added Casey. "Flying big ships means you have to get creative to get kills."

"Hahaha you fat boy pilots and your pesky turrets," laughed Melissa.

Sean was obviously not having this as he started turning red and gritting his teeth together.

"Turret kills are not a thing. That would be like claiming the Leviathan has a certain number of kills." Sean then jabbed a finger at the board and barked, "Last I checked it was not on the kill board."

"Well then I still have one kill," quipped Chris.

"I'll give that to ya, Chris," Mike mused. "In a different world you would probably have been a good fighter pilot. Let's toast to Chris's lone kill!"

Sean stood up and stuck his finger out at Chris. "Listen, I am not toasting to some smuggler kid who thinks he has a kill. Chris, you're not an Earth Force pilot—you're barely a pilot at all! You're a smuggler, about one step above the pirates we axed today!" yelled Sean.

Chris was speechless, as he had not realized how angry Sean was getting. That being said, Sean's words had cut straight through the booze and lit up something inside of him. Mike, meanwhile, seemed to be loving getting under Sean's skin and was chuckling.

"Easy Sean, he's just a kid who lost his whole crew. Chill out," cautioned Melissa.

Chris slowly rose up from his chair and leaned over the table and stared at Sean.

"I am a pilot. Some of us were not lucky enough to be born in a high-class society and go to the academy. I may not be an awesome Raptor pilot, but I am a pilot, and a pretty damn good one too."

Sean composed himself and relaxed a bit, but still leaning over the table, said, "Kid you wouldn't last five minutes on a real mission, even if you had a fully functioning Raptor."

Chris could tell he had some liquid courage running

through his veins and figured what the hell, why not stand his ground. "I think you would be surprised."

Mike added, "I think you two should settle this in the simulator!"

"Ha! That kid isn't even worth my time," replied Sean.

"What's the matter, Maniac Man? You afraid of a smuggler kid?" joked Melissa.

"Well after all that fuss it would be worth watching!" beamed Casey, "I mean the three of us would happily watch a duel between you two."

"You guys can't honestly think the kid would beat me in a duel? I'd be willing to bet I could beat any of you guys in a duel," argued Sean.

"Well let's make it fair. How about if Chris gets a hit on your Raptor he wins?" asked Mike.

"He could get lucky and get a hit in. Doesn't mean he is a pilot," replied Sean.

"Well I don't have nanites helping me out," complained Chris.

"Another sign of you not being a pilot," noted Sean.

"How about two hits?" questioned Mike.

Sean grabbed his chin and stroked his goatee in thought.

"I'll get two hits in, guaranteed," Chris offered.

That's all it took, just a little bit more egging on, and Chris had started chipping away at Sean's ego.

"Done," stated Sean "I'm going to wipe the floor with you kid. Meet me in the simulator room in ten."

With that Sean took his shot, then gulped down the remainder of his beer and walked off at a fast pace.

"Oh shit," thought Chris, "What have I done? Did I just ruin my chance to hang with the pilots or will they want to see me again after this? Who knows?"

"Woohoo, Chris!" exclaimed Mike "That was awesome. It's been a minute since I've seen Sean that fired up!"

"Hahaha ya," added Casey "He's madder than a midget

with a yo-yo."

"All right, boys, there is too much testosterone here. Chris, good luck in your dick measuring contest with Sean. As much as I'd love to see you knock him down a peg, I think I am going to call it a night and head to bed," admitted Melissa.

"You're not going to watch?" asked Chris.

"No, I have seen these duels before and honestly, no offense, but you don't stand a chance. You've been drinking, he has nanites to help out his piloting, and not to mention he is a lieutenant in the Earth Force Navy and a damn good one at that. Good luck though!"

With that Melissa was off. Chris stared at her butt and the way it gently swayed side to side as she walked off. He wondered how she could be so serious and professional and still be so desirable at the same time.

"Earth to Chris, come in Chris," Mike joked, "you have to beat the enemy before you can get the girl."

Casey chimed in, saying, "It's going to be a lot harder to fly the stick if your stick is in the way. Focus, dude!"

Chris shook his head and refocused. Then stated, "All right, there is one thing I need to do before we head to the simulators."

"Chris, you don't have time to rub one out, you can do that after the duel," Mike quipped.

"Haha damn it, Mike! That's not what I'm talking about. Trust me, I need every advantage I can get. Follow me," responded Chris.

The three of them walked back up to the bar where the bartender Bill was cleaning the bar top.

"I see you have been making friends and enemies Chris," commented Bill, "Casey, Mike do you need another round?"

"Ya, I didn't mean to make Sean mad," Chris responded.

"No more drinks Bill, we are going to watch Chris get his ass kicked by Sean in the simulator," laughed Mike. Casey was cracking up as well.

"Ahhh," replied Bill, "Well good luck with that Chris. Sean has a big head but he usually backs it up."

"That's actually why I'm here," stated Chris.

"Oh ya?" responded Bill.

"Ya I need one of those injections badly—you know the ones that sober you up," prodded Chris.

"Oh that's why we're here?" commented Casey in mock disappointment.

Bill gave the three of them a disapproving look.

"Oh come on, Bill, give the kid one. I'd love to see him pull this off," Mike asked as he gestured to Chris.

"All right, but if there is any blowback from the higher ups, I'm saying you authorized it," mused Bill.

"Ya ya, sure," replied Mike.

Bill reached below the bar and pulled out one of the injections he had told Chris about earlier. Then he said, "All right, Chris, give me your arm."

Chris did as he was told and added a "Thank you, Bill" to it.

Bill removed the injection from the packet it was in. It was only about six inches long. He placed one end of it on the underside of Chris's forearm. Next he pressed a button on top. A hissing sound followed and in one second it was all over.

"Well that wasn't so bad," Chris stated.

"Oh just wait," Mike chuckled as both he and Casey shared a smirk.

Chris looked at them like they were being weird and a few seconds later his head began to pound as nausea set in.

"Oh man, what is happening?" Chris asked.

"You're sobering up," replied Bill, "Just hang in there and don't barf. It'll be over in a minute."

The feeling just kept getting worse and worse over the next few seconds and Chris began gagging. It got so bad he had to sit down with his eyes closed holding his head.

"Oh my God this is awful!" Chris shuddered.

Mike and Casey were again laughing. Between glances

Chris even saw Bill had a slight smile on his face.

"I call it the drunk price," comforted Bill. "It basically deters people from getting so drunk they need the injection. If you need the injection, you will pay the drunk price."

Chris sat down and shuddered. It felt like an entire hangover condensed into one concentrated setting. After thirty seconds or so the nausea and headache began to subside. Another twenty seconds later Chris started feeling normal again.

"You all right there, buddy?" asked Casey.

Chris looked up at him and with a smile forming on his face he said, "Ya, now let's go get The Maniac Man!

"Atta boy!" yelled Mike.

With that they started walking out of the Afterburner and toward the turbo lift. If someone had been watching they would have noticed quite the pep in Chris's step.

CHAPTER 15

The doors to the simulator room swooshed open. The room itself was rectangular with standard white floors and ship grey walls. The first thing that struck him was that there were no view screens on the walls, which was unusual. None of the ship's rooms had windows, for obvious reasons, but most had screens that imitated viewports. Chris could tell it was a fairly large space, but the sheer amount of equipment packed into it made things feel tight.

The highlights of the room were six full-sized cockpits sitting in the room hooked up to all kinds of electrical equipment. The room was clearly designed to be a place where all the pilots could train at the same time as if they were actually on a mission. Since the Leviathan could hold five fighters and one cargo ship, that created the need for six simulators.

Chris walked forward and immediately knew which simulator belonged to Sean. Somebody had taken the time to draw "Maniac" on the back of the machine, and Chris had a feeling he was looking right at the artist. Sean was leaning against it, sipping on a beer. Chris was flanked by both Casey and Mike, while Sean had obviously told a couple of friends on the ship about the friendly competition. Chris noticed one of them was a lady. She was talking with Sean and another friend while they waited for Chris to show up. Chris thought, "Is Sean trying to impress that girl?" She kept looking up starry eyed at

Sean and curling her hair.

"Damn, that asshole has a fan club?" muttered Chris.

"Oh ya he does," replied Mike, "People are fascinated by pilots. Maybe it's the danger, maybe it's the sexiness of the ships, I'm not sure, but people are drawn to you. Basically it's not uncommon to have a groupie or three following ya. Call it a perk of the job."

Chris looked at Mike like he was crazy and Mike just winked.

"It's true," added Casey, "but I'll tell you now, it doesn't quite extend the same way to cargo pilots, which is complete bullshit. Just because I'm a little heftier doesn't mean I don't deserve love too!"

"Sure, you just have to pay for it!" chipped back Mike.

Mike and Chris laughed and Mike steered him toward a simulator he could use.

"Damn kid, I thought you would be smarter than this and just not show up!" Sean yelled.

"Sean I would never pass up a chance to fly against a pilot with more ego than skills!" replied Chris.

Sean let out a little laugh and then flicked Chris off. Chris didn't return the gesture as he didn't want to press his luck with Sean, who had the brass's ear. He figured he was already walking on thin ice by egging on one of the ship's pilots.

"So whose simulator do I get to use?" questioned Chris.

"Mine," replied Mike. "Figure it's not right to put someone in Higgin's simulator while he's out of commission."

"Agreed," added Casey.

"So how does this all work? Do I just jump in and take off from the Leviathan? Is Sean on the same ship when the program launches? Do we only have guns? Are there any restrictions?" asked Chris.

Sean took that moment to walk over to Chris, Mike, and Casey. Sure enough, his entourage walked over with him.

"All right, kid, here is how this is going to work. It's a

standard dueling format—not that you'd have any idea what that means, I'm sure, cause you're not a real pilot. We're going to be located ten thousand meters apart, facing each other. Nobody has any missiles as this is just a gun fight," stated Sean.

"So far so good," thought Chris.

"I'm saying we stick with the standard MX-5 lasers, so that means we get four each—not that you would know what a MX-5 is either, Chris."

"Oh I do, on my old ship's turrets we opted for MX-5Cs—they had twice the range," replied Chris in a snarky tone.

"Wow kid, I am impressed with how much you wish you were a real pilot. Maybe reading about what real pilots fly will help you today, but probably not," warned Sean.

"Easy guys, let's save it for the match," cautioned Casey.

"All right, so we are ten thousand meters apart—open space, no obstacles. Just you and me, *mano a mano*, Chris. Deal?" stated Sean.

Chris looked from Casey to Mike for any signs of debauchery taking place that he may have been unaware of, but they both just looked back at him with normal faces. For Mike that meant he had a shit-eating grin on his face and seemed to be loving this whole situation.

"Deal, let's make it happen," replied Chris.

Sean stuck his hand out to shake, and Chris reluctantly took the hand. Luckily, Chris was expecting the death-grip that ensued so he stuck his index and middle fingers out onto Sean's wrist to keep his knuckles from grinding—an old trick Captain Hammerfist had taught him that Chris remembered after the first time Sean almost broke his hand in a shake. Sure enough, Sean attempted to break his hand with the pressure. Chris simply smiled back at him.

"Got a firm grip there Sean—must be your primary hand!" joked Chris as he made an explicit motion with his free hand.

Sean dropped his hand, spat on the floor, and said, "Figures that's where your mind is at. You can crack all the dirty jokes your mind can muster—won't be talking much in a few minutes when I wipe the floor with you."

With that Sean turned and walked toward his machine. Chris shrugged and walked up to his own machine. The canopy was raised and the seat inside the cockpit was ready for him. He hopped over the edge of it one leg at a time and sat down. The seat began to auto contour to his shape and adjusted him for optimum viewing. After it was done Chris made a couple minor adjustments to his height to get everything perfect. Casey leaned over the left edge of the cockpit and Mike was on the right. They both began fastening him in.

That's when it hit Chris. He had no idea what he was about to get himself into. His hands started shaking slightly and a tremble could be heard in his voice.

"Uh Mike and Casey, can you guys show me what the controls are?" asked Chris.

"I thought you knew how to fly?" asked Mike in response.

"Well I have played a lot of video games, Major Sarner gave me a tutorial in the cockpit, and I've flown a Nez class transport ship, but a quick refresher on how this system actually works would be nice," requested Chris.

Mike and Casey both laughed and agreed. After giving him a crash course in the basics—very basics—Chris felt confident he could do what was needed to accomplish the mission of hitting Sean twice.

"All right, you ready to do this?" asked Mike.

"Ya," replied Chris, "but one question before we get started. How come you two are helping me and not Sean? Don't you want him to beat me? You guys are the pilots; I'm just a prisoner slash guest on board this ship."

Mike laughed with Casey and then responded, "Listen, Casey and I have Sean's back any day in a real fight. But Sean could use a good ego check. The way I see it, best case scenario, you get your hits in and Sean's head deflates a little bit. It will be something I can remind him of for years to come. I can imagine it now: we are at the Afterburner and he is spouting off about something he did and I just remind him of the time he lost to a kid from a smuggler ship."

Casey and Chris both laughed at this and then Mike continued, "Worst case scenario you lose to Sean and life goes on. But I'll at least remember when Sean got all flustered over a smuggler who came on board wanting to be a pilot."

"Oh, well that makes sense," acknowledged Chris.

"All right, it's showtime, Chris. Here are your neural communicators," said Mike.

Mike handed Chris two quarter-sized metal dots with blue pulsing lights on them. Chris knew what these were. These two dots would adhere to each temple on his head and provided the simulator with a direct link to the human brain. This way the simulator could provide an artificial background that would look realistic. Normally the aircraft would synchronize with a pilot's nanite package, but neural communicators could be used as an alternative for someone without the nanite package.

The simulator itself was an exact replica of a Raptor cockpit, but to see the projected space in the background these two dots had to link up with your brain. This also provided Chris with his heads-up display so he could get real-time data. As a secondary measure it also drowned out all real noise going on around him so he would feel like he truly was on a mission.

Chris reached up and took the two devices and put them on. He could feel the nano adhesive adhering to his skin and then the nano fibers connecting to his brain. It didn't hurt but it provided a slightly awkward itchy feeling.

"OK Chris, here comes your first space battle in a Raptor. You picked a difficult target so good luck buddy," cheered Casey.

Casey and Mike backed up and they closed the canopy. As soon as it sealed shut Chris's vision all went black.

About a half a second went by and Chris was able to see himself sitting inside a Falcon SF-15 Raptor. There was nothing in the background except stars—a lot of them. The sight was something Chris had seen before, but usually there were at least some objects around, such as a planet, moon, some space facility, or at the very least an asteroid. Chris looked down and focused on his controls inside the raptor. He found he was shaking from the excitement of finally being in a real Raptor simulator—or was that the nervousness of having to face off with Sean? He couldn't tell.

About twenty seconds later a ship popped up in front of him with a red outline around it and it was identified as another Raptor fighter with the name "Maniac" written next to it. Then a familiar looking face popped up on one of the fighter's screens.

"Well kid, you ready to catch that ass whooping you've been looking for?" mocked Sean.

"Oh Maniac, you're a better pilot than I am for sure considering that you have been handed all the training and first-class equipment that the Earth Force can provide. But you'll be surprised what we smugglers can do with far less. I'm going to score at least two hits on you. Probably more," replied Chris.

"Ha! I'll believe it when I see it. Unless you need time to pray or say some last words, let's do this!" exclaimed Sean.

"It's on then!" shouted Chris.

With that Chris throttled up the Raptor to full power and began closing. Even with the inertial dampeners fighting the Gs he still sank back into his seat. Chris was very impressed with how real these simulators made combat feel. He set his four MX-5 lasers to fire in pairs, that way he could fire more quickly, although with less damage, as only two bolts would hit with any one shot. He thought about shooting all four at once but since he only had to hit Sean twice, he figured being able to fire more rapidly would help him since he wouldn't have to wait for all four lasers to cool down at once between shots.

Sean also throttled up his fighter and the ten thousand meters between them began closing rapidly. Chris knew the maximum range of the standard MX-5 laser was five thousand meters, so shooting before then would only deplete the laser's charge and waste a shot.

"This will be easy," Chris thought, "I only have to hit him twice and I'm going to nail him at long range. Sure, he will be able to do the same thing, but he has to destroy me while I only have to get two hits."

Chris placed his index finger on the trigger and watched the distance close. Eight thousand meters, seven thousand meters, six thousand meters—Chris could feel the tension growing. As soon as the distance measurement fell to five thousand meters, Chris saw his targeting reticle turn red, indicating he was locked on and had a good shot. This was important, because at five kilometers away Sean's ship could barely be seen. It was a tiny grey spec in the distance.

As soon as it turned red Chris pressed the trigger hard. As the trigger was pressed, Chris could hear the two inner most lasers cycling and could see the discharge come out from the guns in two red-tinted lines streaking toward Sean.

In the exact same instance Chris pulled the trigger, Sean pulled the trigger as well and four lasers lanced out at Chris. The biggest difference was Sean also fired his maneuvering thrusters, which sent him into a roll to his port side.

Chris watched as his once-red indicator turned back to yellow. In the time between the indicator turning red and Chris firing his first shot, Sean had returned fire and rolled out of the way of Chris's oncoming laser fire. Chris was shocked.

"Nobody can have reflexes that fast," Chris thought. Then he remembered the nanite package that each Earth Force pilot had and realized this was going to be tougher than he thought.

In the same instant that Chris had his revelation his

ship shook from incoming laser fire. All four of Sean's lasers scorched Chris's fighter and Chris watched as his forward armor took the brunt of the damage. At this range the lasers were not particularly powerful, so Chris's Raptor armor took the incoming barrage easily, but it did chip away at what once was armor with 100 percent integrity.

The ships computer estimated Chris's forward armor to have 87 percent of its integrity in place. Chris lined up a second shot and fired again with the outer banks of lasers this time. Again, Sean rolled out of the way, dodging the incoming fire. This continued two more times with Sean sending another return volley at him between shots and scoring hits on Chris's forward armor.

"What the fuck!" Chris thought. Then again, a familiar face showed up on his display.

"You didn't think you could beat The Maniac Man that easily, did you Chris?" joked Sean. "You are going to have to try a lot harder than that to take out a real pilot!" The display cut off with Sean in laughter.

Chris immediately began thinking up a new strategy. At this rate, his forward armor was getting pummeled while he was doing no damage in return. Chris began juking his Raptor to the left, then up, then, down, trying to confuse Sean as to where his ship would be when Sean's indicator turned red. In the meantime, he continued firing shots back at Sean.

Sean, however, looked like a pro, dancing around Chris's shots as the two fighters closed. Chris was in awe at the skill Sean demonstrated. He made juking look like an art, with smooth but quick maneuvers, all the while getting shots in of his own. The good news was that now that Chris was juking as well, Sean's shots were not hitting with the same success. Chris's armor integrity was still falling as a shot or two got in, but at least it was much slower than before. Chris was even able to see the scorch marks on his ship from where the lasers had begun melting away armor.

Chris knew Sean would not be able to avoid his shot forever. As the distance closed, Sean's Raptor began growing in size, and even with his lightning fast reflexes and premier training, physics would take over and he couldn't dodge a shot from close range. Their dance continued until Sean closed to one thousand meters. Chris was fairly confident this would be it for Sean, as his ship was very visible in his targeting reticle now. He pulled the trigger and unleashed the rapid firing lasers in pairs. It was too late, however, as Sean had hit the afterburners of his ship. The blue exhaust flames coming out of Sean's engines changed to red and their trail tripled in length as Sean moved forward at fantastic speeds.

Chris's shots all fell behind Sean and he began pulling up on the stick in an effort to line up the shots properly. The Raptor fighter was maneuverable, but not fast enough. Sean streaked by Chris inverted.

Chris immediately banked his fighter to starboard in an effort to find Sean, who was now behind him. He pulled his stick hard, pushing the Raptor's maneuvering thrusters to their maximum. The Gs were punishing as he struggled to fight his eyelids from closing shut. Chris continued the turn, but Sean was nowhere to be found. He looked left then right, but nothing. He checked his radar and it kept pointing to Sean being behind him somewhere.

Chris changed tactics and banked to the port side in an effort to throw off Sean's anticipation of where Chris would be. Chris felt the shudder through his ship as laser fire impacted his aft and port side armor. He looked down and his armor was holding strong, for now.

"What's the matter kid?" Sean provoked through Chris's comms. "Can't find The Maniac Man?"

Chris changed directions again and put himself in a hard loop, pulling up. Even then he felt another shudder through his ship. This continued for a while as Chris kept trying to get Sean off of his six. Every time he changed directions Sean would get a shot in. After a while Chris looked down at his status screen and saw his rear armor had fallen to 50 percent and his starboard and port side armor was down to 68 and 74 percent integrity, respectively.

Chris knew something had to change or he was going to lose this. Sean's reactions and training were too much for him and he was slowly being picked apart.

Chris leveled off his ship and began a very aggressive barrel role all while changing the direction of his ship randomly.

"Oh what's this you're doing kid?" mocked Sean. "Got a hidden trick up your sleeve for me?"

"Ya, I like to call it the asshole-killing maneuver!" Chris responded and Sean chuckled.

While in the barrel roll Sean was able to get another couple of hits in, but for the most part Sean was struggling to line up a clean shot. Then, without warning, Chris stopped the barrel role and yanked up hard on the stick. Again, punishing G forces hit Chris and he fought to close off the blackness that was enveloping his vision. Chris controlled his breathing and pushed out short breaths while tightening his whole body up. This was a maneuver pilots had been using since the dawn of aviation to deal with the heavy Gs. While it was extremely uncomfortable, Chris found the simulator exerting more than 7 Gs on him. He knew that the real ship had inertial dampers to lessen the loads on the pilot, and that in real life his ship would be experiencing close to 20 Gs.

Chris continued to strain his body, and although he struggled to do much more than maintain his maneuver he did realize Sean hadn't scored anymore hits. Then, out of the corner of his eyes he saw a bit of red flame against the background. It must have been Sean's exhaust trail. He continued to steer in the direction of the exhaust trail, as he knew Sean's ship would be on the other end of it. Unfortunately, Chris also realized his body was failing him. With his vision dimming he realized he was struggling to bring in enough oxygen, and unless he wanted to blackout he was going to have to ease off the Gs.

"Dammit," thought Chris, "Those nanite packages are amazing. Not only do they help with reflexes and targeting but they also help Sean pull more Gs for longer. It just isn't fair."

Chris let off some to lower the Gs and he hoped Sean would have to do the same. It didn't happen though, and the flame he was chasing went out of view. Chris knew Sean was lining him up for another shot, so instead of waiting for the inevitable he leveled off his Raptor and punched the afterburners. While the Gs subsided relative to the hard turning, Chris still was pressed back into his ship's seat as it lurched forward at fantastic speeds. He began changing directions randomly again while still using afterburners to prevent Sean from getting a shot. Sean had taken a second to line Chris back up and realized Chris had hit the afterburner because Chris saw the distance indicator on his heads up display between their ships rapidly increasing.

"Damn kid, I got to give it to you, that was a hell of a maneuver. Most people would have blacked out from it. Even I was pushing myself. But The Maniac Man doesn't lose to wannabe pilots," beamed Sean.

"You're such an asshole," was all Chris could reply.

Chris continued the maneuver, but even with changing directions and using afterburners Sean was able to get a couple more scores. Chris looked at his gauges and saw his engines were running out of juice.

The term afterburners was not exactly an accurate description of modern-day spacecraft engines. It came from the old days when pilots had jet engines and afterburners were a mechanism to quickly add lots of thrust. Pilots would dump excess fuel into the exhaust of a jet engine, causing a massive controlled explosion that would boost the power output significantly. This was great for pilots trying to get somewhere quickly but it cost them massive amounts of their limited fuel supply.

In modern-day spacecraft the engines would simply increase output beyond the full capacity of the fusion engines. This worked great for short bursts of power but caused engine heat to build rapidly. If they overheated too much, engine components could fail—or worse, the reactor would go supercritical and the ship would be destroyed. The good news is fusion engine afterburners didn't use up fuel like the old days, just increased the heat beyond safe limits. So after they reached the heat limit the computer would override pilot input and power would be dialed back to regular capacity to cool off. Once cooled off, the engines could be increased to beyond capacity again.

Chris continued the burn until the computer forcefully cut the overdrive off and began the cooling cycle. Without the added acceleration of the afterburners Chris's acceleration returned to normal levels and Sean began to close back in using his own ship's afterburners.

"What's the matter kid? Trying to run away?" asked Sean.

Chris pulled back on the stick and figured there may be enough space between them to line up a shot or two. Again, the Gs hit him hard and he completed the loop only to see a lot of incoming laser fire. His front armor began absorbing multiple shots, as his indicator said the forward armor was down to roughly 50 percent integrity.

This time though, Chris had another idea. As his targeting indicator turned red, Chris squeezed the trigger but didn't wait to see if he had scored a hit, as he guessed Sean would just roll out of the way like he had last time. So, he maneuvered his indicator to the right of Sean's ship while the trigger was still pressed and another shot fired.

As anticipated, Sean rolled to the left and juked by Chris's first shot. He also returned fire, melting Chris's already depleted forward armor even more.

Chris watched as one of the two lasers he had fired in his second volley scored a hit right on the nose of Sean's Raptor.

He fired three more volleys, but Sean hit his burners and flew past Chris before anymore could land.

"Ha! Looks like The Maniac Man took a hit!" mocked Chris.

"Everyone gets lucky now and then," responded Sean.

Chris continued the turn to try and chase Sean and they began circling each other. At this point, Chris knew he couldn't reel Sean in this way, as Sean could take sustained Gs for longer thanks to his nanite enhancements. Though he didn't have to beat Sean this way, Chris needed to allow his engines to cool enough to hit afterburners again. He figured he would perform the same maneuver, score one more hit, and win the simulator battle. They looped around each other a few times as Sean began closing in on him.

Chris saw his afterburner indicator turn green, meaning his engines had returned to normal temperatures, so he punched it while leveling out his fighter. Then he began changing directions again while the simulated Gs pushed his body.

"You know Chris, you're actually lucky you're not a pilot under my wing. Besides the fact that I would kick your ass every day, you would immediately be given the call sign 'Kid,' " laughed Sean.

"Honestly," Chris spoke through clenched teeth as the Gs rocked him, "I'd take that for the opportunity."

"That's the first intelligent thing you've said all day," mocked Sean.

Chris was doing a good job changing directions, because Sean was unable to score additional damage this time. He saw the distance between Sean and him grow like it had the first time, but not as much. Chris figured Sean had anticipated his maneuver and was giving chase to stay on his tail.

When Chris was almost out of afterburners he pulled up on the stick and began another G-intensive loop. When he had rotated 180 degrees he lined his targeting indicator up on Sean, as he did before.

Sean sent another volley of laser fire at Chris and it hit

hard. At the same time Chris saw his indicator turn red, he fired, held the trigger down and steered to the right of Sean's ship, firing additional shots.

Sean, as anticipated, rolled out of the way, but instead of going to his left like before he rolled the opposite direction, causing Chris's follow-up shots to drag in the wrong direction.

"Ha!" Sean spouted, "You didn't think that would work twice, did ya?"

Chris didn't respond and instead he steered his ship in the direction Sean had rolled to and gave chase. He wasn't able to line up his shot, as Sean had used his afterburners to fly past Chris and again get in another circling battle. Chris did notice on his heads-up display that his forward armor had fallen to critical integrity levels at 19 percent. Any further hits on the front could possibly start causing system failures.

Chris began racking his brain to come up with new ideas. Unfortunately, pulling Gs and trying to avoid getting shot didn't leave a lot of time for him to contemplate new strategies.

As anticipated, Sean was eventually able to close the loop on Chris and he began pummeling Chris's rear armor again. Chris changed directions once, twice, and even a third time to no avail. Sean had wreaked havoc on Chris's rear and side armor as well. The rear was down to 13 percent integrity and his sides were not that much better.

"Hey Chris, I was feeling bad about picking on ya and figured I'd give you the opportunity to give up and cry uncle if you want?" asked Sean

"Hell no," replied Chris as he once again hit the afterburners.

"All right, your loss. I'm sure this strategy will pay off for you this time," mocked Sean.

Chris figured since Sean had rolled right last time he would probably go the other direction this time. He wasn't sure but figured he had a 50 percent chance, which was a lot better than just trying to delay the inevitable.

What Chris didn't realize was Sean anticipated his

maneuver and was very close behind. Chris let off the after-burners and began his loop. As he was feeling the Gs he felt his ship shudder from one laser impact, then another. As the second hit registered on his heads-up display he heard an explosion behind him. He looked down at his damage display and noticed his number three engine was destroyed.

"Shit!" thought Chris, "How am I going to take Sean out with only three engines?"

"Well, looks like this is the end, kid," Sean laughed. "No way are you going to be able to get me now!"

Chris then remembered Mike talking about how Sean had quite the ego. He began trying to figure out how he could use that against Sean.

Chris changed directions in the loop and instead pushed the stick forward, starting an inverted loop. He began feeling pressure in his head and his vision began to redden as the blood rushed into his head. Another explosion rocked his ship as the number two engine was taken offline by Sean's laser fire. Sean was on his six and Chris knew it was now or never for him and his Raptor. Chris then hit afterburners in the middle of the inverted loop. He had to relax the stick some, as the Gs would have been far too much for his body to maintain. Now, with only two engines remaining, both on full afterburner, his Raptor lurched forward with great speed. Sean however matched his move and was very close behind.

Sean came in over the comm: "Two engines down kid; any last words?"

"Ya, look what I can do that you can't," replied Chris.

Chris had set his afterburners to continue firing and while holding the stick in between his legs so his ship would maintain the inverted loop, he put up a double-handed middle finger salute toward the camera inside the cockpit that was recording his communication.

"See, no hands," laughed Chris.

Sean, upon seeing both of Chris's hands flicking him off

while maintaining an inverted loop, knew there was no way he could let the kid think this would go unpunished. So Sean did what came naturally to him and set his afterburner to keep firing while positioning the stick in between his legs and flicking Chris off with both hands.

Chris meanwhile had cut his visual feed after Sean saw him flick him off. Chris knew Sean wouldn't be able to resist returning the gesture. The instant Chris saw Sean's hands start to come up on his communications display in rapid succession he cut off the afterburners, set main engine thrust to zero, and engaged the forward maneuvering jets to slow his ship as hard as he could.

The Gs shifted and Chris felt like his eyes would pop out of his head and his face would be pulled off. His Raptor rapidly lost speed and Chris watched, waiting for the instant his prey would become visible in front of him.

Sean, meanwhile, in the middle of his salute realized Chris had done all he could to bring his Raptor to a full stop. Even with the nanites helping Sean's reactions he still had to get his hands back on the controls. Sean did and rapidly cut the thrust of the afterburners and engines. He looked back up and saw he was overtaking Chris's ship, which was just beneath him.

Chris saw Sean's Raptor come into view above him. He pulled up on his stick and did his best to bring Sean into his sights. As he was bringing the nose of the raptor up he toggled his lasers to fire in bursts of four, or all at once. This meant each time he pulled the trigger all four cannons would fire but he would not be able to fire while the lasers cycled between shots. Chris was OK with this because he figured he would only get one shot anyway and with all four laser banks firing at once it would maximize his chances of a hit.

Sean must have realized that there was no way he could stop in time, so instead of trying to stay behind Chris he gave up and instead applied full throttle and hit his afterburners in an attempt to avoid any shots and put some distance between him and Chris.

Chris watched as Sean's fighter lurched forward with red exhaust trails extending out of his four engines. This only helped Chris as his sights lined up perfectly on Sean's Raptor's belly. His sights went red and Chris pulled the trigger.

Chris heard all four lasers cycle at once just as Sean fired his maneuvering thrusters to roll out of Chris's line of sight. This maneuver had worked multiple times before at much greater distances, but at the almost point-blank range it could only avoid some of Chris's fire. Two of the four lasers lit up Sean's aft armor and Chris mentally relaxed. Physically he kept his sights lined up on Sean's ship and figured he would fire at him again after his lasers cycled.

Chris knew he had won. He hit Sean twice, technically three times if you included the fact that two of his four lasers hit on his most recent shot. Even though he knew Sean would be able to finish off his damaged ship in a dogfight to the end, the bet had been that Chris couldn't hit Sean twice.

Chris saw his lasers had finished their cooling cycle, so he lined up another shot at Sean's Raptor, which was getting smaller as the distances increased. As he fired his next shot, Sean's Raptor disappeared. Chris assumed this meant the simulator battle was over. He threw up his hands in a cheer and saw two familiar faces show up on his comms display.

"You did it!" yelled Mike and Casey, who were looking at him from outside his simulator.

Chris laid back into his chair as the simulator came to an end. For a split second his vision was totally black and then the real world of him sitting in a simulator came back to him. The canopy opened up with a hydraulic hissing sound and Mike and Casey were cheering and laughing.

Chris pulled off his neural communicators and reached up to pull himself out of the simulator cockpit. He hadn't realized it, but with all the stress he had broken out in a sweat. He almost slipped pulling himself out of the simulator cockpit, but Casey grabbed his hand and pulled him up.

"Well done, little buddy," cheered Mike. "You just made Casey and I one hundred credits."

"I did?" questioned Chris.

"Ya, we made a bet with Sean's crew over there after you logged in," replied Casey.

Chris hopped out of the simulator and gave Casey and Mike a high five. Then he saw something out of the corner of his eye. Someone was standing at the entrance of the simulator room. As his eyes focused he realized it was Melissa. She smiled at him, and then in a smooth motion disappeared around the corner.

"Yes!" thought Chris. "She did care, ha!"

A few seconds later, after the celebrating died, down Chris saw a large figure moving toward him. It was none other than Sean with a stern face. He walked up to Chris in a menacing manner, and when he was about one foot away he stopped and stared down at Chris.

Chris got real nervous, but stood his ground and returned a stare at Sean. You could have heard a pin drop during the stare down. Then Sean, with a quick motion, stuck out his hand for Chris to shake. Chris looked down and then back up at Sean. He shook Sean's hand in return.

"I know when I am beat, and you got me," admitted Sean. "Don't get me wrong, I'd still kick your ass all over space if it was a real fight, but that trick was pretty good. I'll admit, for a smuggler kid, you are clever. Next time I won't fall for the no-hands trick."

"Thanks Maniac," said Chris, who used Sean's call sign, "and next time I'm going to get more than three shots in."

Sean smirked at that and the two released hands. Sean turned around and with his entourage made his way back to the turbo lift.

"Well, I got to admit," sighed Casey, "today was a wild day.

First one of our wing gets hurt, then a captured smuggler kid joins us for drinks, pisses off our second in command, and wins a bet in a simulator battle he had no business being in."

"Yep," added Mike, "sounds like we need to do another round of shots to celebrate!"

With that Chris, Casey, and Mike made their way to the turbo lift and back to the Afterburner.

CHAPTER 16

The next day for Chris was much more entertaining. Not only had he established himself as able to operate a Raptor (albeit clumsily), someone up high had heard about his exploits. The day after winning the bet against Lieutenant Quick he received an electronic message from Commander Schafer.

"Mr. Skylander, I hear you've taken an interest in our simulators. While their use was unauthorized, I understand you're a professional pilot in the civilian world. I can only guess you were trying to maintain your pilot skills for your eventual reintroduction into the labor market. It's good to hear you are taking into consideration the fact you will need to find new employment when this mission has concluded.

Consequently, I'm going to authorize your continued usage of the crew's simulators under a few conditions: First and foremost, you are not to interfere with crew training. Second, classified systems will be locked out to you and shall remain so. Finally, this is a privilege that can be taken away. Think of it as an extra incentive to walk the straight and narrow while on this ship."

Chris couldn't believe it; he had assumed he would get in trouble for the fiasco the previous day if the brass had found out. While it would have been worth it, he wouldn't have been surprised to find himself getting chewed out, or even visiting the detention cells again for a brief time. Instead they granted him access? They knew perfectly well a Raptor was nothing like a Nez class cargo ship. The sim time would be almost useless to a civilian pilot. Still, he wasn't going to look a gift horse in the mouth, especially not for something he had dreamed about since being a kid.

He went back to the simulators within hours of receiving the message. The operator saw him coming and smiled at his approach. He was a bigger guy, maybe six foot three and 230 pounds, and might have been intimidating if he didn't have such a kind face.

"Back so soon? I had a feeling you might be," the operator said at his approach

"Couldn't help it—you all have a heckuva setup down here. I'm just grateful the commander is letting me use this equipment. More than grateful, to be honest—ecstatic is more the right word," responded Chris

"I was a little surprised you were allowed as well, but it's not my place to judge. It's a beautiful thing down here, though. Not quite the real deal, but I'll take what I can get. Name's Woodford, but you can just call me Craig when nobody's around," he said as he reached out to shake Chris's hand. Chris immediately noticed the rank insignia on Major Woodford's sleeve. Craig saw him react to the rank as if he was used to the look of surprise on Chris's face.

"Not all support crew are enlisted. A few years ago I was bonafide pilot," he said as he slapped his chest. "A damned good one too. Had a little mishap in training, however, and they pulled my medical. Couldn't really blame them—inner ear just can't take the Gs anymore. I still know my way around simulations, though, plus I've always had a knack for electronics. Figure if I can't fly them anymore this is the next best thing. So, looking to take one of babies out for a ride?"

"Absolutely! One question though, where were you yesterday? I didn't see you in all the commotion?" Chris asked.

"Oh, I don't get into all that nonsense. One big ego

measuring contest if you ask me. I always preferred to let my flying do the talking. So when I see a bunch of half-inebriated pilots come storming down the hallway I prefer to stay in the background," responded Craig. "Now, if you want to enjoy a good bourbon with someone," he said with a big smile, "then I'm your guy. Now my understanding is that the XO has authorized you to do some training down here. Not sure what flying a Raptor has to do with civilian flying, but I do as I'm told."

And with that Craig made his way to the control station in the back of the room. It was funny that Chris had never considered the effort it took to make a system like this work. He told himself right then and there he would make sure to show proper respect to Craig, just like he did Whistler.

Chris began with asking Craig to recreate famous battle sequences that he could participate in. While this was incredible, Chris found himself quickly overwhelmed and confused with everything going on. Real combat wasn't like in video games. Rapid fire orders were being dished out and wing tactics employed. If you weren't paying attention you'd be left behind—or worse, isolated and destroyed.

Craig seemed to expect this, however, and after Chris was destroyed for the nth time he made the comment: "Hey ace, if you want to take a break from getting blown up all the time, might I suggest some training modules?"

Chris was a little off-put that Craig would suggest he need to learn how to fly, but after reflecting on how poorly he'd been doing he quickly changed his attitude.

"Ya, getting the idea I could use some pointers," he chipped back.

"That's an understatement. Let's start you with some basics. Then maybe we'll hit some wing tactics and theory," stated Craig.

Chris wasn't even upset at the jab, saying back, "That sounds awesome! Is Commander Schafer going to be cool with that though?"

"Hmmm . . ." questioned Craig, "Let's just keep some of this between you and me, how about? What he doesn't know won't hurt him. Besides, what are they going to do? Pull my flight slot? Nobody else knows how to run this system anyways. I think my job is safe."

With that Craig took Chris back to basics. Chris quickly dropped his ego, as it became very clear Craig knew his stuff. After only a few lessons he found himself addicted, training in Raptors for hours every day. Luckily Craig seemed to enjoy teaching a pupil, and was game for the intense training. He did have to kick Chris out though from time to time, so Major Sarner and his team could prep for whatever mission they had next. Chris didn't mind though.

Honestly, there was not a lot for Chris to do on board the Leviathan besides the simulators. He had gone to the Afterburner lounge every night but his pilot friends were not there when he went. He enjoyed talking to the bartender Bill but that was not going to entertain him for long. Stacey had shared several meals with Chris and seemed to be doing a lot better. She was ready to get off the Leviathan though, and couldn't wait to go back to Earth to see her family. After that Chris made sure to go to the gym to start training his body in case Sean shoved him unexpectedly in the hallway again. In the back of his mind he was hoping that he may run into Melissa again, which never happened. Basically the simulator was a way for him to get lost in his own world.

As he spent more time training, he began to formulate a plan for how he might actually be able to make Zion pay for all he had done. He had fully intended to take up Commander Sarner's suggestion of applying to the academy. If he kept training in the sims with Craig, he'd be a shoo-in for a fighter pilot slot. They wouldn't be able to say no—at least Chris hoped. By the time he did that, however, Zion would probably be long gone. With three destroyers chasing him, Zion probably wouldn't survive for very long.

With that in mind, Chris began thinking of an alternate plan—a way for him to make Zion pay, and do it sooner rather than later. It was bold, stupid, and would probably land him in a cell once more, but it might be the only way for him to avenge his father.

Life continued on like this until one day when Chris found himself eating a slice of pepperoni pizza in the cafeteria. He was halfway done with the slice and was enjoying the legendary combination of pepperoni, tomato sauce, and mozzarella cheese when the alarms went off.

"Battle stations! Red alert, this is not a drill," boomed a computer voice over the speakers in the cafeteria.

The lighting even switched to a red tinted lighting to improve night vision. This was just in case the power went out.

Chris didn't waste time finishing his pizza and instead ran toward the turbo lift. He figured the cleaning bots would come by and take care of his wasted food on their time.

When he got in the turbo lift he immediately hit the button to be sent to the observation deck. The lift zoomed to the correct destination and Chris waited impatiently as the doors seemed to slowly open. He rushed out, turning himself sideways to decrease his width, and squeezed out of the lift. As anticipated Chris saw the observation deck was empty. He quickly went to the center console in the room and began typing in his commands so he could see the whole battle scene come into view.

As the walls reset to follow his commands Chris waited impatiently.

"Come on," he thought and watched as the walls became transparent, showing the situation going on around him. When they finally finished showing the scene, Chris was able to see the Leviathan was just coming out of subspace. As the Leviathan passed through the event horizon the space around the ship came into view at the observation deck. Chris could see the familiar-looking sun in the distance. It was not as bright as it normally was when near Earth, which meant they had come out of subspace somewhere a good distance further from the sun than Earth. Stars began populating the black sky around him until he looked at the starboard side of the Leviathan. A very large tan-colored gas giant planet could be seen with vast rings around it. Chris knew this meant they had come out of subspace somewhere around the planet Saturn. Saturn's many moons began coming into view as the resolution of the planet increased and the computers had a couple more seconds to sharpen up.

Chris redirected his attention to the forward part of the ship to find the action. Chris knew that it was common practice to get to red alert when emerging from subspace, especially when you knew or anticipated danger ahead. Chris obviously was not given a mission briefing, but he could pick up a lot of information by just sitting on the observation deck. He knew the captain would be monitoring what he looked at, but also knew the captain never said he couldn't look around.

By now the observation deck had finished loading the scenery around him and Chris could see what lay ahead. It was another Poseidon class destroyer that, upon zooming the optics in, appeared to be in bad shape.

"That must be Zion's ship," thought Chris. He assumed after being on the run for days it must have slowly been taking damage and since there were no friendly ports for it to go to, it slowly began wearing down.

Chris knew it still had its weapons capabilities, but several sections of the hull were scorched black and holes could be seen in some of them, meaning the hull had been breached more than once.

Chris looked to his left side and watched as another Poseidon class destroyer emerged from a subspace portal ahead of the Leviathan. It was the E. F. Mustang. After that he noticed yet another Poseidon destroyer that was engaged in battle already with Zion's ship. Fighters from both sides swarmed around the ship, trading blows. It was too far away and was at a bad angle for Chris to see its name, but the ship's computer had already identified it as the E. F. Olympia.

The next thing Chris noticed were fighters beginning to launch from the Leviathan itself. The first Raptor was on full afterburner as it left the hangar. That must have been Major Sarner, the wing commander himself. Soon after that another fighter went out and began forming up on the wing commander. Chris guessed that must have been Sean. Chris counted as a third, and then fourth fighter went out, guessing it must have been Melissa and Mike. Now he sat waiting and hoping the fifth fighter would not emerge. That would wreck Chris's plan.

Chris watched as a fifth ship made its way out of the bay. For a second his heart sank as he thought the last Raptor had left the bay. To Chris's delight it was the Tumbler, flown by Casey. "Yes!" thought Chris, then he wondered. "What would they need the Tumbler for?"

Oh well, it didn't matter. Chris watched with satisfaction as the four Raptors and the Tumbler began flying in formation on their way into the battle happening far ahead of the Leviathan. With three Earth Force Poseidon destroyers and their fighter compliments versus the one damaged Poseidon destroyer Zion had, Chris liked the odds.

With that Chris reached out through his neural communications network to Stacey. Nowadays people didn't use cell phones. They had implants that allowed a person to call or talk to another person far away. The communication still moved at the speed of light, so a call to someone on Earth from the Leviathan would still have insane amounts of lag, but effectively Chris could contact anyone on the ship who gave him permission. His neural communications system could even display artificial images on his retina.

Chris waited for Stacey to respond and he saw a dialing

graphic in the upper right-hand corner of his right eye.

A few seconds later Stacey responded and Chris heard her say, "What's up, Chris?"

"I need to talk to you in person. Where are you?" asked Chris.

"I'm in the room. Why do you need to talk now, during the ship's battle? Are you OK?" Stacey questioned.

"Yes, I'm fine, I'll be down in a second, but I need you to put on your jumpsuit and help me do something," explained Chris as he began sprinting toward the turbo lift.

"Ok . . . You are sounding weird though, what is going on? What could you need me to do for you in the middle of a battle?" Stacey again questioned.

Chris hit the button to send the turbo lift toward his quarters and responded with, "I'll explain when I get there. Just be ready to move ASAP."

"OK . . ." sighed Stacey in a suspicious tone.

Chris felt like it was taking forever to get off the turbo lift but in reality only a few seconds had gone by. He exited the lift and began sprinting to his and Stacey's quarters. He ran up to the door and the biometric sensors opened the door, knowing it was him.

He was greeted by Stacey, who had a concerned look on her face. To her credit, however, she was dressed and ready to go.

Chris began, "OK Stacey, I know what I am about to say is going to sound crazy to you. But I need a huge favor."

"Chris, you are already sounding crazy to me. We're in the middle of a battle right now. What do you have going on in that head of yours?"

"Stacey, I have been trying to figure out a way to make an impact on this ship. I have nothing else going for me in this world. I have nowhere else to go to after we get dropped off by this ship and no solid future prospects or credits," explained Chris.

"Well Chris, I can probably help you get on your feet when we get off this ship. It's not much, but it's something. Maybe I can get you a job as ship's mechanic," comforted Stacey.

Chris stared at her with a dumb expression, then smiled slightly and expressed, "Listen, Stacey, I really appreciate that, but I have no official credentials, no real job history, and have been labeled a smuggler. You and I both know the chances of me getting a job and living a quality life are pretty low. However, just hear me out—I think I have come up with a way to help myself, and more importantly the crew of this ship. As an added bonus I may be able to get back at Zion as well."

Stacey laughed and sighed, "Now this I have got to hear."

Chris began explaining his plan to Stacey and the looks on her face went from interested to shocked. Chris was not sure if he had ever seen someone's eyes get so wide. When he got done explaining she sat there slack-jawed.

Chris paused and waited for her to collect her thoughts. After a few seconds he asked, "So will you help me?"

"Are you serious? Absolutely not. That is probably the worst idea you have ever had. No way am I going to help you piss off everyone on this ship on the small chance that you may—and I do mean to emphasize, may—be able to help," shouted Stacey.

"Stacey, you have to! I have nobody else who will help me and if this doesn't work I'm screwed anyway," explained Chris.

"No, no way Chris, there has to be another way for you to make it in this system," comforted Stacey.

Chris exhaled and looked at the floor in grief. Then he looked back up at Stacey. Chris reached out and grabbed her hands. Then in a soft tone Chris articulated, "Stacey, I have been thinking about this for days—ever since we were taken aboard this ship. I know in my heart this is the right thing to do and it's not something I take lightly. Josh's," Chris paused, "my father's dying words were 'Do not look back, Chris. Be bold. Your destiny lies ahead of you.' I think he was onto something and this is how I face my destiny."

Stacey looked at Chris for a second, contemplating what Chris had told her. Then she took her hands back and turned around.

She then quietly stated, "Chris, if I do this, we could both go to jail for the rest of our lives. I'm just not sure it's the right thing to do. Listen, I loved Josh, and you know I respected him, but I'm not sure this is what he meant by those words. I don't want to risk your life and mine on such a risky plan."

Chris had been holding a trump card in his pocket. He knew Stacey was on the fence about the idea and he waited to play it. Chris was not mad at her or disappointed. Any good friend would have given the advice Stacey gave, but this was not a normal situation that normal people went through. This was a crappy deck of cards to be dealt and Chris knew he would have to go big to find his happiness.

Chris then stated with conviction, "Stacey, I saved both of our lives arguably more than once escaping from Zion and his pirates. This is your chance to save my life. I'm asking you to take a risk on me. If it doesn't work I'll say I threatened you and you didn't want to do it."

Stacey interrupted Chris, "Stop, Chris, I'm not going to abandon you and I don't need you to lie for me. I will do this since I do owe you one, and in a way, it is probably something Josh would have done—or at the very least it is something he would have thought of as well. I'll make it happen, Chris, to the best of my ability."

"Awesome!" replied Chris, "Thank you so much, Stacey!" He gave her a hug, which she returned, and then began to make his way back to the turbo lift with her.

Stacey announced, "Chris, just so we are clear, after this we are even!"

Chris laughed then said, "Sounds great to me Stacey!"

With that they both set off to the turbo lift.

Both Stacey and Chris exited the turbo lift together at the

entrance of the hangar bay. It was very chaotic, as ship personnel were moving back and forth, performing their jobs with efficiency and urgency. Chris was counting on this, as he and Stacey had not been given access to the hangar bay.

"So how do we play this out?" asked Stacey.

Chris motioned her to follow him and he began walking purposefully down the hallway, not trying to enter the hangar.

"We need to make it look like we know exactly what we are doing. Make sure you keep your head up and focus on something in front of you, as if it were your job to work on that thing you are walking to," explained Chris. "We are going to wait till someone passes us in the hallway and then turn around behind them. We will stay a couple paces back and hope they are headed into the hangar. As they go in and the doors open, we will follow behind them as if we had business to attend to in the hangar."

"All right, but the ship's sensors will pick us up and notify the bridge there are unauthorized personnel in the hangar," argued Stacey.

"True, and I have no doubt we will get reprimanded for it, but they are in the middle of a battle right now and worrying about what two civilians are doing on board the ship is something that will be on the back burner," stated Chris.

"All right, Chris, that does make sense. I'll follow your lead on this one since this is your cockamamie plan," said Stacey with a wink.

Chris responded with, "Remember, just look like you know what you are doing and people will usually leave you alone. We have our ship jumpsuits on so we will really only stand out if we look like tourists walking around and looking at everything."

With that they kept walking down the hall until they saw a group of four mechanics walking the opposite direction. Chris assumed they were probably headed into the hangar so after they passed he lightly grabbed Stacey's arm and they did a 180 degree turn. The mechanics were moving at a very brisk walking pace, so Chris pushed himself and Stacey to keep up. They were literally six feet behind the mechanics, who were very busy talking about the tasks they needed to get done to prep for the fighters' return.

Chris noticed the hangar doors coming up on the right and he unconsciously began holding his breath. As they got closer the hangar doors automatically began opening for the mechanics. The big metal doors opened with an audible whirring sound as the motors moved the massive structures.

Sure enough, a couple of seconds later the mechanics turned to the right and began walking through the doors. Chris and Stacey turned to follow the mechanics before the hangar doors began to close. As Stacey and he walked through he heard an audible chirp from one of the door sensors, which meant unauthorized personnel had just entered the hangar. Luckily for them there were so many other loud noises and lights flashing that the noise from the sensors went unnoticed. Chris knew, though, that a signal had been sent to the bridge noting the unauthorized access of civilians. From here on there was no turning back. At the very least there would be a stern talking to from the XO and more likely they would be spending some time in the brig.

As they entered Chris saw the lone remaining Raptor docked on his right. Chris knew that was Corporal Higgins's Raptor. It was the one that was badly damaged and now was without a pilot. Chris had been counting on it remaining behind for the rest of the missions. Whistler and his crew had done as they said and fixed the ship up completely. It was clean and looked fully repaired and ready to go. All it needed was a pilot.

Chris immediately began walking with purpose toward it. He looked at Stacey and stated, "Remember, just act calm and with purpose. We belong out here on this Raptor."

She just nodded and kept walking toward the space

superiority fighter. Chris saw the many people moving around him and several people clanking in exosuits. The people still in the bay were prepping it for the return of the four Raptors and Casey's Tumbler. For the most part they were ignoring the unused Raptor in the corner.

As Chris and Stacey reached the nose of the Raptor Chris heard someone yell, "Hey Chris!"

"Oh shit!" Chris thought, "I'm busted and I didn't even make it inside the Raptor."

He turned his head as Stacey kept walking toward the Raptor. It was Whistler, who was about thirty meters away working on some of the armaments the Raptors used. Whistler didn't look mad, just more curious than anything. So Chris did what he figured anyone who belonged here would do and he waved at Whistler. Whistler gave him a confused look but then waved back and carried on with what he was doing. Chris turned his head back toward the Raptor and rejoined Stacey.

Many people would be surprised to know that military equipment typically has no security features of any kind. The conventional thought has always been that the last thing command wants is equipment delayed or grounded because of security systems. Whether it be forgetting the password, a sweaty finger on a fingerprint scanner, losing keys, whatever, there has just never been a system adequate for the purpose. As a result, the military dictate has always been to simply restrict access to the equipment. During his stay on the Leviathan, Chris had learned that the Raptors were no exception. They were on an Earth Force Destroyer, in an access-controlled fighter bay, surrounded by Earth Force personnel. Nobody ever considered that someone would be stupid enough to try to steal one—until today.

Chris saw the loading ladder a few meters away, motioned Stacey toward it, and began running his hand along the hull of the Raptor as if he was performing a preflight inspection. Along the way he disconnected electrical hookups, removed

COSMIC GATE

protective covers, and collected lockout pins. So far so good. He took a moment to see how Stacey was doing. To her credit, she had deactivated the magnetic hold-downs and was already rolling the ladder toward the aircraft.

This was it. If Chris turned back now he would probably be fine and receive a verbal reprimand. If he committed to the next stage, however, there would be no going back. In fact, he thought, this may be the last time he ever saw a spaceship. Then he shook his head to get those thoughts out of his mind. It was too late now to feel bad; it was time to execute.

Chris looked around one more time to make sure nobody was directly staring at him and Stacey. He was good to go.

As the metal ladder approached the Raptor, Chris grabbed the other side of it and they gently rested its padded surface up against the Raptor.

"Are you sure I can't talk you out of this Chris?" commented Stacey.

"I'm sure," replied Chris.

"Well in that case, make Josh proud, and please be careful. I'll do whatever I can to protect you afterward but I'll likely be in the brig with you and unable to help. Please don't get killed out there, Chris," articulated Stacey with a touch of fear in her voice and her held tilted downward.

"Relax, Stacey, I don't know why but this just feels right," stated Chris and he began quickly working his way up the ladder.

He hopped from the ladder into the padded seat. He flipped the power button and the cockpit lit up like a Christmas tree. This was it. It only took a second, but it felt like minutes were going by until the Raptor's main screen flashed "online."

Chris looked down at Stacey, who was pulling the ladder away from the Raptor, and gave her a quick salute, which made Stacey smile.

He hit the button to close the canopy and began to fire up the reactor that powered all the main systems on board the star fighter. He heard the hydraulics working as the canopy fell around him and sealed the inside of the fighter from space. Chris knew it would only be a matter of seconds now before people started wondering what was going on. It was one thing to be in the bay looking at a Raptor; it was another to pretend that powering up a Raptor would go unnoticed by the technicians in the bay.

Sure enough, people began looking at Chris's Raptor and pointing. They had to know something was wrong. Not only were there no orders for this Raptor to fly, but the person inside of it lacked a space suit or helmet, which was standard issue for the pilots.

A few more seconds went by and Chris noticed his Raptor was fully online. He took a moment to take it all in. He was about to live his dream and fly a space superiority fighter for Earth Force. Well that last part was a bit of an exaggeration as Earth Force didn't bless this in any way, shape, or form. Still, Chris knew he would be helping Earth Force—or at least, he thought he was helping. The fact that he was breaking the law and living his dream all at once had his nerves firing like crazy. He was shaking he was so excited. He also wished he had gone to the restroom one more time before hopping on board, as he had to pee so badly. He took one deep breath and exhaled. That helped calm him some, but he was so nervous it couldn't solve the problem completely.

Chris looked at his system displays and everything was in the green. His ship was loaded, functioning normally, and ready to go. He looked up and saw several mechanics yelling at him and waving their arms. He could see several of them with red faces and their mouths moving, saying, "Get out of there!" and "What are you doing?"

With that Chris looked to his left and right to make sure his Raptor was clear of personnel. Although mechanics were surrounding his plane, they at least were smart enough to keep their distance in case Chris decided to start maneuvering the plane. He reached down and started hitting buttons to fire his maneuvering thrusters.

The Raptor began to lift off the floor of the hangar bay slowly. After he reached a height of about five meters off the ground he began pointing the nose toward the external hangar door. Mechanics at this point had given up on trying to stop him and instead were getting out of his way. Chris obviously had no intention of hurting them or running into any of their equipment so he made sure to provide plenty of space and time for them to move. People in exosuits were clanking out of the way, assuming he was going crazy and would blast into them.

He then began to nudge the ship forward slowly, watching as the external hangar doors began to grow in size as he approached. His Raptor was moving at about two meters per second and Chris did a quick double check of all his systems. He then thanked himself for spending so much time in the simulators that he could pull this stunt off.

As the external hangar doors approached on Chris's left side he began pointing the Raptor at them.

Modern day destroyers like the Leviathan had massive hangar doors. When the fighters launched they remained open in case the fighters needed to retreat back inside quickly. Now this could, as one would imagine, be a major problem for the mechanics and ship support personnel inside the hangar, as they would get sucked out. To combat this the ship generated a temporary force field at the external hangar doors. The force field drew massive amounts of energy but was very effective at sealing the atmosphere in, while allowing ships with the right transponder codes to move through it freely. A friendly fighter could fly through the force field and the field would contour itself around the ship without letting atmosphere escape. However, if an enemy fighter were to try to go through it, it would either be destroyed by the force field, or, if it had enough mass and inertia, it could bring down the force field around it.

As Chris oriented the nose of his Raptor at the force field he said a silent prayer. If the captain wanted to, he could in theory tell the force field not to allow Chris's ship to move through. He knew that was unlikely, however, as either the field could damage Chris's ship and make it crash, damaging the Leviathan and Chris's Raptor, or Chris would break through the field, causing everything in the hangar to get sucked out into space.

Chris looked to his left, where his ship had been before he moved it toward the door. He could see Stacey in the distance being hauled away in handcuffs, while additional security personnel filled up the hangar, training their small arms on his ship. They were telling him via hand signals and screaming, he assumed, to stop what he was doing and park the ship.

Chris laughed in his head as he knew it was too late for that. Instead, he looked forward again at the transparent force field and reached his arm down to begin throttling up his main engines. Chris moved the throttle forward slightly and the ship lurched forward.

As the ship approached the force field Chris had a butt-puckering moment. The forward part of his ship hit the force field, and without a sound, his ship smoothly went through the field. About a second later he was in space, for the first time, in an Earth Force fighter.

CHAPTER 17

As soon as Chris cleared the force field he did what all fighter pilots did out of the hangar bay, he punched the afterburners for a couple seconds to accelerate to cruising speeds. As the afterburners pushed him into his seat he heard himself yell, "WOOOOOHOOOOOOOO!!!!!!!"

The adrenaline flowing through his body gave him a tremendous feeling of invincibility and he honestly couldn't think of a time in his life when he had been happier. All was good in the universe, as Chris had found where he belonged—kind of. After about five seconds of bliss the real world came back to him in the form of a flashing indicator on one of his displays.

Chris activated the display to see who was contacting him and a familiar looking clean-shaven face popped up on his display screen.

"Chis Skylander, this is Commander Shafer of the E.F. Leviathan. You have committed treason and stolen property of the Earth Force government. On top of that you are in an active war zone. You are hereby ordered to stand down immediately and return to the Leviathan's hangar."

"Treason?" responded Chris. "Guys, I am here to help. After we deal with these Gate Keepers scum bags I'll land the ship, no problem. In the meantime, why don't you give me a target to shoot?"

Chris looked down at his radar display and saw that Zion's

ship and the main battle was off on his port side. He began maneuvering his Raptor to head in that direction.

"Chris, I am only going to ask you one more time. Return to the Leviathan immediately. Any other action will be viewed as hostile and we will deal with you with force," Ben stated in a venomous tone.

"Listen, Commander Shafer, I know what I have done, but I am here to help, nothing more. If you won't help me, then I'll do my best on my own to take down some bad guys," replied Chris.

Commander Shafer cursed and then ceased the transmission. At this point, Chris had enough of being reprimanded and had begun heading toward the main battle. What he saw ahead of him and what was on his radar, however, were much different than what he had seen when still in the observation deck. It honestly took him a moment to understand just what he was looking at.

Many kilometers ahead of him was Zion's destroyer, the Iceni. It was in even worse shape than before. It was hardly even functional at this point, and the people on board appeared to be evacuating. He started to get excited that he might be able to land some of the finishing blows on Zion, when he noticed something else.

There was debris floating close to the Iceni, and when he focused on it his eyes went wide with shock. The computer identified the spinning objects as the wreckage of the E.F. Olympia.

The Olympia had somehow lost the battle with the Iceni, despite outnumbering it three to one, and outgunning it with a better trained crew and better maintained ship. Worse yet, its reactor had gone supercritical. Chris hoped the crew had gotten to the escape pods in time, but typically escape pods didn't survive thermonuclear radiation blasts at close range in the vacuum of space.

"How did this happen?" Chris wondered.

Things only got worse from there as the computer continued to identify additional wreckage in space, this time in the
form of a floating husk shaped like a Poseidon class destroyer. The wreckage was identified by the computer as the E. F.
Mustang. Chris realized it must have been destroyed without
the fusion reactors going supercritical or the wreckage would
have been in many more pieces. Instead it had been turned to
Swiss cheese, with multiple sections missing completely. He
hoped some of the crew had made it to sealed compartments
or the escape pods.

Again Chris thought, "How had the Iceni destroyed a second Poseidon class destroyer!?"

None of this made sense to him. He simply couldn't understand how the situation had changed so drastically. Earth
Force had this one in the bag, with three destroyers and their
compliment of fighters up against one banged-up destroyer
and about a dozen skimmers.

The next thing Chris noticed, to his relief, was a dozen or so
Earth Force fighters remaining. Even better, the Leviathan's
compliment of four fighters and a Tumbler appeared to all be
intact as their wing was engaged in combat with the skimmers
around the Iceni. Several of the fighters had taken different
degrees of damage, but they were still functioning.

Chris then noticed about halfway between the Iceni and
the Leviathan was the Tumbler piloted by Husky aka Sergeant
Casey Hogan. He seemed to be hustling back to the Leviathan.

Just then another indicator flashed on one of his display
screens and Chris knew it was the Leviathan contacting him
again. Reluctantly he reached down and hit the button to answer the incoming communication.

As soon as he did, to Chris's surprise, Captain Erik Spear's
face popped up in the display.

"Umm hi Captain Spear," greeted Chris.

"Son, you are flying into a very dangerous situation. You're
in an active warzone, piloting a craft you aren't trained to

operate, with no one to protect you. I'm asking you as the captain of the Leviathan to return to the ship as you are in grave danger, and throwing your life away will not help anyone. You can still make this right, Chris," explained the captain.

Chris replied, "Listen, Captain. I respect the hell out of you, but I don't have anything else waiting for me in this universe and this is my chance to exact revenge on Zion. I've always wanted to pilot a ship for the Earth Force, you had a spare, and there's a guy down there who needs killing. I'm not going to let these scum retreat and get away. It's time to get revenge on Zion. He killed my father!"

Chris yelled that last part a bit unexpectedly. Captain Spear did not seem offended by it. He looked down for half a second, then looked back up and said solemnly, "Chris, Zion is no longer in the area. He has escaped."

Chris gasped and then said, "That's impossible! The Iceni is in front of me! I see it on radar."

Captain Spear looked into the camera and explained, "Chris, he escaped and is on board a different ship now. It is too late to get him. Return to base and we will deal with the fallout of your actions and this battle. The best thing you can do is come back safely with an undamaged Raptor."

Chris's feelings of joy and excitement began to quickly dissipate. He couldn't believe it. After all this effort to get out here and fight Zion and his minions and he wasn't here? All that was left was a critically damaged destroyer and several Skimmers that the Earth Force fighters were engaged with. Chances were by the time he got there, they would already be destroyed by Wing Commander Sarner and his wing along with the fighters from the E. F. Olympia and the E.F. Mustang. What then was left for him to do?

"Dammit, was this all for nothing?" Chris pondered.

Chris began to reply to Captain Spear and tell him he was coming home when he noticed four more wormholes open up right behind Husky's Tumbler.

Four of the Gate Keepers' Skimmers began to emerge from the subspace portals. Instead of telling Captain Spear he was returning, he looked down at the display with the captain's face on it, grinned, and beamed, "Time to kick some ass and save lives!"

With that Chris cut the transmission and hit the afterburners. His ship lurched forward at fantastic speed. The inertial dampeners strained to keep Chris from blacking out. Chris felt the crushing forces against his chest, but he hung on.

What Chris saw was four enemy Skimmers jumping in to take out Husky's Tumbler. The rest of the Earth Force fighters were too far away to help in time as they were engaged with the remaining pirates. If Chris didn't help, Husky was probably doomed.

Chris toggled his weapon selection over to missiles and he watched as a yellow triangle on his heads-up display started working its way over toward the first Skimmer to emerge from subspace. While he was waiting for the target lock to acquire, Chris also switched fire to dual mode. This meant that when he pulled the trigger two missiles would fire instead of just one. The target lock felt like it was taking forever but in reality it had locked on in just over a second.

As soon as the targeting reticle turned red it meant that Chris had acquired a lock, and he immediately pressed the trigger. Chris felt the slight shudder as two Lancer class missiles rocketed out from under the wings of the Raptor.

Lancer missiles were the Earth Force's most common missile. They were fairly maneuverable but didn't pack a lot of punch. The guidance system they used was radar based, so a radar lock was required to successfully launch them.

Chris wasted no time targeting the next Skimmer and repeating the same sequence of events. Acquire target, fire pair of missiles. While he was doing this, Wing Commander John Sarner popped up in his heads-up display.

"Chris, what the hell are you doing?" asked Major Sarner

"Shooting at bad guys, sir," replied Chris as he squeezed the trigger, launching two more Lancer missiles. Chris mentally noted that he had used four of his missiles at this point.

"That's the problem," commented Major Sarner. Chris was amazed to see the wing commander communicating with him as he was in a dogfight of his own. Sarner paused for a moment to take an evasive action. "You're supposed to be tucked in safe and sound on the Leviathan," he then finished.

"Change of plans sir. I couldn't stand by and let you guys have all the fun," explained Chris.

"This is not fun, Chris, this is war. I know I cannot talk you into returning to the ship. I understand the captain and XO have already tried. On top of that I have my hands full and can't deal with whatever you're trying to prove. So I'll say this: turn around and run. You cannot handle four Skimmers on your own. My team will be heading there in a minute after we finish up our current engagement," commanded Major Sarner.

"Negative, Wing Commander," answered Chris as he fired another pair of missiles at the third target. "That Tumbler isn't going to last long against four Skimmers and you won't make it here in time. I'll hold them off long enough for you to help out."

Wing Commander Sarner finished the conversation with a resigned sigh and then a hopeful, "Good luck Chris. Give them hell!"

"Yes sir," Chris acknowledged.

Chris achieved target lock on the last of the four skimmers and as he was pressing the trigger, launching two more missiles, another familiar-looking face popped up on the display.

"Kid, I gotta admit, you have balls," joked Lieutenant Quick aka Maniac. "Don't get me wrong, you are a huge dumbass and I'm going to laugh watching you sit in a cell for this stunt if you don't get blown up. Till then, good luck trying to get as many kills as me. I have five already and I'm not done."

"Thanks, Maniac, for the support, I guess?" questioned Chris.

Maniac smirked in his screen and then cut off the transmission.

Chris watched as all eight of his Lancer missiles tracked their four targets. He was still a solid twenty kilometers away from his targets and his afterburners had cut out. Instead of afterburners he was still accelerating at 100 percent nominal thrust toward his targets. He didn't want to use the burners again, as then he would have built up so much speed he would have to spend a long time trying to turn around to face the fighters after he passed them. Meanwhile, Husky was burning toward him and the Leviathan at full speed, but was still sixteen kilometers away.

By now the Skimmers had fully emerged from their subspace portals, taken inventory of their surroundings, and become aware of the missiles coming at them. The two in the lead began deploying countermeasures to scramble their radar signatures while the two in the back began firing at Husky's Tumbler. The Tumbler, though being a slow, lightly armed ship, was at least tough. It had an impressive number of countermeasures and it would take many rounds of laser fire to bring down her armor. Chris was hoping the eight incoming missiles would be able to provide Husky the time he needed to get back, or at least hold on until more help could arrive.

Chris saw he was being contacted on a private communication line. He toggled the display and Husky himself showed up, wide-eyed and looking stressed out. Sergeant Casey Hogan aka Husky exclaimed, "Chris, am I glad to see you! This is on a private line as I know the command staff is super pissed, but I wanted to at least let you know that I am thankful you're trying to save my ass."

"No problem Husky, I'll do what I can," replied Chris.

"Thanks, I'll try to help you out when the dust settles from this, if we both make it—though this old girl has a few tricks up her sleeve and won't give up easily," explained Husky.

With that Chris saw a different zoomed-up display in his cockpit showing Husky's Tumbler. Its turrets began unleashing laser fire on the incoming Skimmers. Unfortunately, he also saw streaks coming from multiple hostiles, indicating the Skimmers had launched missiles of their own.

Chris began getting another target lock on the first Skimmer. The missiles Chris had launched would either hit any second now, or miss their targets. Chris watched in anticipation. If the first pair missed, he would fire two more. Chris had twenty missiles on board, so supply was not an issue at the moment.

Chris watched as the first two missiles did their best to collide head on with the first Skimmer. Its pilot shifted the Skimmer to the right in an effort to dodge the missiles and it was partially successful. Only one of the two missiles impacted it, causing significant damage to its forward armor but not taking it out of the fight. Chris's display read an estimated 57 percent hull integrity for the first Skimmer. With that, his targeting reticle went red again as he achieved lock and fired two more missiles on their way.

Chris cut his acceleration at this point, as he was approaching fast, and he began tracking the second of the Skimmers. It had done an even better job than the first and was able to dodge both missiles, allowing it to hammer away at the retreating Tumbler. As Chris achieved lock again he fired two more missiles, hopefully distracting it.

The third Skimmer didn't fair so well. It had received some laser fire from Husky's Tumbler and its forward armor was lightly depleted. This, combined with the Skimmer pilot's overconfidence, led to his doom. He misjudged the closing rate of the incoming missiles, probably because of the distracting laser fire, and when he tried to pull up to avoid the incoming missiles it was too little too late. Both Lancer missiles slammed into the front of the Skimmer, detonating their payloads in close proximity. The forward armor on the Skimmer could not take the amount of punishment it had received and gave way, causing the structure of the ship to disintegrate. The pilot couldn't eject as his whole cockpit was engulfed in flames and his body atomized from the explosion.

Chris cheered as he knew his odds of success had just gone up. He watched as the last two missiles from his first salvo closed in on their target. The fourth Skimmer had already begun evading the missiles, probably because he had just seen what happened to his friend. The first of the two missiles missed completely, and the second only did slightly better. It too missed, but was close enough to the target that its proximity sensors detonated the warhead anyway and the fringe explosion was able to do a light amount of damage to the evading Skimmer.

Meanwhile, the enemy missiles had closed on Husky's tumbler. Chris counted six missiles incoming, too many for any fighter to fend off. A tumbler wasn't a fighter, however, as Chris immediately learned. Just as the missiles closed on their target, the space around the tumbler lit up. Dozens of countermeasure boxes were ejected, jamming radar and releasing radar-reflecting chaff. In addition, the tumbler's turrets had targeted the missiles and were unloading furiously on them. Easily half of the missiles lost target, and the other half that stayed on target were identified by the computers running the turrets for termination. A few moments later the turrets finished their job. All six missiles were either destroyed or wandering aimlessly into space.

Chris cheered silently as he began toggling his weapons over to lasers, as the range was getting too close for more missiles. He also began decelerating, as he was really going to overshoot his targets soon if he did not slow down.

With a total of four missiles launched and hunting two of the remaining three Skimmers, Chris began to change the focus of his tactics. The Tumbler being piloted by Husky on its way back to the Leviathan was now in range of Chris's lasers, which meant the trailing fighters would be in range of Chris's lasers in only a couple more seconds.

Chris increased his rate of deceleration and did his best to focus as the inertia threw him forward. He watched as the first Skimmer performed evasive maneuvers in an effort to dodge Chris's second missile attack. For the most part it worked, as the first missile missed. The second, however, hit its target on the belly. While the Skimmer had already been hit from Chris's previous salvo, the belly armor was still relatively un-damaged. After Chris's missile slammed home it tore a huge hole in the belly armor but the Skimmer remained intact and combat capable.

Chris was ready for it and had already lined up his target-ing reticle with the projections of where the Skimmer would be by the time he pulled the trigger. With the sights lined up, Chris pressed the trigger and his lasers began firing two at a time. The bolts lanced out and reached deep into the hole where the previous missile had already done damage. All it took was four total hits from laser fire to melt any remain-ing armor and hit the reactor inside the fighter. His canopy instantly went dark to compensate for the light of the enemy ship's reactor going supercritical and becoming a momentary star in the dark of space.

"Yes!" shouted Chris as he realized he just gotten his first kill by laser fire. Granted, he had gotten the element of sur-prise over his foes while piloting a fighter with far more fire-power, but the exhilaration was real nonetheless.

The celebration was short lived however as his computer warned him he was being targeted by one of the Skimmers. It was the second Skimmer, which had avoided a total of four missiles at this point. Chris knew this pilot was either very lucky or had some impressive piloting skills. Some of Zion's people were ex-Earth Force, so it didn't surprise him that he'd face some good pilots. He hesitated momentarily as he thought back to the last time he had faced an Earth Force pilot, albeit in the simulators.

Chris killed the thought quickly, thinking back to his father's words, "Fear is the mind-killer." He then began tracking the second Skimmer and the two faced each other head on. The other Skimmer appeared to be ignoring Chris and instead was pouring laser fire at Husky's Tumbler. Chris did a quick check and saw Husky's estimated hull integrity was at 67 percent. This meant he was taking a lot of hits, but was OK for at least a little while longer.

As Chris stared down the Skimmer approaching him, the two began to play a game of chicken. Chris was pretty confident he could win this, as his ship was better armed and armored compared to the Skimmer he was going up against. If the two shot each other an equal number of times, Chris would be victorious, as his ship had more armor and firepower. Plus, if the other pilot was Earth Force, he'd have the nanite package enhancements, giving him an edge in maneuverability and reaction times. If Chris could lure him into a slugfest, however, it would negate the other pilot's advantages. So Chris mentally said, "All right, you want to see who gives up first? Let's do this!"

Chris fired his laser in alternating bursts of two at a time. His first two bolts hit, melting away armor. At the same time the oncoming pirate must have pulled the trigger as well because Chris's ship rocked slightly as two bolts of energy reached out and hit his ship. This shudder must have affected both him and the pirate he was shooting at, because Chris's next shot missed, along with the pirate's shot at him. Then the two realigned, facing each other, and they both began pouring on the firepower again. Chris was hit by another two bolts, and with a look out of the corner of his eye he read his own forward armor integrity at slightly over 80 percent. Meanwhile, the Skimmer he was shooting at could not hold on as long. Its armor had fallen to almost 50 percent integrity.

Chris knew his theory about who could last longer in this fight had paid off, and so instead of trying to avoid the oncoming laser fire, Chris kept the triggers depressed and poured on the fire. The Skimmer pilot was not foolish enough to continue the game of chicken and instead began to maneuver, avoiding Chris's fire for all it could. As the Skimmer dodged, Chris did his best to keep the cycling lasers on him. Chris hit him with a few more shots as the two ships flew past each other.

As they were passing each other, Husky came over his comm system and with fear in his tone exclaimed, "Chris, I need some help here! This guy is tearing me apart!"

"All right, hang in there. I'll try to take the heat off you!" Chris yelled back.

Chris had begun his turn to chase the Skimmer who had just flown past him, but instead maneuvered his ship to take on the Skimmer that was harassing Husky.

Chris saw he was just over three clicks away from the Skimmer that was pounding on Husky so he throttled up his engines to close the distance further. With another glance he saw that Husky's integrity had fallen to 40 percent, which meant bad things were going to start happening soon. Chris also knew that the Skimmer that had flown past him would be turning around and firing at him. He felt a sinking feeling in his stomach as he realized this was most likely exactly what the enemy had planned.

Putting those thoughts out of his head he lined up his sights as best he could on the Skimmer chasing Husky and began unleashing single blasts from his four laser cannons. Chris had switched to single fire mode in an attempt to distract the Skimmer with all the laser fire. He was hoping that it would concentrate on evading him instead of attacking the Tumbler.

The tactic didn't work for the first couple of seconds, but after several successful hits the Skimmer pulled up and began evading. This worked in Chris's favor, though, as Chris was able to continue steering his ship at the evading Skimmer. He kept the trigger pressed the whole time as round after round of energy blast escaped his cannons. Several more of those shots found home on the fleeing Skimmer, melting significant chunks of its rear armor. Chris read the target's rear armor integrity at just below 50 percent.

He lined up additional shots and kept firing. His own ship began rocking left and right, however, which ruined his accuracy. Chris looked at his radar to see what had happened and realized the Skimmer that had flown past him was now on his six and was unleashing its own version of devastation on him.

Thus began a dance between the two Skimmers, Husky's Tumbler, and Chris's Raptor. Husky's Tumbler was trying to get back to the Leviathan, the forward-most Skimmer was trying to avoid Chris while getting a shot or two in at the Tumbler, Chris was trying to shoot the foremost Skimmer while avoiding damage from the Skimmer behind him, and last but not least, the Skimmer in the back was trying to take Chris out before Chris could take his wingman out.

Chris dodged left and right, all the while pulling the trigger in between changes of direction. Chris had switched his laser fire up so that all four laser cannons fired at once. This increased the amount of cycle time between shots, but as he only had brief windows to line up and fire this wasn't a problem. More importantly, the few shots he took would be significantly more powerful. The tactic worked somewhat well, but Chris realized he was not getting enough damage on his target quickly and it was still peppering away at Husky's dangerously thin armor. Chris decided it was time to do something bold.

He decided to allow the aft Skimmer to get shots in on Chris while Chris made sure not to focus on dodging and just focus on hitting the Skimmer harassing Husky. Chris keyed up his comms and threatened the pirate ships, "Hold still, you sons of bitches, I have some justice I'm trying to dispense!"

Chris fired and all four lances shot out at the Skimmer, damaging it further. Chris could see the black spots where armor had melted and sparks were flying out of the Skimmer. It was in bad shape but still serviceable. Chris watched as the pilot turned the Skimmer toward the Tumbler to fire some additional shots off. Chris lined up his sights and pulled the trigger just as he felt his ship rock from incoming laser fire. Chris saw his rear armor was holding at an estimated 43 percent integrity but dropping fast. Even worse, he saw Husky's rear armor had fallen to an estimated 14 percent strength. If Chris didn't act right now his new friend was going to die. Chris knew that Tumblers didn't come equipped with ejection seats, as they were not supposed to be getting into gunfights. With that he made a snap judgment, and ignoring the skimmer pummeling his rear armor, he lined up for one more shot.

A bright orange flash exploded in front of Chris as he nailed the Skimmer with all four cannons. That Skimmer wouldn't be harassing Husky any longer. Unfortunately, Chris still had a Skimmer on his six who continued to press the trigger as well. Chris's ship jolted from the incoming fire and warning claxons went off, indicating that critical systems were getting damaged.

Chris pulled up on the stick while at the same time hitting the afterburners in an attempt to evade the more maneuverable Skimmer. His ship lurched forward and up, giving Chris a chance to assess the damage. His rear armor was down to 20 percent integrity and the number three engine was leaking coolant and only working at half capacity.

Chris pushed the afterburners until the computer forced him to cut them off and cool. The problem with having a Skimmer on his six was a big one. The Skimmer was naturally a more maneuverable ship, so outmaneuvering it was probably not going to work. In addition, Chris didn't have a proper space suit or a nanite package to help with the Gs. So even if his ship could physically outmaneuver the Skimmer on his six it wouldn't matter because Chris's body couldn't handle the stress.

Chris had a feeling he was going to have to get lucky somehow to walk away from this fight. He figured he would drag this Skimmer on his six away from the Tumbler and hit the eject button right before his ship blew up. This way, by the time the last remaining Skimmer got him, it would be too late to get the Tumbler, which would hopefully be safe and sound in the Leviathan's hangar bay—or at least very close to the Leviathan, which would provide cover fire if the Skimmer came close.

Chris's ship weaved up, down, left, and right and it worked for a few seconds before the Skimmer got in another couple of shots. Even more warning claxons were going off now. Chris could see that the number three engine was completely destroyed and his armor had fallen to 5 percent integrity. Guidance systems were damaged and his reactor was threatening to lose containment.

This was it—another couple of shots and Chris would have to eject or be killed in a massive fiery explosion. Chris hit the afterburners one more time in an attempt to buy some additional time and it worked. Chris saw the amber glow of a laser narrowly missing his Raptor. Chris pulled up on the stick, straining from the pressure of the G forces. He then straightened out the ship, inverted himself, and as the afterburners cut out again he pulled up, bringing the ship back around in an attempt to avoid incoming fire. It had worked and he bought himself a few more seconds.

Chris knew he couldn't hold on forever though, and lifted the warning guard around the ejection handle. He hoped the canopy held its seal, as his lack of a space suit meant he faced a cold death in vacuum if it didn't. He continued to steer in an evasive manner but wanted his hand on the ejection handle to ensure he left before the reactor went.

Chris heard the warning siren that meant the enemy had

acquired a lock on him and held his breath as he waited for the shudder that meant he was hit. Once he felt that he would just lift the handle and the computer would take care of the ejection sequence.

He continued holding his breadth and maneuvering when the warning siren cut off. Chris looked down at his radar and the red dot representing the Skimmer on his six disappeared. Chris looked to his back left, where he thought the Skimmer was, and saw an orange explosion.

"You're lucky I have impeccable timing, Chris," came the wing commander's voice over the comms.

Chris exhaled in a sigh of relief. The wing commander had launched his own volley of missiles at the Skimmer and they both hit, destroying the Skimmer instantly.

"Thank you," replied Chris over the comm. "That was too close for comfort."

"Dammit, Chris, you almost broke that shiny Raptor you stole. The least you could do is return it in the same shape you found it in. Whistler is going to be pissed," laughed Joker aka Sergeant Mike Carpenter.

"Stow it, Joker," ordered Major Sarner over the comms. "He has a lot of explaining to do and we will take his crime of theft seriously."

"Roger that," muttered Joker.

"Chris, are you going to be able to land that thing or do you need assistance?" questioned Major Sarner.

"I'm kind of banged up a bit, but it won't be a problem to land sir," informed Chris.

"Good, the team and I are going to escort you in and assist if you have problems," commanded Major Sarner.

Chris knew what that meant. The time to pay for his actions was now and they were going to escort him back to base and make sure he landed that fighter whether he liked it or not. This was a lot less about his safety and a lot more about security of Earth Force property.

Chris maneuvered the joystick and brought the nose of the craft around toward the Leviathan. Chris then throttled up the Raptor's three remaining engines and began closing in on the Leviathan. It would only take a few minutes to get back and Chris wished it would have taken longer. He was tired but very proud of himself. He had shot down three of the enemy and saved Husky's life. Not bad for a smuggler kid on his first and only mission, who had no business in the Earth Force. He was sure, however, Captain Spear and his command staff would not see it that way.

Then he started thinking, "Well hey, since this is my last time flying a Raptor for the rest of my life I should probably have some fun." So Chris did a barrel roll, then another in the opposite direction before a voice came over the comm.

"Knock it off, Chris." It was the wing commander. "The last thing I need is for you to damage that ship even more. Plus, if you're not joyriding your way back to the Leviathan the captain might believe that you actually feel bad for stealing his ship."

Chris acknowledged the command and stopped the barrel rolls. Instead, he figured he should take in the view. To his left and right the wing formed up on him in a V configuration. He was the center point of the V, which was normally the position where the wing commander flew. However, since they were watching him in case he made any foolish moves, they kept him in front of them. Chris had to admit it was cool to be flying in a wing in the wing commander's position.

He continued watching as the Leviathan went from a tiny ship in the distance to a larger and larger ship in front of him. The vessel was an awesome sight to see and Chris still couldn't figure out how Zion had taken out two of them from the time Chris had left the observation deck to the time he actually stole the Raptor. The Poseidon class destroyer, at 420 meters long, was a majestic spaceship with a commanding presence. Its three large sections bristling with plasma and laser cannons were nothing to sneeze at.

As the wing approached the destroyer Major Sarner called to the Leviathan, "Permission to land?"

"Permission granted," came a navigational officer on board the command deck.

Chris slowed his craft down to landing speeds and began the approach pattern that would take him into the Leviathan's hangar bay. He watched in awe as the giant size of the destroyer kept getting larger and more details became visible. He felt a pang of regret as he realized Major Woodford would probably have some explaining to do. Nobody was going to believe Chris had learned how to do everything he'd just done on his own. It was with that thought that he passed through the force field separating the bay from space and engaged his maneuvering thrusters to slowly position the ship in its designated landing spot.

He looked around and saw the mechanics scrambling around prepping and waiting for their assigned fighters to get back. Chris could see Husky's Tumbler already docked. It was in pretty bad shape, as it had scorch marks all over it. Some had even managed to penetrate to the inner hull.

As he put the Raptor in the right location he maneuvered it so the nose would face the external hangar doors. This was common practice for pilots so they could get out faster if they needed to scramble the fighters. As the Raptor lowered down to the hangar floor he began to notice all of the infantry men with small arms ready in case he decided to continue his minor rebellion.

Chris had no intention of messing around further, however, as he really did just want to help out, in his way. After the ship touched down he began the sequence of shutting the Raptor down. After a few seconds of shutting systems off he heard stairs press up against the side of his ship.

He opened the canopy and found two marines pointing weapons at him. They immediately and loudly gave him orders to exit the craft.

"Relax guys, I'm going to comply," explained Chris.

They didn't muscle him around as he pulled himself up out of the cockpit but they watched him very closely in case he did something stupid.

As Chris made his way to the bottom of the stairs two more marines greeted him at the bottom.

"Put your hands behind your back," ordered one marine with a dark fireman's mustache on an otherwise clean-shaven face.

Chris complied wordlessly and the marine walked around him then cuffed him.

"What's the matter? No comments about foreplay this time?" whispered the marine.

"Huh?" questioned Chris.

"Last time you came out of the escape pod you had all sorts of hilarious comments. Now you are just going to follow orders and not make me laugh? Hmm . . . disappointing. Pick up your game Chris," explained the marine.

Then it hit him. This must have been the marine in the T-800 suit he thought he saw chuckling at his jokes when he was arrested coming out of the escape pods.

"You going to give me the date rape drug again? Or you going to let me stay awake this time so you can gaze into my eyes?" joked Chris.

"Ha! There it is," laughed the marine quietly.

With that the marine pushed Chris forward and another marine grabbed his right arm. Whistler was the next to walk up to him and the guards stopped for a second.

"Damn it, Chris, you are just like the others. Take one of my perfect-looking Raptors, fly it around, smash it all up, and bring it back here expecting me to fix it. Typical flyboy—if they ever let you out of the cell and into a fighter again you will fit in fine with the pilots," mocked Whistler.

"Sorry, Whistler, was just trying to help," replied Chris.

Whistler had already stopped talking to him though and was ordering his mechanics to get to work. Chris looked back at his Raptor and he could definitely see there was some significant damage done to the backside—nothing Whistler couldn't handle though.

At this point a couple of other Raptors had made it in the docking bay and were landing as well. One looked relatively undamaged but the other was in as bad a shape as Chris's. At least his ship wouldn't be the only Raptor getting repairs. The two marines escorted him to the hangar doors, where Chris ran into a scowling Commander Ben Shafer. The commander didn't say anything though, just looked at him with disappointment. In retrospect, he would have preferred a dressing down; the silence cut more than he would have imagined.

"What is there to say?" thought Chris. "What's done is done."

At least he had the chance to fly a Raptor and put three of Zion's men in the grave. With that thought he steeled himself against whatever the Earth Force was going to do to him. He had fulfilled his dream, and in a way avenged his father. Though Brad and Zion still breathed, it would be a problem for another day. With that the marines escorted him down to the brig. As they approached the familiar holding cells, he saw Stacey sitting in a cell waiting for him. The marines opened a cell door across from her, tossed him in, and closed the door behind him. Instead of leaving him without a word this time, the marine with the mustache stayed behind for a second.

"Look, you two, I'll be honest—you're going to be here for a while. Not just because you fucked up colossally, but because the captain has a lot to deal with. So make yourself comfortable." And with that he walked off.

To his surprise, Stacey was the first one to talk, "Chris, you realize this is the THIRD time you've gotten me locked up, right? I seriously hope it was worth it out there."

To his surprise he heard himself laugh a little, and then

he filled her in on all that had happened. It comforted him to see her smile as he told her about taking out the enemy ships. He hadn't known what it would do to him to take another human's life, and seeing her reaction was good. All in all it was a great to have her there to talk about what had happened.

"Wow! Well it sounds like we saved one of the pilot's lives! That makes it kind of worth it to be in this cell," exclaimed Stacey when he was all done.

"It was definitely worth it," replied Chris.

CHAPTER 18

Chris found himself in the now-familiar position of lying in his cell bed staring at the ceiling. Its plain texture and white color were a perfect canvas for him to replay the events of the day upon. All the sights, smells, and tactile inputs were burned into his memory. It took the first hour for him just to stop shaking from adrenaline. Just as he found himself starting to calm down he heard the clang of a door opening. He sat up and noticed that Stacey in the cell opposite to him had done the same thing.

Chris got up and walked over to the steel pillars in the front of the cell, craning his neck to see who was coming by for a visit. Sure enough, a familiar sight strolled up with a big smile on his bearded face.

"Chris! Just the man I have been needing to see!" greeted Sergeant Casey Hogan, aka Husky.

"Hi Sergeant," returned Chris.

"Whoa, that won't do my friend," said Casey.

"What's that?" asked Chris.

"Any man who saved my life," Casey said as he stuck out his hand, "should call me by my first name."

Chris smiled back and returned the handshake.

"Well you would have done the same for me and I was happy to do so Casey," returned Chris.

"Wow, you really did save his life," chimed in Stacey from

the other cell.

"Well yeah, I told you that," stated Chris.

"Yes but you pilot types tend to exaggerate. You guys take a simple task and glorify it like it's something amazing, so I wasn't sure," replied Stacey.

Chris and Casey feigned shock on their faces.

"Oh don't give me that look, you know it's true," added Stacey.

"Slander!" yelled Casey.

"Ya, I never exaggerate anything!" retorted Chris.

Stacey rolled her eyes and waved her hand at them in a way that said, "Whatever."

Casey turned his head back to Chris and explained, "Seriously, dude, I am grateful. If you ever get out of here and need a favor, even a big one, I owe you."

"Well, speaking of getting out of here, do you think I ever will? How pissed off is everyone?" asked Chris.

"Oh they are pissed. Some of the officer's faces turned so red I didn't know it was possible for a human to look like that," laughed Casey before continuing, "I can't speak to the details as it's not my place and I have to respect the chain of command even if I owe you my life. But I will tell you this: I put in every good word I could. I explained that if you hadn't stole that Raptor I wouldn't be here and we would also be down a Tumbler."

"Oh boy, I hope they know I didn't do it to piss them off. I did it because I really thought I could help, even if I knew they would never let me," assured Chris.

"They know your motivations, I think, but honestly I don't think you will be getting out of here until we dock at port. I asked them to let you out now—heck, I told them you should fly with us again until we get a replacement pilot," comforted Casey.

"Really?" asked Chris.

"Really," replied Casey, "But don't get your hopes up because they scoffed at that idea and dismissed me."

"Damn," muttered Chris.

"Yeah, it sucks. You really have them in a mess, and it's pretty funny actually," laughed Casey.

"What do you mean?" asked Chris.

"Well they are having a hell of a time trying to decide what to charge you with and how to punish you. On one hand you have a civilian who disobeyed direct orders to not enter the hangar, then he stole an Earth Force Raptor right out from under their noses. Imagine how the captain is going to try to explain that to his superiors," stressed Casey.

"Oh wow, I didn't think of that part," empathized Chris.

"Ha! I'm sure you didn't. On the other hand that civilian did what needed to be done for the benefit of the whole Earth Force. He flew that Raptor well, knocking out three enemy ships—which, nice job by the way." Casey fist bumped Chris. "By doing so you saved Earth Force personnel and a very expensive Tumbler ship, all because we were down a pilot and nobody else could fly that Raptor. So you did something bad in order to do a lot of good," contended Casey.

"Well that was the point of doing all of that," answered Chris.

Casey laughed again and stated, "Yeah and I'm sure you didn't have any fun doing it."

They both laughed at that and Stacey chimed in, "Oh, pilots have fun flying spaceships? Never would have guessed."

"It was strictly for business purposes," alleged Chris.

They continued talking for another minute and Casey asked Chris about how he pulled off the heist. Chris explained the whole thing and Casey thanked them both again for doing what they did. Then he left and said he would do everything he could to get them out of trouble, but not to expect much. With that he left.

Stacey and Chris laid around their cells for a while longer before the doors opened again. They both walked up to the steel pillars to see who was coming this time. To Chris's surprise the first person he saw was Master Sergeant Melissa Lawson, followed shortly by Sergeant Mike Carpenter.

"Well if it isn't the infamous Raptor bandit Chris Skylander," greeted Melissa.

Chris smiled at that name.

Then Mike added, "And his infamous sidekick the evil Stacey Fields."

Stacey laughed at that one.

"Hi guys, how is the free life treating ya?" greeted Chris.

"Life out here is great! You ought to try it, Chris!" joked Mike.

Melissa smacked his shoulder for the comment.

Stacey said, "Thank you for doing that Melissa. I was wondering how I could reach him from inside this cell." The ladies shared a smile between themselves.

"Must be nice," Chris laughed, "What can I do for you guys?"

"I just wanted to come down here and thank you for saving my friend," explained Melissa, "I have to admit Chris, that was well played."

Chris's heart fluttered as his crush finally said something positive toward him. As usual, though, his brain turned to mush and he replied with, "Uh, thanks."

At least he followed it up with a smile and she returned the gesture. Chris thought, "Wow, she is beautiful."

"Yeah and I came down here to hear how you pulled it off! That shit must have been crazy!" joked Mike.

Melissa smacked his arm again.

"Oh yeah, and to thank you for saving my friend, blah blah blah," muttered Mike.

They all laughed and Melissa added, "Mike struggles to express his gratitude but if Casey wasn't here he wouldn't have anyone to laugh at his jokes."

"Whoa, plenty of people appreciate my comedic humor," defended Mike.

Melissa rolled her eyes and crossed her arms.

"Well seriously I do want to hear how this whole thing went down after we launched. It has to be a good story," explained Mike.

Chris and Stacey told the story again for them and both of the pilots seemed to be impressed.

"Damn, Chris, you have balls of steel, and I'm damn impressed with Ms. Fields as well," laughed Mike.

"Thanks, but I have a serious question for you guys," explained Chris.

"Yeah? What?" asked Mike.

"When I was on the observation deck before I went down to grab Stacey and well, steal the Raptor, I was watching the whole battle. We had a three-to-one destroyer advantage, better-trained crew, and a greater number of more advanced fighters. When I emerged from the Leviathan all hell had broken loose. Multiple fighters were down, and more importantly, two of the three destroyers were completely destroyed. What happened?" asked Chris.

The looks on both Mike and Melissa's faces went from cheery to horrified. They looked at each other. Clearly neither knew what to say.

"Guys?" questioned Chris.

Mike seemed to get his thoughts together first. He turned to Chris after another moment of consideration and began speaking in a serious tone that was unfamiliar to Chris.

"It was terrifying," he stated. "It was so big and it came out of subspace with so much power. We didn't stand a chance."

"Mike!" Melissa shouted. "Enough!"

She looked at Chris, and despite her emotions, which were clearly triggered, she managed to calmly say, "We cannot talk about that. It is on a need-to-know basis, and despite your heroics, you are not authorized."

"Oh," muttered Chris as he shared a look of shock with Stacey.

"What happened out there?" thought Chris. "What could

have done that to multiple Poseidon destroyers and managed to scare two Raptor pilots?"

"Sorry, you guys," said Mike. "Can we talk about something else? Like Melissa said, we can't talk about that."

After Mike said that he seemed to get a hold of himself and return to his more light-hearted form.

"Of course," replied Stacey.

There was an awkward silence for a couple of seconds before Mike started making quips.

"Chris, we are going to have to give you a call sign if you keep pulling off crazy stuff like that," joked Mike.

"I was thinking it should be 'The Terminator' or 'The Assassin' or how about 'Thor' 'cause I bring down the hammer!" beamed Chris.

Stacey rolled her eyes and Melissa just laughed. Mike gave Chris a dumb look and then said, "I was thinking more like 'Bananas' cause you would have to be bananas to try to pull off that stunt."

"How about 'Dumbass?' " asked Stacey. " 'Cause you would have to be a dumbass to try to steal from Earth Force."

"Truthful, but a bit too direct," explained Mike.

"Hey, easy guys," said Chris, but they ignored him.

"What about Sergeant Insano?" chimed in Melissa.

"Cuckoo works," added Mike.

"Guys," Chris repeated.

"I thought Looney Tune was appropriate," admitted Stacey

"Oh! What about Wackadoodledoo?" asked Melissa

"Um, guys!" repeated Chris.

"Fine! Bananas it is!" stated Mike.

"Wait, no!" protested Chris.

"I'm good with Bananas," beamed Melissa.

"Bananas does seem oddly appropriate," stated Stacey.

Chris looked at Stacey and declared, "You can't be helping them, Stacey!? You're not a pilot and you helped me pull this off."

"Ya but look where that got me," replied Stacey, "I listened to a man who was bananas and now I'm in jail."

Stacey and Mike laughed and Chris thought, "God no! I am not going to be called Bananas!"

"Well it is settled," professed Mike, "If you ever get out of here, Bananas, the first round at the bar is on us."

Chris started banging his head on the bars of the jail cell.

"Speaking of getting out of here," pried Stacey, "Any word yet? Or are we stuck here for life?"

Melissa actually waved off Mike and fielded this question, "We have debriefed our superiors on this and they know our opinions. Both Mike and I think what you did out there was a good thing, even if you had to do it by, well, breaking a lot of Earth Force laws. We told them our opinions but you have to understand, we're pretty low on the totem pole and this issue will only be resolved by the brass."

"What she said," added Mike.

Stacey and Chris exhaled in disappointment, but what else could they expect.

"Thank you guys for trying," comforted Stacey.

"It's the least we can do for a guy who saved one of our wingmen and the lady who enabled him," replied Melissa.

The four of them talked for a few more minutes and eventually Mike and Melissa took their leave.

Nothing happened for another couple of hours or so until the doors opened up again. This time four marines walked through the doors and up to the cell. Chris recognized one of the marines with the fireman's mustache as the guy who was laughing at his jokes as he was arrested both times.

"Stacey Fields," boomed a different marine, "by the orders of Captain Erik Spear you are hereby released from prison and are to be confined to your quarters until further notice."

"What about Chris?" asked Stacey.

"I do not have any orders for him, ma'am, just you," he replied.

"Well I'm not going anywhere without him," stated Stacey.

"Stacey, just go. I'll be fine and there is no point in you staying down here with me," admitted Chris.

She gave him a look of protest and he gave her a familiar stubborn look back.

"Besides, you can do more for me on the outside than sitting in here. I expect you to visit when you can," added Chris.

"Fine, I guess that's true," sighed Stacey.

She got up as the marines opened up the cell door.

She walked through the doors and two marines took their place at each side of her to begin escorting her back to her quarters. They began walking toward the holding block's main door. Chris watched this happening but noticed one of the four marines stayed back. It was the guy with the mustache. Chris watched him as he watched Stacey walk out of the holding block. When she finally exited and the door shut behind her the marine who stayed back turned around and walked up to Chris's cell.

Chris really wasn't sure what to think at this point. Was that marine going to do something good or bad to Chris? Maybe he was passing on a message, or maybe he was going to torture Chris and that's why they took Stacey out of the cell.

Chris took a step back as the marine walked up to the cell and extended an arm toward him. Once Chris realized there was no weapon and the marine was just extending his arm for a handshake Chris relaxed and shook the man's hand.

"Thank you, Chris," said the marine.

"You're welcome, but what for? My jokes?" asked Chris as he let go of his hand.

The marine chuckled and then explained, "Yes, for the jokes as well. This place can get boring and the humor makes it better. However, that is not the main reason I am thanking you. The boys and I want to thank you for saving our lives."

"Oh yeah? When did I do that?"

"Did you think that Tumbler you saved was empty?"

laughed the marine, "Thirty some odd marines and I were on board, and if you hadn't stolen that Raptor and escaped, we wouldn't be here."

"Oh," was all that Chris could say as he realized what he had done. "Well, you are very welcome . . ." Chris said it in a way that asked for the man's name.

"Corporal Brian Beis is my name, but you can call me Beis, as my friends do," returned Beis.

"Well, great to put a name to the face finally, Beis, and I'm glad I could help you and your men out," commented Chris.

"Yep, me too," replied Beis.

"Well I suppose you have no idea when I am getting out of here either, do you?" asked Chris.

"Nope, that's way above my pay grade, but I have a feeling you will know before too long," replied Beis.

"Oh yeah? Why is that?" questioned Chris.

"Cause they just took your roommate away, and despite this being the military, things move pretty quickly on board this individual ship. Captain Spear and his XO don't usually waste time," explained Beis.

"Well one can only—" started Chris, but he was interrupted by a signal that came into Beis's comms device.

"Standby, Chris," stated Beis as he opened up a communication link with someone. Chris knew the marines had built-in nanite packages that could enable them to receive messages from others internally so nobody else could hear.

Chris waited a moment and watched Beis tilt his head as he listened to the message. Beis sported a Mohawk that stayed straight and rigid despite the tilt in his head.

When it was finished Beis looked back at Chris and asserted, "Well, like I said, I don't think you will have to wait long. I must be going, Chris; thank you again."

"You're welcome," returned Chris as Beis had already turned and begun walking out of the holding cell.

Beis exited the cell and Chris was left to contemplate his

own existence alone. The wait was not long, however, and once again Chris heard doors open up. Three figures stood in the doorway as Chris craned his neck to see who was coming. The figures walked in an authoritative manner down a few stairs with one leading and two flanking the leader. As they stepped into the light Chris immediately recognized the three of them.

The figure in front was none other than Captain Erik Spear. Over Captain Spear's left shoulder was Wing Commander John Sarner and over the captain's right shoulder was Commander Ben Shafer.

"Oh shit," thought Chris as he gulped. "This cannot be a good thing. Are they about to sentence me to death?"

The three walked up to Chris's cell and Chris threw up a salute as he didn't know what else to do. The commander and the wing commander had their hands behind their backs and were looking forward, but not directly at Chris. Captain Spear, however, was looking directly at Chris and he cleared his throat but did not return the salute.

"Mr. Skylander," began Captain Spear, "you have had quite the adventure on board my vessel."

"Yes sir, sorry sir," returned Chris.

"I should have probably denied your access to the observation deck after I saw you observing our battles, but I must admit, I never thought you would use the information you gained from it to steal a combat craft and endanger your life and the crew's life," continued the captain.

Chris was about to say something back when Major Sarner gave him a throat cutting motion so Chris just stood there with a guilty look on his face.

"What you did was reckless, dangerous, foolish, and I will admit somewhat brave, although I'm still not sure that was your intention," explained the captain. "My XO and I both tried to get you to return to the Leviathan, which you refused to do. Normally I would be charging you for treason for those actions."

Chris thought, "Dammit, treason? I was just trying to help.

Wait—he said 'normally.' "

Then Chris asked, "So you are not charging me with treason?"

"Well since you are not a member of the Earth Force Navy and therefore I'm not your commander you did not commit treason, so you will not be punished for treason," explained the captain. "However, you did still steal property from this ship, which is a crime that is punishable with severe prison time."

"I'm sorry, sir, I have nothing left in this world and I was just trying to save lives and take out Zion," retorted Chris.

Captain Spear just looked at him. Those brown eyes felt like lasers digging into Chris's head.

"Please don't punish Stacey for this. I used the fact that I saved her life earlier as leverage to get her to help me. She honestly tried to talk me out of it. I'm the one who deserves to be locked up for life, but please don't wreck her life as well," begged Chris.

Captain Spear's face was rigid as stone. Finally, though, the edge of his lip betrayed him as it curled up in a slight smile.

"What happens to Stacey will depend on you, Chris," mused the captain.

"Me?" asked Chris.

"Yes," stated the captain in a calm tone. "Despite my natural instincts to keep you locked up in that cell until you can be tried for your crimes, you have convinced many of my crew that you honestly had good intentions. Many crewman who have directly interacted with you think I should turn a blind eye to this situation, or at the very least be," he paused, "lenient."

Chris looked up in hope. He started to speak but the three officers gave him a look that said, "Shut up."

"Chris, I try to stick to the book as much as I can. I get the feeling that when I am dealing with you it will be difficult to do so. You are not the only person on board this ship that does these off-the-rail activities," accused the captain as he glanced over his shoulder at Major Sarner.

"With that in mind," continued the captain, "I am going to offer you one chance to make your wrongs a right."

"Whatever you need, Captain," burst Chris.

"Good," pondered Captain Spear as he looked at Chris through a lens of judgment. "Because what you are going to have to do will not be easy. In fact, it is because of this difficult situation that you are going to be given this opportunity. Desperate times call for desperate measures, and indeed these times are desperate."

Chris looked at the captain in anticipation. "What could he be offering?" thought Chris.

"Yourself and Ms. Fields will be conditionally pardoned for all of your previous crimes," offered the captain, "in turn, you will swear yourself in to the Earth Force Navy, temporarily." The captain emphasized the word "temporarily." "You will agree to follow the chain of command to the letter and will be replacing our injured pilot Corporal Higgins. We are down a pilot right now and need all the firepower we can get. You proved that you can be useful in your earlier stunt, and I'm hoping with some proper direction we can harness that usefulness for the mission. I'm not going to lie, Chris, things are bad, and we need all the help we can get."

Chris's jaw felt like it was going to hit the floor, then smash through that and hit the bottom of the ship. He had just been offered the chance to legitimately, if only temporarily, fly for Captain Spear's fighter wing on the Leviathan under Major John Sarner. Thoughts and emotions began flooding into Chris's head. He honestly thought for a second that he might be dreaming until Major Sarner cleared his throat in an attempt to get Chris to pay attention.

"Oh yes!" shouted Chris. "I'm your guy, or pilot, um sir! I'll do whatever is asked!"

"I expect nothing less than complete obedience, Chris.

Do not disappoint me again. If you do, you can expect to be brought up on charges and will spend the rest of your days behind bars. XO, will you do the honors?" asked the captain.

Commander Shafer stepped forward and replaced Captain Spear as the figure closest to Chris. The XO then unlocked Chris's cell door, opened it, and commanded, "Chris, raise your right hand and repeat after me."

Chris raised his right hand and stood with a very rigid posture.

Commander Ben Shafer then proceeded to have Chris repeat back the standard enlisted oath for the Earth Force Military.

Chris stated, "I, Chris Skylander, do solemnly swear that I will support and defend the Constitution of the United Countries of Earth against all enemies, foreign and domestic; that I will bear true faith and allegiance to the same; and that I will obey the orders of the President of the United Countries of Earth and the orders of the officers appointed over me, according to the regulations and the Uniform Code of Military Justice. So help me God."

Before stepping back behind the captain, the XO warned, "Chris, I won't lie. I think we are wasting our time with you. I expect you to prove me wrong."

"Yes sir!" barked Chris as he began walking through the prison door. In his head Chris thought, "Well, great, another XO who has it out for me. Started this off on the right foot."

After he made it out of the cell he turned to the captain and asked, "Sirs, can I ask why we are in desperate times? You basically stated that you could use my help, which I appreciate and will give, but why do you guys need me?"

Captain Spear cleared his throat before he began speaking. The dimples in his cheeks were the only thing betraying his serious expression. "Chris, as I know you are aware, we came into that last fight with overwhelming odds and firepower. We had a three-to-one capital ship advantage, newer and better-equipped fighters, and a better-trained crew, yet when the battle was over we were the only capital ship to survive."

"Yeah I noticed that but couldn't figure it out and the crew wouldn't tell me what happened," replied Chris.

"What I am about to tell you, Chris, is highly classified information that cannot leave this room. Do you understand, Chris?" stated the captain with a raised eyebrow.

Chris nodded with a serious expression on his face.

"Shortly after the fight began we were winning and we launched our Tumbler to recover some very important items from the Iceni. Everything was going according to plan at first. It docked with the Iceni and we were able to extract one of our two objectives. That's when things went wrong. Chris, are you familiar with Zion and his past?" asked Captain Spear.

"I know he used to be an admiral in Earth Force's Navy," responded Chris.

"He was not just an admiral, he was a centurion admiral and he was in charge of one of the special projects divisions. His division was involved in, among other things, some important top-secret science projects. When he left, he staged a very well-thought-out rebellion. It nearly worked and cut off Earth Force leadership from access to our navy. Lucky for us, some brave and loyal people in Earth Force were able to limit the amount of people, equipment, and ships he took with him. Many of them paid for this with their lives. Despite their work, however, he still managed to escape with the most powerful warship ever created by mankind. We have not seen an appearance of this ship since our battle around Saturn where a research base was destroyed. The media is unaware of this ship and our government has been telling them it is just the Iceni that is causing trouble. In reality there is a new class of military capital ship called the Cleaver," explained Captain Spear.

"Hold up, there is a class of ship more deadly than a Poseidon destroyer?" questioned Chris.

"That is correct, and the ship was designed for a special purpose related to the devices held on board the Iceni. That information is need-to-know at the moment, but the point is Zion was in charge of the construction of this ship and during his rebellion he commandeered the Cleaver along with a few Poseidon class destroyers. The Iceni was the last of the destroyers he still had in his possession and we were confident we could handle the situation," stated the captain.

"So the Cleaver showed up and that's what messed up our task force?" asked Chris.

"Correct. The Tumbler we had was docked with the Iceni and had already brought one of the two devices on board when the Cleaver came out of subspace. I assumed it would immediately go after the Tumbler docked to the Iceni. In an effort to save the Tumbler I gave the order for Sergeant Hogan to abort his mission, gather the marines, leave the second device on board the Iceni, and get out of range of the Cleaver. The Olympia and her Captain immediately moved in and tried to position themselves between the Tumbler and the Cleaver. They fought like heroes but at the end of the day the firepower of the Cleaver was too much and the Olympia's fusion reactor went supercritical," admitted the captain.

"It happened too quickly. The firepower of the Cleaver is, well, overwhelming," added Major Sarner with a blank stare on his face.

Chris could tell this was not an easy conversation for the command staff, so he didn't press the situation.

The captain then continued, "Sergeant Hogan was able to detach his Tumbler and avoid the explosion but I was almost positive he would be the Cleaver's next target. Instead the Cleaver deployed fighters and its own Tumbler. It was much closer to the Iceni than either the Mustang or our ship the Leviathan. The Cleaver's Tumbler docked with the Iceni and the Mustang and Leviathan rushed into the battle to try and stop it. As we got in range the Cleaver moved in between its

Tumbler and our ships. We opened fire on the Cleaver and it returned fire at primarily the Mustang. Round after round of plasma impacted the Mustang. The Cleaver had more firepower than both the Mustang and Leviathan, and more armor as well."

"Jesus, there is a ship out there with more than twice the firepower of a Poseidon?" interrupted Chris.

"Yes," responded the captain. "After the Cleaver's Tumbler launched from the Iceni it landed in the Cleaver's bay with, we assume, the second device. It was at that point that the Mustang had taken too much damage and the captain had given the order to abandon ship. After that the Cleaver went back into subspace and disappeared before we could track it."

"Wow," was all Chris could mutter.

"Shortly after that," continued the captain, "was when we realized an unauthorized Raptor had made it out of our hangar bay. The rest I'm sure you are quite aware of."

Chris looked down in confusion. So many things were going through his head. What were the devices? What did a Cleaver ship look like? How had Zion pulled this rebellion off? Why go through all this? Was it really a religious thing like the news said?

Then he looked up at the captain and asked, "So Casey made it back with one of the devices. What does it do?"

"That is on a need-to-know basis, Chris," replied Captain Spear.

"OK, well I'm assuming you need me to help attack the Cleaver?" asked Chris.

"That is the gist of it," replied the XO.

"Well sirs, I'll do my best to make sure you don't regret this decision. What do you want me to do? Are we going into battle again now?"

Major Sarner smiled as he saw the excitement in Chris's eyes. However, it was the captain who spoke up, "Easy, Chris. Your first mission is going to be up in med bay. After that, stay tuned for a briefing. I'll notify you when that is scheduled."

"Med bay? But I'm not hurt," stated Chris.

"Yeah but you won't be much of a pilot unless you get the nanite package the rest of us have," chimed in Major Sarner.

"Wait, I get to have the same nanite packages an Earth Force pilot gets?" beamed Chris.

"That is what the captain just said, and he isn't in the habit of repeating himself," mused Major Sarner.

"Yes!" boomed Chris as he threw up a fist in the air, then realized the rest of them were not in a celebratory mood at the moment and had lost many of their fellow soldiers. "Oh, sorry, sirs," Chris added.

In his head though he was pumped. This was one of the most advanced nanite packages known to man. Chris had never dreamed of having the capabilities it would offer him.

"Well you won't have to worry about me disobeying orders, sirs," explained Chris as he threw up a sloppy salute. "I'm on my way to sick bay."

They nodded and Major Sarner mentioned, "Your second mission is to report to me after med bay and I'll teach you a proper salute. Till then, get to med bay ASAP."

Chris turned around and with that he ran off toward the turbo lift.

CHAPTER 19

With a ding, the turbo lift came to a stop and Chris knew he was at his destination. The lift doors slid open and what everyone called med bay stretched out in front of him.

Clean and white seemed to be the theme, Chris noted mentally. There was not a speck of dirt to be found on any of the walls, the floor, or the ceiling. It made sense for a place that was required to be a very sterile environment, but the visual was still spooky.

Chris walked forward to where a crewman was sitting at what appeared to be a registration desk. He could see little nano-machines cleaning after his footsteps as he walked forward. It was kind of creepy, but hospitals tended to be that way for Chris, as he had never enjoyed visiting them. Something about either himself or someone close to him being ill or injured every time he visited likely caused his general feeling of unease.

Chris shook off these thoughts and tried to stop focusing on the machines cleaning up after him. Instead he greeted the pretty face that awaited at the reception desk.

"Hello there," greeted Chris to a lady who seemed to be in her early thirties with fiery hair. She looked up at him with hazel eyes that complemented her many freckles. She was a thin girl with pale skin that looked like it hadn't seen the sun in a long time. Still, on a warship she was easy on the eyes.

"How can I help you?" she responded with a giggly tone and a smile.

"Well I was told to come up here by the captain. The name's Chris," he returned.

She batted her eyes and blurted, "Oh! You're that guy! I'll get the doctor out in just a minute. Feel free to have a seat over there." The lady pointed her finger with a long red nail on it toward several seats.

Chris turned to go sit down but then hesitated and turned back toward the lady and said, "The name's Chris Skylander. I'm the newest pilot on board the Leviathan. What's your name?"

She looked up at him, smiled, and immediately shot out, "Private First Class Jenifer Reed!"

Chris began making small talk with her. His confidence was sky high at the moment and his new position amongst the crew was fueling that confidence. They continued chatting for a couple of minutes and Chris thought about asking her to join him for a drink at the Afterburner. Sure, she was a bit older than him, but it wasn't too far of a stretch. Besides, it's not like he had anyone else's attention at the moment.

Right when he was about to ask her out he heard a voice from behind in an almost scolding tone say, "Mr. Skylander."

Chris turned around to see another lady in her forties with brunette hair and a medical tablet in her hands. She wore a very serious expression and was borderline intimidating with her hair pulled back in a ponytail. Her height at just over five feet tall and light blue eyes betrayed the serious look she was portraying.

"Yes ma'am," Chris shot back in an instant.

The lady seemed to relax a bit as if his attention was all that was needed to satisfy her.

"Please come with me. I'm your doctor for this appointment."

With that she turned around and began walking through a

door that led further into the depths of the medical bay. Chris looked at Jenifer, nodded, and with a smirk said, "Nice talking to you, Jennifer. Hopefully I'll see you later."

"Hopefully," she giggled and then went back to her computer screen.

In his head Chris thought, "Man, was she into me?" He contemplated this for all of about ten seconds before he walked past a room that had a name he recognized on it. "Andy Higgins" was written on the placard next to the door of the room.

Chris stopped there and asked, "Excuse me, Doctor, is this where the pilot who was injured is staying?"

The doctor stopped, turned around, and nodded.

"Is he OK?" Chris added.

"He is OK for now and resting as comfortably as we can make him," she returned.

"Would it be possible for me to visit him and talk to him?" asked Chris.

The doctor gave him a weird look.

"I'm actually going to be flying his Raptor and I wanted to thank him," he continued.

"Unfortunately you can't right now. He is resting in a medically induced coma. He suffered third-degree burns all over his body and," she hesitated, "he will be receiving a new arm and leg when they are regrown."

Chris had a puzzled look at first until he realized what she was saying. That shot had burned his body and must have melted his arm and leg off. Chris shuddered thinking about that. At least nowadays with the medical technology Earth Force had access to, limbs could be regrown in a couple of weeks and then surgically reattached. Still though, Chris had heard burns were a terribly painful injury, which would explain the medically induced coma. Chris had heard there was no amount or type of drug that could take that pain away.

"I understand," Chris told the doctor.

They continued walking down a hallway until the doctor turned and motioned for Chris to enter a room. He did so and she followed him in, immediately walking to a computer terminal.

"OK," she declared, "My name is Doctor Spartan and I'll be taking care of you today. Please have a seat on that table."

Chris looked at her badge and read that her first name was Kelly. "Nice to meet you," he replied.

She had been looking down at her terminal when she introduced herself so Chris didn't offer her a handshake. This lady seemed a bit oblivious to social norms, but Chris figured that was probably the doctor in her. She did seem intelligent and serious and Chris figured those were better traits to have in a doctor than friendliness.

She went over Chris's medical history with him and asked him a few basic questions about his health. After the initial review was done she cautioned, "Have you ever received a nano-injection similar to the one we have for you today?"

Chris thought about it for a second and then stated, "No."

"All right, you are scheduled to receive a standard issue Earth Force pilot package. Normally people receive this at the academy but lucky for you we keep a few extra on board this ship in case we need to issue replacement nanites," explained Dr. Spartan. "I'm going to inject this into your neck, and from there the nanites will do the work."

"Do the work?" asked Chris.

"Yes, they will integrate into your brain stem mostly, but some will make their way into your eyes, organs, and nervous system. Just a heads up, it is common for people to feel disoriented and lose their senses temporarily. Basically, I am going to have you lay down because you will not be able to function properly for a few minutes while the nanites make their way to their positions, install, and integrate themselves with your body," comforted Dr. Spartan.

"Umm that doesn't sound pleasant," commented Chris.

"It's not usually," chided the doctor with a smile on her face. She chuckled a bit then said, "Relax, everyone in the military these days has the injections. They are very safe, but the first few minutes after an injection suck."

Chris laughed at her description. "At least she was honest," he thought.

He laid his head back on the table. Its cool surface, along with the tension from the imminent procedure, gave him goose bumps. He tried his best, however, to relax and focus on all the benefits these nanites had given Sean during their simulator battle.

Dr. Spartan walked up to him with the injection in her hands. Then she looked down at him with a smile and asked, "Any last questions before the injection?"

She lifted the device and placed it against his neck.

"Nope," Chris responded.

"All right, well hang on. This should all be over in under five minutes," she replied.

She pressed the button and Chris could feel something penetrate his skin. It wasn't very painful. In fact, it itched more than anything. Nothing happened for a solid five to ten seconds when all of the sudden a tingling started all over his body.

"Oh boy," Chris muttered.

"How do you feel?" asked Dr. Spartan.

"Tingly—oh wait, oh shit! I can't see!" Chris responded as his vision literally went black.

"Relax, Mr. Skylander, that is the nanites connecting to your visual sensory organs. During integration certain senses are taken offline temporarily," calmed the doctor.

This freaked Chris out. He was fine with the tingling, but no vision? Chris realized there was nothing he could do, though, so he just prayed the doctor was right. He began breathing in a labored fashion as the tingling went away and a burning sensation began around him.

"OK now I feel like I'm burning up! Is this normal?" exclaimed Chris loudly.

"Yes, that is the nanites connecting to your nervous system and the stem of your brain. Relax and don't fight it; it will go faster," comforted the doctor in an unconcerned tone.

About thirty seconds went by and Chris's vision started working again as if it had never stopped. The burning pain began to go away and Chris thought everything was over. That is until all of a sudden he couldn't hear. The doctor mouthed something to him but Chris couldn't understand and gave her a weird look and pointed at his ear. She actually laughed and then smiled at him. With her hands she motioned for him to calm down again.

Then she put a timer up on the wall that had a countdown. She set it for three minutes and when it got down to two and a half his hearing came back.

"What's that timer for? I can hear again," asked Chris.

"The system should be completely installed by the time it finishes counting down. You should feel normal at that point," Dr. Spartan answered.

"Oh thank God," moaned Chris.

It was very weird having your senses messed with and weird sensations going on in your body. Chris felt like he had taken a lot of drugs and they were taking their toll on his system. After the timer finished, Chris had to admit he was feeling back to normal.

"OK," confirmed Dr. Spartan, "The nanites are installed. Now it's time to boot the system up for the first time."

"OK, what do I do?" replied Chris.

"Ha, you take it easy there, champ. Once the boot starts the software will install and things should function normally in about ten seconds."

Sure enough, numbers and patterns began running across Chris's vision. He couldn't make sense of any of it and wondered how he was going to be able to use all of these nanite enhancements. Again, just like the doctor had mentioned, things went back to normal in about ten seconds.

"All right, now that it is all installed let's turn it on," explained Dr. Spartan.

"OK," replied Chris in a questioning tone.

"Just think about turning it on and your mind will automatically handle the rest," added Doctor Spartan.

Chris did as she asked and an internal heads-up display appeared in the corner of his eye. At first he had green indicators that said everything was installed successfully, and then it switched to saying functioning nominally.

Chris could feel a surge of energy in his body and excitement in him began to build.

"OK Chris, everything is finished. Looks like all of your bio readings are within nominal ranges. You're good to go. Just be aware that you may be a bit tired over the next twenty-four hours as the nanites recondition your nerves, muscles, and other internal systems. You won't be Superman, but you should notice your reaction, speed, and strength will be greater than before. I encourage you to see what your new limits are, but I don't want you doing too much too quickly."

"Awesome!" exclaimed Chris.

"Now get out of here and go get some sleep if you can," ordered Dr. Spartan.

With that Chris got up and made his way out of the room. He was excited and feeling great. He decided it was time to go back to Corporal Reed and ask her out on that date.

As he rounded the corner to the receptionist's desk he put on a big smile. Unfortunately for Chris some Marine was already talking to her and she was clearly interested in the conversation.

"Dammit," thought Chris, "this is just my luck. Oh well, I guess I'll head to the Spacer's Café for a bite, and then the Afterburner for a beer."

Instead of interrupting their conversation Chris made his

way to the turbo lift and hit the button for the Spacer's Café. Before the doors closed he looked back and saw Jennifer Reed waving at him with a big smile. She yelled, "Goodbye Chris! Nice to meet you!"

Chris winked back at her and as the doors closed he couldn't help but notice the scowl on the marine's face.

"Wow," Chris thought. "This ship just got even more fun."

CHAPTER 20

The doors swung open and Chris was greeted with the smooth, calm jazz music that seemed to be forever playing at the Afterburner lounge. He walked in and immediately spotted Mike and Casey sitting at the bar. He began walking forward while at the same time flexing his hands. He could feel energy moving through his system and began thinking perhaps he should have gone and hit the gym up instead to test his new abilities. The doctor had warned him though to take it easy for a day so instead he figured he would try to link up with the pilots.

Chris was going to try and surprise Mike and Casey but the bartender Bill Bronx gave him away by nodding his head at Chris as he approached the bar. Mike and Casey turned around and in unison they yelled, "Chris!"

They all shook hands and greeted each other like old comrades. Chris knew he was wearing a grin a mile wide, and didn't care. Mike then turned around to Bill and shouted, "Give this man a beer!"

"And a shot for all of us!" added Casey.

"OK, beers and shots coming right up," responded Bill.

Mike turned back toward Chris and blurted out, "Bananas! You are going to fly the next mission with us! Congrats on being a temporary pilot!"

Then Casey added, "Yeah man, congrats. Also I heard

Bananas was your new call sign and I have to admit it fits."
Both Mike and Casey laughed.

Chris shook his head in embarrassment, but despite
his new call sign, for the first time in a while he felt like he
belonged.

"Thank you guys for the endearing call sign," Chris
acknowledged.

"You're welcome!" Mike returned. "We got the notice you
had been temporarily sworn in and all the pilots were pumped
that you would be allowed to help—except Sean, of course. He
was saltier than a sardine's ass that they let you in. Probably
just scared you'll give him a run for his money, right?"

"Wait, you mean everybody else? Even Melissa was happy
about what happened?" asked Chris.

Casey laughed and said, "Yep, even Melissa. Now you will
have another chance to get shut down by her!"

Mike burst in with, "Chris, I want you to know a problem
came up with you being a pilot, but don't worry Casey and I
already figured out how to fix it."

"Oh yeah?" replied Chris in a worried tone.

"Yeah," added Casey.

"When we heard you were going to be flying with us we
immediately realized you didn't have a rank," explained Mike.

"Wouldn't I be an ensign since that is the lowest rank?"
questioned Chris.

"Well one would think that, but you are not an actual member of the Earth Force Navy. So technically you're not even an
ensign," mused Casey.

Chris was immediately thinking, "I don't like where this is
going," while wearing a confused look on his face.

"That is why Casey and I thought long and hard for you
Chris. We have decided you will be ranked, Intern!" laughed
Mike.

"Intern Chris 'Bananas' Skylander!" added Casey.

With that everyone raised a glass in the air and Casey

handed Chris his shot.

"To Intern Bananas!" cheered Mike and everyone at the bar toasted to Chris.

Chris couldn't believe that was going to be what the crew referred to him as, but hey, he would take it.

Chris downed his shot and he immediately noticed something scrolling across the top of his field of vision. It was a notification that stated, "Alcohol filtering engaged."

He instinctually blinked and reached to rub at his eye. It truly alarmed him to have a message pop up in the middle of his vision. He was going to have get used to his body having an operating system.

"Somebody just get their first notification?" Mike said with a light jab to Chris's midsection. "Better get used to being a walking, pissing computer, because you're locked in now. Those nanites are actively boosting your liver enzymes to process out the alcohol. They can't totally eliminate the effects—"

"Thank you Jesus!" shouted Casey.

"But you can consider yourself the equivalent of a German heavyweight wrestler when it comes to alcohol tolerance," finished Mike.

"Cool," was all Chris could manage.

Everyone continued sharing their drinks and Chris could tell he was no longer a taboo subject to the other crewmen on the ship. Many of them came by to thank him, especially the marines on board the Tumbler. Even Whistler stopped in for a quick beer and mentioned he approved of the brass's decision to let him out of the cell to help stop Zion.

Chris stayed at the Afterburner talking with his newfound companions for a good couple of hours. Eventually everyone cleared out before getting too rowdy. Everyone knew that they could go to battle stations at any moment and nobody wanted to "pay the drunk price" to sober up.

Chris finished his beer and made his way back to the turbo lift. He figured he could use a good night of sleep and was hoping he would get it. He was already yawning when he exited the turbo lift and he began walking down the hallway toward his quarters. When he rounded the corner to his doorway he was shocked to see Commander Ben Shafer standing at his door with his hands behind his back.

"Sir," Chris blurted out. "Uh, what can I do for you?"

"Good evening, Mr. Skylander," opened the commander.

"Oh, good evening sir," replied Chris.

"I would say let's go in your quarters and have a discussion, but I believe your roommate is in there sleeping. So instead, why don't you take a walk with me?" asked the commander.

"Sounds good to me," replied Chris in an uncertain tone.

They began walking down the hallway side by side, Commander Shafer still keeping his arms behind his back walking in a very rigid military style posture. Everything about Ben seemed to be prim and proper. It was something Chris couldn't stand about him—probably because it reminded Chris of his old XO Brad Singer, although Chris knew it wasn't fair to judge Commander Shafer that way.

After they rounded a bend in the hallway Chris started, "So what is this about, sir?"

Commander Ben Shafer continued to look forward and began speaking in a tempered tone, as if he didn't want many to hear what he had to say. "I understand that you've had a very rough week leading up to this point. Between meeting Zion, losing your old crew, watching a member of your old crew betray you, and then escaping from Zion's own ship the Iceni . . . Well, for lack of a better word you've had a colorful week."

Chris winced a little bit at the usage of the word "colorful" to describe his week, but he didn't get angry as he was pretty sure that was not the commander's intent. They kept walking down the white hallways of the ship.

Commander Shafer continued, "You have also," he paused "been able to distinguish yourself on board the Leviathan, if you look at it under the right lens."

"Uh, thank you, sir," replied Chris in an almost questioning tone.

Chris could tell the XO was trying to get to a point but wasn't sure how to break it to him.

"Sir, if there is anything you need me to do, you just have to ask," stated Chris.

They rounded the next corner and continued.

"Well it is not anything that you need to do, but rather information that I believe you should know about. And instead of hearing it from someone else, I believe it should come from the command staff of the Leviathan," explained Commander Shafer.

"Okaaay," Chris said, drawing out the word.

The commander at this point stopped and turned to Chris. Chris reciprocated the gesture and looked Ben in the eyes.

Ben continued, "I know you have been watching our actions on the command deck, trying to piece together the puzzle of what Zion is doing, and what pissed him off badly enough to get you involved and eliminate your crew. I know you also are concerned about what the Earth Force Navy is doing to stop Zion. Well, Chris, I am going to give you a briefing that all the department heads aboard the ship will be giving a version of to the crew first thing in the morning. Crew members already know some or most of this information, but they'll be getting the full picture as a result of the briefing.

"Additionally, these events are so big that the Earth Force Navy and our government, the United Countries of Earth, can no longer cover them up or deny them. Speaking honestly, that's fine with me since these events will likely forever change the history of our species for better or for worse. As a result, much of this information is going to become public information in approximately four to six hours. However, civilians will receive a more edited version."

Chris gulped and thought, "What the heck is he about to tell me?"

"I received Captain Spear's blessing to give you this information now, but like I said, the department heads will be briefing the crew and it is going to be public information soon. On top of that, I wanted to give you this briefing personally. You'll see why when you read this report," Ben explained.

With that Commander Shafer's hands came around from his back and he handed a tablet to Chris.

Chris reached out and accepted the tablet from Commander Shafer. He was about to read what files it had on it when the XO interrupted again, "I've put together a quick little slideshow based on the briefing that will be going out to the crew members."

"Thank you, sir," returned Chris.

Chris thought to himself, "Well even though the XO has a stick up his butt sometimes, this is pretty cool of him."

Chris saw the tablet showed a timeline starting at the current day and stretching back into the early 2000s.

Commander Shafer began, "Even though this conflict has been going on for weeks, the origins of this story begin long ago, at a time not even Earth Force command is aware of. Hundreds of years ago, back in the time of the United States government, a group of civilians accidentally uncovered what we now know is an alien artifact. At the time, scientists guessed the object had been there for a very long time based on the surrounding area, perhaps even thousands of years. The discovery of the object occurred in the 2040s and no, it was not a spaceship that we used to create some radical technologies from."

While talking, Ben had zoomed in on the 2040s and selected the first picture, showing scientists in white lab coats gathered around a strange object. They appeared to be at the bottom of a construction site. Chris could see concrete pilings and exposed rebar around them. Ben then began scrolling through pictures while talking.

"In fact, little was done with the artifact other than storing it because the object appeared to have no value other than groups of unintelligible markings. For decades we tried applying power to it, or to use it in various experiments, but other than puzzling scientists there was nothing that the people at the time could use it for. Instead, it was stored for over a hundred years. What we didn't realize at the time was that the alien writing was actually a series of complex math equations that gave us clues into how subspace worked. In the early 2150s one of our mathematicians was finally able to make some sense of the markings. He was able to decode and understand one of the first equations the artifact presented."

At this point Chris found himself staring at a scientist sporting an impressive moustache. He was standing behind the artifact smiling. The caption below stated, "Dr. Jack Cleaver." He couldn't believe what he was seeing.

"Wait, Cleaver—that's the name of the big ship Zion has that you told me about earlier," noticed Chris.

"That is correct. The ship was named after the man who discovered the answer to the first equation. After Dr. Cleaver solved the equation they were able to input the answer into the alien artifact and we hoped it would do something fantastic. Instead, all it did was present us with another mathematical riddle. This process continued for years while the time and money invested into figuring out what the artifact had to show us vastly increased. We found out later that whoever left this artifact here did it so that when an intelligent species was ready, they would be guided in their development.

Over time the artifact began teaching our scientists the theory behind subspace. The last equation we solved happened in 2208 A.D. If you know your history, that is two years before subspace was first discovered. That's because it took us two years to build the first prototype subspace drive that worked."

"Wait, so you're telling me the Ancients Theory is true!?" asked Chris in an incredulous tone.

Commander Shafer responded, "Yes, while I'm not a fan of conspiracy theories, that one is surprisingly accurate. I'm sure the government at the time had a field day figuring out not only how the information leaked out, but how to cover it up. Anyways, after we solved this final equation the artifact presented us with one last bundle of knowledge before it stopped working all together. Now it sits as a dormant object hidden away somewhere in a top-secret military warehouse on Earth.

"That last bundle of knowledge the object gave us was that this object was only the first of three objects that were left in this solar system. It told us to find the other two objects and then we could begin our path toward ascension. It also explained that the second alien artifact would be able to open a portal through which we could travel the stars. The purpose of the third object remains unknown.

"Finally, the object gave us more markings. What were thought at the time to be more math equations turned out to be coordinates for the remaining devices' approximate locations, which happened to be in the Asteroid Belt."

"Whoa, so we've known where these things were? We went and got them, right?" asked Chris.

"Not so fast," answered Ben. "Even after being given the approximate location it still took a long time to find the devices. They had been implanted in the Asteroid Belt ages ago, so after countless years of orbiting the sun, their exact location remained unknown. After searching for decades we finally were able to locate the devices. Shortly before we located the devices Zion staged his rebellion. We believe he did this after we were able to narrow down the search since he knew we were close to finding them. This is where you come in.

"Your old crew happened to come across our excavation ship in the Asteroid Belt right after Zion had disabled it. We didn't send a large force in hopes it would go unnoticed. We knew he had spies, and if we had sent a large force he would have seen it and moved to intercept it. However, Zion's spy network was larger than we had thought, and he was still able to figure out that we had found the two remaining devices. So he did what he had planned to do, which was to capture them. We suspect he laid an ambush and had a group of pirates nearby who lay in wait with their systems powered down. When the time was right, they disabled the communications systems and engines of the Big Guppy, then bugged out in order to let Zion know the exact location without sending transmissions.

"Anyways this is when you and your crew showed up. You know the rest of that story, which brings us to where we are today. When we spotted the Iceni in our latest engagement we launched our Tumbler full of marines to secure the remaining two alien artifacts. We were only able to capture one of the two objects, however. The Cleaver intercepted the other. We quickly discovered the device we captured happened to be the second device. More importantly, when we retrieved it we found it had been activated. This, of course, means Zion has the third device on his ship and we are assuming the second device provided him more information on the nature of his third device.

"When the second device was activated it sent a signal out. That signal has been traveling through our solar system, and if it hasn't already, it will soon find the supposed portal. Once this happens, according to the information we have, the portal will activate. We don't know how long activation will take, but when it does we will be able to pick up the portal's signal an equal amount of time later. When our sensors pick up its location, we will be launching the fleet to investigate. Zion, we are assuming, will be doing the same thing. Based on educated guesses from the information we have gathered from the objects, we expect to know the location of the portal in six to ten hours.

"Once the portal is activated and we receive the return signal, there will be no way to hide this from civilians. We believe universities around the solar system will detect the return signal and train high-powered telescopes on the origin. As a result, the Earth Force is already prepping an emergency briefing to civilian authorities and the President of the United Countries of Earth will be calling a system-wide press conference to break the news. Civilians will not receive a briefing on Zion or his rebels, but they will be informed of the portal's existence. Anything beyond the portal's existence is considered highly classified, and any leak will be punished accordingly. Our mission is to capture Zion and the Cleaver. After that we need to secure the portal and await further orders.

"Again, some of what you have read will become public knowledge shortly. However, much will not be, so your discretion is required."

Chris looked up at Ben and nodded to signify his understanding.

Commander Shafer then stated, "I felt like you deserved to hear this from the command staff since it has personally impacted your life and we had answers. I want you to know that your crew's sacrifice was not in vain. If you had not shown up when you did and tried to steal those objects, Zion and his Gate Keepers cult would have both objects, all of his ships, and probably be long gone. Instead you delayed his recovery of the objects and sent out a distress beacon that notified us of his latest position at the time. Basically it is because of you and your crew that we are still in this fight."

"Damn," was all that Chris could mutter. So many thoughts were going on in his mind. This almost felt like a dream. "How the hell did I get caught up in this situation?" thought Chris. "Who are these aliens? Why did they drop these objects off? Why did my crew have to stumble upon the objects Zion was searching for? What does this mean for humanity? Where does that portal lead?" he asked himself.

"I know you have a lot of questions, but I want you to save those questions for our briefing. You will be notified when the time is right. Get some sleep if you can, Chris. Our call to action will be coming shortly. Till then I must return to my duties," said the commander as he took the tablet back.

Ben could tell Chris was in shock at learning the story. He put a comforting arm on his shoulder, gave him a slight squeeze in support, and then walked off.

Chris, standing in shock in the hallway, shook his head in a vain attempt to rid his mind of the thoughts going through it. He was very happy the commander had gone out of his way to prepare this briefing for him. That's not something Brad would have done. Even though Ben followed the rules to the letter, he actually did care about his crew. He even cared about those who were not officially a part of it. For that, Chris gained respect for Commander Shafer and promised himself he would remember that the next time the commander pissed him off.

After staring at the wall for a minute in contemplation of the recent news Chris made his way back to his quarters. He laid down in his bunk to get some shut eye. Unfortunately for Chris, with all the news he had heard his mind was racing and he knew sleep would not come easily. It seemed like just when he thought life couldn't get any crazier, it did.

CHAPTER 21

Chris lay in his bed staring at the ceiling attempting to sleep for what must have been the third straight hour. Stacey slept soundly in a bed near him. He listened to her soft breathing and noticed it had a rhythm to it. At some point he must have finally dozed off because the next thing he knew he shot awake with a loud beeping noise playing internally in his head.

"Woah!" he thought as he sat up and quickly gained his senses. It felt like he had just awakened from a nightmare, adrenaline pulsing. He looked and saw that Stacey was still sleeping soundly in the bed next to him. Then he sat there, stupidly looking around the dark room for a moment, trying to figure out what caused the noise before the realization struck him: "The nanites!"

Chris realized they were able to function as a biological alarm clock if needed. That would take some getting used to.

The culprit of his rude awakening quickly popped up in his internal display. It was a message from Major Sarner. Chris opened it up with a mental thought and a video image of Major John Sarner was displayed on his retina.

"Chris, meet us in the briefing room in five minutes. It's go time for the team and we need to get you and the wing up to speed before our next mission," ordered Major Sarner.

Chris responded quietly with a, "Yes sir."

He hopped up out of bed and over to where his dresser was

located. When he reached in he was surprised to see there was a green jumpsuit inside. "Holy shit!" blurted out Chris.

Stacey must have heard because she made a moaning sound and rolled over to sleep face down.

He put the green jumpsuit on and zipped it up. Sure enough he looked to the right side and it had a black patch over his right pec muscle that read "C. Skylander" in white-stitched lettering. On his left shoulder there was a patch that had the familiar 72nd Flying Panthers. This, of course, was Major John Sarner's wing on board the Leviathan.

"Awesome!" thought Chris, making sure not to bother Stacey anymore.

Chris finished getting himself together and walked out of his quarters in the hallway. He was about to begin walking forward when he realized he didn't know where he was going. He mentally dialed up Major Sarner again and asked where he was supposed to be. He had never been to the pilot briefing room, and didn't know where it was.

The major scolded him for taking a long time to report to the briefing room and then told him how to get directions.

"Jeez, I'm late already?" Chris thought.

It was pretty neat though, because the major explained all he had to do was talk to the ship's computer and it would send him directions. Shortly thereafter, an artificial green arrow showed up in his vision highlighting the path he had to take.

Chris made his way to the turbo lift and his vision automatically highlighted the button he needed to press. He pressed the button and the turbo lift sent him flying in the correct direction. Several seconds later it came to a stop and the doors whooshed open. From there Chris made his way down the hallway to a room that was closed. On one side of the door was a placard with the label "Briefing Room."

Chris pressed the open button and a small but tech-intense room with several familiar faces greeted him.

Major Sarner was in the front of the room with a wall full

of graphics being displayed at his back. He even had a small podium on one side of that wall from which he apparently conducted the briefings. In between Major Sarner and the door Chris was about to walk through were several rows of plush leather seats. Most of them were empty minus the four occupied chairs. In those chairs at various locations were the three remaining members of Wing Commander Sarner's wing, along with Sergeant Hogan. Chris wasn't sure what the extra empty seats were for but he wasn't about to embarrass himself by asking.

"Glad to see you felt like joining us today, Chris," greeted the wing commander.

Chris walked through the door and made his way to the nearest unoccupied seat.

Lieutenant Quick made sure to add with an eye roll to cap the gesture off, "You're late."

"Sorry sirs," was all that Chris could muster but this seemed to be more than enough for the rest of the team. Chris was unsure how the heck they all had gotten there faster than him but that would be a mystery to solve another day.

Major Sarner spoke up again, "As you all know, we have had a field promotion or acquisition. I'm pretty sure you all know him already but just in case this is temporary pilot Chris Skylander."

"Whoa, my apologies, Major, but that is not entirely accurate," Mike chimed in.

The wing commander gave him a quizzical look and even Chris didn't know where Mike was going.

"This is not temporary pilot Chis Skylander, this is Intern Chris Skylander, call sign Bananas!" Mike blurted out.

The rest of the room laughed and even Major Sarner couldn't help himself but chuckle a bit.

"All right, everyone knock it off; we have some serious business to discuss," ordered Major Sarner.

Chris tried to sit down in the nearest seat in the back of the room when Major Sarner added, "Chris, sit up front here right next to me."

"Yes sir," replied Chris although he knew that he was literally being treated like the new kid in class.

Chris made his way forward and sat down. Sean was in the row behind him and leaned forward and whispered, "Intern sounds like a nice rank for you, kid."

Chris ignored it and kept looking forward at the wing commander.

"As you all know, the last mission didn't go as planned for us. Now we are having to react to the situation, which is never a good thing. A lot has changed though, since our last mission, and I'm now cleared to fully brief everyone," said Major Sarner.

"So you're not going to conveniently forget to tell us about a massive Poseidon-killing ship running around out there?" asked Lieutenant Quick. Mike and Melissa chuckled at the obvious outburst directed at command. They had clearly read their briefing materials the night before.

"Stow it, Lieutenant," was all that Major Sarner replied.

A graphic of a massive-sized ship began to be displayed on the wall behind Major Sarner. It broke down the ship into several sections highlighted by different technical information on the ship. In comparison to the Poseidon destroyer, the new Cleaver was over twice as long.

"What we have here is the latest creation the special project division was working on. It is called the Cleaver and it is a deadly new class of ship that has been under development," began Major Sarner.

A couple of jaws dropped in the audience as the pilots were able to take a good look at the beast in front of them without worrying about getting shot at like before.

Major Sarner continued, "At twelve hundred meters long the Cleaver class ship is over twice the length of the Poseidon and it has well over four times the mass. Some other technically relevant information is that the ship is designed to house up to five wings of fighters and three Tumblers, which again is much larger than the wing a Poseidon destroyer can hold."

Chris's jaw was now slack as he thought of how big this ship must have been to be able to hold and service that many other ships.

"It has a weapons load out of twenty laser cannons, twenty plasma cannons for capital ships, and ten rail guns—not to mention various point defense and flak turrets," continued the major. "Basically, this thing is a fortress of destruction."

"No shit," muttered Mike.

The major gave him a look but nothing more.

"So how do we kill something that big?" asked Chris. "Nukes?"

"Nobody uses nukes, dumbass," commented Sean in a condescending tone that caused Chris's blood to get hot.

"Lieutenant Quick, if I need your help giving a briefing I will ask for it," Sarner shot in a tone that elicited a grunt and frown from Sean. "To answer your question, Chris, while nukes are exceptionally powerful, they're slow-moving compared to lasers and rail guns. Ships could easily pick them off long before they got close. If someone was dumb enough to try to deliver one via bomber it would be a suicide mission. In space there is no matter to dampen the radiation so the resulting blast would fry any electronics in the area and cook any human pilots in the vicinity with gamma rays. As a result, they're seldom part of a spaceship's arsenal except in specialized missions. So to answer your first question, I'm afraid overwhelming conventional firepower will be the solution we use against this enemy."

"When did we design this ship and how exactly did Zion get a hold of it?" asked Sean.

"Well, Lieutenant, if you'd read your briefing you'd know the answer to that," Sarner quickly replied to the chuckles of others in the room, Chris included. "But for the sake of expediency, I'll give you the short version. This ship was built with the 'devices' in mind. Earth Force knew that if the rumored portal was real then we would need a capital ship capable of standing on its own far from Earth. Unlike the colony ships of the past, this ship would need to be armed in case we ran into another species of equivalent or even greater technology. With Zion overseeing the project he had unlimited access to it."

Major Sarner spent several more minutes going over the technical specifications of the Cleaver. One of the key things he noted was how the Cleaver was not using older generation fighters like the Skimmer and instead had a full complement of Raptors and Lightnings on board.

After a while Sean must have been getting bored because he spat out, "So what's the actual mission?"

"Another good question," replied the major, ignoring Sean's snarky tone. "As you all know we were able to recover one of the two devices. What we didn't know last mission was that the device we recovered had already been activated. As you are already aware, when it was activated this device sent out a signal that will soon reach its destination, if it hasn't already. Now we do not know where its destination is until we detect it with our sensors, but based on our intelligence findings we think that it will be found in the very near future. That is why we want our squadron ready and the Leviathan prepped for action. Once Earth Force command picks up this portal signal we will jump to the location ASAP."

"Is the Cleaver at the location now?" asked Mike.

"Probably not, but we have a feeling just like us it will go there as soon as they detect the signal. We can only hope we beat them to it and are ready for when they get there," replied Major Sarner.

"So what does this portal do?" questioned Casey Hogan.

This last question made the major a bit uncomfortable. He sighed and then began explaining, "We believe the portal has been a part of our solar system for thousands of years, and has the ability to generate a wormhole to somewhere we've never been. Kind of like our subspace drives, but much, much more powerful. We believe this portal will change the course of human history as we know it."

"Will we know where the wormhole will take us when we get there?" asked Chris.

"No, but we'd expect it connects us to another solar system or even another galaxy. Wherever it goes, there's a good chance there will be intelligent life waiting for us. On that note, we also need to be prepared, in case opening the wormhole provides a way for an invader to come to our little home in the galaxy," returned Major Sarner. The room was dead silent at this point. After a moment Mike finally broke the silence.

"So what do Zion and the Gate Keepers want with this wormhole? Are they really just a bunch of religious nuts who believe the aliens are our gods? That's what the news says."

"Zion and his cultlike following are definitely crazy. It's doubtful they're doing this for religious purposes, but their exact motivation is unknown," returned Major Sarner.

"Ha! More like we do not need to know," quipped Sean.

The major just ignored him.

"Twenty-four hours ago I was not aware that aliens existed. Now they do! That is pretty awesome!" beamed Chris.

"Easy there, Chris. We know aliens existed at one point in this galaxy, but we do not know if they're still alive now," returned Major Sarner.

"What does it take to destroy this Cleaver ship? How many Poseidons does Earth Force believe will be required?" pondered Sean.

"Command estimates that at least four, preferably five Poseidon destroyers will be required along with their complements of fighters to bring down a fully operational Cleaver class vessel," returned Major Sarner.

"So does command plan on bringing that many ships to the table?" questioned Sean again.

The pilots immediately began chirping amongst themselves in doubt.

"Pilots!" boomed the wing commander and the pilots shut up, "Command is taking this very seriously. We are currently vectoring in ten Poseidon class destroyers with up to an additional three after resources are freed up."

"Damn," whispered Sean in surprise.

"Whoa, I have never seen that many Poseidon class vessels at one time," blurted out Mike.

Then Major Sarner explained, "So this is the mission. Once we figure out where this wormhole is located we are going to jump to that location, secure it as quickly as possible, and wait for the Cleaver to arrive. If it does arrive and doesn't surrender peacefully, then we'll have to take it out at all costs. We cannot let it get through that portal."

"I know this is crazy, but I feel like I have to ask," questioned Chris, "What if aliens show up? I mean, you said that the portal could go two ways?"

"It isn't crazy, Chris, but all of our pilots and command personnel are fully trained in first contact protocol. As far as you're concerned, if that happens just don't do anything unless told and let our leadership handle things. Now, any other questions?" stated Major Sarner.

Nobody raised their hands or had any questions.

"All right, this is the part that gets a bit tricky," Wing Commander Sarner revealed, "because nobody knows exactly when we will detect the signal and nobody knows exactly where it will be coming from. Ships will be arriving at different times. Once each Poseidon vessel arrives it will launch its fighter wings. Then it will form a defensive perimeter around the wormhole. The goal is to get at least five Poseidon class ships into position before the Cleaver arrives, which is what command recommends is needed to stop the Cleaver."

The display behind the wing commander showed a graphic of five ships moving in around a circle at the center labeled "portal."

"From there, with fighters already launched and in

formation, we hold the line and wait for the Cleaver until relieved from duty," continued Major Sarner. "Any questions?"

Chris thought of a couple but didn't want to sound nervous so he kept his mouth shut. Mike, however, did not show any restraint.

"What are the chances we get lined up before the Cleaver arrives?" asked Mike.

"Unknown at this time," responded the wing commander.

The pilots began grumbling at that response but for the most part remained on board.

"All right," began the wing commander again. "After additional ships arrive they will form up in the perimeter. If you do not encounter any resistance, which is unlikely, after two hours you will be relieved of your shift. As I said before there will be ten Poseidon vessels vectoring into position with us. The names of those vessels in addition to the Leviathan are the E.F. Expedition, Iowa, Britain, Oxford, Hamilton, Paris, Lion, Pontiac, and Ranger."

"Holy shit that's a lot of capital ships," thought Chris.

"If there is nothing else, pilots, then report to the ready room! Dismissed!" barked Major Sarner.

With that all of the pilots sitting in their chairs except Chris got up, saluted, and started shuffling down the center aisle. The wing commander saluted them back. Chris, realizing he had missed the memo, stood up and threw the best salute he could muster at the wing commander. Major Sarner saluted back and said, "We still have to work on that salute."

"Come on, Chris!" shouted Mike as he waved at Chris to join him and the other pilots.

Chris began a brisk-paced walk toward Mike. Mike himself turned around and started jogging after the other pilots. With that Chris picked up the pace and followed him toward the ready room.

CHAPTER 22

A s it turned out, the jog from the briefing room to the ready room was a pretty short one for the pilots. After making their way out of the briefing room, down a hallway, then through another door, Chris found himself in what looked like a locker room and command center all in one. The pilots referred to it as the ready room. On one side was a row of equipment lockers with seats. Each locker was huge and had a pilot's name and call sign on it, showing who was assigned to it. Inside the lockers were all sorts of gear for each pilot. Chris noticed one of the lockers next to Mike had what looked like printer paper taped to it. The printer paper had "Intern Bananas" written on it in bold letters.

"Oh crap, this has become official," thought Chris.

Chris walked over to the seat in front of his locker and continued to survey the scene. On the other side of the room was a wall with several graphics being displayed, much like the ones shown in the briefing room. It displayed the ship's status and other parameters of the mission they were about to embark upon. Chris also noticed to one side there was a hall leading to full-sized restrooms with showers. Chris could tell the Earth Force spared no expense for its pilots. The last major thing Chris noticed was a large red door on the opposite side of the room he had walked in from, with the word "Hangar" labeled above it.

Chris must have looked lost in his own world because Mike finally gestured at him, "Sit down, I'll help you out after I get all set up."

Chris sat down and watched as all the pilots began suiting up, putting on their spacesuits and other combat accessories. Chris tried to pay attention as he was sure he would be next. Just then some old school rock and roll started playing. The guys, and even Master Sergeant Lawson, all seemed to be getting into it. Chris was about to ask Lieutenant Quick a question, but before he could get a word out Sean stated, "Not now, kid. Everyone has a pregame ritual and you don't want to jinx us."

Chris went back to observing as the team in their busy preparations kept suiting up. He could tell Sean was right. Mike was wearing some kind of antique headphones with a wire coming out of them. He bobbed his head while putting on gear. Casey was doing a little miniworkout prior to putting on his gear, starting with pushups, sit ups, and a pull-up bar he'd hidden in the corner. Sarner was intently writing some kind of note. Sean was looking at himself in a mirror, adjusting his hair with the suit pulled up to the waist. Strangely enough, Melissa didn't seem to be doing anything. After a second Chris realized she was meditating!

After a few minutes of watching, Chris figured it was time for him to start getting prepped on his own. He noticed that the first thing everyone did including Melissa was strip off their jumpsuits and get into just their underwear. It was all he could do to not keep stealing glances at her out of the corner of his eyes. From there things got interesting. Chris reached forward and opened the locker he was assigned.

As he stood in awe looking at his suit, Mike walked over to him from his own locker with the headphones around his neck and began instructing him on what to do. It was pretty simple, but the amount of technology at Chris's disposal was awe inspiring. Chris began putting on a standard issue Earth

Force pilot suit, which was an impressive piece of kit. First off, as Mike explained, it was airtight and capable of supporting him in the cold emptiness of space. At the same time, it was extremely light and flexible. The last thing a pilot needed during the heat of battle was a heavy cumbersome suit that prevented free movement. Mike continued to tell him about how the suit was resistant to small arms fire as well, but not to count on it in a real firefight, if that ever happened. After the suit was on it automatically began tightening up in certain areas and loosening in others to fit Chris properly.

"Wow, is this smart material?" asked Chris.

"Yep, this suit is smarter than you are, Chris," joked Mike back at him.

Mike continued showing Chris the process. Next up were the boots and gloves that would help seal Chris off from the vacuum of space were he to eject. From there Mike continued explaining how the oxygen system worked and how the suit could recycle the air he had for hours at a time. There were more details but Chris's mind began wandering some before Mike reached into the locker and grabbed something interesting.

"This here is your combat knife," stated Mike. "It has a monomolecular edge."

Chris looked at the eight-inch long blade as Mike pulled it from its sheath.

"What does that mean?" asked Chris.

"Well, it basically means this blade is sharp as hell. You can cut through almost anything with this bad boy before it dulls," responded Mike.

"Oh nice! Let's test it out!" burst Chris.

"Umm how about no, Chris. We have to be ready for this mission, and honestly, if you get to the point where you need your knife, you fucked up," laughed Mike.

Chris thought about it for a second and confessed, "Yeah, I guess that's true."

Then Mike put the knife back in the sheath and strapped it to Chris's left leg around the calf. From there Mike reached into the locker again. Low and behold he pulled out something Chris was finally familiar with. It was none other than a Laz Tech laser pistol.

Mike probed, "Have you ever seen one of these?" as he held up the weapon with a smirk on his face.

"Actually that's the first and only piece of equipment you've shown me so far that I do know about!" beamed Chris.

"Oh really?" pried Mike.

"Using a pistol in video games doesn't count," joked Sean.

"Actually I shot a man with one last week," replied Chris in an unconcerned voice. He figured this would probably be one of the few times he would impress any of them.

The rest of the pilots all looked at him with an "Are you serious?" expression that quickly changed to an "Oh shit, he is serious" expression.

Chris smirked internally, as pilots lived off of their egos and he had finally checked them for once. Chris was pretty sure he was the only person in the ready room that had shot a man with the pistol.

"Well, all right then, Chris, you and the major are the only ones who have done that before," commented Casey from a few seats over.

Chris was surprised to hear Major John Sarner had shot someone with a pistol, but upon further examination the major was the only one who wasn't concerned with Chris's previous statement and instead seemed to be in his own world getting suited up for flight.

"Ha, yeah, I guess I don't have to show you how to use this then," stated Mike. "Still, if you find yourself using this pistol or the knife, you have fucked up. The only weapons you should be using are the ones attached to your Raptor."

"You mean Higgins's Raptor," added Sean with a hint of distain in his voice.

"Of course," replied Mike as if it wasn't an issue at all.

The last major piece of kit that Chris was introduced to was his helmet. Chris was surprised by how much it looked like an old fighter pilot's helmet from back in the early twenty-first century. It had the 72nd Flying Panthers emblem on it and tinted glass where the eyes went and a standard mask for breathing. Chris was not too impressed.

"It kind of looks old," muttered Chris.

"Well it's not," replied Mike. "This helmet's primary purpose is to keep your head intact and you breathing. That's why it is made of the same Duranium metal that your ship's armor is made of, and the visor is transparametal, same as a Raptor's cockpit canopy. You see, in the old days these helmets were full of advanced hardware and software, and in many smuggler vessels that's how it is today. But in the Earth Force navy we have the latest and greatest nanite software packages, which automatically interface with your fighter through this helmet. Any visuals or information needed are displayed on your visor, retina, or cockpit heads-up display, based on your preference. So the need for computers built into your helmets doesn't exist for us."

"Damn, that's impressive," responded Chris.

"No shit, Sherlock," laughed Sean.

Mike put the helmet on Chris and it automatically adjusted to the size and shape of his head. Then he removed it again and told him, "No need to just sit with this on, put it on when it's go time! Between you and me, it makes us look cool walking out there with the helmets at our side."

At this point Chris had noticed that all the other pilots were fully suited up with their helmets off and waiting in their seats in front of their lockers. Mike finished up all the little adjustments to Chris's suit and told him he was ready to go.

"Now you just have to hurry up and wait," joked Mike.

"Get used to it, Bananas. It's part of being in the military," laughed Casey.

"He won't have to; he is temporary. Higgins will heal and will be back," provoked Sean.

"Relax, Sean. He's doing everything he can to help us. How about you act like an officer for once and build him up instead of tearing him down every chance you get," spat Melissa in a slightly scolding tone.

To Chris's surprise, after a grunt from Sean, this seemed to work and he shut up.

Chris sat in his chair thinking about all the stuff that had happened to lead up to this point. In his head he said, "Dad, look at me now. I know it's unbelievable, but I am a real pilot in the Earth Force, about to go on a critical mission that could determine the future of humanity. I just wish you could have been here in person to see it." A tear began forming in the corner of his eye, but Chris subtly wiped it away quickly. There was no room for weakness right now, and he couldn't stand the thought of someone in this room seeing him tear up.

As if on cue, Sean stood up and changed the music and started shouting to fire people up. He switched it to an old rock song from back in the twentieth century. Chris had never heard it before, but his internal display said it was called Long Tall Sally by Little Richard. Heads were bobbing and the team was singing along, all except for Major Sarner, who looked with an approving grin at his team. Mike then started playing his air guitar. Chris could tell the whole team was getting pumped up and ready to go to war.

Shortly after the song began Sean reached into his locker and pulled out a small bag. Chris saw from his seat that the bag had the label "Red Man" on it. Sean reached in and grabbed a big handful of something that looked pretty gross to Chris. Then to Chris's surprise he put a handful of the stuff into his mouth. Sean's cheek bulged outward every time he bit down and chewed on the stuff. He then handed the bag to Major Sarner, who shook his head. Next up was Melissa, who made a raspberry sound with her mouth and waved him off.

"Yes sir," replied Chris with a sloppy salute and a grin on his face as he stole another look at Rachel watching from below.

Whistler rolled his eyes and groaned, "No, Chris, you're thinking with the wrong head already." Whistler turned around and as he walked down the stairs he commented, "Lord, why do all the pilots just think about girls and shooting other ships."

Chris blushed a bit as Whistler called him out in front of Rachel. Then he put his helmet on and pushed the button to close the canopy as Rachel and Whistler pulled back the stairs. He glanced over one more time when the canopy was closed and the stairs were far enough away. Whistler and Rachel both flashed him a thumbs-up, saying he was good to go.

Chris then began the startup procedure getting everything ready.

About ten seconds later Chris heard a voice over his comms, "All right, everyone is online and ships are ready to go!" Chris quickly recognized the voice as that of his wing commander. "I just got word, however, that this is a longer than usual jump. Everyone get their systems operational but be prepared to sit tight for a minute."

Chris double checked everything in his cockpit and all systems were showing green, meaning they were good to go. Chris remembered Mike telling him military life was all, "Hurry up and wait." Chris was starting to realize Mike wasn't joking, as there was a lot of that going on today.

About twenty or so minutes later Chris felt the transition from subspace into normal space. It was a weird thing, as nobody could really quantify how people could tell from inside a ship with no windows. But for some reason you could feel the universe around you changing slightly. Some scientists argued it was the gravimetric waves changing their effects on you. Others argued it was a magnetic force interacting with your body that gave the transition away. Chris didn't know the real answer but the point was he could just feel it.

"It's go time, Panthers," came the wing commander over the comms.

With that Chris throttled up the reactor and his Raptor slowly began lifting off the hangar deck. At the same time, the massive external hangar doors began opening. Chris could see the faint glow of the force field filling in the gaps between the doors as they widened.

"All right pilots, line up. Chris, you will be the last fighter out and will be on the furthest left side of the V formation," ordered the wing commander.

"Yes sir," responded Chris.

The doors fully opened and Chris watched as Major Sarner was the first one out. As he left he hit his afterburners and disappeared from sight. Next up was Maniac aka Sean Quick, then Ice Queen aka Melissa Lawson, and finally Joker aka Mike Carpenter. Chris knew that meant he was next so he lined up his ship, gave it some throttle, and after passing through the force field, hit his burners. He was pressed back into his seat hard as his heads-up display highlighted his wing's formation ahead of him and automatically highlighted a course to follow to form up with his wing.

CHAPTER 23

Chris let off the afterburners and relaxed a bit as he maneuvered his ship into formation. As soon as he formed up with his wing he took a second to look around. There were no planetary bodies anywhere in sight, which he didn't find surprising. What he did find surprising was that other than stars, everything else was pitch black. The light reflected off the other ships was noticeably dimmer, meaning they were very far away from the Sun, alone in the emptiness of space. Chris could feel his skin tingling. Something seemed off about this place. It was definitely somewhere that mankind had no bases and probably had never visited up to this point.

"Where the hell are we?" Chris thought.

It took Chris a moment to realize, with the assistance of his nanites, the slightly brighter star relative to the rest of them near the top of his canopy was Sol.

Just then a message came in and Chris, along with the whole wing of fighters, took the incoming transmission. The face that popped up on his display belonged to none other than Captain Erik Spear.

"All right, Panther wing, listen up. Here is the situation," started the captain. "The signal came from far below the ecliptic plane of our solar system, about 30 Astronomical Units from the sun. Roughly the distance of our sun to the orbit of Neptune. As such, that is where we are all located now."

"Dang," Chris thought. Everywhere he'd ever been had roughly been on the ecliptic plane of the solar system. Being 30 AU below it was like falling way, way underneath the map and seeing the world above him. Before he could ponder this further, however, Captain Spear continued.

"We are currently the second ship to arrive here, as the Iowa beat us by a minute. Check your scanners, as there are going to be many more ships arriving from subspace. We do not believe all of them will be friendly, either. So keep your heads on a swivel and begin securing the area starting with the portal. Captain Spear out."

"Roger that, Captain," responded Apocalypse, which was Major Sarner's call sign, "You heard him, boys. Let's secure this portal."

"Holy shit!" exclaimed Maniac, "The portal is at our eight o'clock low! I've never seen anything that big other than a moon or planet!!"

"Keep it cool, Panther wing. Let's head toward it while maintaining formation," ordered the wing commander.

As Chris's wing maneuvered into position the portal came into view right in front of him. Chris's jaw dropped in awe of what he was seeing. The thing they were calling the "portal" was a massive structure. Chris was unsure if it was a ship, a device, or a space station, but whatever it was it was huge. It was a massive ring-shaped structure that measured roughly ten kilometers in diameter. The center of the ring-shaped structure was empty, but you could not see stars, just a jet-black emptiness that seemed unnatural and left Chris with an uneasy feeling. It wasn't one solid piece, however. Instead, the ring was made up of eight different pieces of structure that moved along the outer circumference of the ring. These structures were larger than any Poseidon ship and were moving around the circumference at thousands of kilometers per hour. What made the construction even crazier was the four smaller structures were moving in a clockwise direction around the circumference while the four larger pieces moved counter-clockwise. The half that moved clockwise were slightly closer to the center of the ring while the counterclockwise sections were a bit farther away from the center. This way, when they came to the same spot in their rotations the pieces of structure didn't collide. They just looked like they almost touched but passed by each other. It was a crazy sight to see and nothing like anything the Earth Force Navy had in its arsenal.

"Look," Joker mentioned, "the middle of the ring is just black. I wonder why we can't see stars from the other side in the center."

"Let's close on that object," ordered Apocalypse, "but keep a couple of clicks of distance between you and it. I don't think it has any defense mechanisms but I don't want to find out."

Everyone acknowledged the order and began approaching the portal. They were still very far away but it was so big it could still be seen clearly by the naked eye.

Chris checked his scanners and could see the Iowa was at his ten o'clock. It was too small to be anything other than a spec in the distance at this point but using his nanites and ships cameras Chris saw that it had launched its wing of fighters as well. Both Poseidons had retained their Tumblers but Chris knew they were staged and ready to launch at a moment's notice. They would be used if the Cleaver showed up and the Earth Force was able to successfully disable it. The marines on board would then attempt to regain control of Earth's most prized space vessel.

Major Sarner and the Panthers continued flying toward the portal, leaving the Leviathan behind, as it was not nearly as fast as the fighters, but all ships were converging on the massive structure.

Chris was still in awe of it. Apparently it had been constructed by the aliens known as the Ancients thousands if not millions of years ago. Chris couldn't believe this thing had been out here the whole time, inactive and hidden, just waiting for someone to press the "on" button.

"Heads up, we have another subspace signature coming in," said Commander Ben Shafer over the comms.

Chris checked his scanners and looked up. Sure enough at his two o'clock a bright spec of light began to appear as a subspace portal opened up. Chris tensed up in anticipation of whoever was coming through that portal. He wondered if the rest of the wing was as nervous as he was.

Chris couldn't visually see what was coming out of that subspace portal since it was very far away, so he kept his eyes glued to the sensor's display. An unknown object began emerging and his scanners quickly recognized it as a Poseidon class vessel. Shortly after that his sensors picked up the transponder signal that identified it as the E. F. Hamilton.

Chris exhaled in relief, as it was a friendly vessel. That also increased the odds of success for the team, as that meant they had three Poseidons in system already. They needed at least one, preferably two more before they could take down the Cleaver, according to the briefing.

Chris overheard the command chat as the captain of the Hamilton exchanged greetings with the Iowa and the Leviathan. Shortly after it arrived Chris's sensors began picking up the readings of the Hamilton's fighters launching from its fighter bays.

The next thirty seconds were pretty uneventful as everybody continued to close on the main portal, which had now been designated the Colossus Portal. It continued to grow in the field of view as Chris and his fighter wing got closer.

"Heads up, team, we have another subspace signature coming in. It's a massive one as well. This may be our main objective," came the voice of the captain of the Iowa.

Chris didn't know who the man was but it didn't matter. They all had the same objective.

He continued looking ahead as his scanners starting picking up the swirling blue and white signatures of a giant subspace portal opening up. The scanners showed the subspace portal was coming from the far side of the Colossus Portal, meaning it was on the opposite side of the Leviathan relative to the Colossus Portal. In addition, Chris noticed that there were roughly 50 other smaller subspace portals opening up around the big one on the scanners.

Chris watched as the scanners started identifying the ships on his heads-up display.

"OK boys this is it," reported Apocalypse over the comms, "The Cleaver has arrived and it's bringing a compliment of roughly fifty fighters. Looks like they're all Skimmers as well."

"I thought that ship could only carry five wings of fighters," asked Joker, "and weren't they supposed to have the latest types of fighters? Not the old Skimmer classes?"

"I guess these were the leftover ships he has," speculated Wing Commander Apocalypse, "He probably still has the main compliment of fighters in the Cleaver's bay."

"Shit," shuddered Maniac, "You're telling me we have fifteen fighters and three Poseidon ships against a Cleaver class ship with an escort of fifty fighters, not to mention possibly twenty-five in reserve in its docking bay? We can't take that many!"

"Come on, Maniac, I thought you were the best pilot in the fleet. Should be easy for you," mocked Ice Queen over the comms.

"I'm great, not stupid," returned Maniac, "We need to fall back until we can even the odds."

"Easy, Panthers, maintain course and remain calm. The enemy force has arrived but we still have a lot of ships coming in to back us up," soothed Apocalypse in a calm voice.

Chris could tell that Major Sarner was the real deal as he could hear some of the pilots getting antsy. He couldn't blame them either; unless more backup arrived they were flying into a meat grinder. Chris guessed Major Sarner must have faced odds like these before.

"All right, let's hit the burners team," ordered the wing commander.

Panther wing accelerated in unison as they closed on the Cleaver and its huge compliment of fighters. They were the furthest away from the Cleaver and didn't want to let the Iowa's or Hamilton's wings engage without their support.

Just then another subspace signature began to appear on radar. Chris checked his scanners and it was the E.F Ranger. It was the closest of the Poseidon ships to the Cleaver but still had enough distance and time to launch its own wing of fighters.

"That will help even the odds," Chris comforted over the comms.

"Yeah, it's still fifty versus twenty," returned Maniac, "Your math doesn't add up well for us, Bananas!"

Chris began getting nervous as they passed by the Colossus Portal and began closing in on the Cleaver, which was still just a spec in the distance. The Colossus Portal freaked him out with its jet-black center. There were so many unknowns regarding it. Chris was sure scientists would be pouring into the area should they win today's battle for the chance to study the object.

"The Cleaver is launching fighters. They look like a combination of Raptors and Lightning fast attack fighters," came an unfamiliar voice over the comms. Chris's computer identified it as wing commander of the E.F. Iowa's fighters.

Chris checked his scanners again and he saw that the enemy fighters were forming a perimeter around the Cleaver and that his wing, along with the Iowa's and Hamilton's, were meeting up to synchronize their attacks. Chris figured nobody wanted one wing of fighters going in alone as they would be overwhelmed quickly.

Just then a familiar southern-accented voice came over the comms, broadcasting on all frequencies, as far as Chris could tell.

"Gentleman, there is no need for this fight to happen. As a former admiral in the Earth Force I can assure you I do not have hostile intentions, but will defend myself if forced to."

"Ignore this shit, pilots," commented Apocalypse over the wing's frequency.

Zion continued, "Your leaders have deceived you. They want you to think I am the bloodthirsty head of some religious cult who worships aliens and wants to kill you. That is simply not true. Your leaders are the bloodthirsty ones, focused on expanding out of this system and attempting to subjugate whatever lives on the other side of this portal. That is exactly what the Cleaver was designed to do. That is not why the Ancients left us these devices and why I cannot let them carry out such a foolish mission. Furthermore, the idea that we could dominate any race as advanced as the Ancients is ridiculous. Instead, I offer an alternative. Join me and together we can meet the elder race that has run this galaxy for millennia. I have on board the third alien device. I bet your commanders didn't tell you what it can do, because if they did, you'd realize I was right. This device will allow us to communicate with the Ancients once we're on the other side of the portal. Think about it—the first device gave us subspace, the second device activated this incredible portal, and the third will allow us to connect with its makers. This has been our destiny. But if you can't bring yourselves to join our mission of ascension, at least spare the bloodshed and let us pass in peace."

A couple of seconds passed as Zion's words sank in. Then another voice began, "This is Captain Spear of the E.F. Leviathan. You are illegally in possession of Earth Force property, and have committed treason, murder, and desertion while being so. Zion, you are hereby ordered to power down and prepare for boarding. If you do so, you have my word you will not be harmed while being taken into custody. Any other action will be taken as hostile and we will be forced to retaliate."

Zion returned, "I can see you still think your purpose is more important than that of the Ancients who created this portal. You fools still think you know what is best for this galaxy. We are just a small part of a giant picture. How can you be so arrogant as to think we know better than the Ancients?" Zion exhaled a big breath then continued, "All right, all fighters engage. I didn't want to destroy you, but I will do what is necessary to carry the human race to its destiny."

With that Zion cut off his transmission.

"Why didn't command tell us that device could allow us to communicate with the Ancients?" asked Joker.

"It doesn't matter," returned Apocalypse. "We have a job to do."

At this point the fighter wings from the Iowa, Leviathan, and Hamilton had met up, and with the Ranger deploying its own fighters they began their attack on Zion's charging force. The Cleaver was at full burn, heading toward the Colossus Portal, and for some reason had only launched ten of its fighters.

"New contact on sensors!" shouted Maniac, "It's coming from behind the Cleaver."

Chris could see the swirling portal in the far distance opening up as his own fighter got closer and closer to the Cleaver and its dozens of fighters.

"Holy shit! It's the E.F. Expedition!" beamed Joker. "She is right on top of the Cleaver!"

Chris could hear several cheers as the pilots shouted in encouragement at their reinforcements.

"Bet that asshole didn't see that coming," added Joker.

Chris watched ahead and saw red and green flashes ahead of him as the Expedition opened fire on the Cleaver. Lasers and plasma cannons could be seen in the distance as the ships began clashing with each other like two huge titans. They were trading blow for blow as armor began melting away on both ships.

"OK pilots, we are coming into missile range. Acquire your targets and fire when you get a lock. It's go time boys!" ordered the wing commander.

Chris watched as his ship's computer synced up with the rest of the wings to coordinate missile strikes. This way two pilots didn't waste their salvos on the same targets and instead were able to hit different ones.

Chris watched as the targeting reticule turned red, signifying it had a lock, and pulled the trigger.

Two Lancer missiles shot forward and began tracking their target. Chris thumbed the targeting button on his joystick and the computer began acquiring a lock on the next enemy Skimmer. Before it could do so, however, Chris heard warning claxons going off on his own ship. His heads-up display began flashing warning signs to him saying "Missile Lock" in red. Then it quickly switched to "Incoming Missile" with the claxons changing tone to signify the difference in status. Chris knew this meant the enemies had acquired a lock and fired their own missiles at him.

Chris looked at the distance display and decided he had enough time to get one more volley of missiles off before he would have to begin maneuvering to dodge the incoming missiles—at least that's what he hoped he would be able to do. Chris thanked Craig Woodford in his head for the extra training he had received in the simulators.

As soon as the targeting reticle turned red Chris fired his second salvo of missiles at the Skimmer. He watched as the pair of missiles quickly out-accelerated his own fighter and flew with insane speed at the enemy.

Chris had been training in the simulator a lot lately, although compared to a standard Earth Force pilot it would have been scratching the surface. That being said, he had learned that many standard engagements had two phases for fighter pilots. There was phase one, as Craig had put it, which was the initial standoff. Basically fighters would launch missiles at each other and then begin maneuvering in an attempt to avoid the other ship's oncoming missiles, all the while closing in on the enemy. Phase two was about the dogfight that followed. There was no phase three, as somebody was usually dead or disabled at the end of phase two.

Chris immediately performed a quarter roll and pulled up on the stick. The G forces were tremendous and he sank into the supportive leather gravity chair. Chris could tell the nanites were helping him out as the seven Gs smashing him into the seat tried to sink all of his blood to his feet but failed. His vision remained completely clear—no tunnel vision. He could tell he was not at the limit.

This maneuvering was done to hopefully out-handle an enemy missile. Pilots knew their ships couldn't out-accelerate a missile. The missiles had a much higher thrust-to-weight ratio and needed to be going faster than ships to catch up to them. This speed, however, came at the cost of maneuverability, and an expert pilot could take advantage of this fact. So between chaff, which was a way to distract the missile's radar, and his maneuverability, a pilot gambled that he could avoid the radar-guided missile.

Chris watched as his first salvo of missiles hit his target and the enemy dot on his radar disappeared. There was no time to celebrate though, as there were two incoming missiles that would hit his ship in two seconds unless he did something to prevent it. Two seconds with nanites, however, was a long time in a dogfight.

Chris immediately rolled 180 degrees again. He could feel the nanites helping him make the precise movements through his joystick that would carry out the move he had pictured in his head. This was in addition to practicing the maneuver in the simulator. He then pulled up hard while at the same time using his thumb to fire the radar-confusing chaff his fighter carried on board. Despite the inertial dampeners working their hardest Chris sank into his chair and registered ten Gs in his heads-up display. Even with the nanites and the aid of his flight suit, the edges of his vision were beginning to creep in. He knew if he blacked out here he may never wake up.

Chris watched as he saw two streaks move behind his fighter. He exhaled as the missile lock warnings stopped and his heads-up display flashed the words "Missile Evaded," which made him realize he had just dodged his first pair of missiles. Even if the missiles didn't detonate on his chaff, they didn't have the fuel to execute a 180 degree turn, reacquire his ship, slow down, then accelerate and track him again. In addition to dodging the missiles Chris had also got his first real fighter pilot kill as a member of Earth Force. It wasn't anything fancy, but slamming two missiles into an enemy Skimmer felt good. Unfortunately, the second salvo he had launched had missed, as the enemy Skimmer had done a similar set of evasive maneuvers and was beginning to track Chris for round two of the engagement.

Chris performed a quick situational check just to make sure his wing was still alive. Command had given him the ability to check on his wingmen, but not all the fighters in the fleet, as he was not in any type of command. He saw that all the fighters in his wing were still alive and fighting, but that Joker had fallen to 70 percent hull integrity, as estimated by his computer. Chris guessed that Mike had not been 100 percent successful in avoiding the incoming missile fire. Most missiles utilized a proximity fuse and therefore didn't need to directly hit to do damage. With no atmosphere to slow down shrapnel, the effective radius of a missile detonation was larger than one would typically expect.

Chris lined up his targeting reticle on the Skimmer he had missed earlier and noticed that the enemy pilot was doing the same thing to him. The distance between the two was rapidly closing and Chris figured there wouldn't be time for another missile lock. So he mentally switched into dogfight mode, and brought his lasers to bear.

Chris entered range and again watched as his reticle was lined up. He pulled the trigger and two of his four lasers fired at once. Chris mentally scolded himself for not setting them to quad fire mode, as that would have hit even harder At this range his lasers would not do a lot of damage, so two additional lasers would have helped. Chris also felt a slight shudder as one of the two lasers the enemy Skimmer had fired gashed into his Raptor's front armor.

Chris pulled the trigger again to fire the next two lasers and at the same time a white flash came out of nowhere. It would have blinded him if not for his Raptor's canopy instantly going completely dark, save for a white glow off to his left. Chris instinctually pulled up to avoid any more laser fire from the enemy. One of the features Craig had told Chris about their Raptors was their electro-chromatic canopies that could darken nearly instantly to prevent the pilot from being blinded. On top of that, his nanites could augment his pupils to react more quickly than a normal human, helping aid the darkening of the canopy. In addition, the nanites helped his eyes adjust back to normal more quickly.

"What the hell just happened?" asked Chris as the flash began to decrease and the canopy began slowly letting light in again.

"We lost the Expedition!" shouted Maniac over the comms.

Chris scanned his radar and sure enough the Expedition, which had just jumped in and began fighting with the Cleaver, was gone. Its reactor must have gone supercritical, and that was the flash Chris had seen. Modern ships used fusion reactors to power their systems. These fusion reactors counted on electromagnetic containment fields to control and contain the plasma at their core. Should these containment fields become damaged while the reactor was operating, the reaction could run away, causing a multikiloton release of energy and radiation.

As the flash dissipated Chris started getting his situational

awareness back. His canopy returned to near-normal conditions and he could see the shock wave from the explosion
working its way outward. His fears had been realized though,
as the Cleaver remained intact, moving toward the Colossus
Portal.

"My God, it's happening again," murmured Maniac.

"Keep it together, Panthers," returned Apocalypse.

Before Chris could admire the beautiful shockwave, the
Skimmer pilot Chris had been fighting with reacquired Chris
and began peppering him with laser fire. Chris brought his
ship back around and decided to play a game of chicken with
the Skimmer pilot as he switched his laser fire into quad mode.
Chris had played this game before with a Skimmer and knew
he could win it, even though it would cost him armor from his
ship.

He began firing away with all four of his Raptor's lasers at
once. The ship's lasers could be heard as they cycled between
shots. Simultaneously he was hit with a full-on barrage on his
ship's nose. Warning claxons could be heard, encouraging
him to stop whatever the hell he was doing immediately. He
kept on the triggers, however.

"This is the Ranger," began a voice over the comms, "We're
in range and opening fire on the Cleaver."

Chris assumed that must have been an officer on the
Ranger's bridge. Chris continued firing as he heard a similar statement from another officer saying the Hamilton had
opened fire on the Cleaver as well.

After the fourth straight hit Chris watched as the Skimmer
pilot he was attacking pulled up on his stick and got out of
the chicken match with Chris. Chris had lost 30 percent of
his armor at this point up front, but the enemy had fallen to
an estimated 40 percent hull integrity and was bailing out of
their fight.

Chris began tracking the targeting reticle that led the enemy Skimmer, showing where Christian needed to fire to hit

the target. Before he could fire a shot, though, someone came in over the comms.

"I can't shake this guy," came a female voice. "He's on my six. I need someone to help or I'm not going to make it!"

Chris quickly recognized it as Melissa's voice and with a thought his nanites highlighted her ship and the enemy shooting at her on the display.

"I'm on my way to help but I need twenty seconds to get there!" shouted Maniac.

"I'm on my way too! Hang in there Ice!" added Apocalypse.

Chris and his nanites instantly did the math and he realized he was less than two seconds away and he could help now. He stopped tracking the Skimmer he was working on and let him go. No way would he let his dream girl down now.

"Bank left, Ice Queen, I'm moving in to help!" ordered Chris.

"Bananas?" questioned Ice Queen in a very surprised tone.

She may have been surprised but that didn't stop her from following his command. Chris immediately began tracking the Skimmer that was beating on Ice Queen and within another second he was in range. He toggled his lasers over to single-fire mode as he figured more shots with less cycle time would distract the enemy Skimmer, causing its own fire to miss his wing mate, whose hull was down to an estimated 50 percent integrity.

He pulled the trigger and laser fire shot out of his craft. At this range and with only single shots from each laser cannon the damage was not devastating but the distraction began working. After three direct hits from Chris the Skimmer broke off his attack on Ice Queen and began dodging.

"Thanks, Bananas," said Ice Queen.

Chris switched to dual fire mode as he wanted to start hitting with some weight on the next shots as he fought.

"This is Captain John Johnston of E.F. Oxford. We are on station," announced a voice over the intercom.

A quick glance at his radar showed the E.F. Oxford had jumped into the battle. Unfortunately it was even further behind the Leviathan so it couldn't help much in the short run.

As he began hitting the Skimmer that had been beating on Ice Queen, he watched a giant flame shoot out of the tail end of the Skimmer as it turned away from Chris.

"Wow," thought Chris. "This guy is running away from me. Ha!"

Chris began using his own afterburners but he quickly realized the other guy's faster Skimmer was putting distance on Chris, even with the added power. That's when Chris realized what he should have already been doing—something any experienced pilot would have already done.

Chris fired two Lancer class missiles at the fleeing enemy, since his computer had already acquired a lock.

The two missiles reached out toward the fleeing Skimmer, but Chris did not stop there. As the Skimmer began his own evasive maneuvers and deployment of chaff Chris launched two more at the enemy. He quickly did an ammo check and realized he was down to ten Lancer missiles of the twenty he had started with on board.

The pilot was probably a pirate of some kind without the nanites that Earth Force pilots had, but in his defense he was a natural at the helm. The first two missiles completely missed as they got distracted by the chaff.

Luckily for Chris the second set of missiles came in from a better angle and the pilot he was chasing was going so fast he couldn't maneuver very well as the G forces would be crushing.

One of the two missiles got distracted by the chaff but the other hit home. Chris watched a fiery explosion in front of him and thought this dogfight was over. To his surprise the computer quickly showed him that the enemy had maintained 20 percent hull integrity.

"Damn, this bastard is tough," thought Chris.

Chris also noticed as the explosion dissipated that the

engines of the fleeing Skimmer had taken the brunt of the damage and looked to be destroyed or at the very least severely damaged.

The wounded Skimmer began drifting and could only make minor course corrections. Still, given enough time he could bring his lasers to bear and that meant Chris knew what he needed to do.

He began pouring laser fire into the wounded ship. It only took two shots before Chris saw an explosion. As the fighter exploded Chris noticed a little escape pod coming from the ship. The pilot had ejected. That was fine by Chris, he had just notched his second kill of the day while saving his favorite girl.

CHAPTER 24

Chris brought his fighter around and hit the burners, as he had put some distance between his fighter and the rest of the battle while chasing his last kill. As he was pressed once again in the chair he took a moment to analyze the situation in front of him. While things had been going well for Chris, to his dismay the rest of the battle was not going well for Earth Force.

Of the twenty fighters Earth Force had actively engaged in combat, not counting the five additional fighters from the Oxford that were on the way, only fifteen remained. Chris only hoped the pilots of the five lost Earth Force fighters had managed to eject. The good news was there were only twenty-eight Skimmers left of the initial fifty that had jumped in with the Cleaver. Clearly the Earth Force pilots had superior training and technology compared to the pirates and it was showing, but the numbers advantage the enemy had was taking its toll on Earth Force. From there the news only got worse. The Cleaver had launched ten of its Raptors and they were staying close to the Cleaver in guard formations. While they were not attacking Earth Force fighters, they had remained undamaged themselves.

After pounding the E. F. Expedition and making its reactor go supercritical, the Cleaver had continued its charge toward the Colossus Portal nearly unscathed. The Ranger and

Hamilton had engaged the Cleaver next with the Iowa close behind. The Leviathan was the next closest, followed by the Oxford.

With only two Poseidon class vessels in range of the Cleaver the friendly firepower was not doing enough. The Ranger, while still fighting, had taken a beating. Its estimated hull integrity was at 32 percent. The Hamilton, which had also come into range, was down to 58 percent estimated hull integrity. Meanwhile, the Cleaver had an estimated 82 percent integrity.

Chris next did a quick scan of his own wing and saw that Apocalypse and Maniac were still doing well, Ice Queen had been damaged, but Joker was in trouble.

"I need help guys!" yelled Joker over the comms.

Chris checked his heads-up display and saw he was too far out to help Joker.

"Roger that, Joker, I'm on my way. Hang in there!" replied Maniac.

"He's all over me. I'm losing engines and I can't shake him! Hurry up or I'm a goner!" screamed Joker.

After being at full burn for several seconds, Chris had to cycle off his burners before the reactor overheated.

"Dammit!" Chris yelled to himself as he was still too far away.

"Just another few seconds!" Maniac pleaded.

"I can't take it, I'm—"Joker screamed until he went silent.

Chris saw a small fireball explode in front of him in the distance. His scanners identified it as Joker's ship. The blip on the radar where Joker had been disappeared, and Chris had no idea if Joker had made it out.

"You motherfucker!" cursed Maniac and he went into a rage over the comms. "This guy is all mine!"

Instead of chasing after Maniac to help exact revenge upon Joker's assailant, Chris decided it would be smartest if he went after the nearest enemy Skimmer instead.

With his lasers set on dual fire mode and his reactor cooled sufficiently he once again hit the burners and began closing on his enemy. At that point he heard the captain of the Ranger check in.

"We can't take much more, Command. The Ranger has been disabled and we continue to take fire. We are dead in the water until we can get repairs."

As Chris was closing he noticed the Ranger's hull integrity had fallen to an estimated 8 percent. Between the missing chunks of hull he saw blue and white arcs from damaged conduits being exposed to space.

"Damn that thing is shot up. The Ranger fought right up until the end." Chris thought. He hoped for the crew's sake that Zion would leave the now-harmless ship alone and move on.

Chris knew that one of two things could cause a ship to be disabled. Chris hoped it had just been the engines that had failed. The other thing that could cause a ship to be disabled was a reactor failure. That was much worse, as the reactor powered weapons, navigation, communications, engines, jump drives and most importantly, life support. Without it, the Ranger was on borrowed time. In addition to that, a reactor failure could lead to a containment issue, which at the very least involved radiation, which was deadly to the crew. At worst, the reactor could go supercritical and cause a mini thermonuclear explosion, as it had on the Expedition.

Meanwhile Chris had found another Skimmer and once again acquired missile lock. As before, two Lancer missiles shot out from his ship and began homing in on their target. Chris had been on his afterburners but made sure to dial back the power as to not overshoot his prey.

The Skimmer he had targeted must have noticed the lock because he began maneuvering quickly and launching countermeasures of his own. Chris was still slowing his ship to prevent him from completely overtaking the enemy and began tracking the ship with his lasers.

One missile had clearly gotten distracted by the chaff coming out of the Skimmer as it completely missed the target, but his other missile, for whatever reason, was better able to track the enemy. It didn't slam home, however, as the Skimmer pilot had been performing aggressive evasive maneuvers. Instead, being an intelligent warhead, it realized that it was not going to directly impact the Skimmer and would pass by the ship at roughly three meters distance. When the missile's computer realized this was the best it was going to do, it made the correct decision to explode and hammer the enemy Skimmer with a shockwave and exploding shrapnel.

Chris watched as this knocked the Skimmer into an erratic flight path, spinning out of control. While it didn't kill the Skimmer it did bring its hull integrity down to roughly 50 percent and likely damaged some critical systems along the way.

Chris was moving in for the kill and began firing pairs of lasers at the enemy ship with reckless abandon. The thin amount of Duranium armor on the Skimmer began melting away at the impact of Chris's lasers blasts. The out-of-control Skimmer was doing his best to regain control of his ship but Chris was confident he could finish the job before the enemy could right himself.

After the third cycle of lasers fired from Chris's ship, his targeting reticle shuddered. Chris looked to his left and saw armor beginning to melt off his left wing. Again his ship shuddered from an impact and Chris realized a different enemy Skimmer had lined up on his six and was beginning to wreak havoc on Chris's armor. Chris was ready for this, however, and honestly felt lucky to have made it this far before falling into some else's sights.

He decided to disengage his original target and begin evasive maneuvering. Left and right he began rolling and turning. For the most part he was pretty successful in evading fire. Despite the faster and more maneuverable Skimmer having the drop on him, his piloting with nanite assists seemed to be leveling the playing field. The dance went on for about ten more seconds without either side having an advantage. Chris thought things were going well until he realized another Skimmer had acquired him and began hammering away at his ship.

In a bit of a panic Chris jumped on the comms, "I need some help here guys. I have two bogeys on me and I don't think I can shake them."

"I'm on my way, Bananas! Bank hard to starboard 90 degrees and hit the burners!" responded Maniac.

Chris did as instructed, narrowly avoiding more laser blasts as he saw the amber-colored streak go by his cockpit canopy. As he sank into his seat from the Gs his computer highlighted Maniac's incoming Raptor, and to Chris's delight, Maniac was bringing the pain.

Four Lancer missiles narrowly flew past Chris's fighter. If Chris didn't know that Maniac was a trained professional on his team he might have suspected those missiles were aimed at him. Chris knew that Maniac, despite being a salty asshole, was also an elite killer.

Two of the four missiles slammed home and one of the two Skimmers disappeared off radar. The other one avoided the missiles coming at him but had to disengage Chris as Maniac had begun using his lasers to finish the job.

Chris let off the after burners and did a quick glance at his computer to see how things were going. Again, it wasn't good. The Hamilton was down to 16 percent hull integrity and was suffering extensive system damage while the Cleaver still had an estimated 62 percent hull integrity. Maniac and Apocalypse had taken some damage but were still very much in the fight. Ice Queen, however had taken a heavy beating, and her fighter couldn't take much more. She was still fighting, though, and Chris knew that was all they could ask for. The Leviathan and Iowa were almost in place, forming a blockade of the Colossus

Portal, while the Oxford was somewhat behind. Unfortunately the Cleaver was making a strong push forward with its entire fighter compliment still in play.

Just then Chris heard warning claxons go off and he realized someone off to his starboard side had acquired a lock on him. He rolled toward the incoming enemy Skimmer and watched as the distances between him and the freshly launched enemy missile decreased. At the right time Chris pulled back sharply on the stick and began a high-G maneuver as chaff poured out of his Raptor. Chris watched as the enemy missile streaked safely beneath his ship thanks to the ships cameras and his nanite software. With the aid of his nanites he could actually see a projected image through the bottom of the ship.

The enemy Skimmer pilot either must have been a rookie or was very confident in his targeting systems because he didn't follow up his missile shot with laser fire. Chris would make him pay for that mistake as he kicked his ship around to bring the enemy into his normal field of vision.

The enemy Skimmer began banking his ship to the starboard side and turning to reacquire Chris. Chris hoped he would be able to finish the job this time, as his last few engagements kept getting interrupted. He knew this was common in a big dogfight and it was therefore important to deal out whatever damage was available to you and move on when the time was right. Eventually the damage would add up and the enemy would be defeated. As Chris began the downward half of his loop he acquired his target and began firing off lasers blasts. The enemy Skimmer was doing the same thing and both pilots missed with their first two blasts.

Chris was ready to play another game of chicken with this guy and he switched his lasers into quad mode. Even with his depleted armor he was pretty sure he could finish the job. The two ships traded one barrage with three of the four of Chris's lasers hitting home. Chris waited as his lasers cycled even as the enemy's two shots hit his Raptor. He would probably get one or two more shots in before they passed each other.

Then, before he could press the trigger a second time, a laser blast from above smashed into the nose of his ship, melting already damaged armor even more. This moved Chris out of position slightly and prevented him from firing again at the Skimmer. The damage didn't end there, however, as one of his four laser banks went offline due to the direct hit. In addition his navigation systems and radar had been damaged. They were not offline, but his computer told him they were not functioning at 100 percent and that there may be blind spots.

Chris didn't wait around to see what would happen next. Instead, he aborted his attack, hit the afterburners, and pulled up into another high-G maneuver. He was doing everything he could to make his ship hard to hit while he figured out who had just attacked him.

"Suck it, Earth Force scum!" Chris heard from a familiar voice over the comms. It must have been the enemy Skimmer firing on Chris who was broadcasting openly. Chris's mind raced for a minute trying to identify the familiar voice. He realized he knew the voice very well as he completed the high-G evasive maneuver.

After he came to this realization, a jolt of rage began permeating through Chris. He mentally told the computer to target the Skimmer that was shooting at him and the computer responded by presenting the position of the hostile ship on Chris's sensor display. The enemy Skimmer only managed to get that one shot off before Chris began evasive maneuvering. They began circling each other with the enemy ship in the slightly superior position since it had gotten the drop on Chris.

Chris, without taking his hands off the stick mentally opened up his comms and responded in a venomous tone while allowing his face to be displayed. "Brad Singer, you piece of shit."

"Chris?" Brad responded with confusion as he chased Chris's Raptor.

Chris continued avoiding fire and responded between breaths, "I have been waiting for this day ever since we got off the Puddle Jumper. Stacey will be happy to hear that our former XO's blood will be scattered amongst the stars and that my father's killer lives no more, because today you're going to die."

"Ha! Is the little boy still hurt from losing his daddy?" instigated Brad in a mock whiny voice. "Oh hell, grow up Chris. I told you before and I'll tell you again: in this world you either learn to survive or die. I chose to survive, and I even got to pilot this here fighter as a result. I still don't know why you think I should have stood there and died like your daddy but I'll tell you what," Brad grunted as he continued maneuvering, "Straighten your ship out and I'll make all the pain go away. You'll even get to see daddy again!" Brad began laughing in between maneuvers.

"Fuck you Brad!" yelled Chris as he disengaged his comms.

Chris continued his evasive maneuvering, and to Chris's surprise he found he was doing it with ease. Chris started realizing the advantage the nanite package was providing him. Between the nanites and the cameras on the external portion of the hull that were tracking the enemy Skimmer chasing him, Chris was instinctually able to dodge the incoming fire that Brad was dishing out. It was something truly amazing that he'd never been able to do before.

He straightened out and then began dodge left, then right, then a barrel roll to the right, then he began a loop, all while Brad chased him, firing shots from his lasers in an attempt to destroy Chris. His confidence in the nanites and his Raptor continued growing.

"Hold still, you little shit!" taunted Brad in frustration.

Before Chris could respond to the taunt, his canopy went dark from a very intense white flash. Chris knew this was

another Skimmer when he noticed an object out of the corner of his eye. It looked like an escape pod.

Chris targeted it, matched its speed, and approached the pod. Sure enough, the computer identified it as Brad's. An escape pod was just the cockpit of the fighter jettisoned from the fuselage, so he knew Brad could see him coming. An evil smile began to curl up the edge of Chris's lips as he got close enough to visually see the man inside the transparametal canopy.

Inside was a pilot with a look of panic on his face, waving his hands frantically.

"Chris, I'm sorry! I was just doing what I needed to survive!" pleaded Brad in a panicked voice over the comms.

With his ship in front of Brad's escape pod canopy Chris began feeling at the dog tags he had on his neck. The three tags were from his birth father and mother, and Josh Hammerfist. All three were given to Chris by Josh as he lay in front of Chris, dying from the laser wound Brad inflicted upon him.

"Like you said, Brad, you either learn to survive or die. Well, I told you when we were on the bridge of the Puddle Jumper I would look you in the eyes when I killed you. Those last shots that blew up your raptor were for our crew. This one, however," Chris paused, then through clenched teeth growled, "is for me!"

Chris pressed the trigger button and his three remaining lasers burned through the transparametal cockpit incinerating everything inside. Chris's only regret was that it wasn't a slower, more painful death. A tear slid down his cheek as his own internal mission was now halfway completed. Thinking of his family reminded him of how alone he was in this world. Zion was all that remained on his list now.

CHAPTER 25

"Chris get your ass back in the game here, we need your help!" yelled Apocalypse.

Chris had been distantly aware of someone yelling his name while he burned through Brad's escape pod, but it hadn't registered. As his lasers cooled, however, so did he, and his brain began to process the urgent commands coming to him. He acknowledged the command and throttled up his Raptor while looking around to assess the situation. His own ship was at an estimated 51 percent integrity, while Maniac and Wing Commander Apocalypse were roughly the same. Melissa was in critical condition with 27 percent integrity. The Iowa and Leviathan had formed a blockade of the Colossus Portal with the Oxford rushing to join them. Chris looked and realized that even with the Oxford's fighters the good guys were down to twelve Raptors.

The Cleaver had fallen to 53 percent integrity and was making a hard charge through the blockade toward the portal. The enemy fighters that had stayed close to it were in the thick of the fight now, but they had only lost two of their number.

As Chris was flying toward the remainder of the enemy fighters he saw off to his two o'clock another subspace portal opening up. To the delight of Earth Force personnel, a Poseidon class vessel began emerging.

"This is the captain of the E.F. Paris. We are on station.

The Cleaver is dead ahead and we are engaging while launching fighters," came an unfamiliar voice over the comms.

The Cleaver was only minutes away from the portal being blockaded by the Leviathan and Iowa. The Paris was on the Cleaver's tail in pursuit. Chris hoped they could lay down enough fire to finish the Cleaver while not getting destroyed themselves.

Chris picked up the nearest enemy fighter and realized it was another Raptor. He was too far away for a missile lock so he hit his burners.

As he was getting closer Chris noticed that all the enemy Raptors had disengaged and were heading back toward the Cleaver.

Then another familiar voice with a southern accent came over the comms, "I see you met up with your old pal, Chris," Zion chuckled. "Well, family reunions can be a bit hostile sometimes. Regardless, it's time for me to go. A pity you were never able to see the light."

"What do you want, Zion?" rumbled Chris.

"Oh, just wanted to give you the chance to take Brad's place. Answer to a higher calling and join me as we ascend and meet with our Ancient brothers and sisters. It could provide meaning for your former crew's sacrifice," Zion replied.

"Seriously, fuck off, Zion. You're crazy to think I would join you," Chris shot back immediately.

Zion chuckled with a throaty laugh, "I figured you would say as much. Just know this, Chris. I did what I had to do to pull off this plan at any cost. I now follow a higher calling. You, however, have signed yourself up with people who want nothing but death, destruction, and control. You'll see what I mean in due time. Till then," Zion gave a half-assed salute, "Enjoy your new patrons. Maybe I'll see you on the other side of the portal."

With that the transmission went out.

The Cleaver began engaging the remaining blockading

Poseidon vessels. Unfortunately for Earth Force, only the Iowa and Leviathan stood in Zion's way. The Oxford and Paris were pursuing as well, but wouldn't be within weapons range in time.

As Chris was closing in on the Cleaver another message came through the comms. It was none other than Captain Spear himself, "All ships, the remaining Raptors are landing on the Cleaver while the Skimmers cover them. The Cleaver is making a push to gain access to the Colossus Portal. We must stop him at all costs. Engage the Cleaver directly and try to disable to engines. If we can slow them down we can buy time for more allied ships to get here and support."

"You heard the captain! All fighters attack the Cleaver!" added Major Sarner.

Chris was already hard on the afterburners, heading back into the fray. He was very nervous about a close-up engagement with the Cleaver. Fighting capital ships was very different from fighting other fighters or bombers. With all the point defense and flak cannons it could be a very short-lived engagement if Chris was reckless.

Chris decided to lock onto the Cleaver and fire all his remaining missiles. It was likely a futile effort as the point defense weapons on the ship would destroy most if not all of them. Furthermore, even if they all hit they couldn't bring down the Cleaver, as its sheer mass was just too much. There was always the chance, though, that a warhead could find just the right spot to slow the ship down, and Chris had to take that chance.

Typically, fighters did not engage capital ships at all as they were not equipped to take them out. It would take hours of laser fire to do enough damage to destroy a capital ship and a fighter could never last that long. One of two strategies were typically employed when attacking a capital ship. The first strategy was the most common for Earth Force: bring in bigger, more powerful capital ships with their own heavy weapons and armor. Earth Force was used to doing this because it always had the biggest and best ships around.

The other strategy was to use bombers. This method was also very effective, especially because losing a bomber was not nearly as costly as losing a capital ship. The bombers had special torpedoes on board that packed a massive explosive warhead. One issue was that these torpedoes, when shot from far away, could be destroyed by the point defense cannons before reaching their targets. As a result, bombers were heavily armored and built to be able to shrug off lots of hits from flack and point defense cannons while they got in close to deliver their payload. Unfortunately, however, there were no bombers around so it was up to the remaining Raptors and Poseidon destroyers to take care of Zion's flag ship.

Chris fired his remaining missiles in pairs of two as fast as he could. They reached out in front of his fighter with their rocket engines burning bright.

In a way, the sight before him was a beautiful thing to behold. It was the definition of a space opera. Capital ships were firing green plasma blasts at each other while the remaining fighters circled around each other or made strafing runs at a capital ship while trying to avoid fire. Tracer rounds from various cannons and the amber glow from lasers lit up space in a beautiful silent symphony.

Chris watched as his missiles were taken out one by one by point defenses as they got closer to the Cleaver. In the end only one of his missiles made it through. While it destroyed the area of the ship it impacted, the damage was not enough to make a real difference.

Chris began slowing his fighter at this point, as he began to make his strafing run. He had switched his cannon fire into quad mode when Melissa came up over the comms, "I've lost my engines! I am dead in the water for now, but my ship is intact. Good luck, guys. Get that bastard for me!"

"Chris, switch your cannons into quad fire mode and hit

that ship as best you can. If you start taking damage from the defense cannons get out of there, regroup, and make another run. You will be able to do more damage in the long run that way as opposed to one all-out assault that gets you killed," ordered Apocalypse.

"Roger that," Chris replied as he verified his ship was in quad fire mode. In reality though, Chris knew one of his lasers was offline and three was all he would be able to muster.

Chris noticed that all the enemy Raptors had retreated back on board the Cleaver and the few remaining enemy Skimmers were jumping out.

Chris lined up his ship on the aft section of the giant ship, and as he entered range he pulled the trigger. Three amber streaks launched themselves at the Cleaver, but at this range the damage wouldn't even register. Still, something was better than nothing.

As he got closer, Chris couldn't believe the size of the Cleaver. At over a kilometer long it was very intimidating and the two Poseidon destroyers defending the portal looked like children swatting at an adult. The ship just had a menacing look to it. Despite all the firepower they were launching at it, it was returning just as much and it was getting very close to the event horizon in the middle of the Colossus Portal.

Chris pulled up hard as one of the point defense cannons began spraying his ship with enemy fire. The hits sounded like a hundred sledgehammers hitting the outer hull of his ship all in a span of a second. He knew he'd lost armor and would lose more if he didn't get out of there quickly. As he pulled up he hit the burners to get out of range as fast as possible.

Chris rolled his ship around again, let off the afterburners, and pulled up to bring his Raptor around for another strafing run. As he was turning toward the Cleaver he saw the Leviathan and the Iowa firing away while taking damage of their own. Chris was pretty sure the fight would come down to the wire if none of the capital ships bailed out.

Once the Cleaver was back into view Chris targeted the defense cannon that had briefly pounded his ship. He pulled the trigger and his lasers reached out, melting armor around the cannon. The cannon again "noticed" Chris, pointing back at him, and began rattling away tiny rail gun rounds. Chris dodged left and right, only taking minor amounts of damage, and in the end the point defense cannon lost the mini battle between the two. Chris's lasers melted it to the point where it failed.

After the cannon ceased to function Chris continued randomly strafing the Cleaver until once again he was under too much fire and had to abort his attack run. The Cleaver's cannons were smart and redirected fire to cover the old cannon's turf. In addition, his ship had taken significant damage and he was beginning to worry about the increased incoming fire.

"Hit him with everything you have pilots!" yelled Captain Spear over the comms.

Chris brought his fighter around for another run and began lining up his targeting reticle, waiting till he was in range. He could see a Raptor in front of him making a strafing run and his computer identified it as Apocalypse's fighter. The major made his strafing run look like an art form. He dodged left and right almost as if he could anticipate the incoming fire from defenses. This made Chris realize how much he still had to learn.

As Chris came into range he began firing away at the Cleaver once more. As his lasers cycled for another shot he noticed a burst of acceleration from the Cleaver. It launched itself forward once again, moving out of range of Chris's laser fire and past the remaining blockade.

Chris looked ahead of the Cleaver's path and watched as a small white light began expanding in the middle of the black nothingness at the center of the Colossus Portal. The white light expanded with the familiar swirling blue of a subspace portal.

"Shit!" thought Chris as he realized the Cleaver was escaping. He slammed his left hand on the canopy transparametal in frustration.

Several more plasma cannons hit the Cleaver but it wasn't enough. The front of the ship began entering the event horizon and Chris realized they weren't going to complete their mission.

The Cleaver dove into the event horizon, and as the last of it went through, the portal began to close behind it. Then, after all was done, the Colossus Portal remained as if nothing had happened at all. It just sat there spinning, waiting for the next ship that wished to go through.

"All pilots, we have failed and the Cleaver has escaped. For those fighters that have taken damage you are cleared to return to base. The rest will remain on patrol and await further orders," came Captain Spear over the comms.

Chris and Earth Force had failed the mission. Zion had escaped to an unknown location.

"We can enter the portal and chase him down!" exclaimed Chris over the comms.

"Stand down Chris," returned Apocalypse.

"Negative, pilot," added a member of the E.F. Iowa's command staff. "We don't know what is on the other side of that portal and your jump drive is not equipped to go through that kind of wormhole."

Chris shook his head in disgust. He was tired and frustrated. Zion had escaped and nobody was going to do anything about it, at least in the short term.

He brought his fighter around and as the Iowa came into view he realized how badly the fight had gone for the Earth Force ships. Internal sections of the hull were open to space. He could see fires venting out of the ship before being extinguished by the cold and emptiness of space. Electrical arcs of energy could be seen randomly firing between exposed conduits. From there it only got worse. Little figures floated around near the edge of the damaged sections. Chris knew these were the unlucky spacers who happen to be in the wrong place at the wrong time when the Iowa took damage. He realized with that kind of damage it would be tough for Earth Force ships to chase the Cleaver anyways.

Chris turned his ship away from the carnage and searched for Apocalypse. Once he found the wing commander, Chris formed up on his wing, Maniac on the opposite side. They flew toward the Leviathan, which was in only a slightly better situation than the Iowa. Scars of black could be seen all over the large ship from plasma blasts. Engineering sections toward the aft of the ship had taken the majority of damage. Two of the Leviathan's four engines were no longer functioning.

"Chris, you did well today. I want you to land first as Maniac and I have not taken as much damage. We will escort Husky as he recovers any pilots and begins salvage ops."

Chris felt a flash of guilt move through him. With all of the action going on he had forgotten about seeing Joker disappear amid a ball of fire.

"Roger that Apocalypse," returned Chris. "Permission to land Leviathan?"

"Granted," came the comms officer on the bridge.

Chris maneuvered out of formation as Maniac and Apocalypse flew toward Husky's Tumbler, which had already started to clean up.

Chris lined up his Raptor with the hangar bay door on the Leviathan. He approached the door, and as it grew in his field of vision he could see people inside scrambling to get the hangar bay ready.

Chris slowed the Raptor and moved through the shielded door. He brought the Raptor to the position he had taken off from, and with the help of the people guiding him brought it down to rest. Once the Raptor settled he powered down the fighter and opened the canopy.

Chris exhaled as someone quickly brought up the rolling

stairs toward the cockpit. Chris looked up as he was undoing his seat belt to see a familiar face coming up the stairs.

"Welcome back Chris," said Rachel. She was covered with sweat and dirt, which clashed with the face full of makeup that he'd seen before he left. Apparently things must have been pretty bad on board the Leviathan, and she'd been busy working hard.

Chris pulled off his helmet and replied, "Thanks," as he looked at her. She was already gone though, working on her next job.

Chris leaned his head back against the headrest and closed his eyes. He mentally thanked God for making it and then lifted himself up to get out the cockpit.

Before Chris could get out on to the roll up stairs he heard a voice shouting at him.

"Dammit, Chris! The one thing I told you to do was not mess up this ship. What do you go and do? Mess up the Raptor and sign me up for double shifts. It's like you're already an Earth Force pilot," yelled Whistler as he walked toward the stairs.

Chris smiled as he walked down the stairs and answered, "Um, it's not that bad, Whistler. I brought her back under her own power."

Whistler put a hand on Chris's shoulder and turned him around and hit Chris with a, "Not that bad!?"

Chris looked at the ship he had been flying. It was a mess. Black streaks of burn marks were all over. Metal had sagged in multiple places. Up front, where one of his lasers used to be, was a charred, melted barrel. Wires had been exposed in a few areas, which made Chris thankful that the ship had redundant wiring and systems that would automatically reroute based on damage taken. Toward the aft portion of the ship the engine structures looked like an old dart board. Chunks here and there were missing and pock marks were everywhere. Chris was amazed at the ruggedness of his Raptor and also thankful he didn't need to restore it to working order.

"It's nothing you can't handle Whistler. You will have this thing back in tip-top shape in no time!" replied Chris.

Whistler just shook his head and began rounding up his crew.

"Glad you made it back Chris. Now get out of my way. Some of us have real jobs to do that require hard work," mocked Whistler as he got started.

Chris turned around and made his way to the ready room. He needed a shower.

CHAPTER 26

Chris headed straight back to the ready room to dump all his gear. As he pulled his equipment off he realized he was drenched in sweat and decided to take full advantage of the shower facilities adjacent to the ready room. He heard a commotion outside, but surprisingly nobody else took a shower. By the time he got done, in fact, the room was cleared again, leaving him all alone. "Oh well," he thought, "they must prefer to shower in their own quarters." He had just gotten a fresh jumpsuit on and was heading to the Spacer's Cafe for a bite to eat when he received a communication from Major Sarner.

"Chris, where the hell are you? Meet us in the briefing room ASAP for the debrief!"

Chris apologized and was about to ask about Mike when Major Sarner cut off the communication. Instead Chris saw the familiar highlighted path outlined in his vision that steered him toward the briefing room. At the same time he realized that was why nobody else had taken a shower. They had all dumped their gear and gone straight to the briefing room for the debrief.

Chris made his way quickly there, and as he got close enough to the front of the door it automatically slid open.

Seven figures were inside and they turned their heads toward Chris.

Captain Spear and XO Shafer were already facing Chris

with the pilots standing opposite, with their heads turned. Chris quickly saw Wing Commander John Sarner, Lieutenant Sean Quick, Sergeant Casey Hogan, Master Sergeant Melissa Lawson, and Craig Woodford. Chris felt a pit in his stomach as they were all wearing serious expressions and Mike was nowhere to be seen.

"Umm so, Mike, did he make it?" questioned Chris. His heart began beating rapidly as he thought his fears might become reality.

"Sergeant Carpenter is alive and healthy, but is recovering in sick bay right now. We expect him to be fit for duty shortly. Just needed to get some minor work done after the toll the battle took on his body," returned Captain Spear.

Chris exhaled in relief and walked up to the team.

"Don't worry, that asshole is tougher than he looks," added Lieutenant Quick.

Ben and the captain seemed to disapprove of the joke based on their expressions but were happy enough to let it slide since all of their pilots were safe.

"We can go see him after the debriefing," explained Master Sergeant Lawson with a smile.

The captain motioned for the pilots to take their seats. As the last few butts made their way into chairs he began talking.

"As you all know, we were unable to destroy the Cleaver. We have failed to achieve our primary objective but all is not lost. We have secured the portal, which has officially been designated the Colossus Portal by high command and it will be studied intensely beginning immediately. Pilots, despite all the bad news and destruction, there is some good that will come out of this. We were able to eliminate many of Zion's forces, and without supply ships he will have to be careful and conserve his resources wherever he is going. Exploration missions are being organized now and I expect our first ship to go through the portal within forty-eight hours."

"Sir, will we be heading through?" asked Sean.

"Yes, most likely, but not until this ship has been repaired," replied the captain. "We estimate that we will be fully functional within two months."

"So we won't be the first Earth Force pilots to go through?" probed Sean.

"Nope, not this time Lieutenant," returned the captain.

Sean sighed in disappointment but was smart enough to keep his mouth shut.

The captain cleared his throat again and continued, "Pilots, I want to thank you for your sacrifice and hard work in the name of duty. You saved a lot of lives out there today and without your work we may not be here having this discussion. With that, the XO and I will take our leave as there is still much to be done around here. I'll leave the wing commander to continue your debriefing."

The captain and XO saluted and all the pilots stood up in unison and returned the salute.

After they left the briefing room Major Sarner continued debriefing the team. They talked tactics and maneuvers throughout the battle, especially the things pilots did wrong. Chris could tell each pilot hated going over the bad stuff, but they understood that failing a mission would not go without consequences. During these discussions Chris could hear his father in his head saying, "You learn more from your failures than your successes." Chris had always responded, "So learning is for losers?" to which Josh would only shake his head.

Chris eagerly awaited his turn for feedback, but it did not come. Eventually he could tell they were wrapping up, so he raised his hand to ask about it:

"Sir, we didn't cover anything regarding my portion out there. Why not?"

Major Sarner's response cut him to the core: "Well Chris, your flying was so sloppy and untrained that there would be nothing to learn from. On top of that you're not getting back in the cockpit anytime soon, so the training would be wasted.

Don't get me wrong; your help was appreciated. You've just got a long ways to go before becoming an Earth Force pilot. Besides, your flight data recorder was damaged in the fight and the data was unrecoverable."

Chris was shocked by the response, and it sort of hurt that despite his efforts with Major Woodford they still thought so little of him. The debriefing came to an end and Chris got up to go check on Mike, get some food, and take a nap. He was pretty tired after a rough day of flying, and since the Leviathan was scheduled to dock at Lunar Space Station in twenty-four hours he figured why not rest up. Besides, the pilots had agreed to meet up at the Afterburner at 20:00 hours to celebrate their victory. On the way out the door, however, Major Sarner stopped him and told him to wait. Once the other pilots had cleared out he spoke quietly.

"Chris, we do actually need to talk about your flying out there. Specifically, what you did that couldn't be said in front of the others. Your flying wasn't actually bad—squad tactics yes, but flying no. The real problem, however, is what you did with Brad. You know what you did was a war crime right? You shot an unarmed combatant in a fucking escape pod, man!"

Chris tried to sputter out a response in defense but was silenced by a one-armed shove into the wall and a major in his face.

"Don't talk! This is the part where you shut up and listen! I know you two had history. He killed people you cared about, your father even, but this is war and you were temporarily enlisted in the Earth Force. There are certain rules you have to follow when you wear our badge and fly our ships, or you will be tried for war crimes in front of a human rights board. But seeing as how you aren't a member of the military in the first place, it would cause more problems than it would solve for our betters to pursue that particular avenue. So count yourself lucky, again, that you will be getting off light. I swear, you've got the luck of the Irish. Your flight records are damaged and that's the story. Got it?"

Chris nodded quickly.

"Good. I like you Chris, and I understand your reasons. That's why I had Whistler pull your flight records. But that shit can't happen again. What happened between you and Brad stays with the two of us, Whistler, and nobody else. Now go get some food and rest. You look like you need it."

With that the major walked off and Chris found himself alone in the briefing room. He no longer had any appetite; he needed to think. After several minutes of mentally kicking himself for disappointing Major Sarner he decided to go check on Mike.

Mike was sitting up in a medical bed talking with Sean, Casey, Melissa, and of course Major Sarner when Chris walked in. Several systems monitoring his vitals beeping and chirping in different tones in the background could be heard over the conversation.

"Damn, you had me worried Mike!" opened Chris when Mike looked over to see him entering the room.

"Well trust me, I was a bit worried myself," replied Mike as he winced from some injuries. "But I knew Casey here wouldn't forget about me, and once I regained consciousness and realized I was still alive I just waited for you guys to pick me up."

"Are you OK, physically?" asked Chris as Mike continued wincing.

"Ya it's mostly just my ego that took a hit. Worst part about this is the intern made it back with his Raptor in one piece while mine is in a million pieces out in space."

The other pilots laughed and Sean added, "Oh don't worry I'll remind you about this the rest of your life."

Mike shook his head in disgust but then smiled again as he was happy to be alive and able to catch the crap that his friends were going to throw his way.

"Well I am glad to see you again, Mike. That was a hell of a battle out there," Chris stated.

"You got that right, Bananas. The team did some mighty fine flying out there," returned Mike.

With that the pilots kept talking for another few minutes before Mike said he had had enough of sick bay and wanted to get some rest in his quarters. The rest of the pilots went their separate ways and Chris was left with just himself and a decision about whether to get some food or get some rest.

He decided to skip the meal and head straight for his quarters. He was completely lost in thought as he opened the door, only to be greeted by an emotional, pissed-off looking Stacey.

"What's wrong?" he exclaimed.

"What's wrong?" she shot back. "Gigantic space battle you don't belong in, flying a ship you don't know how to fly, in a part of space nobody's been before, and you don't think to maybe send me a 'Hey Stacey, I'm not dead, you can stop worrying.' "

Upon reflection Chris had seen a bunch of messages on his internal display but ignored them when he got the call to get to the debrief.

"Look, I'm not your mother," she continued "but I'm also the only family you've got, unfortunately, so it's kinda my job to watch out for you."

With that they just stood for a moment and stared at each other awkwardly. Then Stacey gave him a hug. After he returned the embrace and a couple seconds passed Stacey asked, "So how many kills did you get?"

"Three! You should have seen it Stacey!" Suddenly he remembered his last kill and his expression changed sharply. "I also . . ." he paused. "I also gave Brad what he deserved."

The conversation continued on this track for almost an hour, with Chris telling Stacey every detail except one. He left out the part about killing Brad while helpless in his escape pod. He wanted to tell her, but after the talk with Major Sarner he figured it would be best if she just thought he died in the initial explosion. Eventually the fatigue hit him, and he dropped down on his bunk for a much-needed nap. Before he drifted off, he made a note to himself to remember Stacey more. She was right; she wasn't his mother, but she was the last person alive to connect him to his past. That was worth something. And with that he drifted off . . .

CHAPTER 27

Several hours later, Chris pressed the button in the turbo lift that would take him to the Afterburner lounge. The doors closed and he could feel himself being moved ever so subtly. His nap came easily but after he woke up and got ready he and Stacey had talked some more. That talk left Chris with a lot on his mind.

She told him that they were to get off the Leviathan once they reached Lunar Space Station and that she was going to meet up with her sister on Mars after that. She told Chris he was welcome to come with her, and stay until he was able to find a job. Chris knew this path would be hard and not one that he wanted, but at least it was an option. It sure beat being dropped off at Lunar Space Station with a week's worth of credits, hoping for a job, before he would need to start begging. So, in the end he had agreed to accompany her.

That meant that in less than a day, he would walk off the Leviathan and never again be a part of her crew. It also meant that his days of piloting a spaceship were also coming to an end. This made Chris sad, but he thought, "Hey, not everyone goes from flying a smuggler ship to flying a Raptor for Earth Force. Heck, most people never fly for the Earth Force period."

Major Sarner hadn't said anything about the Space Academy and getting a slot for him since they were touring the hangar. Chris would bring it up at the Afterburner if the chance presented itself, but was afraid that after the stunts he had pulled over the past week the opportunity would be off the table.

All of this meant Chris found himself wondering if this was his last meeting with the 72nd Flying Panthers and the crew of the Leviathan.

The doors from the turbo lift opened up and Chris was once again treated to the familiar sight of Afterburner lounge. Its soft jazz music and warm atmosphere welcomed him in and seemed to make all of his troubles disappear. Chris knew it was the perfect spot to forget about one's problems.

The Afterburner was a bit crowded today but not full. Chris had asked earlier if they should be celebrating. Even though the pilots had all made it, there were a number of crewmen who had died in the fight with the Cleaver. Mike told him that there was a common understanding on board the ship. Everyone dealt with their victories and losses in different ways and that the Afterburner was not a place to judge others. While the pilots celebrated their victory, a mechanic, or an officer may be there to mourn the loss of a close friend or crewmate. Other people dealt with losses in other ways and while at the Afterburner, no serious judgment would be imposed.

So with that Chris spotted the Flying Panthers sitting at a polished wooden table. All the pilots were there, even Mike, who was sporting some new bandages. Next to Mike he spotted a sixth chair available and empty. This brought a smile to Chris's face as he realized they saved a spot for him.

"I thought you guys said twenty hundred hours!" opened Chris.

"We did!" returned Casey.

"Well I am only one minute late and you guys are already here with beers in hand. Nobody looks like they just got here, either," questioned Chris.

"Oh crap, we forgot to tell the new guy," joked Major Sarner.

"Forgot to tell me what?" asked Chris.

"Well, Chris, when we say a certain time, everyone knows that pilots love beer so we get to the Burner at least a half hour before we said we would get there. Especially after a victory!" explained Mike.

"Last I checked, that was not a victory?" questioned Chris.

"Living to fight another day is always a victory," returned Mike.

"Oh," muttered Chris with understanding.

The team laughed and got up from their seats to greet Chris. Chris exchanged handshakes and hugs with Mike, Casey, and Melissa.

When it was Major Sarner's turn Chris wasn't sure what to do. The major stood there staring at him and then quickly gave him a salute. Chris immediately returned it and a smile came to the major's mouth as he reached out a hand. Chris returned the handshake and then looked up to see Lieutenant Quick staring down at him.

It was an awkward moment as Chris realized as he didn't know what to do.

Then Sean spoke, "Chris, I have to admit: for a pencil-neck smuggler, you're not half bad at flying," and with that Sean stuck his hand out.

That was it, Chris realized. That was Sean's attempt to make amends. It wouldn't get any better so he went with it. Chris returned the handshake and Sean didn't even try to break his wrist this time.

"Glad to be able to fly with this crew," replied Chris.

"All right enough of this mushy stuff. Chris, grab a round for your wingmen," ordered Lieutenant Quick.

"On it!" returned Chris. He put in an order for some pub food as well as he was starving and he'd heard about Bill Bronx's cooking skills. "Damned fine eatin," as Casey had put it.

Chris came back with six beers and the crew sat down to tell war stories. Bill stopped by a few minutes in to drop off some delicious-looking pub grub, to which Chris dug in heartily.

The team continued going over the combat stories and how things had played out. Beers after beers were downed and the stories got more and more exaggerated.

After a few rounds Sean spoke up, "All right, ladies and gentlemen."

"What gentlemen?" asked Mike.

"Well the major's here, so, you know," replied Sean.

The major chuckled but otherwise remained silent, sipping on his brew.

"Oh here he goes," added Melissa.

"Here goes what?" questioned Chris.

"The dick-measuring competition," responded Melissa.

There were some chuckles but Sean continued, "It's time to add up the kill count and play the game," as he pointed to the kill board.

Sure enough on the wall was an old paper list that had all five fighter pilots' names on the board. It included Corporal Higgins. Next to each name was a number. The paper had a title on top that read, "Kill count."

"Wow, is that a list of all of your kills?" asked Chris.

"All of the kills from this campaign, not all time," explained Mike.

Sean got up and walked over to the paper, which had an erasable pen next to it. The rest of the crew followed.

"Now being the best pilot on the ship, I'll go first," started Sean.

"Whoa there, young whipper snapper," interrupted Major Sarner. "You're good, but I am the master. I was a seasoned pro before you ever saw a Raptor."

Melissa just looked at Chris and said, "Here it goes," but she chuckled and was enjoying the display.

"I said best, not oldest there, Gandalf," Sean continued.

"But as a result of my superior abilities, on the last mission I was able to destroy five of those traitorous bastards." With that he erased his kill count, which was eleven, and now wrote the number sixteen.

"Major, what did you get?" asked Sean.

"I also got five kills on that mission," replied Major Sarner with a smirk.

Sean went to the board and erased the twelve next to his name and put a seventeen there.

"Damn," muttered Sean under his breath.

"Well it appears you still have not achieved the top ace status," added Casey.

Sean shook his head but took it good naturedly. Then he asked Melissa, "How many kills did you get?"

Melissa took a pull from her beer and said, "Three."

Sean went to the board, erased the eight next to her name, and changed it to an eleven.

"Damn," thought Chris, "Melissa may not look deadly but she is." He was shocked that this team had been able to kill so many people in this campaign and so far they had only lost one pilot and one Raptor, at least that Chris was aware of.

Then a big grin opened up on Sean's face.

Chris heard Mike mutter, "Fuck, here it goes."

"Mike, how did you do, old buddy?" questioned Sean.

Mike drank his beer, exhaled, and replied, "I killed one."

Sean, Casey, and Melissa, all laughed at that response. Even Major Sarner chuckled and Chris did as well quietly.

"Oh man, I remember my first time flying," added Sean after he got himself under control.

Mike flipped him off but took it good naturedly.

Sean erased the six next to Mike's name and started to write seven but stopped.

"What are you doing?" questioned Mike.

"Well, I have an issue, but maybe the wing commander can settle this for me," began Sean.

"What can I do for you, Lieutenant?" asked Major Sarner between pulls on his beer.

"If you are flying and shoot someone down, but then get shot down, does that still count as a kill?" questioned Sean sarcastically.

Everyone laughed at Mike's expense again, but Sean gave him the seventh kill in the end.

"Ya, ya, ya," added Mike, "Remember this Chris. Pilots are assholes—every one of them."

"Well I think that about wraps this one up," finished Sean.

"Whoa there, sir," began Casey. "I believe you are forgetting someone."

Sean looked at him quizzically and stood there.

"Yes he is!" said Mike as he set down his beer and grabbed the pen out of Sean's hand.

"Whoa, this is for the Flying Panthers," explained Sean.

"Yeah well we had an official intern with us," returned Casey.

Sean accepted this and moved aside after Major Sarner gave a nod approving of the coming gesture.

Mike wrote in "Bananas" and asked, "Well, Chris, how many did you kill?"

"Three!" Chris yelled proudly.

Then Mike put a six next to his name.

"He said three?" questioned Sean.

"Ya, but he killed three on his first outing as well. So that means he is at six for the campaign."

Sean accepted this with a nod and with that Chris was officially on the Top Ace board.

"Well thanks guys," added Chris.

"Don't thank us so quickly," returned Melissa, "the worst is yet to come."

"Yeah, I'm not looking forward to this," warned Mike

The major looked at Sean and said, "Well, big guy, since you tied me you can get the shots for everyone."

Sean complied and went to get the bartender's attention.

"It's times like this that make me glad to be flying in a transport ship," explained Casey.

"What is he doing?" Chris asked as he took another sip of his beer.

Mike looked at Chris with a worried expression. Then he stated, "Chris, as part of the 72nd Flying Panthers, the rule is whoever kills the most sets the standard. Since Sean and Major Sarner each got five kills, that is the standard. Since you and Melissa killed three each, you have to drink two shots of whatever Sean picks."

"Oh shit, two shots in a row," Chris said with worry on his face. Then he realized what that meant for Mike and began to laugh.

"I see you figured it out," returned Mike.

"Can't wait to watch you take four in a row, Mike!" laughed Casey as he sipped his beer.

Chris's stomach twisted with just the thought of trying to keep down four shots.

A few minutes later Sean returned with fourteen shots of whiskey.

"That's a lot more shots than we need," explained Melissa.

"Nope, I counted correctly," replied Sean with a smile. Then he explained, "First shot is for all of us. It is to toast Corporal Higgins. Since he didn't make it through this campaign in flying shape, we will all take one to toast to his health and recovery. The remaining eight shots will be for you lackeys," laughed Sean as he passed them out.

"You bastard," returned Mike, but he knew he had to do it.

Chris took a deep breath and grabbed the first shot Sean had passed out.

Major Sarner started the toast, "To Higgins, he is a damn fine pilot and I look forward to having him on my wing again," and he raised his glass.

Everyone replied, "To Higgins!"

With that Chris took his first shot of whiskey. It burned going down but Chris was able to handle it. A small notification came up in his vision and it stated that his nanites had begun filtering out the alcohol.

That's when Sean added, "Oh ya, turn off that filtering, you pussies. We are celebrating tonight."

With a mental thought Chris found himself able to switch off the system and the same icon that came up in his vision now had a slash through it with red letters instead of green.

Next the pilots began lining their respective shots up. Melissa volunteered to take her shots first. Like the nickname she was given she took both shots in a row with ice in her veins. It was as if she had done this time and time again and she never grimaced. Chris watched probably a little too intensely as she adjusted her flowing blond hair from taking the shots.

"All right, lover boy, you're up," mocked Sean with a grin.

Chris exhaled and mentally prepared himself. He knew he couldn't throw up. Not now.

He reached for the first shot, breathed in, and took the shot. Chris quickly swallowed and reached for the second. The whiskey began burning as it went down but Chris figured best to get the second one down before the full burn began. The second shot touched his lips and he threw it back and downed it. The burning intensified and Chris found himself pounding his chest a bit with his hand in a fist. His eyes began watering a bit as he exhaled but he knew after the first few moments he was going to make it.

"Wow!" Chris exclaimed with relief. His stomach was turning but as he took a sip from his beer as a chaser things began to calm down.

"Damn, Bananas isn't half bad!" laughed Casey Hogan.

The team clapped their hands or slapped the table and seemed to be impressed. After a few seconds of recognition the table's attention turned toward Mike.

Mike sat there, focused in on the four shots of whiskey that had been presented to him.

"Come on, Joker. After this you will never let me get four kills on you," egged on Sean.

"Yeah, no kidding. If you do I'll have to shoot you down," Mike joked.

"Don't worry, Sean, I'll swing by and pick you up," added Casey.

Mike leaned over and sat his head on the table in front of the shots. Then he took a deep breath, exhaled some, and grabbed the first one.

Everyone, even Major Sarner, watched with interest. Chris looked around and several other tables were staring at the commotion.

Mike was a Joker, but Mike also knew how to drink. Considering he had already done one shot for Higgins, adding another one or two wouldn't be a problem. But four in a row would be a sight to see.

Mike downed the first one, then picked up a second one and then downed it right away. The crowd cheered after the accomplishment. Then he grabbed a third one, and stared at it for a second before leaning back and taking it. Mike's face cringed and Chris could only imagine what three in a row felt like.

"Oh God," came Casey in disgust of what he was witnessing. Apparently, Casey wasn't kidding when he said he was glad he didn't have to participate.

Then Mike reached for the fourth shot of whiskey and the crowd cheered impatiently.

"Do it!" shouted the crowd.

Mike took the fourth one and threw it down. His other hand was on his chest and his face was scrunched up. Finally he exhaled, but before he could all the way, his cheeks bulged up as if something was trying to escape his mouth. People made disgusted faces and Casey almost threw up himself from having to watch.

Mike then slowly began swallowing whatever had come up in his mouth and that was it. Casey jumped up and ran to the nearest trash can with his own cheeks bulging and threw up into it.

People laughed all around the table and the pilots cheered and handed Mike his beer as he finished his efforts to keep the whiskey down.

"That is why Casey flies transports!" mocked Mike.

Casey, who had finished, flipped him off while he cleaned his face up.

The night went on and Craig stopped by for a quick drink as well before returning to duty. Chris noticed Bill Bronx pull out a bottle he'd never seen from underneath the bar when Craig ordered his drink. Eventually Major Sarner was the first of the pilots to get up and leave.

"Well Panthers, it's about time to hit the dusty trail for this guy. I'll see you in the morning," stated Major Sarner.

Chris had asked earlier in the night if anything had come up regarding Earth Force academy and the major told him no, nothing, but to keep an eye on his email as he may be contacted in the future.

Chris bid the major good night and so did everyone else at the table. After that the crew kept on drinking and the next domino to fall was Melissa.

The bar had quieted down some, so she was able to talk without shouting. She got up from her chair, and with a smile on her face said, "Boys, it's time for me to get some beauty sleep. Enjoy the rest of the night."

Everyone said goodnight to her as well, and before she turned away to head to her cabin she added, "Oh Chris," she walked over to him, "just wanted to thank you properly for saving my life out there."

Chris looked up into her beautiful brown eyes and managed to mutter, "Uh, anytime." At least he added his own smile to the mix, which was pretty easy considering how intoxicated he was.

She leaned over and went to plant a kiss on his cheek. But as she did, Chris turned into the kiss and kissed her back.

She didn't freak out and pull away but instead lingered for a second. It didn't go any further than a kiss, but it was all Chris could want in that moment.

After a couple of seconds she pulled away and had a big smile on her face. "Good night boys," she added before walking off toward the turbo lift.

Chris watched as if under a spell, her hips swaying back and forth. Then reality came back to him and he saw Sean, Casey, and Mike slack-jawed at the table.

"Damn, Bananas, you son of a bitch," exclaimed Mike in surprise.

"I had no idea we were living with a playa. Shit, not even Sean has managed that one," added Casey.

"I've got to hand it to him, well done, Intern," returned Sean.

Chris was officially on cloud nine by now, solidifying this night as the best in his life. Luckily for Chris, he and the pilots were still drinking.

Eventually, after catching a lot of jokes and congrats about Melissa everyone had enough and retired to their rooms. Chris couldn't recall a night where sleep had come so easily to him and the dreams were so pleasant.

At 0800 the next day Chris awoke to his mental alarm. He shook off the sleep and was surprised he didn't have a hangover. He mentally thanked himself for turning back on his nanites after he left the Afterburner. They really could work wonders if you'd had too much to drink. He really hoped they wouldn't deactivate them when he left; they could give him a huge leg up in the civilian world. He did his morning routine and packed a small duffle bag with some spare clothes the Leviathan crew said he could have, along with some trinkets he had picked up since joining the crew. That was it though; everything Chris owned was in that duffle bag or in a small account in a bank.

It was all coming to an end now and Stacey was ready to get off the Leviathan, which had docked at Lunar Space Station not twenty minutes prior.

"You ready?" asked Stacey with a smile and a sense of excitement in her tone.

"Why are you so perky?" replied Chris.

"Cause this is the first time in a long time that I get to see my family and not be stuck on board this ship. This, for better or worse, will be a new chapter in my life," she explained.

Chris realized that Stacey did have something to look forward to in the near future and the thought of her being happy made him somewhat happier in return—even though this adventure would probably be a lot more boring than the last few days for Chris.

"Yep, I am ready Stacey. Let's do this," announced Chris. He had tried to inject some enthusiasm into his voice and hoped it worked.

Chris and Stacey made their way to the turbo lift. All the while Stacey was telling Chris about her family and the property they had on Mars and what it was like to live there. Chris pretended to be interested by adding an "Oh" or an "I see" or a "That's cool." It's not that Chris was trying to be rude, but he wanted to cherish every last moment on board the Leviathan. He would have the rest of his hopefully long life to figure out what Mars was like, but only another few minutes to enjoy the Leviathan.

The turbo lift would take them to the main docking port, which was what people used to get on and off the ship when it was resupplying at a station. From there Chris would walk down the hallway, exit the Leviathan, enter the space way, which was a long tube connecting the docking port of the Leviathan to one of the many docking ports of Lunar Space Station, and enter the station.

The lift doors opened to a busy scene of personnel moving

back and forth with various tasks being executed.

Chris paused for a second after he stepped out of the tur-bo lift. Once he went through the doors to the space way that would be it—no more Earth Force Navy, no more Leviathan, no more Flying Panthers, and finally, Zion would forever be out of Chris's reach.

He must have been standing there for several seconds be-cause he snapped out of it with Stacey snapping her fingers in his face, saying, "Chris, hello, anybody home?"

Chris apologized and Stacey laughed and in a cheerful voice said, "Come on, I'm going to buy you some breakfast as soon as we get on the station. When was the last time you had some real eggs and bacon? And no I am not talking about the frozen stuff on the ship, I mean freshly made."

Chris thought about it and it had been a while. So he shrugged his shoulders in an "I don't know" gesture and pro-ceeded forward. Stacey was almost skipping she was so ex-cited to get off the ship. Chris made sure not to drag his feet but he certainly wouldn't run off the ship.

As they approached the docking port door Chris noticed the XO Ben Shafer and Wing Commander John Sarner were there. This got Chris's attention, as he was certain those two had better things to do than stand around watching people coming to and from the Leviathan. He wondered what they were doing since if they needed to get a hold of him or anyone else in the crew they could via their nanite package.

Stacey and Chris continued forward and Stacey waved at the two senior officers. Chris pasted a smile on his face and waved as well. He thought about saluting but figured he was just a civilian again and they probably were doing something important.

Commander Shafer cleared his throat as they walked by and Chris stopped.

"Mr. Skylander," came the XO in his crisp and to-the-point voice. Chris laughed inside and remembered that this man probably never relaxes.

Stacey stopped as well and Chris turned and walked up to the XO.

"Yes sir, what can I do for you? Come to wish me good luck on my future civilian life?" asked Chris.

The XO stared at him with a dumb look. The major then stepped in and spoke up, "Chris, no, we didn't come down here to wish you luck. Something more important has happened that you may be interested in."

This surprised Chris and he scrunched his eyebrows up in confusion. Ben's hands, which were of course behind his back, came forward and he handed a tablet to Chris. Then he stated, "Chris, an important communication came through and the major and I figured it would be best if I delivered this to you in person." Again Chris had to reevaluate the XO. He may have had a stick up his butt, but Chris really respected his upfront attitude.

Chris took the tablet and began reading. It was addressed to Mr. Skylander and it read as follows: "Mr. Chris Skylander, Based on some outstanding recommendations from Captain Erik Spear of the E.F. Leviathan and his highly decorated Wing Commander Major John Sarner, along with an excellent service record when called upon, I would like to extend you the following offer." Chris saw that the message was signed by Centurion Admiral Olds.

Chris's heart began beating at a million miles per hour as he wanted to see where this was going. He clicked on the attachment labeled "Offer Letter" that was underneath the message.

The attachment opened up and it was an official letter that read as follows: "Dear Mr. Skylander, Congratulations! On behalf of the Dean of the Earth Force Academy, Centurion Admiral Robin Olds, it is my pleasure to announce your appointment to the United Countries of Earth, Earth Force Academy as a member of the Class of 2273. You will be joining a select group of our planet's finest young people as you take this challenging and rewarding step toward becoming a professional Earth Force soldier. Due to the unique circumstances regarding your situation and because the current class has already begun you can accept this letter by signing at the bottom and reporting to the Earth Force Academy office of admissions at 0600 tomorrow morning." The letter was signed "Sincerely, Edward Houser, Director of Admissions."

Chris's jaw hit the floor and then kept going. He couldn't believe it and quickly read the letter again just to make sure he saw it correctly. His eyes began to water but he quickly tried to stop them as he didn't want to show that emotion in front of his former commanding officers. Stacey must have been reading over his shoulder because she shouted for joy and tears came to her eyes as well.

"Well, Chris, what do you think? Do you want to live a civilian life, which will probably be filled with hard work and just reward on Mars? Or do you want to join us on a thankless journey that'll probably get you killed?" asked Major Sarner.

Chris was about to respond when he remembered he had already committed to going with Stacey, who for all intents and purposes was his only family left. Chris looked back at Stacey and was about to ask what she thought. Before he could though, Stacey exclaimed through tears of happiness, "Oh don't even think about it! This has been your dream for as long as I have known you!"

"But what about you?" returned Chris. "What will you do?"

"I'll be fine," Stacey responded with a bit of laughter. "It will be cheaper paying for transport for one anyways. Just promise me that you will visit one day when you are an officer and get some leave."

"I promise," Chris replied.

Then he turned and signed the bottom of the tablet. The tablet accepted his signature and Chris handed it back to the XO.

Chris held his hand up in a gesture to shake the XO's hand and Commander Shafer obliged.

Then Chris looked to Major Sarner, who stuck his hand out to congratulate Chris. Chris took his hand, shook it, and then couldn't help himself and hugged the major, stating, "Thank you sir! Thank you so much for this. I won't disappoint you."

The major chuckled and replied, "All right, easy Chris. We'll see how much you want to thank me when you're a week or two into the depths of the Academy. It ain't exactly pilot summer camp."

Then Chris realized he had a problem and stated, "Um sirs, I have no idea how I am going to get from here to Earth and be ready at 0600 tomorrow morning. What should I do?"

"Well Chris," began the XO, "this is where I take my leave. Congratulations on the opportunity and please, whatever you do, play this one by the books. I don't think we can handle any more of your messes. I'll leave you and Major Sarner to work out the last step."

With that the XO walked toward the turbo lift.

The major started, "Chris, I have a transport shuttle reserved for us in the hangar bay of the Leviathan and I'll be dropping you off personally."

Chris blinked in surprise. "Well all right then, let's do this!" he shouted.

Chris turned back to Stacey once again. They said their goodbyes and exchanged hugs more than once. Chris promised to visit again and told her he would stay in touch. Then the major said it was time to go.

With that Chris and Major Sarner made their way back to the turbo lift and pressed the button.

"You made the right call Chris. The Earth Force is the best and toughest thing I have ever done with my life. That being said I would do it over and over again," explained Major Sarner.

"Well I know deep down it's what I have to do. Besides,

someone has to catch Zion," replied Chris.

The major laughed as the turbo lift doors opened and as they walked in he replied, "Well we will see if he is still around when you graduate. By then I'll probably have shot down all the bad guys and you will have a long, boring career."

Chris laughed at that one and responded with, "I have a feeling Zion will be a pain for longer than that. Besides, who knows what we are going to find on the other side of the Colossus Portal. I have a feeling they are going to need all the pilots they can get."

Major Sarner smiled at that, and with a whoosh the doors to the turbo lift closed and the two were rushed away toward the Leviathan's hangar bay. Upon reaching the transport ship a familiar face greeted him at the controls.

"You know I was a little confused when they said I'd be flying to the academy" came Casey's voice, "but when I saw you come into the hangar it all made sense. You've earned it, pal. Now sit back and enjoy the ride."

"Oh I will, and I'll be back—and when I do I won't be the rank of intern!"

EPILOGUE

"Status report?" asked Admiral Zion.

"All systems nominal. We have jumped into the new system with no issues, sir," replied the navigation officer.

"Perform a system scan. I want to know everything about this system. Look for any habitable planets," ordered Admiral Zion, then continued, "Engineering, has the device been able to identify any Ancients in this system?

An engineering officer responded, "No Admiral, just like the last two systems the device is not reacting. It appears to be operating nominally, just no Ancients in this system to communicate with."

"Damn, where the hell are they?" Zion thought. He had been hoping to make contact with the Ancients in the very first system they jumped to after escaping the Earth Force fleet at Sol. After exiting the portal in the new system, however, and realizing there were no intelligent life forms in the system they had begun repairing the ship. Nobody said it would be easy to find the Ancients. Their hopes had been lifted soon afterward when scans of the new star system had located two more jump points out of the new star system. These were unlike the Colossus Portal in that they appeared to be naturally occurring wormholes.

After making initial repairs and picking one of the two jump points in the new system the Cleaver made another jump successfully, only to once again find no Ancients or intelligent life. As before however, scans quickly located yet another portal. Once they had thoroughly scanned the system they were in, his crew and ship made their next jump, bringing them to the system they were in now.

"Shall I launch a patrol of the system, Admiral?" asked Commander Reagan Force.

"Yes, Commander, and have Lieutenant Wolver take a wing to the opposite side of the system and run a patrol route. I want to know everything in the system is of no value before we move on. No blind spots outside of our sensor range," ordered Admiral Aken Zion.

"As you wish, Admiral," replied Commander Force.

With that the flight commander walked off the bridge to prep his pilots for the upcoming mission.

The admiral turned back to his viewing screen to contemplate his next move. If there were no Ancients here or targets of interest he would search for another jump point that could lead to another unexplored system. Even if he had to do this another hundred times it would not deter him from his goals.

"Contact!" announced the officer at the sensors station.

"What is it?" asked Admiral Zion.

"It appears to be a small ship, standby . . . Make that twelve contacts, no, twenty and counting . . ." explained the sensor station officer. A few seconds went by before he turned to the admiral with a pale face, "My God sir, we're picking up over three hundred contacts."

ABOUT THE AUTHOR

Rolf Brunckhorst is an avid fan of science fiction books, movies, and video games, especially anything involving space. Cosmic Gate is his first attempt at creating a story. Outside of science fiction, Rolf is happily married to his wife Linnea and they live with their Great Dane Max.

CPSIA information can be obtained
at www.ICGtesting.com
Printed in the USA
BVHW071459120421
604733BV00002B/171